Praise for

Prisoner of the Queen

"E. Knight is back with another tale from the Tudor Court. Think you've read everything about the Tudors? Ms. Knight shows that there is much more to love . . . Filled with court intrigue and passion, this book will have you wanting to read more about her heroine, Katherine Grey, sister of Queen Jane Grey!

—Meg Wessel, *A Bookish Affair*

"Eliza Knight once again tells the story of the little known royal relation with a personal panache and flair for the dramatic that serves to elevate one given a mediocre place in the annals of history to astronomical heights in the fictional arena. Vibrant characters, mind-bending plot twists, and a fluid yet breakneck pace are all trademarks of authoress Knight that fans of her books have come to know as her signature hallmarks of excellence."

—Frishawn Rasheed, *WTF Are You Reading?*

"*Prisoner of the Queen* is top shelf historical fiction. Anyone as addicted to Tudor history as I am will love escaping into this heartbreaking yet touching look at a woman taking her own life into her hands and making her own choices despite what tragedies may come."

—Colleen Turner, *Historical Tapestry*

D0905927

Prisoner of the Queen

Prisoner of the Queen

TALES FROM THE TUDOR COURT

E. KNIGHT

LAKE UNION
PUBLISHING

3 1740 12000 5354

This is a work of fiction. Names, characters, organizations, places, events, and incidents are either products of the author's imagination or are used fictitiously.

Text copyright © 2014 E. Knight
All rights reserved.

No part of this work may be reproduced, or stored in a retrieval system, or transmitted in any form or by any means, electronic, mechanical, photocopying, recording, or otherwise, without written permission of the publisher.

Published by Lake Union Publishing, Seattle
www.apub.com

Amazon, the Amazon logo, and Lake Union Publishing, are trademarks of Amazon.com, Inc., or its affiliates.

ISBN-10: 1503945561
ISBN-13: 9781503945562

Cover design by Elsie Lyons

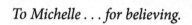

To Michelle . . . for believing.

Table of Contents

Cast of Characters

The court of Henry VIII is vast in occupancy, and for this story, while I've used a number of its inhabitants and key players, I have also, for the sake of the reader's sanity, taken the liberty to neglect a few. Even still, the number of characters within this book is staggering and, as such, necessitated an introduction of sorts. Additionally, many people in history had the same names, so it can become confusing who is who.

Main Characters

Katherine (Kat) Grey (Pembroke), Countess of Hertford; grand-niece of Henry VIII; daughter of Frances Brandon and Henry Grey; sister of Jane Grey and Mary Grey.

Edward (Beau, Ned) Seymour, Lord Beauchamp; Earl of Hertford; eldest son of Anne Seymour and Edward Seymour; nephew of Queen Jane Seymour; husband of Katherine Grey.

Mrs. Helen, companion and maid to Katherine Grey; fictional.

Jane Grey (Dudley), The Nine-Days Queen; daughter of Frances Brandon and Henry Grey; grandniece of Henry VIII; sister of Katherine Grey and Mary Grey.

Mary Grey, grandniece of Henry VIII; daughter of Frances Brandon and Henry Grey; sister of Jane Grey and Katherine Grey.

Frances Brandon, Duchess of Suffolk; niece of Henry VIII; daughter of Mary Tudor and Charles Brandon; mother of Jane Grey, Katherine Grey, and Mary Grey; wife of Henry Grey.

Henry Grey, Duke of Suffolk; husband of Frances Brandon; father of Jane Grey, Katherine Grey, and Mary Grey.

Anne Seymour, Duchess of Somerset; widow of Edward Seymour; sister-by-marriage of Queen Jane Seymour.

Jane Seymour, daughter of Anne Seymour and Edward Seymour; sister of Edward (Ned) Seymour; close friend of Katherine Grey.

Mary I (Mary Tudor), Queen of England; daughter of Henry VIII and Catherine of Aragon; cousin of Jane Grey, Katherine Grey, and Mary Grey.

Elizabeth I (Elizabeth), Queen of England; daughter of Henry VIII and Anne Boleyn; cousin of Jane Grey, Katherine Grey, and Mary Grey; also known as Good Queen Bess, Gloriana, and the Virgin Queen.

SECONDARY CHARACTERS

William Cecil, chief advisor of Elizabeth I.

Robert (Robin) Dudley, Earl of Leicester; ardent admirer of Elizabeth I's; brother of Guildford Dudley; son of the Duke of Northumberland, who played a major role in Jane Grey's ascent to the throne.

Guildford Dudley, husband of Jane Grey; son of the Duke of Northumberland.

Katherine Brandon, Duchess of Suffolk; stepmother of Frances Brandon; step-grandmother of Jane Grey, Katherine Grey, and Mary Grey.

Henry Herbert, first husband of Katherine Grey; son of the Earl of Pembroke, who played a major role in Jane Grey's ascent to the throne.

Bess St. Loe, Bess of Hardwick; Countess of Shrewsbury; wife of William St. Loe; a lady of Elizabeth I's bedchamber; sometimes confidante of Katherine Grey.

Jane Dormer, Countess of Feria; wife of Ambassador de Feria.

Ambassador de Feria, Spanish ambassador; husband of Jane Dormer.

Adrian Stokes, Master of the Horse to and lover (husband) of Frances Brandon.

Ambassador de Quadra, Spanish ambassador; replaced de Feria.

Arabel, Katherine's toy spaniel dog.

Beau, Katherine's greyhound.

Rex, Katherine's toy spaniel dog.

Stew, Katherine's pet monkey.

Edward Warner, Lieutenant of the Tower.

Lord Arundel, Keeper of the Palace at Nonsuch; uncle of Katherine Grey.

John Grey, uncle (and guardian) of imprisoned Katherine Grey.

John Wentworth, guardian of imprisoned Katherine Grey.

William Petre, guardian of imprisoned Katherine Grey.

Sir Owen Hopton, guardian of imprisoned Katherine Grey.

Prologue

THE YEAR OF OUR LORD 1568

I have served three queens in my life. One was my sister, one was my savior, and one was my bitterest enemy.

I've seen a queen fall from power in just nine days. I've watched a queen die of heartbreak and neglect. And I've threatened a queen with my very existence, for I, too, am of royal blood.

And yet, for most of my life, I've done the bidding of queens. I've nodded my head, curtsied, acquiesced, given up my hopes and dreams. Mourned the death of loved ones taken before their time. Even in the face of brutal loss, I have listened and obeyed, understanding that in all things, the sovereign always wins.

But I tell you, the queen has not won this time. Even now, at the hour of my death, I have prevailed over her. There are those who see me as her victim, but I have triumphed where others failed. You see, my love has conquered the commands of a royal crown.

For love, I carved for myself a little peace and happiness from this life, and what love I have known makes it all worthwhile. It was *mine*. It is still mine, this love. Love that I would never have known if I were a queen. Love that the queen herself has never known and never will.

So I shall rejoice, knowing that I would do it all once again. Knowing that there are some things in this life that we cannot let another control. We cannot bend to another's will at the risk of losing who we are. We must defy them. Keep sacred the matters of our hearts, our very souls. And that is why not even death will take this victory from me. My love, my private triumph, will live on even when I am gone.

For I am Lady Katherine Grey, and this is my story . . .

Chapter One

Draw near good minds that sadly marks,
the sway of worldly broils,
And hear what I at large can say,
of troubling times and toils.
Which did befall in foreign land,
'tween two of noble race . . .
—Thomas Churchyard, Elizabethan Soldier and Poet

AUGUST 25, 1548

Sudeley Castle reared up into the sky. The imposing height of the towers showed that this was a household of importance. That of Dowager Queen Catherine, to be exact. The only wife of Henry VIII to have outlived him—number six.

A groom lifted me from my horse and settled me on the ground, where my slippers crunched on gravel.

"There you are, my little lady."

I flashed him the most ladylike smile I could muster at the age of eight, before turning to await Mrs. Helen, my governess, as she, too, was helped from her horse. I tried not to giggle when she nearly lost her footing. Mrs. Helen was not used to riding such a long distance.

The great doors of the castle opened, and with long, graceful strides, Thomas Seymour, Lord Sudeley, who was my older sister's guardian, along with Her Grace, came to greet us. He was tall, with a handsome face, dark hair, and eyes that sparkled with merriment. His clothing was ornate—a doublet embroidered with gold and studded with pearls—and cut to show off his figure.

"Lady Katherine, a pleasure it is to have you here." He made a bow, and I endeavored to curtsy just so. He came forward and chucked me on the chin. "You are a darling girl, aren't you? Your sister is in our back gardens. Do you think you can find her?" His eyes shifted to Mrs. Helen. "Her Grace is not feeling well, so close to her time. Our midwife says it won't be more than a week. She's taken to her bed."

I glanced from one adult to the other, wishing I knew what they were talking about. Worry wrinkled my brow.

"Run along now, my lady." Mrs. Helen straightened the skirts of my sky-blue gown and made sure my hair was tucked properly under my pearl-studded cap, then she walked into the castle with Lord Sudeley. Maybe she could make the dowager queen feel better. She always made me feel better when I was ill.

I ran over the grounds until I came to the garden gate and was ushered through by two guards. It was a magnificent place—full of bright, colorful flowers of yellow, pink, white, and red. Butterflies flitted back and forth, guiding us to a maze that begged to be explored. I was fascinated and turned in a circle to take it all in.

But where was Jane?

I put a hand to my forehead, shielding my eyes from the summer sun.

"Jane!" I waved when I caught sight of my older sister, whose attention was wrapped in her task of drawing in the garden, yellow skirts spread out around her in waves. She sat below a weeping willow tree, its branches brushing the ground like fingertips with each gentle breeze.

She glanced at me, her face lighting up. "Katherine! You came!" She rolled up her drawing and rushed toward me, skirts lifted in one hand, slippers sinking into the lush green grass of the lawn.

We embraced, and I took comfort in her strength. It'd been a little over a month since we'd last seen each other. Nothing was the same now that she'd moved out of Bradgate Manor to be fostered with Dowager Queen Catherine. I missed her dearly. The nursery was empty without her. The only company I had now was that of our younger sister, Mary, a small babe. Indeed, the whole of the manor seemed bereft without Jane's presence. I prayed that when my time came to be fostered out, Mother and Father would let me go with Jane.

"Happy Birthday, Kat. How does it feel to be eight summers?" Jane smiled with glee. She rocked on her heels and hid her drawing behind her back.

I tapped my chin and pursed my lower lip, thinking on the matter. "Not much different than seven, I suppose. Mayhap not any different than your eleven summers."

Jane laughed and looked behind me. "Did Mother and Father come with you?"

I shook my head, knowing that Jane would be disappointed. "They had other matters to attend to." They *always* had other matters to attend to—children were a kind of property, and there was no great sense in idling time away with them before they were grown to a useful age. Even at eight, I knew that. Still, there were others, like the dowager queen, who seemed to take delight in the household's children. Shame colored my cheeks for thinking such disloyal thoughts regarding my parents.

"Oh," Jane said, the light in her eyes dimming. "What of our sister, Mary?"

I shook my head, sad to see her discontent. I wanted us to be happy today, not somber, as it had been so long—and it was a day to celebrate!

I peeked at the rolled parchment in her hand. "What were you drawing?"

"'Tis nothing, really."

Soft footsteps behind us startled me.

I whirled around to see our cousin, Princess Elizabeth.

"Of that you can be sure . . . The sketchings of an eleven-year-old are nothing to be admired," she said in husky tones.

At nearly fifteen and lithe of figure, she towered above us. Her hair, golden red, looked to be set afire by the sun. Her eyes held a scorn in them I had not encountered before. A gown of gold bedecked in jewels shimmered in the light. Elegant and regal. She reminded me so much of a portrait of her father, Henry VIII, I'd seen in my mother's solar—only much more feminine.

I straightened my spine in an effort to appear taller. The effect I hoped for was not achieved. "I did not see you there. Apologies, Cousin." I offered her a smile, trying, in spite of her disposition, to remain kind.

"Yes, well, I do not live with Queen Catherine any longer—like some others do." If possible, her glare intensified as she looked on Jane. "So I would not expect you to think I was here. But unlike some, I actually belong at Sudeley, and love Her Grace, and so I've come to pay my respects and check on her health."

Her tone was sour, her face pinched. And with her words, I recalled a hastily scribbled note from Jane, something about trouble with Lord Sudeley, that he and Elizabeth had been caught doing something naughty.

"Our living arrangements are no fault of my own." Jane's tone came off accusatory, and she straightened her shoulders.

I gasped that she would insinuate Elizabeth was to blame for her current situation. Even if she were, how was I to know? For certes, I'd done many naughty things. Mrs. Helen was always yelling at me about putting frogs in her pockets or salt in her milk.

Elizabeth reached out and yanked on a lock of Jane's golden hair that hung loose from her hood. Jane yelped, and Elizabeth snickered, reaching out to yank again.

I moved to stand between the two, to protect Jane, but Elizabeth only shoved me aside. I stumbled, my legs getting caught in my skirts, and I fell with a grunt, my elbow striking a rock that protruded from the ground. I rubbed at the tender flesh in an effort to take away the sting.

"Do not attempt to intervene, Kat," Elizabeth spat at me. Her hands were placed upon her slender hips, and she looked down at me as if I were a slug to be crushed. "'Twould be a waste of your silly time. I am the daughter of a great king, sister to our current king. You are both nothing to me." Her gaze turned back to Jane. "You will never be anything. Just the Grey sisters. Pawns in the schemes of many."

"At least our mother has never been called a witch!" Jane taunted.

My mouth fell open at Jane's insult, and I grew faint with fear. The hatred that sizzled in Elizabeth's dark eyes was enough to give me nightmares. She lashed out, her palm connecting with Jane's cheek, leaving angry, red stripes.

"I could see you hanged for that," Elizabeth threatened. "Pawns should keep their mouths shut."

Before either of us could reply, Elizabeth spun on her heel and marched toward the garden gate.

Pawns? What could she mean? The only pawns I knew of were the little pieces at the front of the chessboard—the ones that were usually sacrificed for the gains of the bishops, knights, rooks, queens, and kings. All of a sudden, the meaning of her words became clear, and I blanched. Would we truly be sacrificed for others' gains?

Such a thought had never crossed my mind. I glanced at Jane, who stared after Elizabeth, a determined expression on her face.

When Jane turned back to me, she smiled, although it didn't reach her eyes. She held out a hand and pulled me to my feet. I swallowed back my tears, resolving to be just as strong as my sister.

"What have we ever done to deserve such animosity from Elizabeth?" I asked Jane.

Jane brushed a few grass stems off my gown. "She is jealous, 'tis all. Her life is not her own. Her fortune is given, then ripped away. I am where she wants to be. I am who she wants to be."

I furrowed my brow, not understanding. "But she is a princess."

"And supposedly, so are we."

My mouth opened, forming a small O. Mother always lamented we were princesses of the blood, but Elizabeth was a true princess, daughter of a king and queen. Why should she be jealous of us? We were, as she said, just the Grey sisters. What power did we have?

Jane frowned down at her drawing and marched toward the pond where ducks and swans floated in complete accord.

Why could we—Jane, Elizabeth, and I—not be like the ducks and swans?

Jane unrolled the drawing, and when I realized her intent, I ran toward her, shouting, "No, Jane! Don't!"

But it was too late. She let the drawing fall from her hands into the murky water. As I reached her side, breathless, I caught sight of what she'd drawn. A beautiful rendition of us both, smiling, content. To see us now, one would not think it possible. We both stood, watching the drawing, our eyes riveted on its delicate journey upon the water.

Tears blurred my vision. I wiped them away and saw from the corner of my eye that Jane did the same.

I slipped my hand around her waist, and she sank against me. There we stood, two sisters, stoic in our vigilance. At least we had each other. We could take comfort in that much.

I prayed it would always be this way. And yet, somehow, with the new knowledge imparted on me by Elizabeth . . . I had my doubts.

I was aware now that my position in the realm could be ill used for purposes not of my own choosing. This truth resonated deep within—and I resented *and* appreciated Elizabeth for telling me. I had a feeling such knowledge would have a profound effect on who I was.

And Jane was never the same again.

LONDON, ENGLAND
MAY 5, 1553

Heads on spikes protruded from the top of London Bridge in macabre welcome to any who entered the formidable city.

London.

For years, the name of England's capital city had been a thing of wonder to me, a magical place were the elite lived and made merry with royals.

A sultry blast of air whipped at my gown and with it brought the scent of decay. I gagged as delicately as I could and lifted my orange-and-clove pomander to my nose. Despite the stench and the incessant buzzing of flies, my eyes remained riveted on the impaled heads.

I tried to count them, but by the time I reached twenty-three, we'd passed the chilling sight.

Our king was only a boy and already a formidable ruler. I shuddered at the thought. We were headed his way. If I forgot some form of etiquette, would he slice off my head?

No, that could not be the case—or at least, so I hoped. We were family, after all. Family didn't kill family. But wait . . . Realization dawned on me, and I nearly choked on the air I breathed, for hadn't the king's own father—the great Henry VIII—done that very thing?

And hadn't this young boy king cast his own sisters, my cousins Elizabeth and Mary, out of the line of succession? For that was the reason we were headed to London, this place of putrid heads—heads that I'd never dared see even while sleeping.

Neither Mother nor Father had warned of the monstrous display that greeted every person upon entering the city. Not even my sister Jane had mentioned it to me, and she'd been visiting court for nearly six years.

But Jane sat high-and-mighty on her horse, much changed in the past few years. She boasted of her intelligence and how she would rule her kingdom. At home, she forced our younger sister Mary and me to play her ladies-in-waiting.

Swelling so, her head would be too large to be placed on a spike. It pained me to think on how close we had once been.

I flashed a glance at Mary. Tears had gathered in her close-set eyes. She blinked them away before they could spill and fiddled with her overlarge riding gloves. Mary was a tiny little girl, even for her young age of seven. Her eyes were warm and kind, and she had a mind for numbers and languages, but her body didn't grow. I'd heard Mother once threaten to stretch Mary on the rack to make her limbs longer, but the horrifying deed had never been done. Mary was safe for the time being from Mother's temper. At the moment, it was dear Jane who bore the brunt of Mother's ire. She had a great task laid at her feet—but I didn't know what it was. I'd only heard the hushed whispers, her voice raised to Mother and Father.

A crow cawed overhead and swooped down toward me. I bit my lip instead of screeching and ducked, praying the bird would not defecate on my new gown of soft sage-colored wool. I stroked my fingers over the seed pearls lining my stomacher and then reached up to touch the square neckline, the creamy, ruffled lace at my wrists falling back to reveal the new pearl bracelet Mother had gifted me with just this morning.

I turned in my saddle, trying to get another peek at the heads. I didn't know why I was so fascinated. They were truly revolting, but there was something about them that drew my attention and held it.

Lips parted in question, I turned to my mother, who rode beside me, her stoic gaze cast over the streets of London as if she owned the city. I hoped to catch her eye, as we children were only supposed to speak when spoken to. Seeming to sense my questions, she turned to me and, in clipped tones, said, "Traitors, Katherine. You see what they do to those who oppose the crown? You'd best heed your king or *queen* before your conscience." Her brows rose in challenge, and her gaze flicked to Jane. "Else your head gets skewered."

Mother's words left a foreboding chill in my blood. Frances, Duchess of Suffolk, daughter of "the French queen," niece of the great Henry VIII—my mother—was a formidable, unforgiving woman.

How easily it seemed life in this realm could be forfeited to those in greater power. My gaze wandered back to the heads. What had they done to be called traitors? Who were they? Had they left families behind? Or was there no one to mourn their passing?

I recalled a time when I was much younger. A servant had stolen some of Mother's jewels—precious jewels the late Queen Jane Seymour had bequeathed her. I'd never seen Mother so angry. But it was not she who'd scared the sin out of me on that day, but Father, Henry Grey, Duke of Suffolk—so titled only because my uncles, the young half brothers of my mother, had died of the sweat before they reached their majority, leaving my mother with the only claim to the inheritance.

In the face of someone daring to thieve in his home, Father raged, his face red, spittle flying from his thin lips. The servant in question, a young man who looked half-starved, was dragged down the steps of Bradgate Manor and to the center of the court-yard, where he was tossed to the ground and stripped of his wool shirt.

Mother had ushered my sisters and me to the courtyard to wit-ness the servant's punishment, all the while lamenting of treachery and sin.

The servant, on his knees, pleaded with my father, prayed to God, and prayed for mercy. But he must have seen something in my father's eyes, something that told him praying would do no good, for he quickly muttered, "To Jesu, I commend my soul," which even I knew was what was muttered by those expecting death.

One of Father's retainers rushed forth with a dreadful-looking weapon: a scourge. The whip had several lengths of corded leather, each end fitted with sharp rocks. When the first stroke hit the young man's back, he screeched in pain, the sound reverberating in my head, as the flesh was torn from his back and angry divots bled like rivers over his flesh.

I tried to hide my eyes against Jane's shoulder, just as Mary had buried her face in my skirts, but Jane pushed me off, her eyes narrowed, distant.

"Kat, 'tis the way of things. The vermin should not have stolen from us." She spoke with a superior calm—like a mother to a way-ward child. "And now we must relish his punishment."

But I did not relish it. And judging from Jane's face, she didn't, either. She accepted it. How could I take pleasure in the pain of another? For certes, he'd stolen my mother's precious jewels, but were pretty stones worth a man's life?

Seeing the crushed expression on my face, Jane scoffed, but I could see her disdain was only a facade, a pose to make herself feel better. "For shame, Kat. We are princesses of the blood! In line for the throne! You cannot pity a mere commoner who would dare to steal from you. 'Tis akin to treason."

I didn't understand then, and even today, I still thought many punishments did not fit their crimes. Mayhap 'twas a good thing Jane was the eldest—a potential queen had to be severe in such matters. Jane would make a better queen than I, if it ever came to that, because a queen must be strict about things like punishment.

Besides, Jane's marriage would have to be an advantageous one. I should like to marry a handsome courtier who read me poems.

We turned down the Strand, and I admired the view of the houses that backed up to the Thames. The streets were jammed with merchants, wagons, people, and horses. The stench was beyond anything I'd ever experienced, even when walking near the muck pile at Bradgate. I wrinkled my nose. This was something altogether different: a mixture of offal, rotten food, bodily filth, and dead things. I squinted my eyes and could almost see poisonous vapors wafting up from the cobblestone street.

Even the pomander I held to my nose could not block the stench.

"Could ye spare a coin, pretty thing?"

I twisted, wobbling atop the horse, toward the sound of the voice and the rough tug on my skirt. I gripped the reins so tightly they bit through the leather of my gloves. A toothless woman with a craggy face and slimy hair, the skin of her face smudged black with dirt, offered up a horrid, gummy smile.

My horse whinnied and yanked on the reins, swinging his head with agitation and stomping his feet. I opened my mouth to speak, but the horse was so unnerved, his movements so jerky and uncontrolled that I feared he'd throw me. The woman started to tear a piece of fabric from my underskirt of gold cloth, her dirty hands smudging my gown, leaving stains of brown in slashing patterns.

"Let her go, you old wretch!" one of my father's guards shouted, his mount surging forward. With his horsewhip, he slapped at the woman's shoulders.

"I should've known not to expect charity from the likes of you! Greedy . . . dog hearted . . . ," she mumbled as she wandered away, clutching her sore shoulder.

My heart beat erratically, and my throat was tight. Tears welled in my eyes. Not that the event itself was all that traumatic, but it was so unexpected. The fear of being thrown, pulled off my horse, my clothes stripped off me. A body left naked and vulnerable in the streets.

"Come, Katherine, do not let one of God's ungracious creatures unnerve you." Mother's voice was harsh, provoked by the insolence of my assailant. "Remember, you are a princess of the blood. Chin up, shoulders back."

With that, she clucked her tongue and nudged her mount forward, signaling for our entourage to continue the journey through London.

I followed behind but found myself searching the crowd for the old beggar woman. Was she so poor she had to steal a piece of my clothing? Was her plight so awful that to make it better, she would see me suffer? I felt suddenly naïve. At Bradgate, I was sheltered from the most base of lowly humans, and yet I had been taught to sew shirts for the poor, attend the sick, and deliver food to the hungry. But those whom we served in Leicester had respect for us as their noble overlords, and to assault us would never cross their minds. Were things so different in London? Was noble blood not admired in this great city as it was in the country?

For the remainder of the ride, my nerves jumped at every sudden shout, and each time my leg brushed another rider, I lurched in the opposite direction, making my horse prance about wildly.

I received several stern glances from our retainers and Mother. When we reached Dorset House, immense relief flooded me. I would be safe behind the gates.

To my disappointment, though, Jane and Mother left us behind to meet Father at court. Oh, how I wanted to see the glamour that was the royal castle, to meet the king and all the courtiers!

I pursed my lips in a pout when Mother bade me to stay but was rewarded with only a clipped, "Your time will come," before they left me to my endless studies.

MAY 10, 1553

There was much to explore in our new home, and I'd taken to traversing the grounds and castle corridors every second that I could.

Upon our arrival in London, many courtiers visited Dorset House. A number of them were formidable looking, and all spoke in hushed tones. Today, I'd seen at least five men arrive within minutes of each other. Their attire was rich and formal. It had taken only minutes for me to convince my tutor I needed to use the privy—oh, how I loathed my studies—and only five more for me to ferret out the men's whereabouts.

Father's study.

The door was tightly closed, and in the dimly lit hall, a strip of light seeped from beneath the door. The muffled voices of several men sounded from within, then the angry tones of my father. What could they be discussing?

I glanced around the corridor, making sure I was alone, then knelt at the floor, putting my eye to the keyhole. From what I could see, they all stood around the table, jabbing their fingers at each other in an effort to be heard. Whatever it was they discussed was important.

I turned my ear to the keyhole, closed my eyes, and held my breath, as I'd learned that was the best way to eavesdrop.

"No, I say! I'll not have her marry a man of such low birth," Father said.

"With all due respect, Your Grace, as members of the king's council, we do heartily impress upon you the urgency of such a match." I did not recognize the speaker.

I knelt back on my heels and chewed my lip. Marriage? Whose wedding were they planning? Jane's? Should I tell her what I'd heard?

"Lady Katherine!" Mr. Aylmer's voice echoed in the hallway.

I dropped to my hands and knees and patted around the floor. "Good sir, I seem to have lost my earring." I glanced up at him with practiced, doe-eyed innocence. "I think it may have fallen beneath this door." I tumbled onto my backside with a light laugh. "I seem to have tripped over something here."

My tutor, having never thought me capable of much, rushed forward and dropped to his knees. While he felt around on the floor, I plucked off my earring and made an effort to slip my fingers just beneath the door.

"I've found it!" I said with glee.

Mr. Aylmer grunted his annoyance and stood, offering me a hand. "Let us return to your studies."

But little good returning did, as my mind was still on what I'd heard behind my father's closed door.

MAY 19, 1553

"Mother, no! I cannot!" Dear God, what I'd heard had not only been about Jane, but me as well!

Mother's salon was dark, as gloomy as the news she'd delivered. The curtains were drawn, and a dozen candles blazed on the chandelier that hung from the plastered ceiling. I imagined them crashing down on me, burning Dorset House to the ground.

Mother slammed a hand down on her carved-oak writing desk, which made a loud cracking noise as if the wood would splinter beneath her palm. She fixed her narrowed gaze on me.

I had never raised my voice to Mother before, and I sincerely regretted doing so. This would for certes lead to a most awful punishment.

"Katherine, do not quibble like a babe in swaddling clothes. You will obey. Lord Henry is the son of the Earl of Pembroke, and so shall he inherit his father's title. He is a suitable husband for you, and your sister Jane shall be glad to have your company on her wedding day, as will Catherine Dudley, who is to be married to Lord Hastings."

But Jane is fifteen, and I am only twelve . . . I felt betrayed, for Mother had always promised we'd not be married until at least age sixteen. I did not voice these objections, for doing so would only have gained me a stinging slap.

I glanced around the room at the rich furnishings, the oak-paneled walls, brightly colored tapestries, and portraits of lords and ladies passed, whose images caught the light of the candles, making shadows dance across their faces. I avoided my mother's gaze for as long as I could, until I heard the click of her nails in irritation against her desk.

The sweet rolls Cook had given me as I passed through the kitchens felt like a solid block in my belly. I would rather be studying Greek and translating the Old Testament from Latin into French than standing here before my mother discussing the imminent demise of my youth—and considering how I loathed Latin . . .

I swallowed hard. The idea of marrying was deplorable, even if it would be during the same ceremony as my sister and the Dudley girl. I had so many years yet to live. I had not been to court, and I had hoped Mother would take me when next she went. I wanted to attend the royal joust and feast. Listen to courtiers read their poems of love and make merry with other young ladies. But now I should never get the chance. Now I would be a married woman. Shut up in a dark castle somewhere, breeding heirs to an earldom.

I was powerless to stop the creasing of my brow or the frown on my lips. But when Mother's own brows drew together, I did my best to wipe the disappointment from my features.

"'Tis the way of things, Katherine. Do not question it. Your father and your future father-by-marriage have negotiated a good marriage contract, which will only succeed in furthering your future and the future of our families in this realm. You will present yourself to your new family as you've been raised. Do not cause your father, me, or, indeed, your cousin King Edward any embarrassment."

The duchess sat stoically upon her cushioned chair, her back so straight her spine might snap if she moved too quickly. Her chin was thrust forward, shoulders squared. Her beauty radiated behind her creamy, saggy flesh, and streaks of gray sliced through her vibrant auburn hair, pulled severely back beneath her head-dress. When Mother was young, she'd kept her willowy figure with rigorous daily walks in the garden and by pecking at her food, but the stress of birthing babies and her position—life in the court, even—seemed to have ravaged her.

I vowed at that moment not to let courtly intrigue ravage me, too. I would have to figure out a way to save myself, though. Did Mother try and fail? Would I fail, too?

There was no question of Mother's upbringing or of her importance, being the daughter of Henry VIII's sister. She was a true princess.

Whenever she looked upon me, I felt lacking, as though she wished I were someone else—perhaps more like Jane. More interested in studies and religion. More poised. But I was not. I was only myself.

I bit the inside of my cheek, hands wringing at my waist. "Will I have to . . ." I trailed off, not wanting my mother to know the extent of my knowledge on marital relations. I spent many a good minute listening in on conversations I should not have heard. A bad habit that would surely get me a lashing, but 'twas the way in which I garnered information. No one bothered mincing words when sweet, naïve Katherine was around—they so readily assumed I'd understood nothing.

Mother's eyes narrowed as she tried to discern my meaning. "Will you what?" Her voice was exasperated, and I sensed her limited patience was running out. "You will be a dutiful wife, Katherine. You will do your duty as your husband instructs. You will make your family proud. You are a princess of the blood. Start acting as such."

I sucked in a ragged breath and lowered my gaze to the floor. So it shall be . . .

"When?" *When will my imprisonment begin?* Because marriage was a prison, was it not?

"The day after tomorrow." Mother waved her hand at me in dismissal and turned to read a rolled parchment on her writing desk.

My world crashed down around me. How could she dismiss me thus when she had delivered such a sentence of death?

"Wh-what?" My mouth fell open in outrage. My earlier conviction to never raise my voice at my mother was tossed to the fire. That was hardly enough time to acclimate myself to the idea of marriage!

Mother did not look up this time but simply shook her head as if she'd already given up and arguing was futile. "Are you deaf, girl? Two days. Now go. You must finish your studies."

"But—"

Mother slammed down the parchment. I jumped. Her gaze flicked to mine, anger flashing in her eyes. Her voice was low and menacing, her words clipped. "But what?"

I did not know how to voice my concerns. Were two days enough to pack my things? Would I get a chance to speak to my betrothed before we were wed? Did he have the same aspirations as I? Where would I live? Would I ever see my family again? Why had she broken her promise? My mind was a whirl, and I could not concentrate, let alone find the words to bring forth.

Mother, again, drummed her nails against the polished oak of her desk, click, click, click, and the clock on her mantle chimed five times as I looked about frantically, trying to pull myself together. To be fair, Lord Henry was not the worst of grooms. He was mercifully close to my age, and I did know him, if only sparingly. He was a quiet sort and awkward with his limbs. Still as much a boy as I was just a girl.

With a sigh of resignation, I shook my head. "'Tis nothing, Mother. I thank you and their lordships for having arranged so advantageous a marriage for me."

"That is more like it. You should show your gratitude, Katherine. People will be much more likely to appease your needs if you should use proper manners and etiquette. Your pretty face will only last so long."

I nodded, feigning complete agreement. 'Twas a trick I'd learned to use to my advantage already. When she again dismissed me, I walked from the room in search of Mrs. Helen. She would answer my questions, and she would do so with patience and love. She would embrace me and ease my fears.

And I would endeavor to enter this imprisonment with the dignity expected of a princess of the blood—or else suffer for it.

Chapter Two

To whose mishaps and hateful fate,
a world hit self gives place.
Not long ago the case so stood,
a knight of great estate
In native soil by destiny's lot
a Lady's favor gave . . .
—*Thomas Churchyard, Elizabethan Soldier and Poet*

MAY 21, 1553

My eyes stung. My head felt heavy. Even forcing my eyelids closed with my fingers, sleep had refused to find me the prior night. Instead, I'd lain in bed, staring at the stone walls. I counted over two hundred cracks in the white plaster ceiling by the window. Made imaginary patterns out of the swirling embroidery on my bed curtains.

'Twas my wedding day, but I would not be a happy bride. After the feast, I would travel with my new husband to Baynard's Castle, where I would reside under his family's care—as if being fostered out to a guardian and not a woman wedded. My only saving grace was that their castle was in London. In truth, it was only a short float down the Thames, and so I would be able to see my family often—I hoped.

I rubbed my eyes. My betrothed and I had met before, briefly, last spring. I'd paid him no mind, not anticipating our fate. My sister Jane had made Henry's acquaintance at court on occasion when he'd accompanied his father, Lord Pembroke, and she had described him as quite an oaf. At age fourteen, Henry was gangly of leg and arm and stout in the belly. He howled when he laughed and dribbled grease on his soft face when he ate.

Not what I'd dreamed of when I fantasized about my future husband. Biting my lip, I also lamented becoming a wife at age twelve.

Mrs. Helen bustled into the room and flung open the drapes, the screeching of the iron rings on the rod making my head ache. The bleak, gray sky seemed fitting. Clouds hung over the horizon, mixing with the London fog.

"Close the drapes, Mrs. Helen. There is no cause to wake today," I said with a pout.

"Oh, my lady, but there is! Today is your wedding day. And even if you are not so excited to marry, you should be pleased and pretty for your sister."

I gave an unladylike snort. Jane was marrying Guildford Dudley. Mother had lamented on and on about him not being a true prince of the blood and not good enough for her daughter. But Father had insisted.

Jane was also not pleased with her groom. She had always held herself above others, and I could never have imagined she would marry the fourth son of a common man who'd risen himself to power and was now a duke. Not when Father had groomed her to marry a king. I could only imagine what plans my sire had put into place to see such a thing happen, and how disappointment must now run thick through his veins.

His princess, his means to a kingdom, would marry a lowly commoner.

According to Jane, the Duke of Northumberland—Guildford's father—had attained his status only with treachery. He'd had a hand in many a courtier's demise. Even the king's own Lord Protector had not been safe from Northumberland's climb for power. The Lord Protector, His Grace, the Duke of Somerset, dear brother to the late Queen Jane Seymour, had been executed for some fabricated charge of treason the boor Northumberland had pinned on him. Jane said she was surprised Northumberland hadn't been arrested himself.

So while my companion, Mrs. Helen, lamented over my sour face, I found it necessary given that I, through my sister Jane, should be linked to such a man.

I was happy to take a slobbering oaf such as Henry over a Dudley.

From down the hall, raised voices echoed, and something shattered.

"Your sister's having a time of it this morning," Mrs. Helen muttered.

"Why?"

"Well . . . 'Tis not my place to say. I shan't be named a gossip." Mrs. Helen pursed her lips and pulled from the wardrobe a linen chemise, an ivory stomacher threaded with gold and gems, an ivory gown embroidered with gold thread in floral patterns and matching slashed sleeves from which gold tissue silk would be pulled. She placed the costly and beautiful items gently on the settle at the foot of my bed.

"Mrs. Helen, I promise not to name you a gossip. Now, go on, do tell." Kept in the dark so often, I was eager to hear what the maid had to say. From what I'd learned, the servants knew *everything*.

And had not Mother taught me that in order to stay ahead of the game, one must know *all* the players' secrets?

Mrs. Helen busied herself with pulling out pins that would fasten my gown to me and connect the various pieces. It felt like an eternity before she finally said, "Her Most Gracious Duchess— your mother—has been up in arms all morning about the wedding. Got your sister into quite a temper. Word has it that young King Edward is ill again." Mrs. Helen crossed herself and mumbled a prayer. "Your father and the Earl of Pembroke, your soon-to-be father-by-marriage, have been having secret meetings."

"What secret meetings?" I blurted out, then quickly covered my mouth. I didn't want Mrs. Helen to think I'd become too excited by what she shared and hence stop talking. I pretended to pick a speck off my coverlet.

"Arranging Jane's marriage the way they have . . ."

I knew Mrs. Helen referred to the plotting I'd overheard. Talk of kings and queens. Mrs. Helen wouldn't come right out and say that my parents were plotting against the crown, but even still, her words were clear.

"Your mother is not too happy. Imagine that lowborn Dudley boy as . . . a ruler? For shame." Mrs. Helen clucked her tongue. "Your sister deserves someone better. Leaves tongues wagging, it does, to have your sister marrying a fourth son. The boy will inherit nothing, unless, of course, your father's made sure the marriage contract stipulates something for the two of them. As it stands, you'll be a countess, but I guess none of that really matters much when you consider Jane may be queen."

Mrs. Helen crossed herself again and for a moment stared off into space. Her words resonated deep within me. Could Jane truly be queen? A plot to steal the throne? Princess Mary Tudor would surely retaliate. And Princess Elizabeth would gladly seek vengeance were she thrust aside once more, with Jane taking her place.

Suddenly, the sense of doom that seemed to cloud over this entire prospect of marriage and how hurriedly it was put together made me light-headed. 'Twas treason for Father to be party to such a plot.

"You mustn't—" I started to say, but my throat was so tight, so constricted I couldn't get the words out. I wanted to warn her not to whisper of such things to anyone else, lest she brought the wrath of God and the king down on our heads.

"Now, dear, don't worry. Things will work out in the end. 'Tis God's will we must trust in." Mrs. Helen poured a cup of watered ale and handed it to me. "And I shan't be telling anyone what I heard either."

The ale was bitter, sour, and warm on my tongue.

"Come now," Mrs. Helen said. "Start your morning ablutions, else your mother find you still abed and redden your hide."

Although Mother hadn't reddened my hide since I was a young child, I wasn't going to risk it. If the sounds coming from down the hall were any indication, Mother was in rare form already with Jane's antics.

"Where is Mary?" I asked, fearful that my younger sister might accidentally cross my angry mother's path. The poor girl was never spared, and while she had a canny knack for avoiding our mother, I still wanted to be certain.

"Oh, the little Lady Mary is with Cook and the others in the kitchen. Saw her traipse in there earlier this morning. She does love to busy herself with making preserves, and from what I hear, Cook is making a delicious peach preserve for the folks to feast on after the wedding."

The thought of peaches, let alone syrupy sweet peach preserves, turned my stomach, and this time, I did rush to the chamber pot. I wiped the back of my mouth with my sleeve and closed my eyes as Mrs. Helen pressed a cool, damp cloth to the back of my neck.

"You're a nervous little bride, love. Do not worry overmuch. Your husband will be kind to you, and luckily, he's just a boy. You shan't have to grow up yet."

I turned and buried my face against my maid's ample breasts. "But, Mrs. Helen, I started my courses two months ago. For certes, they will expect me to begin my duties as a wife." I wailed loud on this last part, for I did not want to fulfill my duties, not at all!

"Oh, hush, love. I heard tell your father struck a bargain that you shan't consummate the marriage until you reach your six-teenth year. No need for tears. Dry them up."

And indeed, with her words, my tears dissipated. My mother may have turned into a shell of herself, a woman fearful of court intrigues and party to the plots of my easily persuaded father in his constant search for power, but she had found a way to honor her promise that we not truly marry until we were at least sixteen. Mother must have fought for me behind closed doors and won.

Knowing she'd done so sent a current of sadness rushing through me. I wished at that moment that I'd been closer to her, for now, I would leave her home for good. I wished I'd listened to her more, had tried to make her happy in at least some small way.

But the past was the past, and there was nothing I could do to change it. Only give her what she wanted, and that was an obedi-ent daughter. Now I had to worry about how my future husband's family would treat me.

The sound of horses' hooves outside my window jarred me from staring at the wall.

The arguing had stopped down the hall, and I could only imagine how mortified Jane would be with puffy eyes for her wed-ding ceremony. Since living with the dowager queen, Catherine Parr, before the great woman passed, Jane had become quite pre-occupied with her appearance, often lamenting that a lady's job was to appear always composed and arrayed in the latest fashion to show others that she cared for herself and would not accept being abused in any way.

Even I had taken to plucking my brows with silver tweezers, as Jane did.

From below, I heard my father's booming voice ordering our staff about. It was time to leave. The River Thames beckoned us to depart, to float down the river and never return.

Footsteps rushed past just outside my door. I stood, smoothed my hands down my stomacher and over my skirts. The ivory silk of my gown and gold threads shimmered in what little sunlight passed through the window.

I stood to contemplate my room one last time. Would I never sleep here again? I ran my hand along the thick brocade of my bed curtains and over the carved oak of the footboard. All my personal belongings had been packed, and nothing of me remained here, except my memories.

Jane, Mary, my parents, our personal attendants, and I walked along the wooden deck to the quay, where my father's barge waited to take us to Durham House for the triple ceremony. The sun had burned through the clouds and shone bright now, and mixed with the fishy smell of the Thames came the scents of lavender, peaches, roses, and rosemary from our gardens.

A slight breeze blew, ruffling my skirts, and I instinctively reached up to steady my headdress, not wanting it to come unpinned and ruin my hair—Mother would never forgive me. From the corner of my eye, I saw Jane doing the same.

She turned to look at me, deep-purple stains beneath her eyes, her face pinched. I wanted nothing more than to pull her to me and hug her, like I had that day at Sudeley when she'd thrown her drawing into the pond, but Jane was no longer one to be consoled, nor would she want me to pity her. Her eyes narrowed, seeing the tender thoughts crossing my countenance.

"Do not pity me, dear sister." Her voice was soft, not at all what I was used to from her. For an instant, the girl I'd once known returned. "We shall both endure a similar fate."

A swift wind blew. My lips parted in question, but I did not speak, for Jane continued close to my ear as the barge lurched forward, both of us gripping the rail. "The king is sick. He will soon walk with God, and I've been told I shall be queen. 'Tis not my place, Kat, 'tis not truly what I want, but it may be God's will—and who am I to disregard God's will?"

"But—" My voice came out a little shrill. What had come over Jane? This was madness.

"Hush. Do not make a scene." Her eyes flicked to the servants and to our parents, who stared out over the river at the landscape. "They've made their choice. They've made my choices for me."

London's tightly woven together timber buildings of wattle and daub sat among immaculate grand brick or stone homes and palaces. Smoke curled up from buildings, and birds flew in circles around the tops of the bridges. I shuddered, recalling the heads those birds were most likely feasting on.

"I am doing my duty for God. For country. For England. 'Tis what King Edward wants. What he proclaimed." Jane paused, as if in thought. "Princess Mary is most unforgiving. She is displeased with being ousted from the line. I fear when things fall into place, Mary will not let us live, knowing we are a threat to her succession." Jane turned her gaze toward the opposite shore. "Perhaps I shall not be a wife for long."

I felt sick. My head pounded. Why did Jane sound so certain? Mother would not let us die . . . would she?

"Jane, 'tis only wedding jitters weighing upon your soul. Come, let us be merry today! You shall be a wife! And to a handsome courtier!" I attempted to cheer her, though my own mood was bleak.

Jane smiled bitterly, a puff of breath escaping her lips. "Oh, Kat, you are so young."

I had only been trying to cheer her, hoping her future husband's handsomeness at least was pleasing, even if his pedigree was not. I gave Jane a bright smile, hoping to ease one from her. "Not *so* young. You forget, I am to be married, too."

Jane's eyes clouded, and her face cleared of emotion. "Aye, and the only one between us marrying someone worthy of a princess of the blood."

I wanted to ask her why Mother and Father had insisted on Guildford Dudley as her groom. I wanted to know why they had likewise arranged a marriage between me and Pembroke's heir. Why now? Why the urgency? But I didn't ask, either because I was afraid of the answer or because her eyes had become distant as she looked down into the river as it passed us by.

We arrived at the quay outside Durham, greeted by an army of servants who led us into the house. I was overwhelmed by the number of guests, the formalities. The triple wedding was lavish, the ceremony long. My groom's palms were sweaty and his pallor sickly. He informed me he'd just risen from his sickbed and that if it were up to him, he would have remained in it. He made no added remark about how long he would have remained, implying he might rather have died there than marry me. Part of me wished he had stayed abed, as I would now have to worry about catching whatever illness he had. Good thing I'd had the sense to tell Mrs. Helen to pack the herbs, flowers, and roots I dabbled with in making mixtures for healing, a hobby since I was old enough to pick flowers. And a hobby that had helped to heal many of our tenants.

The feast, dancing, and entertainments went well into the evening—our hosts doing their utmost to showcase their wealth. Every courtier was present, and it had even been rumored that we newly married couples would be graced with the king's presence.

But alas, he did not join us, adding weight to Jane's earlier comments on his health.

The noble guests feasted upon fresh-baked loaves of bread, with steam still rising from the crusty tops, and fresh butter, cheeses, grapes, apples, sweetmeats, almonds, and even olives imported from Spain. My eyes grew wide at the roasted peacock adorning the trestle table, dressed with purple, blue, and green plumes spread wide. My mouth watered at the platters of roasted capon, salmon with pomegranate seeds, cherry hearts, pickled carrots, peas cooked with milk and ginger, roasted pig stuffed with cheese and chestnuts, stewed beef cooked in wine, currants, and onions.

With the ceremony complete, I was ready to partake in all the glory that was an opulent wedding feast. I washed down the savory meal with one smooth and delectable goblet of free-flowing red wine after another—I not used to such finery, as Mother preferred us to drink watered ale.

Suspended above the trestle table to promote fertility hung wreaths of rosemary, lavender, marjoram, and sage. The sweet scents comforted me, as did the tender looks from Mrs. Helen, who served me still. We had feasts on certain saint days at Bradgate, but never as elaborate as this. Here was my first taste of courtly life. My first taste of wealth and the royal blood that flowed in my veins. I found I rather enjoyed the opulence, but all the same, my mind was drawn back to the beggar woman who'd felt the need to rip fabric from my underskirts to feed herself.

"Mrs. Helen?" I waved her over from where she loitered against the wall. I pursed my lips as I gazed about the room. So much fare was left over, and each person's belly was swollen from gluttony. "Would you approach Cook about seeing that any foodstuffs left be given to the poor?"

Mrs. Helen curtsied and then disappeared into the crowd, just as seed cakes, elderflower cake, apple-raisin pudding, and preserves were placed on the tables. I pressed a hand to my full belly and groaned, my head swirling slightly. My gown had grown tight from filling myself with food and drink, and I would be sick if I ate another bite.

I turned to look at Henry, grease dribbling down his fat chin. Disappointment burrowed within my soul. He was just as gangly and oafish as Jane had described. I quickly turned away, fearing my revulsion showed. Mrs. Helen soon returned and informed me the poor would indeed be fed on the food we did not consume, and my relief at this distracted me somewhat from Henry.

As the dancing continued, a singular young courtier, handsome in his tousled hair and confident gaze, approached the dais. He was several years older than I. I knew not who he was, but something about him arrested me. I watched his approach with a practiced, bemused face.

When he finally reached us, he bent a leg and offered a deep bow, showing off his musculature—which next to my gangly husband's was very impressive indeed. My insides melted.

"Might I congratulate you on your nuptials, and to such a beautiful bride," the young man said to Henry, his gaze caressing my quickly heating face.

"Thank you, Lord Beauchamp," Henry replied, looking slightly bored and irritated.

Henry's demeanor at once had me bristling. Why should he act so? Perhaps it was his own inadequacies beside this young Lord Beauchamp that made him irritable.

"If it pleases my lord, I would ask to dance with your lady wife."

Henry sat up straighter and glanced over at me. I affected a perfectly bored face, hoping it would ease his insecurities—even though inside I leapt at the chance to finally dance, and with so handsome a partner. I was gifted with a childish, satisfied smile from Henry.

"Be my guest." He swept his hand out in a gesture meant to say he did not truly care, while his beady eyes studied our every move.

I stood stoically and slowly descended the dais to place my hand on Lord Beauchamp's arm.

He leaned close to whisper, "Thank you for agreeing to dance with me."

"I did no such thing," I said haughtily.

"Ah, but you did. You could have refused, feigning a megrim or an ache in the stomach and yet you did not." We reached the dance floor, and he spun me to face him. "You also, might I add, affected the most perfect visage of boredom. You must know your young husband well to realize that such an apparent lack of interest would please him and allow you to go with me."

My lip curled at his words. "I merely play the game, my lord. I have been sitting for hours watching all celebrate, and I wished to dance before my limbs became permanently fastened to the chair."

"A lady with an agenda. You will be formidable when you gr—" He cut himself short and looked away.

"When I what, my lord?" My gaze boldly met his, daring him to finish his offensive remark on my age.

His eyes sparked with intensity. "I merely meant to say, when you have had time to ripen with experience."

"I am a woman married, am I not?" Challenging this man was thrilling.

He clamped his lips closed and refused to answer.

"Tell me truly what you think, my lord." My voice sounded breathy, even to me.

"If I were to tell you, it would only anger you."

"'Twill not, I assure you. I have a strong constitution."

"Well, then, I think you a child bride. All in attendance know that your marriage is in name only and that you will not be allowed to con—" Again, he stopped and had the temerity to bite his sensual lower lip.

"Go on," I said with glee, liking how color flooded his face at the unmentionable topic we were discussing. I had not had this much fun in—well, I did not know how long.

"You will not be allowed to be wife in truth, my lady. So I merely meant to say from the beginning that when you are allowed to become a woman, with time, you will be formidable."

I laughed aloud at his discomfort, which drew several gazes our way.

"You will have your disgruntled husband rushing forth to break us apart if you laugh so charmingly again," he remarked.

"You think my laugh charming?" I batted my lashes, wine making me bold.

Lord Beauchamp grew serious as he studied me. "I think you most stunning, my lady."

Now it was my turn for color to fill my cheeks. I had never been flirted with before, and this man was so deliciously forward. Was this how it was at court? I feared I would indeed be a bad wife if such were the case.

"Thank you, my lord."

"I should not be so bold with you on your wedding day." He glanced away, looking agitated.

"But, my lord, you said yourself, 'tis not truly my wedding day."

The intensity of his gaze when it turned on me had my toes curling in my slippers and my heart pounding in my ears.

"'Tis exactly the reason why I should not be so bold. For it only leaves hope for a poor sop like myself."

"Hope?"

He leaned in and whispered, "Hope for a chance at your hand when your time truly does come."

With that, he gave me one final twirl and delivered me, speechless and weak in the knees, back to the dais and a glowering Henry, where I was rooted the rest of the evening, and not so much by any decree but by my own wobbling legs. I drained more wine in an attempt to still my beating heart. But instead of quelling my excitement over my dance and the conversation with the young lord, I merely got myself quite intoxicated.

When the night finally concluded—or at least, when my new guardians deemed it appropriate—I was taken to the barge, along with my groom, to be ushered to Baynard's Castle. I hugged my sister Mary tight and Jane less so, as she was carrying herself too stiffly to allow for much sentiment. I curtsied to my mother and father, who did not appear to need a touch from me. I had to blink rapidly to keep the tears from spilling over. I was not ready to leave, and yet I did not want to stay here. How I wished I could return to Bradgate and a simpler time.

When we reached Baynard's, I was too weary to take in my surroundings and instead allowed myself to be led up to my new chambers without so much as a chaste kiss goodnight to my new husband.

My stomach lurched and my head spun from too much wine. I vowed never to overindulge thusly again. I laid my head upon the downy pillow. Images of Lord Beauchamp danced in my wine-dazed mind. Words my mother had uttered to me a time or two before churned in my mind. *Control, Kat. A woman must always maintain control. Do not allow yourself to be carried away by flights of fancy and pretty words. Your mind is your own and the only place in which you alone are master.*

But I fell asleep with his image behind my eyes despite myself.

Chapter Three

With whom he joined, a hazard great,
his liking led him so:
That neither fear of frowning Gods,
nor dread of earthly woe.
Could make him slay his plighted troth,
such constant mind he bear.
—*Thomas Churchyard, Elizabethan Soldier and Poet*

TOWER OF LONDON
MONDAY, JULY 10, 1553

The king is dead.

Long live Queen Jane.

A shudder passed over me as I glanced in my sister's direction. Today she'd been paraded down the River Thames from Westminster Abbey, stopping along the way for lunch at Durham House with Northumberland and the Privy Council, before embarking again on her royal barge to the Tower of London. Dressed in glorious green velvet royal robes, she held her head high. For as much as she lamented being given the crown, Jane knew she must act the gracious, honored queen.

She reminded me much of the queens of old. In her regal bearing, I glimpsed a touch of my great-uncle Henry VIII, whom I'd seen as a child. She appeared relaxed and comfortable in her new state. After all, she had been born and bred as a royal princess, and I do believe my father had had her coronation in mind from the moment the midwife had slapped her newborn bottom.

Now I was the sister of the queen. *Oh, please, Lord, let this turn out well for all of us.* I knew Princesses Mary and Elizabeth were not happy . . . Even now, rumors abounded of plots to aid the deposed royal children. Even though our mother, the illustrious Duchess of Suffolk, daughter of the late King Henry VIII's sister Mary, had attempted to instill in my sisters' and my own head since birth the understanding that our right to the throne was greater than that of Princess Mary and Princess Elizabeth, I knew it could not be true, for they were the daughters of the king, and we only his grandnieces. No matter how the two past kings tried to repave the line, the fact remained that the princesses had a more direct line than we.

I didn't want to be against Princess Mary and Princess Elizabeth, for I'd no quarrel with either, and I was content always to be in the shadow of a queen myself, but I prayed that Jane's crowning would be good for my family. That we'd not been set on a dangerous path.

I'd heard the fears from Mother's own mouth. Had not Father already compromised himself with court treachery when he aligned himself to Lord Sudeley?

The egotistical Lord Sudeley had plotted to have Jane marry young King Edward and for himself to be married to Princess Elizabeth. Sudeley lost his head for that lunatic scheme four years ago. My father was lucky to have not been executed on that day, and Jane as well, even though she'd been about my age—twelve—at the time. I shuddered to recall that man and the devious plans beneath his chivalrous appearance.

I recalled with bitter remembrance how Jane had changed when she came under Sudeley's care, and our confrontation with Elizabeth in the garden. Always intelligent and sharp of wit, Jane had become cynical and aloof, no longer the sweet older sister I'd once confided in and played with. She grew more like Princess Elizabeth and Princess Mary, her eyes always darting around as if she suspected she'd be attacked or slandered. She was deeply unhappy. Her lips rarely turned up to smile. When I'd stared into her eyes, so cold and distant, I'd felt as though I'd seen a bleak future.

The quarrel between Princess Elizabeth, Jane, and me still played vividly in my mind. She'd called us pawns. She had been right.

Once more, Father now sought to put us all in danger, and there was naught that we could do about it. Even my own mother had not been able to dissuade him. Though Edward VI had named us his immediate heirs in order to preserve Protestant faith in the realm, his own father, Henry VIII, had placed us *after* his own line. Henry's daughters—his blood—had been next in line until Edward's revisions. Not us. My mother had warned Father that—no matter King Edward's wishes—to go against Henry VIII's own daughters would be the ruin of us all, especially because most of England felt Mary Tudor was the rightful heir. Mother was cunning and intuitive. I believed her. And I had never thought my father to be heedless of caution. Nor that he would be capable of flirting so dangerously with treachery—for that was what he was doing. He was pitting Jane, myself, and young Mary against the formidable Tudor princesses to put his daughter on the throne . . .

My fingers played nervously with my skirt, twisting the fabric, wrinkling the delicate folds into a mess Mother would certainly disapprove of.

On the barge, we heard people shout from the shores their approval of Jane's ascension, while Jane made an illustrious progress from Westminster to the Tower of London. She waved at the townsfolk as we passed. But all the while, dark clouds gathered overhead. Big, fat droplets of rain spilled on our heads as we rushed for cover from the quay and through the gates of the Tower. Thunder cracked and lightning streaked across the sky amid the sounds of cannon fire, signifying the queen had arrived. Heralds proclaimed Jane's rule to the crowd, who grew restless and wet, above the sounds of nature and man. I could not have been the only one who saw this as a bad omen.

A shudder passed through me, and I took a long, deep breath to calm myself. We were quickly ushered inside, where maids took linen towels to our persons to dry off the bits of water clinging to our velvet gowns and headdresses, even the tips of our noses.

Jane stood still and stoic as her maids carried out their duties and the other ladies surrounding her giddily talked of the men in their green-and-white livery. I saw in her eyes something was changing, taking root there. Several minutes later, her stolid countenance dropped, and a rare smile crossed her lips.

Jane was a conundrum. For in private, one moment she gave this triumphant smile, and the next moment, fear filled her eyes and her lips pinched together as if she were ill. In the face of others, she remained stoically resolved to take the crown if it was God's will. Her reluctance seemed genuine as did her bouts of joy.

My throat tightened painfully, my chest hurting from not breathing. Father's scheme to take the crown by placing his daughter upon it could get us all killed by Mary Tudor and her followers. Executed. I still recalled the heads on spikes protruding from the top of London Bridge in warning to any who entered the formidable city. *Please let our futures not be grim. Let Jane rule until she's old and gray. Let us all rejoice in this! My sister, Queen of England! We, the most powerful family in the land. There will be feasts, dances, dresses, jewels.* I felt my heart stop just thinking about it all.

For certes, our dear cousins, Princess Mary and Princess Elizabeth, would not stand aside while a usurper took over what they deemed their birthright. But Jane's army and guard would protect us. The council would protect us. *They must!* At least, until they bowed to Princess Mary's rule, for she would not accept Jane without a fight.

I'd heard the servants whisper of Princess Mary gathering troops and preparing to march on London. I'd met my cousin years before. She was an angry woman—embittered with the trials of her station, the wrongs done to her. Behind Mary would be thousands of retainers set on destroying us. We must stand our ground, or we would all be locked in the Tower. We would all be led to the scaffold or the gallows for having gone against her, for having strayed from the Catholic faith she so revered. For we'd all followed Edward VI and his father's Protestant faith devoutly.

Was there any hope in dreaming that London, all of England, would stand for us? For what their child king had decreed?

I folded my hands within my gown to keep anyone from seeing how they trembled. For I was uncertain now . . . The minds of people changed so readily.

Why did King Edward have to die so young? A chill snaked up my spine. Mary would seek her retribution; it was only a matter of time. I might yet follow Edward to an early grave.

Outside, the bells tolled and the sun dipped low toward the horizon around London. Bright orange light shone behind the clustered buildings, and fingers of smoke from chimneys reached up to scratch at the sky. I wished to be out there, anonymous in the streets of London. Anywhere but here in the Tower. We were not prisoners yet, but I was not sure if I would see the light of day beyond these small, stony windows if Mary persuaded the people to her cause.

The room suddenly grew quiet, except for the rustle of gowns. I turned from gazing out the window as a woman of admirable countenance crossed the threshold. Dressed in a gown of black velvet and silver tinsel, she held her head erect, shoulders squared. Her very presence dominated the air I breathed. Her light hair was pulled back tight beneath her headdress. She emanated both poise and grace, but also something else, something much more severe. I recognized her instantly: Lord Beauchamp's mother, the Duchess of Somerset—Lady Anne.

She met my gaze, as I had been staring openly, and I wanted to look away, but I found I could not. Her eyes were cold, and it seemed as though I stared into the very depths of hell. Her lips moved a fraction, and only because I stared did I surmise it was a smile. At that moment, I felt wise and aged beyond my dozen years, for I realized this woman, so painfully thin, skin drawn taut, perhaps had seen hell, had been there and come back all the stronger for it.

I shuddered. *Pray, God, do not let me become so!*

"Your Grace," Northampton spoke with a sneer.

I wanted to slap that evil look from his face. How dare he look down on such a woman?

"We are so glad you were able to answer our summons," the man continued.

"I follow the orders of my king, my nephew, and no one else. And yet, when I arrive, I find he is not the one who summoned me, for how could he, being in his grave?" Her words were clipped, accusing.

Had no one warned the Duchess of Somerset—aunt to King Edward—that he was dead? She was a legendary woman in my mind, having fought so hard for her husband, who, in the end, had been betrayed, executed by the very man who sneered at her now.

"Your Grace, we sent a messenger, but you were not in residence."

"I was visiting friends in the North." Her steady gaze studied each man in the room in turn as if she played a game of chess. "Who wrote the summons?"

"I did, Duchess." Northumberland stepped forward.

"Are you playing king, Your Grace?" Her lips twitched again with the ghost of a smile.

"My lady, I only summoned you to the side of your new queen." He held out his arm, palm up, indicating Jane, who sat beside her new husband, Guildford, in two great polished throne chairs. "Majesty, Queen Jane, the Duchess of Somerset."

The duchess's gaze flicked to Jane, but she did not move. I could scarcely believe it. Would the woman not bow to her sovereign?

Slowly and briefly, she dipped to a curtsy. She did not wait for Jane to tell her to rise. Instead, she stood erect of her own accord, her gaze focused on Jane's.

"I served another Queen Jane before you, Majesty. Would that you could have known her."

My sister's chin lifted defiantly, as if the reminder of the pious mother of our late king, her namesake, was offensive to her.

"I would have you serve me, Your Grace, and your daughter Jane, as well. She and I were both named for the late Queen Jane Seymour," my sixteen-year-old sister managed.

I had to force my mouth to remain closed. Jane appeared intimidated by the duchess, something I'd never seen before. She had felt the need to explain herself. It was odd and unnerving.

"If Your Majesty commands it." Lady Anne's gaze still did not waver.

Jane thrust her chin forward. "I do."

"May I speak freely, Majesty?" The duchess raised a brow in challenge, as if she would make her request no matter Jane's response.

Jane inclined her head in regal fashion, and I suspected it was because she could not find the words to cross her tongue.

"Why is it I bow to you and not the Princess Mary?"

A collective gasp rose up in the room. My mother's eyes widened, and I saw not only fear there, but a deep-rooted respect. I understood then my mother's feelings for the Duchess of Somerset. They'd been longtime friends, or allies at least, from the few recollections my mother had shared of court with me.

Northumberland and my father both took a step forward, as if they would apprehend the duchess, murderous looks on their faces, but Queen Jane held up her hand.

"It was the king's Device for the Succession, his dying edict that the heir to rule in his stead be a true evangelical prince—in my case, a princess—and not return his rule to the breast of Rome." Jane's voice ran cold, as it often did when she spoke of religion, her beliefs. "Do you not agree?"

Her question to the duchess was a challenge, and I watched the interplay with fascination and bated breath.

The duchess pursed her lips and made a clucking noise with her tongue. "Who am I to question the will of the sovereign lord?"

She bowed her head, her gaze cast to the ground, and dipped into a curtsy again. When she rose, I had the distinct impression that she had closed off a part of herself.

"Shall you summon me when your court is ready, Majesty?"

"It is ready now, Your Grace."

The duchess nodded once and then asked to be excused so she might prepare her servants for the move to court.

JULY 11, 1553

Queen for only a day, Jane seemed determined to try and prove
that she could be just as violent in her rule as our late uncle Henry
VIII and his son Edward VI. This morning in London, a young
boy of fifteen summers who shouted out that Mary was the rightful queen was arrested and brought to the Tower. But he wasn't
housed in the opulent, kingly rooms my sister occupied. He was
tossed into the recesses of the dungeon, the dark, the place where
rats, disease, and the whip rule.

All for showing loyalty to someone else. 'Twas treason, true.
But he was only a boy. Can a boy, an ignorant, common boy at that,
be held accountable for something so rash? Would the Princess
Mary treat us this way if she broke through our lines? We were
greater than a common boy . . . Or did that make our fates all the
more precarious?

My sister Mary shuffled into my room, her curved spine causing her to bend forward slightly as she walked, and slumped into
a chair.

"Have you heard the news, Sister?" she asked.

"What news?" I was curious, for Mary was only seven, and
what news could she have heard?

"They've cut off the boy's ears. Left him mutilated." She wrinkled her upturned nose in disgust and fingered her ears.

I was shocked that Jane would authorize such poor treatment.
"Will he be released?" I asked, my voice breathy with horror.

"Yes, and his folly is to be made an example of." Mary sat forward with excitement that for once, she was the one with news
to share. "No one in London, nor the whole of England, will ever
deny Jane's right to rule, unless they want to be earless, too."

I nodded because I could not speak. The idea made me sick.
Mary's joy over it made me sick. She was only seven. Who had
filled her ears with the wonders of violence? The boy was not much

older than I was, and now his appearance was permanently mutilated into something monstrous. Better that he should be hanged than to have to live the rest of his life branded a traitor.

Was Mary merely excited that her own deformed figure was no longer the current topic of ridicule?

I gripped the cross at my throat and mumbled a prayer.

I hoped this was not a sign of the way things would be. That Jane was acting out of fear, that she'd be merciful when her reign was secure. I knew Jane was better than this. She was pious. I'd thought Jane would rule with a gentler hand. Was this Northumberland and the rest of the council's doing, or did she truly harbor such cruelty within her?

JULY 19, 1553

Nine days had passed since I'd been elevated to sister of a queen, but it was clear that status would not last much longer.

The Tower bells tolled relentlessly, in warning and in celebration.

Jane's chamber was a quiet, somber place. Outside, with evening come, the sun shone no longer, and only a few candles were lit within her room.

She said nothing, only stared at the wall, her eyes distant, a forgotten book in her hand. Her husband, Guildford, paced the room with frantic steps. Every once in a while, he knelt before Jane and rested his head, whispering fervently. It was an odd thing to see a man lament at his wife's lap—especially Guildford, who more often than not simply stared at his own reflection, preening like a peacock. He begged for her forgiveness, but for what, I did not know. Even more heartbreaking was that Jane did not acknowledge him, merely stared over his head as if he were not there. When they'd married months prior, she had not wanted to be bound to Guildford Dudley. There was hope they'd grow closer over time, but it was obvious they had not. Whatever vague fondness she'd held for him had dissipated with the impending end to her rule.

Mother and Father had fled the Tower, taking my sister Mary with them and leaving us behind to face the wrath of Mary Tudor. Their daughter the queen—the daughter they'd made queen—and me, always an afterthought.

Jane must know that Princess Mary Tudor would ride on London and take back the city, the country, her throne.

Did she know that she herself would be declared a prisoner?

For the bells did indeed ring out for a new queen—Queen Mary—and with each loud clang, the threat to our lives was brought home.

"You should leave now, Kat. Take your husband and go." Jane's voice was devoid of emotion, and it suddenly hit me—destroying any vestige of childhood innocence I might have had left—that this would be the last time I saw my sister.

My husband, Henry, waited in his own chambers at the Tower for orders from his father, Lord Pembroke, since Pembroke had been an integral man of the council. But there were things I had not told Jane that I'd witnessed at Baynard's Castle. Secret meetings. Men flying up the Strand on horseback in the middle of the night with cryptic missives. Barges leaving Baynard's filled with cloaked figures and heavy wooden chests, their metal locks glinting in the moonlight. A tremendous guilt weighed on my shoulders, for I had not realized until now that Pembroke, my own husband's father, had been working against my sister.

And Mary Tudor was on her way to London.

I remembered Mary from when we'd visited her at Beaulieu as children. Unlike Princess Elizabeth, who was bitter and foul tempered toward me, Mary was always careful to be kind, but behind her kindness was a tightly coiled anger. I had seen it in her nearly black eyes. Hers was an anger that, once released, would not stop until all hell broke loose. I could feel it then, and I felt it now. Felt it in the shouts from the guards throughout the Tower as they called out, "Long live Queen Mary!" Felt it in the ringing of the bells, the intense boom of cannons, and the echoes of London's citizens as they cheered in the streets.

I glanced at Jane, my dear, dear Jane, my mouth in a grim line. She would suffer for this. For all my father's plans for power, for all of Northumberland's greed, she would suffer most.

"Do not look at me so, Kat. I may not have wanted this"—she spread her hand out, indicating her room, the small crown atop her head—"but I certainly did not come to it dragging my feet. I shall deal with the consequences as any royal woman would. I shall be the princess of the blood—the queen—that I am. I will not run from my fate."

I opened my mouth to speak, but nothing came out.

"Go. Lie low for now. Live." She waved me away, and her vacant gaze returned to the wall.

Guildford resumed his pacing, although he added the window to his circuit and peeked outside with frenzied eyes.

"Jane!" I shouted, my voice sounding odd to me—shrill with panic and regret.

Jane shook her head, her glossy eyes cast down to the ground, her white-knuckled grip in her lap betraying her distress. Her bright-green velvet gown looked oddly cheerful against her ener-vated figure. "Kat—" Her voice cracked, and she sucked in a deep breath. "You must remember this moment. You must learn from it, for you will be next when I am gone. See that no man rules over you, that no master calls you to their feet to do their bidding. Be true to yourself, Kat. Feed your mind and your soul, for the most riches to be had in the world are those up here." She tapped a long, slender finger to her temple. "Far more so than the riches of gems and gold. Be a strong princess of the blood."

How like my mother's words were Jane's—to think only of our pedigree.

Before I could respond, there came a loud banging on the door. "My lady!" The chief warder opened the door, his uniform of dark-blue and red trimmings, reminding me that I was not only in the place where monarchs come before their coronation, but also a prison.

"Lady Katherine, you must away now. The bells toll for Queen Mary, but also for the closing of the gates. I shan't say you'd be pleased to spend the night here. Your lord husband and His Lordship Pembroke await you by Traitors' Gate. They sent me up to fetch you. Make haste."

Traitors' Gate. I flinched. Why did they have to call it that? I'd never thought of it before now—now that Jane was considered a traitor to the throne. In fact, our entire family could be perceived thus.

The warder bowed his head toward Jane, and I watched a flash of pity cross his features before he shifted his gaze back to me.

I rushed to Jane and threw my arms around her, tears falling freely onto my cheeks.

"Take this." Jane thrust a book into my hands. I turned it over to see the thread of gold embroidery, Plato's *Phaedo.* "Socrates says in this book that it is only in death we achieve true knowledge, true purity. I have studied my whole life, Kat, to become this being who is knowledgeable in all things, but I still have this body, this silly body that holds me back from what I truly wish to attain. Socrates says, and I believe in his wisdom, that I shall not attain that which I've longed for my whole life until I pass from this body, and my soul is free to learn and absorb the truth."

Emotion choked me. I shook my head because I did not want to believe what she was saying. I did not want to agree with Jane, that she should have to die to attain knowledge. Her eyes were stricken. Fear flashed over her features, and I understood. Jane must tell herself these things to accept her imminent demise.

The incessant tolling of the bells reminded us.

"Do not fret, Kat. Queen Mary will be merciful to you."

I nodded emphatically, biting the inside of my cheek to keep from shrieking that I did not want her to die, and threw my arms around her yet again. Jane's embrace was not as tender, as if she'd already closed herself off, resigned to her fate.

"Godspeed, Jane!" I said against her shoulder.

"God bless Queen Mary," Jane responded, pulling away from me and going to stare out the window.

Her husband bowed to me, sitting heavily in a chair, his face pale, eyes dejected.

I hesitated, not wanting to leave these poor souls to their fates, but I myself could not stay here. I could not be a prisoner. Now that Jane's fate was sealed, I could not allow our line to die with her. I must, for the sake of my family, remain free.

"Make haste, my lady." The warder's voice sounded strained, as if he held back emotion.

I turned from the vision of my sister, straight-backed as she gazed out her tiny window, and left the chamber. It did not go unnoticed by me that the warder locked Jane in as I left, and he saw my narrowed gaze at his actions.

"'Tis the way of things, my lady. Orders from Queen Mary."

Queen Mary. Already, Jane was forgotten.

I nodded, thinking how only just that morning, Jane had been queen. The warder ushered me down the narrow, dark, winding staircase. With each turn he made in front of me, his torch disappeared. I was left in darkness until I caught up and could see again, only for him to turn and send me once more into blackness. I held my skirts high as I ran behind him, afraid that if I failed to keep them clear of my slippered feet, I would trip and fall to my death, and then I'd never leave this place.

The stench of disease, rotting food, and people, urine, feces, and, oddly, salty water filled the Tower like a cloud, and we waded through it, every few feet, a new and grossly exaggerated smell assaulting my nose.

Once at the bottom of the stairs, we exited the White Tower into the inmost ward, the crisp night air hitting my face, and with it, a new smell: panic and fear. Men and women scrambled to exit the Tower—soon to become a prison to my sister and any other traitors who were seen to be against the new queen. Horses whinnied and men shouted out orders.

The warder took my elbow, steering me through the crowds and beneath the portcullis at Wakefield Tower. Once through, his pace quickened, and I had once more to run to keep up, my royal slippers providing no protection against the stone path, sharp bits of rock digging into the soles of my feet.

We entered the darkness of St. Thomas's Tower, the scent of the wharf strong and insulting. Blood rushed through my ears, and my breathing labored with exertion and panic. Before I realized what was happening, my estranged child husband gripped my other elbow and led me to the barge, which housed the Pembroke arms and several retainers.

I collapsed against a cushioned bench as the barge lurched down the Thames much more quickly than I was used to.

As we approached the quay near Baynard's Castle, I heard the quiet whisper of my father-by-marriage to Henry. "Marriage to a traitor's daughter will not do, boy."

But the barge came to a sudden stop, and my body pitched forward, only to be caught by one of the Pembroke retainers, who steadied me.

I was quickly ushered from the barge and to my quarters, wondering if I would be locked inside them, as Jane had been.

What could Lord Pembroke intend? Did he mean to see me cast back into the Tower with my sister? Did he mean for me to suffer as a traitor? Apparently, the exchanged vows and marital contract meant nothing to Lord Pembroke, and young Henry would be powerless to defy his sire even if he wished to do so.

I stood, somber, numb, and barely lucid, as my maids undressed me and put me to bed. To my relief, my room was left unlocked. But my eyes would not close. All I could do was stare at the ceiling and wonder when the guards would rush in to arrest me.

Although I was of royal blood, I *never* wanted to wear the crown. How could I make certain everyone saw that? How could I make certain my father's ambitions were not pressed upon me? I had no royal aspirations! I wanted not to be called Majesty! 'Twas blasphemy!

All I wanted was to live a peaceful life. Serve my sovereign. Dabble with my herbs and poultices. Help those who could not help themselves—whether poor or sickly. Seek love within my marriage, if it was possible, and raise a family.

"I am a most loyal subject!" I exclaimed to the darkened ceiling, wishing Queen Mary could hear my words.

A rustling sound came from beyond my bed. "My lady?"

"'Tis nothing, Mrs. Helen. I was merely saying my prayers."

"God bless, my lady."

"God bless, Mrs. Helen." And indeed, we would need God's blessing.

Chapter Four

For which this second Phoenix may,
with Turtle true compare.
But well away, alas for woe,
his grief thereby began . . .
In prince displeasure throw this prank.
fell low this faithful man.
—Thomas Churchyard, Elizabethan Soldier and Poet

JULY 21, 1553

I had not been arrested . . . yet.

Jane was moved to a smaller chamber in the Queen's House within the Tower walls and Guildford to Beauchamp Tower. Many thought Queen Mary would put him on the other side of the Tower, but it appeared she had some heart after all, as the two buildings were close. Rumor filled the halls that my father would soon be brought to the Tower along with several other council members. 'Twas only a matter of time before Queen Mary had her revenge on those who'd sought to put her aside. When she came to collect Father, would she also toss Mother, me, and little Mary into a dingy, dark cell?

Pray, sweet Jesu, that our good and faithful queen takes mercy on my family!

It was ungodly hot in this place. I could not bear to call it home. Baynard's had never been a true home for me. The walls did not welcome me. There was nowhere that I felt safe. My maids stood around with fans, trying to cool me, and wet cloths were wiped over my brow and neck, but I could not seem to escape this fetid heat. The windows were open, but no air passed through. Outside was worse. Even the gardens were wilting.

While I was glad to have not been arrested, I had been left to languish. My husband and his family had gone to court to serve Her Majesty. Pembroke, the wretch, had left me with the words that my family was traitors and that he would not associate with traitors nor allow his son to remain married to a traitor.

Traitors. His liberal use of the word made me sick to my stomach. People were executed for being traitors, their heads stuck on pikes on London Bridge, and he would toss such an expression toward me? Had he no care for my well-being, my soul, at all? I had done nothing wrong, save be born to a father who would seek power and a mother with royal blood flowing through her veins.

If only I were of an age where I needed no guardian. I could have sought an annulment, run away to the continent. Or rushed off to a convent to live my life in peace with God.

My stomach pained me much. My humors were misaligned. Jane used to tell me of Princess Elizabeth taking to her bed often when they lived together at Dowager Queen Catherine Parr's residence. How Elizabeth complained of headaches and stomach pains. She had then been under the same duress I found myself under now, embroiled in courtly debacle outside her control. Would this be my life? Constantly in turmoil? I could trust no one, not even myself at times, because my fear for my family made me want to toss caution to the wind.

I was in limbo, unsure of what would happen next. Perhaps I would lie in bed until someone ordered me out of it. How else should I proceed? Without my family, I had nothing, and this farce of a family, this Pembroke household, had rejected me.

The Tower was where I should have been. As much as I abhorred the idea, I should have been there to take care of my dear sister. But the great Pembroke would never have allowed that. He might imprison me in his own castle, but he would not see me in the Tower. That would only have made the council and the new queen look on him in a negative light. He would save himself and the rest of his brood by keeping me here. In the dark.

"I wish to rest." I waved away the maids with my hand and stood on weary legs.

The bed was plush, and it beckoned me.

"Shall we undress you, my lady?" Mrs. Helen's voice was soft and comforting. I wanted to run to her, rest my head against her breast and weep, but I knew I could not. That would only have started more talk, and the last thing we needed was more talk.

If only there were someone who could deliver me from this place, from this pain, from this confusion! Flashes of my dance with Lord Beauchamp invaded my mind. A vision of his formidable mother quickly shoved them aside. 'Twas a fanciful thought. He may have been the only man I'd thus far in my life felt understood me, but there was little chance he would come to my rescue. Most likely, he barely remembered me.

Mayhap I should write to my step-grandmother Katherine, Duchess of Suffolk. She had a way of swaying people to her cause, especially now that her two sons, the heirs to the throne, had passed away—and she was no longer considered a threat.

JULY 25, 1553

An urgent letter arrived from my mother. I excused myself from the few servants I'd been advising on herbal remedies to read her missive. She feared my father's imminent arrest and begged me to pray for him. It was as if they had forgotten my sister, who languished without any hope for release other than the queen's change of heart. I burned the letter, hating every word scrawled upon it. My father should have been made to take Jane's place. 'Twas his fault she was imprisoned.

Another letter gave me greater pleasure and eased some of the ache in my head that had been intensified by my mother's news. It was from my step-grandmother, relaying that she would visit in a few days' time. Even better, she would be venturing to Baynard's with Lord Beauchamp's mother, the Duchess of Somerset, and her daughter, Jane Seymour.

The duchesses were both in good standing with Queen Mary— at the moment—and so had been allowed to come to me. A small spark of hope ignited inside me, although I would not allow it to flourish into flames—if I could be put into the queen's favor, perhaps I could ask her to be more lenient on my family, seek pardon for them?

But doing so could put me in a bad light. It was a quandary, a game. My step-grandmother, Lady Katherine, was staunchly evangelical, and Queen Mary might take great offense at our intervention unless she were paired with Lady Anne, whose late sister-by-marriage, Queen Jane Seymour, loving wife of Henry VIII, had been a true friend of the queen, as had Anne herself.

It would be a great risk to ask these women for assistance, but a risk worth taking nevertheless.

I hurried to the castle's chapel to pray. For only God was on my side, it seemed, and perhaps if I reached out to Him, He would

shine His light upon me and inspire mercy within the queen herself for my sister Jane.

JULY 27, 1553

Though I'd been allowed to plant some herbs, the gardens at
Baynard's were pitiful compared with those at Bradgate. But even
still, it was the only place in this vast manor where I felt comforted.
I shooed away a bee, gathering a basket full of lavender. The scent
calmed me, and lavender tisane helped with the exhaustion and
headaches.

But it would take an awful lot of lavender to ease my mind
after the most recent news I'd received. Father had been arrested
as Mother had feared, along with Guildford's brothers and father,
and many other courtiers who were seen to have played a part in
Jane's ascension. I was not surprised, as many, including me, had
wondered only when—not if—the arrests would take place. I was,
however, surprised that my mother and myself had not also been
taken.

Pembroke, my father-by-marriage, had all but guaranteed my
marriage to his son would be dissolved as he gathered men close to
him in secret meetings in efforts to gain the queen's favor. The news
filled me with both elation and foreboding. I disliked Henry. I did
not want to be married to him. But I was also aware that being set
aside—and accused of being a traitor—would place a black mark
on my reputation. I would be a scorned woman set aside and yet
not even a true wife first!

If only I could do something to sabotage his selfish plans—
and yet, doing something like that would only ensure I remained
unhappily wed. Perhaps in time, people would forget that I'd
once been married and set aside. But they'd never forget the

accusations against me and my family—once labeled a traitor, always thought one.

Pembroke's threats and whispered words had visions of heads on spikes running through my mind. It was as if I trod over a field of battle filled with upturned swords. I could not even guess the horrendous things he must have been whispering in the queen's ear about me—and who would deny him? I was sister to the woman who'd tried to usurp her. A princess of the blood. I was naturally Queen Mary's enemy.

She would have to be in an extremely forgiving mood not to reach out with her own two hands to tie the noose around my neck.

Arabel, my little, sweet toy spaniel pup, jumped onto my lap, curled herself within the folds of my skirts, and closed her eyes. I stroked her silky fur. Rex, a pup of the same litter, would not be outdone and came to rest his pretty face upon my slippers. The two soft balls of fur were gifts to me from my father—gifts offered out of guilt, but happily accepted nevertheless.

Rex upended the basket of herbs, stealing a sprig and running off with it. But even his puppy antics could not relieve the grave depression I found myself in. I prayed hourly that my sisters would be kept safe. My knees bore purple bruises from kneeling so long on the stone floor.

I stuffed the spilled herbs back into the basket and set Arabel down, clucking for her and Rex to follow as I headed back into the castle toward the kitchens. A bitter laugh escaped me, drawing attention from several servants who busily scrubbed the floors and walls. Arabel cocked her head, dark-brown eyes gazing into mine, as if she, too, were confused by Pembroke's contradictory schemes. I would have invited scandal by returning home to Bradgate—yet he sought to annul my marriage from his son and send me back himself.

While I waited for my lavender tisane to brew, I stood before the kitchen fire, my gaze fixed on the flames. Mrs. Helen pressed a steamy cup into my hands, and I drank greedily before pulling my mother's missive of a few days before from my sleeve and tossing it onto the hearth. The embers sparked on the parchment, creating red holes, black around the edges, until the entire thing appeared to melt into ashes.

Mother would be visiting the queen with my sister Mary to beg for pardons for Father and Jane. I held out little hope. This queen would surely seek revenge on those who'd gone against her. She'd spent too much of her life—nearly four decades—in a living hell. First she'd watched her mother fill with heartache as her father romped with Anne Boleyn. Then she'd been thrust aside with her mother, not allowed to call herself a princess. Her repeated requests to marry were denied. She'd not been allowed to see her mother, not even on her deathbed. And then her own brother once more pushed her away. Now that she'd obtained what was rightfully hers, Queen Mary would stop at nothing to keep it.

July 30, 1553

My nerves were wound tight for the visitors that should arrive today. The Pembroke household had yet to return, and I was essentially mistress of this place.

My mother did train me to be a lady of the castle when I was grown, and I was actually quite pleased with how well I did preparing rooms, food, drink, and entertainment for my guests. I'd picked rosemary from my garden and slipped it between their sheets, as it was a soothing herb, and I wanted them to be calm instead of chastising me for seeking their company.

They would stay with me for one night only, but despite such a short visit, I had been like a child wanting a sweet for the past couple of days.

My gown was newly made of tinseled silk and lace, a pretty yellowish orange that made me think of springtime flowers and happier times. The Good Lord above knew I had been lacking in small pleasures. Every day I awaited the news of impending doom—whether my own or my family's.

A flurry of footsteps and loud whispers interrupted my thoughts as a half-dozen servants rushed into the great hall, Mrs. Helen among them.

"My lady, your guests are arriving. Their barge has only now pulled up to the quay."

"So soon?" I dropped my embroidery into the basket beside my chair, stood, and rushed, servants following, down the myriad corridors until we reached the door to the gardens. I hurried down the flower-scented paths, the quay in sight.

The two duchesses disembarked with the support of several footmen. Their clothing and jewels sparkling in the sunshine, the women stood tall, stoic, a fearsome duo, and beside them, the young Lady Jane Seymour, Lady Anne's daughter.

I was jealous of her—that this Jane, named for the late queen just like my sister, should stand there free.

The sharp eyes of the Duchess of Somerset found me and looked me over. A hint of a smile touched her lips. My step-grandmother Katherine, for whom I was named, also considered me, albeit with a gaze gentler if somewhat guarded.

"Your Graces, I am honored to have you visit me here at Baynard's," I said with a deep curtsy.

"We are most pleased to join you," the Duchess of Somerset replied with an incline of her head.

"Let me see you, child," Lady Katherine said, twirling her finger to indicate that I should also do so.

I turned in a delicate circle, not wanting to trip on my gown.

"I see marriage has treated you well, dear," she said.

"As well as could be expected for one who is still a maid," I replied quietly.

The women nodded, and Jane looked at me with eyes as sharp and questioning as her mother's.

"We have heard the rumors of Pembroke seeking the queen's permission to annul your marriage on the grounds it was never consummated," Lady Katherine said.

I pressed my lips together and swallowed hard.

"Perhaps you might plead the marriage was consummated if you wish to stay married," Lady Anne stated. "Then the queen—indeed, the pope of Rome, for that is whom we shall end up answering to once more with Mary on the throne—could not offer an annulment."

The idea had merit—though did I truly want to go to the trouble to preserve something I'd never wanted, or should I just let it play out, leaving my fate in God's hands?

I chose not to answer her suggestion and instead changed the subject. "Might you like to walk in the gardens before we dine, or would you like to retire to your rooms for a short rest?"

Neither of the duchesses looked at one another, their gazes steady on me, but they each seemed to come to the same conclusion and did not press the subject.

"Let us walk." Lady Katherine linked her arm with mine, and behind us walked Lady Anne with her daughter. "Baynard's is very beautiful. Did you know it was built by a man named Baynard who was a follower of William the Conqueror?"

"I was not aware, Your Grace. It does have quite an old feel to it, with its dark towers and arrow-slit windows."

"Even the two princes of the Tower lived here for a time before they were taken prisoner."

I was struck numb for a moment with the irony of it. Those two young boys, the sons of Edward IV and Elizabeth Woodville, a future king and a spare, seen as a threat to the crown, had shared the same roof I lived under now. Was it a sign of things to come?

"Did you see many courtiers roaming about Baynard's while your sister was queen?" Lady Anne asked as she came up beside me.

I thought back to those bleak days.

"Yes, His Lordship did have many men coming to the castle to discuss things in private. Secret meetings, missives being passed, messengers in the middle of the night."

The two women exchanged a glance over my head that looked quite meaningful, as if I had spilled some news they wished to hear. A part of me had wondered whether I should share such details, but Lady Katherine was a trusted relation. And Lady Anne was a dear friend of said relation, as well as a cunning woman from whom I thought I might be able to gain some education.

"There is much suspicion about what transpired those short days. The queen will be most appreciative of your knowledge of those men, my dear." Lady Katherine patted my hand.

And would she appreciate Katherine passing the information along, or me for giving it? A twinge of irritation flitted in my mind at the thought. I knew my step-grandmother would be searching for anything she could use to gain favor with the queen. Would I again be a pawn? What was her true motive for helping me?

"Do you recall who the men were?" Lady Anne asked, her voice casual, but her eyes sharp.

My mind raced with questions. Was this their own plan, or had the queen requested the information? Was this how I would be saved, or even elevated at court? I decided I would tell them everything I knew, and what I did not know, I would find out. If they did the queen's bidding, all the better, and if they didn't, Queen Mary would still know that I was loyal to her. I had little to lose, and I had to trust that these women could help me.

"The Privy Council members, minus Northumberland. They did so behind his back, as most suspected he was a party to Father's plotting."

"And your father?"

"He let it be known he was ill and unavailable. The moment that the people seemed unreceptive to Jane's crowning, I think Father knew his plans would fall through."

The women nodded, their lips pursed. Jane skipped ahead to smell a patch of Tudor roses.

"Was Parr of Northampton one of the men in attendance?" Lady Katherine asked.

"Yes, Your Grace."

"You are a good girl, Katherine."

Doubt and guilt riddled my insides. I wanted to share this information with them. I wanted to aid whatever scheme or plot they were hatching, in hopes of saving my sister, but at the same time, I remembered my sister Jane's words, whispered to me when I'd parted from her in the Tower, and fear filled me. Perhaps it would be best if I said no more and went back to my embroidery and lying about in bed and daydreaming in the gardens of a marriage filled with love and little children bouncing around my feet.

Alas, that dream would never be. My husband was ruled too much by his father, Pembroke, and our marriage seemed unlikely to last.

"Why look you so sorrowful?" Lady Katherine asked. She lifted my chin with the tip of her finger and gazed into my eyes. "Do not be afraid, my girl. We shall see that nothing happens to you. We will keep you safe."

"But what of Jane?"

Lady Katherine pursed her lips and shook her head. "I am afraid there is nothing we can do for your sister, save pray to God that Queen Mary has mercy on her."

Mercy . . . What would Mary's mercy be? Already she had an army charging through the country and burning men for lesser deeds than proclaiming themselves the ruling monarch.

"And if you truly wish to be taken from this place, given a new start, perhaps I can be of assistance." Lady Anne's voice was soft but full of confidence. "Perhaps we should go inside and have a glass of wine or cider?" she suggested, her piercing gaze on a gardener who appeared to be doing more than just gardening. "Outside, one is never safe from prying ears."

The four of us went inside, and while Lady Katherine and Lady Anne put their heads together over glasses of deep-red wine, I poured cups of cider for young Jane Seymour and me.

"How do you like being at court?" I asked Jane, curious to hear how court was under a Catholic queen.

"I like it well enough," Jane answered, her eyes flicking to her mother. "But I will admit, if I can count you as a friend and confidant, that I would much prefer to be at home in Hanworth, attending my studies, among other things."

I sighed heavily. "You should indeed count me a friend, Jane, and I will admit to you that I do miss Bradgate, the manor where I grew up. No intrigue assaulted us there. Our days seemed so boring and mundane, and yet now that I have had a small taste of London and court, I yearn for a simpler time when all I had to worry over was when my tutor would let me outside to roam the gardens or to hurry the stable boy into saddling my mare."

Jane laughed. "Yes. I wonder if 'tis part of aging and becoming a woman, or if some country ladies still get to while away their days in leisure." She took a long gulp of her cider and laughed when a bit splashed on her chin.

"I do not know . . . ," I mused. "When we were at Bradgate, I do not recall seeing my mother overmuch. And at the time, I did not even think to see what she was about, unless she was instructing me."

Jane flicked her gaze to the duchesses. "I cannot say the same. My mother is always planning, talking with someone, or writing letters. She has been my whole life. Even at Hanworth, she is a lady of the court first, mother second, and lady of leisure never."

I wished I knew my own mother's character so well. Knowing her pedigree, what she represented to the crown, and the constant plans and plots of my father, however, I knew Mother could not be a country lady of leisure. I only wished I'd had more time with her before marrying to learn how to be a grown woman. To learn to love her for more than simply being my mother.

JULY 31, 1553

"My lady, a messenger arrived for you with this letter."

I looked up from the table in my personal chamber where I ate alone. Mrs. Helen handed me the rolled parchment. I pushed aside my barely touched plate of pheasant and capers.

I set the parchment down on the table and picked up my napkin. "Thank you, Mrs. Helen." I wiped my lips of invisible crumbs. My thumb brushed hesitantly over my mother's seal before I cracked it and turned my gaze to the banked hearth. The few candles lit about my room threw dancing shadows along the walls, and their long, dark fingers pointed, as if beckoning me to unravel the letter and read its contents.

Dear Katherine Pembroke,

I write to you to inform you of our queen's most gracious release of your father from the Tower. We are most pleased that he has been set free and that Queen Mary has seen fit to lift the charge of treason from his head. But with this good news also comes word that will bring sadness to your heart. The queen, in her most infinite wisdom, has found that your sister, Jane the usurper, must remain in the Tower and shall undergo a trial for treason. It is my most fervent wish that you pray for your dear sister, that Her Majesty may be merciful to Jane in her folly, and that Northumberland shall be punished for luring your sister into such deceitful actions.

Your mother,

Frances, Duchess of Suffolk

I should have taken a seat before reading. My knees grew weak, and I stumbled. As I fell backward, Mrs. Helen caught me in her sturdy arms and righted me.

"Come, my lady, let me put you to bed."

Yanking myself from her grasp, I reached to pick up the missive I'd dropped. I crumpled the paper in my hands.

"To the fire with you!" I shouted before tossing the paper into the hearth. I refused to budge, watching the paper smoke and slowly catch fire and only then letting myself be led to bed.

How could my mother be such a traitor—for she was in every sense of the word. She'd gone against her sovereign and her own daughter. And how could my father, the one who had forced this fate upon Jane, be set free while Jane sat imprisoned and facing trial?

The world seemed an awful, unjust place to me then.

If they could do such things to Jane, what would they do to me? I had not half her wit and intelligence, nor had I studied as hard as she to learn when someone might try to fool me into folly.

Chapter Five

And Cesar frowning on the fate,
there was none other but:
But fly the realm or prostrate fall,
full flat at Cesar's foot.
O states by this come learn to stoup,
no stoutness can prevail . . .
—*Thomas Churchyard, Elizabethan Soldier and Poet*

AUGUST 25, 1553

My thirteenth birthday.

But there was no one to celebrate with me. Mother wrote that she planned a visit sometime soon but had to take to the country for a bout of rest.

She said Jane had written a letter to Queen Mary, begging clemency and pardon. She reminded the queen that while she had played a part in herself being proclaimed queen, it was not all her doing, that she would be grateful for any punishment meted out to her, but that she hoped Her Majesty would be kind.

Despite my mother's cordial tone, I bristled with rage. It seemed that, in the past few months, I had aged by years and years. Mrs. Helen appeared to realize this and came to me often with rumors she had heard. I appreciated her diligence in seeking courtly news for me, since my mother only deigned to write infrequently, and the news she imparted was rarely helpful. The two duchesses and I were still in contact, but they were occupied with trying to find their own footing in this new court. Until I was reinstated in the queen's good graces, it would not bode well for them to be seen with me.

I crumpled up Mother's insincere letter and stepped to the hearth. The stones were cold, and ashes had been swept away. This late in August, I begged my servants not to light a fire for fear I would suffocate from the heat.

I reached for the flint and struck it until sparks shot out and my mother's letter went up in flames. I held it, watching as her words melted, but those words were not all that disturbed me.

"My lady!" Mrs. Helen rushed in and wrenched the burning paper from my hands just before it singed my fingers. She threw it onto the stone floor of the hearth and stomped on it. "What are you thinking? Would you hurt yourself?"

I turned absently to my old nursemaid, at once grateful for her presence and irritated by her question. My fingers stung where the flames had licked at my flesh. I examined my hand. It was pink in spots.

I shrugged my shoulders and glanced around for the tisane I'd been sipping. Mug in hand, I willed Mrs. Helen to take her hands from her hips and leave me. Maybe I did want to hurt myself. Maybe I didn't know how else to understand the pain and strife of this world.

But she didn't leave me. Instead, she wet a cloth and took my hand, cooling the spot where I'd burned myself.

"Have you an ointment for burns?"

I shook my head. Why had I not thought to make one? Surely such an ointment would have been useful. But I hadn't made one since arriving, as calming teas and herbs had been my recent passion. My world had been too filled with other, more pressing events to care much about making herbal remedies beyond the ones to ease my own suffering. And truly, my desire for things I once found inspiring had ebbed.

"I'll send for one then."

I did not reply, only turned away from her and walked back to the hearth, my gaze searching for remnants of my mother's letter.

"My dear, Kat, please speak to me." Mrs. Helen's voice held a note of pleading, and when my eyes met her rheumy gaze, wisps of her graying hair falling around her face, it struck me suddenly how much she also appeared to have aged of late.

I closed my eyes briefly and then opened them again. "A letter from my mother."

Mrs. Helen nodded knowingly. "Will she be coming this evening to celebrate your birthday?"

"No, she's gone to the manor in Sheen. I do not know for how long, but she's begged the queen's assistance long enough, she says. Now she must take care of her health, recover, I suppose, so she might try again in a month's time."

Mrs. Helen pursed her lips, but said nothing.

"I know what you are thinking, Mrs. Helen."

"I would never think anything that would displease my lady."

At that moment, Stew, my pet monkey, shrieked and bounded through the room, evidently excited about something. But his timing was such that the shrieks seemed to emanate from Mrs. Helen's own mouth, and I doubled over with laughter that bordered on hysteria.

Mrs. Helen realized why I laughed and made a play at sticking out her tongue at the monkey. "Laugh all you want, my lady. I suppose you are in want of a good jest." She picked up the monkey and chucked him under the chin. "You know your mistress well, Master Stew."

The monkey nodded and then started to groom her hair. When he plucked something from her mane, examined it, and ate it, Mrs. Helen let out a little cry of outrage and pulled the monkey from her shoulder, shooing him away.

"Now we've had our laugh. Will you not tell me what is on your mind?"

"I should like some fresh air that is not so blasted hot." I stuck out my lip, pouting. A walk in the gardens would have been heavenly, but judging from the stifling air inside the castle, I couldn't imagine outside would be any more breathable.

Mrs. Helen waved away an annoying fly. "Let us walk by the quay. The breeze along the water ought to cool you down, and the trees will offer a bit of shade. Perhaps we can find the herbs you'd need to concoct an ointment for burns."

I nodded my acquiescence, and we walked outside. The sun beat down on us, searing my skin even through my gown, until we reached the shaded path by the quay. Swans and ducks floated over the water, and boats drifted by at gentle paces. Odd to see the world passing me by as I stayed cooped up in Baynard's, unsure of my future.

"Tell me, my lady." My maid's voice was soft but firm, and I knew I could no longer hold back what had been eating at my gut and worsening my headaches.

"I've had a coded letter from Jane."

Mrs. Helen's stride did not falter, although her brows did rise. "A coded letter from your sister? Are you sure?"

"Indeed, I am. She used a code we made up as children one time when we were trying to avoid our studies."

"And it held disturbing news?"

I nodded, biting my lip. I stopped and tossed into the water some bread crumbs that I'd gathered from the kitchen on the way out of the castle. Several ducks quickly swam over and bobbed their heads beneath the murky water to snap up the morsels.

"She tells me there are rumors of another rebellion and she is helpless to stop it. A young nobleman named Wyatt wants to proclaim her queen once more. Equally disturbing is that she claims Mother has forsaken her. That the good duchess is having an illicit relationship with her groom. Mother lies when she says she must go to the country to rest. 'Tis so she can be alone with the lowly maggot." Tears of frustration welled in my eyes.

"Another rebellion? And did you say Her Grace is consorting with a groom?" Mrs. Helen had a canny knack of keeping her voice devoid of emotion that I found myself admiring.

"Indeed. The fools never get enough of trying to put Jane back on the throne. They are blind to the fact they cannot win and, in ignoring that, seal her fate. As for Mother, Master of the Horse, to be exact, but yes, she has taken Master Stokes as her lover."

"Poor Jane. Why do you suppose Her Grace has . . ." The breathy question was exactly the same one I had.

"Jane says Mother is most likely doing so because she is lonely and has only ever known the love of a selfish man. Perhaps she desires a gentler hand."

"And do you agree with your sister's assessment?"

I gazed out at the swans as they glided so elegantly across the water. "No."

"What is your opinion on the matter then?"

"Mother knows in her heart that Father and Jane will not be pardoned as the queen promises." A swift breeze came over us, ruffling my hair and spraying river water up in a cooling mist, as if in confirmation of what I'd said.

"My lady! Do not say such things." Mrs. Helen looked scandalized.

I shrugged. "I suppose she is protecting herself. Mother knows that if Father were executed, she could herself be used as a princess of the blood in a marriage bargain, and who knows which side would be the victor? She is aligning herself with a lowly groom so that no one will attempt to make her suffer the fate of her daughter." Horror came over me at my own words. No woman could be that heartless . . . but I feared that in this, my mother truly was.

Mrs. Helen blinked, comprehension lighting her eyes. "My lady," she gulped. "You know too much for a girl of your tender age. Come, let us gather your herbs, and then we will go inside, and I shall read to you from one of your books."

I nodded, because lying in bed while Mrs. Helen read to me sounded lovely, but also because I could not fathom the depth of the words I had just spoken. Mother would protect herself and see us all to a ruinous end.

"And perhaps there might be a birthday surprise inside waiting for you."

"What is it?" I asked, surprised to find myself capable of such sudden joy, my hands coming together in a clap. Mrs. Helen knew the right things to say and do to cheer me.

"Now, it would not be a surprise if I were to tell you." Mrs. Helen's eyes twinkled, and she smiled wide.

"Come now, Mrs. Helen, tell me! Is it a nightingale? A parrot? I have wanted a bird for so very long!"

"Come, then, let us see!" Mrs. Helen gathered her skirts up, and in the playful way she'd had since I was a child, she ran ahead of me.

When we reached the great hall, there stood Jane Seymour and her mother, the duchess, holding a pretty gilded cage from which a nightingale sang a beautiful melody.

"Her name is Cora, after the Greek goddess Persephone," Jane said with a smile as she gazed and cooed at the bird. "That was what she was called before her innocence was taken. I think you and she have much in common. Your beauty is unrivaled, and you've been kidnapped into a world you deem hellish. Have you not?"

Jane's sharp eyes met mine, and I could only nod. Her likening me to the Greek goddess of innocence, who was also queen of the underworld, shook me to my core.

I could not think on it further. Instead, I walked to the cage and cooed to the bird, who turned her soft brown feathered head toward mine and belted out a pretty answer.

"Thank you," I whispered, knowing that Cora would indeed bring me solace. I turned to the duchess. "I do believe I am in need of your assistance."

JANUARY 4, 1554

Fall left as mildly as she'd come—not bothering to cool down until the winter solstice was upon us. Even the leaves of the trees were loath to part with their branches.

But one thing was different: I was no longer in gloomy Baynard's. Soon I would be housed at court with the queen, who promised me an apartment of my own—which had my nerves frayed. Why should the queen wish me so close? For the time being, I remained in Sheen at Charterhouse—my mother's home.

I would begin this year anew. And once again a maid to be bargained with. Pembroke had finally managed to gain an annulment for Henry and me. True to her word, the Duchess of Somerset had eased the passage herself.

"She agreed," I said with an immense sigh of relief.

Lady Anne nodded. "Indeed. I received word Pembroke would approach Queen Mary, and so I arrived at court to attend Her Majesty. I managed to be in the presence chamber when Lord Pembroke was granted an audience. He barely gave me a glance before making his request for an annulment between you and

Henry. He stated the marriage had not been consummated. The queen questioned him, stating she'd heard otherwise."

My eyes widened. "Oh, to have been a fly on the wall when His Lordship heard that!"

Anne smiled at my enthusiasm. "He paled considerably and blubbered for a moment before shouting out that it was impossible. Queen Mary merely raised her brows as if to dare him to speak to her that way again. At that precise moment, when neither queen nor subject spoke, I cleared my throat and bade Her Majesty listen. Queen Mary turned a surprised gaze toward me but inclined her head in acquiescence. Pembroke looked baffled."

"What did you say?"

The duchess flicked her gaze away coyly, as if to say she was not committed to the conversation. "I informed Her Majesty that the marriage between Henry and yourself could not have been valid since you had already been precontracted to my son."

My heart skipped a beat, and I immediately recalled Lord Beauchamp's words when we'd danced on my wedding night: *Hope.* "*Hope for a chance at your hand when your time truly does come . . .*"

A servant knocked upon the door.

"Enter."

"Your Grace, a messenger has arrived for you."

Anne furrowed her brow a moment, then stood. "I shall return in a moment."

I stared after Anne's retreating figure, hoping all was well with her family. But soon my mind wandered back to Beauchamp. Now that I was unmarried, would he indeed claim me as his mother had implied? Handsome as the young man was, I felt myself fill with apprehension.

"Why should I feel uneasy?" I asked Arabel as I scratched behind one of her white fluffy ears. I looked to Stew, who picked at Rex's fur by the hearth, and even Cora cocked her head to listen.

My precious friends, if only they could speak back to me. "Should I not be happy to be wed to such a man? His mother is most loyal to me. I would not have the same issues as I did with Pembroke." *I have not forgotten the dance we shared and how my interest in him was piqued.*

Arabel tilted her head in question, and Cora sang out a pretty tune.

"I know, only words have passed over lips, but 'tis still as good as a betrothal in the queen's eyes, and I've yet to really get to know the young Lord Beauchamp."

Stew scratched his behind and then grossly offered up his tiny fingers for Rex's tasting pleasure. I raised a brow at that and shook my head.

"'Twas not the answer I was looking for, Stew."

I chewed on my lip, for Beau's sister Jane had become increasingly dear to me, as had his formidable mother. How could he be anything other than a decent fellow? Our first meeting had shown him to be quite a flirt, but beneath his outrageous tongue lurked a man who had truly seemed to cherish my company, if only for those few fleeting moments.

Searing pain passed from one temple to the other, and I squeezed my eyes shut. The world spun for a moment, and I shooed Arabel away so I might lay my head back without fear of dropping her to the floor. My megrims were coming more often.

"What is it, my lady? Are you not well?" Mrs. Helen rushed into the room.

I smiled a little at her uncanny knack for knowing when I would need her. "'Tis my head, Mrs. Helen."

"You have not touched your breakfast. Perhaps you are in need of sustenance. Your gowns are sagging. I've had to take them in. You must eat more."

I ignored her, my stomach protesting the idea of food. "It is an odd feeling, Mrs. Helen, being free from marriage and yet not free, since I will most likely be married again."

Mrs. Helen only nodded and handed me a sugared date. I bit into the sweet fruit and chewed slowly. "Mother says she will not allow me to marry again until the union can be consummated, and the Duchess of Somerset agrees. Queen Mary demands that I continue my education and, praise God and His disciples, accept the Roman Catholic faith. I shall journey to court soon to attend her."

"That is nice, my dear. I am sure you will be looked after well."

I nodded and bit into another date. I hoped Mrs. Helen was right. I had not had correspondence with the queen myself and so could not make judgment on how I would be received. Jane still languished in the Tower, along with her husband.

Lady Anne returned, her face pale. She came to stand before me, so tall and straight, her eyes as dark as her gown. "Katherine." Her voice sounded strained. "There is some news."

My stomach churned, and the dates I'd eaten threatened to come back up. I put the other date I'd picked up back on the trencher.

"News of the rebellion orchestrated by a man named Wyatt has reached the queen's ears, as has your father's part in it. They march on London at this moment. Queen Mary's council has succeeded in persuading her to seek out and punish those involved. Your father will be imprisoned once more." She took a steadying breath, and my heart sank. "What's more, your sister Jane and her husband, Guildford, were found guilty of their charge of high treason. Guildford's brothers were also found guilty—all are sentenced to death."

My lungs strained against my held breath. "What?" I choked out. I felt as though the blood of my entire body rushed to my feet. The room spun. "But the queen had said she would grant them pardon."

Anne nodded, her expression anxious.

"What should I do?"

"Pray."

The duchess left within minutes.

But I could not move. I remained in my chair for what seemed like hours. In reality, I had no idea how much time passed.

Mrs. Helen approached, placing a light hand on my shoulder. "Should you like to take a turn about the garden, my lady? I will fetch your mantle. 'Tis not too cold as yet. The fresh air may have your appetite coming back."

I shook my head. How could I walk outside in the fresh air, or even think about eating, when my sister was locked away in the Tower, sentenced to death?

FEBRUARY 1, 1554

"Oh, dear God," I whispered, for I couldn't find my voice. I ran to the chapel, my knees weak, bile rising in my throat, my lungs unable to fill with air. I stumbled over the threshold and down the aisle until I reached the altar, dropping to my knees, ignoring the pain of a jagged piece of stone on the floor cutting into my flesh.

"Our Father, which art in heaven, hallowed be Thy name. Thy kingdom come. Thy will be done in earth, as it is in heaven. Give us this day our daily bread. And forgive us our trespasses, as we forgive them that trespass against us. And lead us not into temptation, but deliver us from evil—" My voice cracked, and a torrent of emotion whipped through me. I could no longer recite the Lord's Prayer as I'd been taught from the moment of my birth, only lament to the Most Holy of Holies, that He have mercy on my sister. "Oh, Jesu, have mercy on us! Oh, Lord God, have mercy!"

I'd just received explanation for Lady Anne's horrible news about Jane and Guildford's sentencing. Thomas Wyatt the Younger, the upstart, who should have been banished from England years before, had undone us all. In attempting to reinstate my sister, he had signed the warrant for her death. Along with my own father!

"Lord, I pray to you! Show the queen my sister's innocence. Do not let her once again be blamed for the evildoing of men!"

My father's actions were perhaps the most vile of treacheries. How could he have joined Wyatt and his rebels?

My hands shook as I held them up in supplication, and tears streamed down my face. I didn't feel the cold, even though I'd left my cape in my chamber. Father's actions were akin to running Jane through with his sword. I sank all the way to the floor, my head resting on the cold stones.

And to think the queen had said she would let Jane go free . . . My sister should never see the light of day again.

To be so utterly out of control . . . To have no say. To be able to do nothing . . .

The rebels were said to be marching on London that very day. They would soon meet with the queen's army, and I prayed the rebels would see their folly, relinquish their weapons, and surrender in peace, for we all knew what the outcome would be should they fight. The queen would win.

FEBRUARY 11, 1554

"My lady, this package has come for you." I sat up in bed as Mrs. Helen handed me a paper-wrapped package tied with twine. "'Tis from your sister. One of the guards delivered it here himself. He said she gave it to him this night and bid him speed it to you. I told him you were abed, but he insisted."

My fingers shook as I took the package. Mrs. Helen lit several candles and then stood expectantly, as though she would watch me open it.

"Leave me," I said quietly.

Mrs. Helen stood a moment longer, assessing me, before she left the room.

I had not slept in days. Not since the queen had finally ruled that Jane, her husband, and my father were all to die.

After Wyatt's rebellion, she could no longer keep them alive without the threat of more rebellions. I was not angry with the queen, for I understood that her hand had been forced. I understood that she had been put to the test, and if she were to continue to rule, my sister must not be on this earth. Men—my own father—had gambled with Jane's life and lost. She had not agreed to the rebellion. Before their treason, the merciful queen had granted Jane a pardon and promised to release her from the Tower as soon as a royal heir was birthed. We'd been so close . . . And now all her promises were shattered.

"Damn you, Father!" I said vehemently to thin air. We, his children, were merely pawns, and now he had lost us to the other side. "Selfish, foolish man."

Jane would die tomorrow.

The recognition of that hit me with the force of a gale wind. I dropped the unopened package onto my bed and rushed from my room. Running from whatever it contained. My mind filled with images of us together as young children, happy, knowing we were there for each other. I could not let her die alone. Not without me.

Down the spiral staircase I flew and out the great doors of the manor toward the stables. The moon lit my way. I cared not for the cold, or that I was only in my night rail. I had to get to Jane. My bare feet froze against the crisp cold of the grass. Sharp rocks protruding from the ground jabbed painfully at the soles of my feet.

"Jane, I'm coming," I vowed, tripping on something in the dark.

My hands came out to catch my fall, pain zinging up my arms as rocks sliced into my palms. I pushed up to my feet, hearing the rush of guards behind me. But still I kept running. I would go to the Tower this night. I would go to her!

Strong hands caught me around the middle, swinging me up into the air. I fought against the force that would hold me back, kicking, punching.

"Let me go! Jane needs me! Put me down, you . . . bastards!" I'd never cursed before, and I didn't even flinch now. "Bloody bastards!"

"My lady, stop," one of the guards urged before my fist found his flesh.

"My lady, you must stop!" another said, helping the first guard to subdue me.

The men carried me, kicking, screaming, into the house, where we were met by Mrs. Helen.

"What on earth are you doing to a princess of the blood? To my lady!" Her voice was strong and broke through my fit of hysteria.

Uncontrollable sobs racked my body, but I had no energy left. The guards set me down, and I took a deep, shuddering breath, trying to calm myself. I was shocked to have reacted in such a violent way, and mortification sank in.

"I'm fine. Simply tired." I tried to be stoic, running hands through my hair and seeing my bloody palms too late.

The guards gazed on me with mixed expressions of sympathy and weariness.

"Oh, my dear," Mrs. Helen said, compassion in her eyes. "Come upstairs."

Mrs. Helen shooed the guards away and ushered me upstairs to my chamber, where she cleaned my hands and feet. I crawled into bed and my kind maid covered me, then ordered my fire to be stoked higher.

I rolled over, unwilling to look at any of the servants. I wanted to be alone in my grief. Mrs. Helen chased everyone from the room, and even she disappeared somewhere.

Something crunched beneath my ribs: Jane's parting gift.

I stroked a hand over the solid front, finding strength in the bold lines of her script.

But how could I open it? To open it seemed like accepting her fate, and the thought made me choke on my heartache.

I curled up in my bed, pillows fluffed behind me, and slowly unwound the twine. The paper fell open, and Jane's favorite tan leather-bound Greek Testament fell into my hands. A breeze came through my bed, ruffling the counterpane and bed curtains. I looked up sharply, expecting to see the ghost of my sister standing at the foot of my bed, but there was nothing there. Not even the shadows formed by the light of my candle danced. It was as if everything in this room waited with bated breath for me to open Jane's Testament. To see if she'd written something for me inside its glorious pages.

There, in Jane's perfectly neat calligraphy, was a letter on the blank pages.

I have sent you, good sister Katherine, a book, which though it be not outwardly trimmed with gold, is inwardly worth more than precious stones.

Trust not that the tenderness of your age shall lengthen your life, for as soon as God wills it, goeth the young as the old.

My good sister, let me entreat you once again to learn to die. Deny the world, defy the devil, and despise the flesh. Delight only in the Lord. Be penitent for your sins, but despair not. Be like the good servant and even in midnight be waking, lest when death cometh, he steal upon you like a thief in the night and you be like the evil servant, found sleeping, or for lack of oil, ye be found like the first foolish wench and like him that had not the wedding garment, ye be out from the marriage.

A smile crept over my lips and I paused in my reading. Jane's reference to the Parable of the Wise and Foolish Virgins was not just a reference to morals and corruption, but to a tender moment in our childhood. It was a moment shortly before she'd been whisked away to court, after which any semblance of a carefree child could no longer be seen—the once joyous smile and singing child transformed to a stoic future queen.

We'd sat one night upon the floor in front of the hearth, and Grandfather Charles Brandon, the great Duke of Suffolk and favored friend of the king, had come to visit. The snow had fallen hard and deep, covering the ground up to one's knees, and so our guests had been bade to stay. His Grace had called all the children—me, my sisters, and our cousins Henry and Charles—to the hearth, where he'd begun to spin a tale.

We'd laughed at his interpretation, as it had been a story already told to us before by the priest one morning during the sermon, but his telling of it had been so fierce, and Grandfather had made the tale more fun than the priest had. He'd even knelt on his knees in a moment of drama and begged the fabled wise virgins for oil, then nimbly jumped to shout his reply of "Nay!"

Curled in bed, I laughed to myself, and for a moment, life's bitterness eased, and I relished what time Jane and I had spent together. In my mind, I embraced her and sent a prayer up to God that He would embrace her, too. I returned to her letter and read further.

As touching my death, rejoice and believe that I shall be delivered from corruption and put-on incorruption, as I am assured that I shall for losing a mortal life and finding an immortal felicity. Pray God grant that you live in His fear and die . . .

I could not make out the next few words, as the ink was smudged, and when I ran my finger over the distorted letters, I thought for a moment I might still be able to feel her tears as they'd fallen on the parchment in her book. Tears sprang from my eyes, and as I batted my lashes to make them go away, a tear of my own mixed with Jane's smudged letters. And then I had to set the letter aside as fear and anguish overtook me, for I would never be able to ask Jane what those words had been. I would never know.

At length, I pressed my chemise to my face to swipe away the tears, pressed my fingers to my temples, and tried to rub away the ache.

I took several steadying breaths and then picked up the Testament again. For Jane. I would read for her, because her words had been so eloquently put together, because I could not abstain from it. I had to read what she had said. I'd known she possessed much wisdom, but I had not envisioned this depth. She truly had been a queen. Whether she was named a usurper or not, Jane could have led this country and tended to the souls of every man, woman, and child.

With that thought, I continued to read her precious words.

. . . neither for love of life nor fear of death, for if you will deny His truth to give length to a weary and corrupt breath, God Himself will deny you and by vengeance make short what you by your soul's loss would prolong. But if you cleave to Him, He will prolong your days to your comfort and for His glory, to which God bring me now, and you hereafter when it shall please Him to call you.

Farewell, good sister. Put your trust only in God, who only must uphold you.

Your loving sister,
Jane Dudley

"Fare thee well, darling sister. May God receive you in His loving hands, and may you know corruption no more," I whispered, closing the book very carefully.

I climbed from bed, clutching her Testament to my breast with one hand and carrying the candle with the other. To my chest I went. The very chest that once held my wedding clothes and now housed only what few jewels I'd been gifted in my short life. I set the candle down on the ground with shaky fingers.

I lifted the lid, and when it creaked, I half expected to see Mrs. Helen jump from some dark corner to inquire what I was doing out of bed. Moving aside several layers of silk yet to be made into a gown, I felt around the cavernous bottom for the latch I knew was hidden there. I opened the secret panel, revealing all the letters Jane had sent me while she was in the Tower, and placed this most precious one, her last to me, so conspicuously written within the pages of her Testament, on top of the others.

I would follow my sister's words, and I would take her Testament out and read it again and again when no one was about.

I sat back and stared down at the simple leather binding, the Greek letters etched on the front: *Novum Testamentum Graecum.*

Jane advised me to never waver from our evangelical faith. To not pretend support of Rome, as Mother and so many others were doing for the queen. Perhaps I should put my faith in something else. Love, if it existed.

To obey Jane's words meant she had not lived in vain, and yet to listen to her words meant to put myself in her shoes and travel to the scaffold shortly thereafter. That in itself seemed a sin.

I pressed a kiss to my lips and placed it on the embroidered letters.

One thing was for certain. I did not want to die.

FEBRUARY 12, 1554

I imagined the bells ringing out, even though I could not hear them in Sheen. The ground rumbled with what I swore was a thousand cannons, but it was simply thunder from the sky, as if God Himself were displeased at the events taking place today.

Jane and her husband were dead. I supposed I should have been grateful the queen had not had their heads put on spikes on London Bridge—though, despite knowing their heads rested in their own arms, the macabre sight of their lifeless eyes atop spikes haunted my vision.

Father would be executed in eleven days' time. I was not so forlorn for him. I thought it a fitting end for a man who'd done nothing but murder his daughter and thrust the rest of his family into danger's path.

I glanced across the table, as Mother had made me attend her this morning to break our fast.

"Why were you not in London with Jane?" My tone was accusatory. I was incensed that she had not gone to Jane in such a time of need.

She didn't even look at me. Instead, she glanced at Master Stokes, whom she now most obviously flaunted in front of everyone.

"Jane is dead. We made our peace a long time ago. She did not wish me there."

Mother's harsh words stole my breath. "Did she tell you thus, or did you make that assumption?"

My mother pursed her lips like she used to before she would pinch me or slam her hand on a table. I watched her take a deep breath before she answered, and while I was impressed that she had found some sort of new control over her temper, I was also irritated.

"She did not need to tell me. She refused to even see her own husband in recent days."

Mother had abandoned Jane.

Indeed, it felt as if all of England had abandoned her. Only a few stepped forward to offer feeble mumblings for the queen to spare Jane's life. How I wish I could have rushed to the Tower and grasped my older sister in my embrace.

"I know what you are thinking, Katherine, and you are a fool." Mother wiped angrily at her mouth with her linen napkin. "She was my daughter. I birthed her, raised her, loved her, and she was taken from me. No mother should have to see her child precede her in death, and yet I have. I did not abandon her in her time of need. I cleaved to the daughters I have left, the ones I *can* protect." She tossed her napkin onto the polished oak dining table and abruptly stood.

My sister Mary, sitting at an oddly leaning angle because of the shape of her spine, choked on her watered ale at Mother's abrupt move. She hacked and spewed, but Mother paid her no attention. Instead, her gaze was fixed on me with a mixture of tense emotions.

For the first time, I considered that my mother might be intimidated by me, though it had always been the other way around. She was resentful that no one had chosen her to be queen, that she was instead skipped over in favor of her children. That had to have been a huge blow to her ego. I almost felt sorry for her. Almost.

I did not let my gaze waver but hoped to convey through my eyes how much I abhorred her part in all this and the utter disgust I felt that she'd abandoned Jane. Mother held my gaze for the span of several breaths, the tension in the room growing palpable. I'd never stood up to her before, never dared. But now with Jane gone, my grief ruled me. My anger thrived. I held no fear for my mother any longer.

My mother glanced away, fumbling with her cup, and cleared her throat. "Do not make me out to be a monster. You are looking in the wrong place for someone to blame. Best you pray."

It was a bitter triumph for me, finally having turned the tables on the formidable Frances Brandon. The bite of bread I'd taken went down harshly in my throat. I watched with resentment as the great Duchess of Suffolk exited the room on the arm of her Master of the Horse.

"Pray I shall," I said to her back—but not loud enough for her to hear me.

Chapter Six

When from the heavens storms do blow,
and striketh down your sail.
From thunder cracks both man and beast
yea Sun and Moon doth fly:
The earth and all that lives below,
do fear the rattling sky.
—*Thomas Churchyard, Elizabethan Soldier and Poet*

JUNE 24, 1558

"Majesty." I curtsied to Queen Mary, who sat dwarfed in the regal chair built for her father. She was covered in jewels, velvets, and lace, and her pinched face had all but disappeared in the mountain of necklaces and her bedecked hood.

"You've a request for us?" she asked in a dull tone.

"Lady Anne Seymour has invited me to accompany her daughter, Jane, as she makes her way to Hanworth House in Middlesex. 'Tis not far from court. And with the recent illnesses, I thought to breathe some country air."

A number of courtiers and many of Queen Mary's ladies had come down with influenza, a disease brought to us from the continent, many suspected by Prince Philip, the queen's own husband, when he was here the year prior. I myself was struck with fever, but only briefly, as Mrs. Helen marched in and fought the illness as if it were the French themselves invading England and she the only savior of our beloved country.

"And has your mother also given permission?" Queen Mary looked hard at me as she always did when she spoke of my mother.

I nodded, not knowing whether that would make Her Majesty wish to turn down my request.

"What is your purpose at Hanworth?"

"Companionship to Jane Seymour." I kept my eyes upon the floor, hoping to appear meek.

"There is no other reason?"

I shook my head.

"Our advisors say we should fear that you live."

Her words shocked me, and I jerked my head up to stare into her black, beady eyes. "I am your most humble and loyal servant, Majesty."

The queen grunted. "And you will stay that way—a humble, loyal *maiden*. There are some poking about to determine your eligibility. Know that I will deny any requests for your hand in marriage as of now."

A maiden. The queen wished me to remain unwed. I swallowed hard and then nodded. A marriage and possibly an heir or two shortly thereafter would have strengthened my claim to the throne. I wanted nothing of the throne. I would have burned the records naming me heir if I could. "As is your desire, Majesty."

"You may go. We will send for you when 'tis time for your return."

"Many thanks, Your Majesty." I curtsied, but she'd already looked past me as if I were nothing to her, which, in all honesty, relieved me. I wanted to be nothing to her. I did not want her to fear me.

Moments later, I climbed into the litter that had been procured for our trip and leaned heavily upon the cushions.

My dear friend Jane Seymour was consumed by a fit of coughing.

"Oh, Jane. Here," I said, pity and sadness in my voice as I pressed a clean handkerchief against her palm.

Her coughing did not abate for several minutes, racking her entire body. She held the linen to her lips, trying to maintain some feminine delicacy. When she pulled it away, the cloth was no longer white, but pink and red with a mixture of blood and sputum.

"'Tis a blessing Queen Mary dismissed you from court for the summer months," Jane said quietly, tucking the soiled linen away.

"Indeed it is."

She shivered and pulled the blanket resting on her legs up around her shoulders. Her normally sharp eyes looked glazed.

"You have a fever," I accused her.

Jane's fevers came and went. Luckily, her vomiting seemed to have eased somewhat. She'd drunk the tinctures I'd made for her, but I could not tell if they bolstered her or not. The cough she'd had for some time did not appear to be improving, and this bout of influenza was making it worse.

"Not overmuch, Kat. 'Tis just the wind."

"Hmm . . ." Her illness was lingering too long. I shuddered to think what could happen to her, but the physicians at court had prescribed fresher air to heal her—and the queen had all but banished from the castle anyone who was ill. All I could do now was pray. Pray that she would get well once again. This court needed her, but most of all, *I* needed her. Without Jane, I would not have known what to do with myself. She was my confidante, but she was more than that. With my own elder sister executed—and oh, dear God in heaven, I missed my sister Jane so—and Mary off with

Mother and her new husband, I was left without a body I could trust. Everyone knew the little shrews about court did nothing but gossip.

Jane had become a sister to me—I think partly because she shared the namesake of my own sweet sister Jane. We were much the same, and in her, I had found a person I could turn to in time of need, and she likewise.

Because Jane was too ill to ride, the litter had been procured for us. A bitter wind swept through the openings of the thick curtains despite the summer season. I tried to close the curtains more and gave Jane my blanket so the wind wouldn't chill her. A thunderstorm had pounded London and the surrounding parts for days now. In our covered, horse-drawn litter, the cool gusts of wind sent shivers up and down my arms, and droplets of rain whipped inside. Wetness seeped into our gowns, making the fabric cling uncomfortably. The duchess's home was not too far from court, mayhap an hour, since she resided on the outskirts of London. I saw a roaring fire in our future.

I looked to Jane, whose eyes were drifting closed. Her lips were bluish, her skin an eerie, pale alabaster.

My throat went dry with fear. "Jane!" I reached out and shook her shoulder, sighing with great thanks when her eyes popped open.

"Are you well, Kat?" Her voice was worried, her eyes stricken.

I searched for something to say. "We are almost there, 'tis all." I could think of nothing else, and I was sorry to have startled her, but for a panicked moment, I'd thought she'd left this earth.

Jane smiled, her eyes tired but still holding a teasing glint. "You are excited, are you not?"

"I confess I am. 'Twill be a nice reprieve from court. The intrigues and constant need to look over one's shoulder do pain my conscience at times."

Jane's face fell slightly, looking sad. "I am sorry 'tis the way of things for you. If only the queen would see you for who you are, and not for what you mean to her throne."

I nodded and looked down to where my hands were gathered in my lap. "'Tis not something I shall ever forget, or be free of. The queen would have me remain a maid, for if I were to marry, I would be even more of a threat to her."

"What makes you think such?" Jane's brows furrowed.

"She has told me."

"The queen must know that you are a most loyal subject. And what of Princess Elizabeth? Does she still bear you ill will?"

"I fear her opinion of me, Jane. She and my elder sister did most dislike each other as children, and Princess Elizabeth often found Jane to be a usurper to her in many ways before she was even crowned queen. She fears much the same from me as she did from my sister, and since Jane . . ." I trailed off, sadness overcoming me, even after all these years.

My friend laid a cold hand upon my cheek. "I understand. My own sisters, Anne and Margaret, are very close to me. I could not imagine if someone were to take them from me."

"'Tis a dangerous thing to be born of noble blood."

"No, 'tis a dangerous thing to play at court, Kat."

Jane's eyes shone with sadness, most likely as she remembered the execution of her own father when she was just eleven, and then that of her uncle. I reflected how the executioner's ax reached so much further than just the neck it touched, to those who shared the blood and tears of the one condemned. We all suffered when one's life was laid forfeit to a monarch, and we were all supposed to trust in God that our Most Gracious Majesty was doing right by us.

But was it right for Queen Mary—God bless her—to burn nearly five hundred God-fearing people because they did not share her beliefs? An acrid reek of burning flesh lingered ceaselessly in the city streets. It was no wonder people whispered, "Bloody

Mary," a wicked name they'd given her, behind their hands. And my sister . . . who most nobly wrote to Her Majesty, begging forgiveness and lamenting that she'd been only a pawn. To have been forgiven and then had Her Majesty rip that pardon away like a child wanting her toy back. Only the toy was my sister's life.

And my father . . . He had been as much a monkey in the game of plotters as my own pet Stew was in his scheme to steal bananas from Cook. Father had never been very good at planning things but had gone along with what others told him—a treasonable offense. It had been obvious to anyone with half a wit that the plan for Jane to be queen had not been an idea of his own making, but Pembroke's and Northumberland's—even though he'd taken part.

Tears pricked my eyes. I must push away these thoughts. I must somehow find my place in this world.

I pulled back the curtain to see puddles covering the ground below. While the sky was still a murky gray, the rain had finally stopped, and fingertips of sun tried to pierce the dark clouds. Up the road, behind a low brick wall, was the manor house, candles lit in the windows as the sun had begun to set.

'Twas ironic that I should come to this place that was once owned by Catherine Parr. My sister Jane visited while in the dowager queen's care, and now here I was visiting it myself, caring for another.

Just as I was about to put the curtain back over the window, the sound of a horse and rider barreling up the road caught my attention. I stuck my head out a little farther, bracing for the sting of raindrops upon my face, but none came.

It was a nobleman, his figure solid and straight upon his horse, wearing a black velvet hat that dipped to the left of his head with bright white plumes held in place by sparkling jewels. A short dark beard graced his chin, and above that was a full-lipped, wide smile. His nose was long and straight, and his piercing hazel eyes gazed into mine.

A spectacular sight.

He pulled his horse up alongside the window and doffed his cap. Recognition hit, and my stomach did a flip. I'd never seen a man with a more handsome smile or whiter teeth. More than a year had passed since we'd last seen each other. Lady Anne had once used a mock betrothal between us to save me from Pembroke. Though it had been a ruse, I'd secretly wished he were mine in truth—ever since he'd captured my heart on the dance floor after my wedding to Henry Pembroke.

"My lady," he said in a deep, smooth voice. He dipped his head in a slight bow, then returned his cap atop his curling dark hair. "Lord Beauchamp at your service once again."

He nudged his horse closer and took one of my hands, which rested on the sill of the litter window, pressing my fingers to his lips. Even through my thick lambskin gloves, I felt the heat of his lips on my skin. A tingling sensation wound its way up my arm, into my chest, and through my body until it settled in my stomach. I let out my breath slowly, so he couldn't tell that I'd been holding it. The rogue! The twinkling of his dark eyes conveyed he knew just how his chivalrous gesture affected me, and he took pleasure in it. It would appear that our courtship just might pick up again. Anticipation flooded me.

"May I have the pleasure of escorting you along your way?"

From behind, Jane snorted and stuck her head out the window. "My goodness, Beau, can we not enter the manor before you try to seduce my dear friend?"

Her voice was filled with teasing, and loving affection, and while she ribbed her brother, she also afforded him her approval of our flirtation. I found it to be very like her.

"Ah, but her beauty has bewitched me. I long to know dear Lady Katherine better."

Heat crept into my cheeks, and I bit the inside of my cheek to calm my racing nerves. I recalled vividly the outrageous way he'd flirted with me at my farce of a wedding to Henry. How I'd dreamed Lord Beauchamp were my groom.

"I thank you, my Lord Beauchamp, it is a pleasure to see you again, especially knowing how your sister is so very fond of you."

"And I am so fond of her." He spoke of Jane but smiled at me.

My breath caught in my throat as I took in his meaning. Years had gone by since we'd danced at my wedding—five, in fact—and he was a man grown now, and I a woman. We'd passed each other at court, but there had been no excuse for conversation, much to my disappointment. I flushed. I'd thought him handsome before, but now . . . he nearly took my breath away. I fidgeted with my gown. What should I say? What should I do? I glanced down at his horse's hooves, suddenly overwhelmed with shyness.

Nothing had ever come of the Duchess of Somerset claiming we were betrothed so my marriage to Henry could not have been legal. From that moment on, Queen Mary had approved of our courtship, but a marriage offer had never been made or accepted, and he'd been abroad the last year, our connection severed. Now, here he was again.

Was there cause to believe we might have a future together? The queen and both of our mothers had approved before. Now that we were of an age to marry and produce heirs, perhaps our mothers could persuade the queen to agree once more. Dear God above, could I hope for such a fate? Beau was more handsome than I remembered, age having given him more distinct, masculine, sensual features.

Time appeared to stand still, and when, from the corner of my eye, I saw Jane turn her gaze from Beau to me, the moment was lost. The flames on my cheeks could not have gotten any hotter. Beau's grin grew wider.

"We shall see you at the house, Brother." With that, Jane slammed the curtain shut and then broke into a fit of coughing.

The banter had been too much for her.

When her breath returned, she said, "You are in love with Beau, are you not?" Her brow rose toward me in challenge, and I was taken aback by her abrupt candidness.

"I am . . . fond of him," I said, pretending to wipe away a piece of lint on my gown. My skirts were damp, and I could feel curls pulling loose from my hood and pushing their way outside my headdress to lie against my forehead and cheeks. I must have looked a fright in front of Lord Beauchamp. No wonder he'd smiled.

Jane reached over and gripped my hand. "You look very beautiful, Kat. My brother saw beyond the windblown hair and soggy gown. Trust me. He only had eyes for your lips and your fiery gaze."

I chuckled at Jane. "So he is not unlike any other man then, looking merely for a little flirtation?"

"Indeed, my darling companion, indeed. I do believe my mother invited him to Hanworth after the queen gave permission for you to accompany me."

"Is that so?" My mind started to crank, the wheels turning, and thoughts of marriage came to the surface once more.

Jane nodded. "She sought your mother's approval, I'm sure."

I licked my lips nervously, and my heart beat rapidly. A small smile started at the corners of my lips and then grew wide. Excitement cascaded through me. My time at Hanworth House was already proving to be quite invigorating to my spirit.

"My lady, Her Grace has requested your presence in the great hall."

I nodded to the maid who'd delivered the message. With shaky hands, I smoothed the wrinkles from my gown. We'd arrived at Hanworth some hours ago and taken much needed rest.

"Are you in need of assistance?" the young maid asked.

While I'd lain abed wondering what this trip would bring about, Mrs. Helen had gone to make the acquaintance of the household servants, which always made our stays at various homes much smoother.

I licked my lips nervously. "No, I am ready. Will Lady Jane be joining me?"

"No, my lady, she is still abed and has begged her mother's pleasure to stay there."

I nodded my understanding and took a step toward the door, somewhat unnerved by how unsteady my legs were. Seeing the duchess wasn't so much what had my nerves acting up. No, it was Beau. Would he be there? What would we say to one another?

I smoothed my flawless skirt for the hundredth time, counted the drop pearls at my waist. "Will you find my companion, Mrs. Helen, and inform her I've been called to the great hall?"

"Indeed, my lady." The maid curtsied and hurried down the corridor in the opposite direction.

Moderately calmer, I descended the curving stair. Voices and music drifted from the great hall, along with the delicious scents of roasted meat and freshly baked bread. My stomach growled loudly, and I realized I had not eaten yet today—a bad habit often affecting me. My face heated at the sound of my stomach protesting the lack of food, even though I was alone. I paused at the foot of the stairs. Perhaps I had better go to the kitchens and pluck a small roll to calm my belly.

"Lady Katherine, will you not join us?" Beau's voice interrupted my contemplation.

I jerked my head up to see him lounging in the doorway to the great hall, his crooked smile directed at me.

"I thought I heard you approach, but you did not enter," he said.

Heat filled my cheeks. "My lord, my apologies, I was just thinking about something."

"Care to share?" He grinned, his countenance welcoming, and I wanted nothing more than to confide in him. But I could not.

"Not particularly."

He chuckled. "Come then, and please, no 'my lord.' Let us be less formal with one another. We have known each other for quite some time, have we not?"

"Indeed, we have."

He took a step toward me. "And have we not been close in the past?"

"Right you are again." My voice came out breathy as my pulse hitched.

Closing the distance between us, he said, "So you agree then?"

I nodded, not really sure what else to do or say.

"May I call you Katherine?" He held out his arm.

I nodded again and took his proffered arm. I had to stop my fingers from massaging the well-formed sinew beneath his surcoat.

"Then I must insist you call me Ned."

"Ned? But you are Beau to everyone else."

"I am Beau to my mother and my siblings. I do not want to be Beau to you."

I frowned, slightly hurt that he didn't want me to be so familiar. Perhaps I had read too much into his flirtations.

"Do not frown so, Katherine." He stopped and turned toward me, bringing my hand to his lips, where he kissed my knuckles, stealing my breath. "Do you find the name Ned offensive?"

"No, 'tis a nice name." I gazed around the great hall, trying to avoid his eyes. The duchess stood by the hearth, discussing something with one of the servants.

"Beau is a name I've had since I was a babe. I would rather a woman of your beauty, a woman I am . . . fond of, call me by a man's name."

My stomach did another little flip.

"You would look at me as a woman does a man, would you not, Katherine?"

Beau was openly flirting with me. The things he said were scandalous. Mother would have dragged me out by my ears. I opened my mouth to speak, not sure any words would come out. I was nearly panting with nervousness and the desire for his lips to press to mine. Wicked thoughts! I dared not speak and only nodded.

"Beau, darling, cease making love to my guest and offer her a glass of honeyed wine." The duchess saved me from embarrassment, and I was grateful, as I was not sure all the decorum I possessed could have kept me from leaning into Ned's arms and pressing my lips to his.

What is wrong with me? I had been raised as a princess of the blood. Straight back, strong chin, stomach sucked in, hips square, feet planted in a ladylike fashion, hands held together in front of my waist, inclines of the head, simple smiles, but emotionless, neutral. Above all things, do not act the fool. And here I was acting like a foolish, common woman—a harlot.

I stepped away from Ned and then, taking measure that he was still entirely too close, took another step away from him.

The duchess approached, and I breathed a sigh of relief. With Lady Anne by my side, I could better weather the storm of emotions raging through my veins. She floated on air, this willowy woman who was once the most prominent in England. Her skin stretched taut over her cheekbones. If she were to smile, she might very well crack, and perhaps that was her reason for not smiling. Indeed, I'd seen her lips quirk perhaps only a dozen times in all the years I'd known her.

She was a sad woman, but driven. Whatever demons chased her when the candles blew out at night, she did not let them rule her during the day.

"Lady Katherine," she said in her smooth, strong voice, "we are honored that you accompanied Jane to Hanworth for the summer."

I dipped into a curtsy. "Your Grace, it is I who am honored to have been invited."

Lady Anne dipped her head.

I accepted a goblet from Ned and sipped at the sweetened wine. "Thank you, my lord."

He narrowed his eyes at me, and I acted as though I did not notice. He may have given me leave to call him Ned in private, but I would not break with custom in front of his mother.

"Lady Katherine, you must tell me everything that is happening at court."

Now this I was very comfortable with speaking of. Though I'd feared her once, the duchess had long now been a trusted ally of mine.

"Princess Elizabeth was recalled to court after her imprisonment for nearly a year. She was to attend the queen in her confinement . . . but it does appear that another phantom pregnancy afflicted Her Majesty." I shook my head, truly saddened for Mary Tudor. She did not deserve the trials she'd gone through as queen after having lived with so much torture as a princess.

Lady Anne's face changed little as she accepted my news. "How does Princess Elizabeth treat you?"

I chewed my lower lip a minute and took another sip of wine. Without food, I felt the wine going straight to my head. I hoped we would eat soon, else I would be light-headed and giddy from drink. "She is cordial to me. We see each other with the queen daily, as we are both in her presence, but I think there is anger she harbors from the past."

"From Jane?"

I nodded, the mere mention of my sister bringing back painful memories.

"Elizabeth is much like her father, I believe," Ned added.

I nodded in agreement. "She has been through much, as Queen Mary has, and I am a constant reminder that some fraction of Protestant England could steal away her inheritance of the throne and give it to me. Many believe her to be a bastard still. I think this weighs heavily on her, but not as heavily as the queen's imprisonment of her. She looks on me and sees that she is treated in an ill manner while I have apartments at court and spend my days with the queen."

Lady Anne gestured for us to sit at the table, where steam wafted off roasted boar and fresh-baked rolls called to me. I sat down and politely took a small portion of the dishes, tasting one bite of each. How I wished to eat with abandon, but decorum would not allow it. I gazed at the duchess's silver plate and saw she had eaten even less than I.

Ned ate in energetic bursts but managed to not spill nor get a bit of grease upon his lips.

"I would make a suggestion to you, Lady Katherine," the duchess said, swirling wine in her goblet. I nodded for her to go on. "Befriend Princess Elizabeth."

I peered at her with curiosity. I did not necessarily take issue with befriending the princess, but it would be a difficult task, as she was more often than not quite aloof with me.

"What do you think I should gain from it? The queen would surely notice, and I do not want to call negative attention to myself, especially in light of speculation constantly being placed on Elizabeth's shoulders."

"'Tis true, Your Grace. I would not wish Katherine put in harm's way."

The duchess raised her brow at Ned's presumptuous use of my Christian name but did not make a comment on it.

"'Tis a fact that Princess Elizabeth could be queen one day, and if the present queen is still suffering from phantom pregnancies and her health becoming more and more unstable, then you should indeed take an interest in gaining friends at court who will be Elizabeth's allies—as well as Elizabeth herself. That is, unless Queen Mary changes her mind and decides to partially honor the Device for the Succession written by her brother and names you her heir."

Her words struck me, cutting off my air, and I forced myself to breathe. If Mary named me next in line, I would run away. Far away. Live in a hovel if I had to. I would not be resigned to the fate of my sister, for I'd not the desire to fight Elizabeth.

Chapter Seven

Where Gods are moved, in soaring clouds
like dusky mantels black:
The troubled air to mortal men,
doth threaten ruin and wrack.
I turn my talk from such discourse,
and treat of that turmoil . . .
—*Thomas Churchyard, Elizabethan Soldier and Poet*

JUNE 25, 1558

I awoke to blinding light. The drapes were drawn open, and through the thick glass, the sun shone brighter than I'd ever seen it. I tossed back the blankets, my feet hitting the chill wood planks of the floor. I jumped from one foot to the other until I found my slippers, still unused to how drafty this castle was, despite summer having arrived.

Padding to the window, I glanced out at the great green expanse that was Hanworth Hall. The grass shone with dew, and a few field flowers popped up here and there. The sun blazed high, and although there was a slight nip to my room this morning, oppressive heat would take over by afternoon.

"Ah, so you have decided to wake. The duchess awaits you in the hall before Mass."

I whirled to see the maid who'd come by the day before standing in the doorway.

"Do you know what today's activities include?" I asked, hoping a ride on horseback or a walk outside was at the forefront.

She clucked her tongue. "For certes, Her Ladyship does not confide in me. Best you find out from her."

I frowned and chose to ignore the curmudgeon. Since I'd given Mrs. Helen the morning off, I let the new maid dress me in a fine gown of black velvet trimmed with burgundy lace.

"How is Lady Jane this morning?" I inquired.

"She is still abed. Had a fit of fever last eve."

My heart sank. Jane always appeared weakest in the morning. I prayed that by afternoon, she would regain her strength.

I hurried to the hall, where the duchess stood, back rigid, with Beau beside her. I was having a hard time thinking of him as Ned, for in truth, he was a Beau to me. His handsome countenance oozed confidence, and his gaze held something of a devilish glint this morning. What was it about courtiers?

I stifled a smile not only because it threatened to curve my lips in a way the duchess would find most unladylike, but also in hopes of warding off the flutter of my stomach whenever I gazed at him.

Evident it was that Ned was his mother's favorite child. She held no great love, it appeared, for any of them, but if one were most in her favor, it was he. Her gaze appeared to soften when she looked at him. I wondered yet again how much she had suffered.

I supposed being the wife of the late Lord Protector, a man executed for treason, could not have been easy.

We were alike in the execution of our family members, and perhaps that was why she did not hold the same disdain for me that she did for other young ladies at court.

"I am pleased you finally decided to grace us with your presence, Lady Katherine." Her voice was clipped, but the look Ned cast my way did much to alleviate any embarrassment I felt at having made them wait.

I curtsied before her, and she inclined her head before leaving the hall.

Ned offered me his arm, and I took it, my fingertips tingling atop his velvet-covered forearm.

"Katherine, I had thought to ask if you wished to go for a ride this morning after we break our fast, but with the heat, you may be more comfortable with perhaps a game of cards instead?"

My eyes widened in panic. I did not know how to play cards! At home, Mother and Father had often played cards, but their priest had advised against us children playing, saying it would lead to idolatry and devilishness. Over the years at court, I'd abstained from playing for fear someone would realize my ignorance. Now there was no help for it.

"I confess, I do not know how to play."

A deep rumble of a laugh came from his chest. "You've never played? Would you care to learn then?"

I glanced up sharply, and my cheeks heated. "You would teach me?"

"If you are of a mind to accept my lessons." His eyes twinkled, and I felt myself leaning closer to him.

"I would be most pleased."

"Your pleasure *is* what I seek," he said in a near whisper.

If 'twas possible, my face grew hotter, until I thought for certes flames would come shooting from my flesh. The man was flirting with me, and while I'd been flirted with many times, never before had a man made me feel so . . . so . . . breathless! I wanted to dance and twirl and sing. So unlike me.

While I enjoyed his company, and even dared to dream of a kiss from this handsome courtier, I was also scared. How could one man make me feel this way? I'd been warned to never align myself with any one man. My duty was to England, and if I were to be joined to a man, it would be of the queen's choosing. Not even my parents were at liberty to make that decision after what had happened with my first marriage. But this was what I wanted, in my secret heart of hearts: a man to love, cherish, start a family with, grow old with.

I held my breath for a few moments to slow my beating heart so that when I finally felt able to answer, I did not squeak like an innocent schoolgirl. "I shall eagerly await your instruction."

The sultry gaze Ned threw my way was anything but innocent. His hooded lids hid a thousand sinful words. I felt it all the way to my toes in a tingling whirlwind. A premonition of our flirtations turning dangerous flitted across my mind, but I pushed it away. I wanted to be happy. I wanted the promise of love that this man seemed to be offering.

Nevertheless, I could not shake the feeling of unease, and when Mass ended, I retired to my room, begging not to be disturbed.

"I suppose I shall forgive you, Lady Katherine." Ned came to stand in front of me while I pegged first one and then another clove into an orange. His hair was tousled, as he'd just come in from a ride, but his eyes twinkled and his full lips curved in a crooked grin.

I raised a brow, momentarily stunned by his proclamation, then smiled. I set the orange on the trestle table in the great hall. A cursory glance showed a few servants on the perimeter, but other than that, we were completely alone. "Whatever for?"

"The death of my father."

His words were shocking, and I gasped, taken aback and at once confounded by the contradiction in his words and his merry expression. I had expected him to say something about not taking up his offer to learn a game of cards that morning.

He must have been teasing me; I could find no other explanation for it. But his words weren't funny. I felt a little addlebrained, as if I were missing a huge piece of a puzzle that I should know. I swallowed, rolling his statement around in my mind.

"How have I anything to do with the death of your father?"

I was suddenly uncomfortable in my own skin. Racking my brain for all clues.

Ned picked up the half-finished pomander and sniffed, closing his eyes a moment in pleasure. "There truly is nothing better than the scent of citrus and cloves, my lady. As to my sire's death, it is not you specifically, but your own father who signed the Lord Protector's death warrant."

Guilt riddled me for my father's sins. How much pain had his schemes caused others and not just myself and my sister? I stared at Ned, my mouth dry.

He plopped the pomander back on the table and smiled. Did the man have no shame? He spoke so flippantly, as if we discussed the weather or the latest hunt. I narrowed my eyes, for I did not follow his line of thinking and did not find humor in his words or the situation as he seemed to. Here I had thought our courtly banters were meaningful, that perhaps . . . something more would come of them. Had I been too naïve?

"I am truly sorry for what transpired, my lord, but I pray you not judge the child for the sins of the father."

His gaze locked with mine, and he picked up the pomander and set it back in my hand, his fingertips brushing my palm, causing a shiver to race over the extended limb.

"Oh, Katherine, I could never blame you, truly. My words come out not in the way I intended. I hoped to make a jest of something that mars both our hearts. I know your father, like mine, was executed for the crime of treason. I meant no harm, my lady, but only to bring up the fact that we have shared a similar past. Perhaps I have gone about it in the wrong way. I pray I have not given offense."

I shook my head, sad in my heart. "I will endeavor not to be offended. But—"

"Yes?"

Despite his excuse that he wished to broach our similar backgrounds, I was still perplexed at this conversation. "There is one subtle difference that you have not mentioned, my lord."

"And what is that, sweet lady?" His eyes were still merry as he smiled at me.

I swallowed back my baser desires. "My father was guilty, and yours was not."

He chuckled softly, lifted a leg to place his foot on the bench where I sat, and leaned forward, his elbows on his bent knee. His overwhelming presence, his size, and his stance all drew my eyes to the strength that converged beneath his silken hose and velvet doublet.

I sucked in my breath, felt my heart jump in my breast.

"'Tis all in the eye of the beholder, my lady. Certainly, my father was not guilty of most of the charges that eventually brought about his death, but he was guilty of things that would have come to light sooner or later."

I wondered at his meaning in that statement. Were there things the Lord Protector had done that were treasonous? Things his son knew of? Ned did not look ashamed. He must have seen the questioning look on my face.

"Do not fret, my lady. 'Twas all for the good of England and for his young nephew. Nothing he would have been ashamed of or changed if God reversed the wheel of time."

His words comforted me, and I smiled. I certainly could not say the same, however, about my own father, and my lips twitched, making my smile feel forced.

Ned took my hand in his and brushed his lips over the knuckles while placing his other hand over his heart. "I am sorry to have been so callous."

My heart skipped a beat, and heat seared a path from my hand to my chest. If I'd had a fan, I would have whipped it open and furiously waved it upon my person. "There is no need to apologize. While we both may be the product of our parents' unions, it does not mean that we are they."

"A very astute observation. However, there are those who would judge us for our sires' deeds."

"Let us pray they do not, since both of our sires were taken forcefully from this earth." While Ned had said his words with a bit of a laugh in his voice, a subtle quirk of lips, my words were more clipped and came off sounding short. I wanted to be carefree and light, but in the end, our pasts were not the same at all. His father had in truth been murdered, and by my own father, who'd also seen to the destruction of my sister, his own daughter. For Ned to have brought up the topic only caused me pain.

I turned away and started to jab cloves into the orange again, taking my frustration out on the fruit and spice.

From the corner of my eye, I saw Ned bow, his face devoid of emotion—which in itself was a message loud and clear that he was distancing himself. "My apologies once more if I have given you offense."

I swiveled my head to face him, opening my mouth to protest, but he turned from me and was gone. The entire meeting left me feeling drained, bereft, and confused. Had he really only meant to find something we had in common and share it? Perhaps he felt sad about his father's death and wanted to seek comfort, and I'd stomped down his emotions and feelings as if they meant nothing.

Prior to that moment, I had been sure a romance was blooming between us. I'd begun to daydream of a wedding day where Ned waited patiently for me to be given to him in God's name. The notion had been broached before, and I desperately wanted it to be broached again.

I frowned down at the oak table, shiny with a new coat of wax the servants had labored to stroke into the wood. Those years before, the promise of a new life had seemed so clear, so bright. Yet nothing had come of it. Granted, Father had most likely destroyed the duchesses' plans, but how, exactly? There was more to be said about my status than even I knew.

I scratched absently at the table. "No one ever tells sweet Katherine anything," I muttered. "She's too young and flighty to bother with such mature talk. Too interested in flower picking and her pets to worry over marriages and alliances."

I breathed a shaky sigh. I couldn't help it if I preferred pleasure over politics. That I enjoyed the warmth, undying loyalty, and love my sweet pets afforded me. How could I be blamed for embracing the sweet scent of jasmine, roses, lavender? Or the thrill of mixing herbs into a tincture I knew would save a life?

Perhaps it was time I did pay more attention to the political side of life. If I was to get what I wanted—to experience love in its true form with the man I wanted to spend my life with—then I would need to listen and plan. Let the outside world continue to think me a capricious, untamed lady.

I would show them in the end.

JUNE 30, 1558

"Oh, the house certainly is much happier when Lord Edward arrives," Mrs. Helen said boisterously as she opened the curtains and started to pull out a fresh chemise, hose, kirtle, skirts, stomacher, and sleeves—matching various shades and shaking her head, thrusting one back in before pulling out another.

"Whatever do you mean?" Since our conversation regarding our fathers, Edward—Ned, as I was to call him—had disappeared from Hanworth for days, much to my dismay, although it had afforded me time to speak with Jane a little about her mother and brother. She'd eyed me too curiously, though, and so I had not dared to bring up the topic again. Not that I did not trust Jane, for I did with all my heart, but the walls had ears. In fact, the floors and paintings and tapestries did, too. I almost let out a laugh thinking of all the eyes blinking through the décor to spy on what one's tongue might let slip.

"Why, he has returned, my lady. And he has requested your presence in the great hall." Mrs. Helen turned with a rust-red skirt, matching sleeves, and a stomacher embroidered with gold, swirling threads. "The gold kirtle, my lady? Or perhaps the green?"

"Gold." I swung my legs over the side of the bed and went to the chamber pot behind a screen to relieve myself. "Why do you think he has requested me?"

I stood to wash my hands, face, and privy parts in the tepid but fresh rose-scented water Mrs. Helen had fixed. She popped her head around the corner, grinning from ear to ear, her gray hair falling in wisps from her hood as it always seemed to do when she was excited.

"You know I do not tell tales, my lady." But judging from the eager look in her eyes, she was bursting to the brim with the desire to tell some now.

Unbidden, the compulsion to tease seized me. "You are right, I should not have asked. It would be a grave sin for one to gossip, and I am morally obligated to see to your soul."

The plump, older woman pursed her lips and narrowed her eyes, studying my face as if trying to discern whether I was jesting.

Unable to hold it in any longer, I laughed and bounded out from behind the screen. "Come now, Mrs. Helen, if you are aware of why a handsome, charming young man has asked for my singular attention, I would hope you would be so kind as to divulge the information."

"Well, perhaps I know naught," she said with a decidedly fake pout.

"Hmm . . ." I tapped my chin and fingered a pearl-lined hairpin on my dressing table, then turned with a mischievous smile. "Would a new bauble loosen your tongue?"

"I could never take such from you, my lady."

"Oh, 'tis a gift. Besides you are the one and only, my most loyal servant and companion."

"Then I shall be glad to accept it, but not on account of telling you all that I know."

"Well met, now spill." I lifted my arms for her to begin dressing.

"He has arrived with a sweet little present for you." Mrs. Helen's voice was muffled with all the pins she held between her lips, as she tucked them each in place, connecting my sleeves to my bodice.

"A present?"

"I shan't tell you what, but you will know that Lord Edward holds you in high regard—and that he knows your mind well."

"Whatever did I do to deserve a present?" Was it a gift of apology for our last encounter?

"I know not, love, but it is obvious he has . . . feelings for you."

"Feelings," I muttered, rolling the idea of it around in my mind. So I had not been completely on my own in coming to that wondrous conclusion.

I looked over my shoulder at Mrs. Helen's progress and hurried her along as she finished pinning my gown together in the back. She placated me with simple murmurings and started pulling my golden puffed sleeves through the slashes of red.

I ran my hand over the silken threads on my stomacher and twisted from right to left to watch the garnets glitter along the center of each golden whirl. The rust-red skirt opened to reveal the satiny gold kirtle, also dimpled with garnets, a gift from Her

Majesty. Mrs. Helen slipped red velvet shoes upon my feet and bade me sit so she could fuss with my hair.

While she brushed it, I shifted uncomfortably.

"Almost finished, my lady," she muttered softly as she placed my gold hood trimmed with pearls and lace upon my head. Next came jewelry, of which I wore relatively little: a garnet-studded gilded velvet choker and matching roses in my ears, the tips of the petals made with tiny garnets. "There now. You are a vision of beauty."

I alighted from the bench, twirled once in a circle, and then, snapping my fingers for Arabel and Rex to follow, made my way down the stone stairs to the great hall. The dogs ran ahead, ostensibly to seek relief in the courtyard and then to raid Cook's kitchen for scraps.

Disappointment flooded me as I entered the well-lit great hall. Summer sunlight filtered through the windows, creating shafts of bright light—so brilliant, in fact, that tiny sparkles of dust danced within the beams. But it wasn't the luminescent vision that disenchanted me—it was that I would not be alone with Ned.

The duchess stood beside her son, as did Jane, Lady Katherine, and . . . Master William Cecil?

Excitement at seeing my step-grandmother tempered my disappointment somewhat, but I blanched at the last guest, not having expected him at all. Was he here to take me back to court? Had Mrs. Helen been misleading me? It was not like her to pull such trickery. Mayhap she was irritated that I chose to sleep in and thought the only way to get me out of bed was to offer up a surprise?

"'Tis good of you to join us, Kat," Lady Katherine said familiarly, despite the company.

I was glad to see her as well, though I worried over her visage. Her skin was pale, purple beneath her eyes, and the bones of her face jutted out as if she'd lost much weight. I was surprised to see her. Her husband, and former gentleman usher—Richard Bertie—was not in attendance. They had fled together to Poland. What had brought her back? Was her return a secret? Mary would certainly persecute her if she found out. The queen burned anyone with an inclination to Protestantism. What suffering had Katherine undergone to appear so haggard? There was so much I wished to speak with her about.

I curtsied to the group and mumbled an apology, citing a headache as the cause of my tardiness. Ned's eyes twinkled as I met his gaze, and a smile tugged at my mouth.

Lady Anne glanced between Ned and me and then stepped into my line of sight. "I believe you are familiar with Master Cecil?"

"Yes, of course. 'Tis a pleasure to see you at Hanworth, Master Cecil."

"Always a delight, my lady," he said, stroking his long, thin beard. He always gave the appearance of seeing through to your very soul, of taking each thought in your mind and dissecting it. I suppose that was why he was such a good ally for the queen. But I knew him to be a man in Princess Elizabeth's circle as well—indeed, he was her surveyor of estates, and so much more. It was well-known that Cecil was a spy.

How many sides did the man work for? And what was he doing here?

"You have missed morning Mass, Lady Katherine. We could not wait," Lady Anne said, almost accusingly.

My eyes widened, and I panicked that Sir William was present to hear of the slip. Would he report to the queen that I had shirked my duties as a good Catholic woman of her court?

"Indeed, I was not well enough to attend this morning, but I did say my prayers upon my prie-dieu." Having a small altar in my chamber was my saving grace . . . else I'd have been seen as completely without morals.

Lady Anne smiled, as if she had hoped I would pass the test. The woman caused me such confusion. I knew she cared for me, but it was hard to tell if her interest in me was because of my friendship with her daughter, my love for her son, or my position at court and what benefits I could provide her.

"Come then, let us break our fast. Cook was anticipating your arrival, Sir William, and has prepared the honey cakes you so enjoy."

Master Cecil chuckled and offered Lady Anne his arm. Ned offered his left arm to me and his right to my step-grandmother.

"Ladies, I would be honored to escort you to the table."

"And we gladly accept, my lord," said Lady Katherine.

I slipped my arm through Ned's, resting my hand upon the inside of his elbow, and felt the heat of his body seep through my fingertips, up my arm, and into my chest.

"Oh, but I nearly forgot. We shall have one more companion for the morning meal," Ned said with a smile in my direction.

I raised a brow in confusion. Whomever could he mean?

A servant stepped from a darkened corner—perhaps the only darkened corner—with a small, squirming bundle in his arms.

My heart leapt as I took in the sight of the white pup, thin of back, sharp of snout, with gorgeous blue eyes and curling black lashes.

"Oh, he is darling! A white greyhound. How gorgeous! What have you named him?" I gushed, reaching out my arms and taking the warm body of the puppy into them, holding him close to my chest and burying my nose against his soft neck. He smelled so sweet, so innocent.

"I have not named him, my lady," Ned said softly. He walked Lady Katherine to the table and pulled out her chair for her, waiting for her to sit before he returned to me.

"Whyever not?" I turned to face Lady Anne, who looked on us wistfully. I wished I could have read her mind, but I feared I would never understand. She had a multifaceted brain, careful compartments like cabinets and filing drawers filled to the brim with knowledge I knew I would never be able to touch.

"He is not mine to name."

My head swiveled back to Ned, excitement trilling in my veins. "For me?" I nuzzled the pup's ears with my nose. "Ned . . . He is so sweet."

"He is yours, my lady. Think of him as a peace offering." Ned's fingers brushed over the silky, soft coat of the puppy's back and, in so doing, stroked my hand as well.

I closed my eyes for a brief second, taking in this perfectly splendid moment in time.

"I shall name him Beau. For he is perfectly sweet, just like you, my lord."

From the corner of my eye, I saw both duchesses and Cecil watch us with interest—though whether or not they approved was not apparent. I could only pray that Ned and I were closer to a support for our union, but I knew that neither his mother, my mother, nor our queen would agree unless it benefitted them somehow. This fact was incredibly disheartening, but I pushed it aside in favor of finding joy in this one moment. My eyes connected with Ned's, our faces only a breath away. I was arrested by his gaze. A passion fired like I'd never experienced before. No speech or action came to me, but my thoughts were a whirl of secret, stolen moments yet to come. All I could do was drink in his face and the vibrant sensations that washed over me. I wished the room would disappear and it could be just us. My lips burned to feel his on mine.

His speech broke the momentary, silent spell, but his whispered words only warmed me more. "Perhaps I should find him a mate and name her Kat so that we might both have sweetness by our sides."

I nodded, at a loss for words, but let my hand drift over his for a second or two as we stroked the puppy's velvet-soft belly.

After breakfast, while everyone went about their duties, I headed upstairs to Jane's room with Beau. I knew she'd gain joy from seeing the puppy, and she'd not been well enough to attend breakfast.

"Oh, Kat, bring him here!" she exclaimed when I entered her bedchamber with the wriggling pup.

Beau leapt onto the bed and licked all over Jane's face. She giggled and buried her nose against his soft fur.

"He smells so sweet," she said.

"His name is Beau."

Jane's eyes lit up. "Any particular reason why?"

I couldn't help but smile wide while I nodded. "He was given to me by your brother."

Jane reached out and gripped my hand in hers. Her fingers were cold despite her flushed face. "He is sweet on you."

"I am sweet on him."

A sadness fell across Jane's face. "I can only hope that one day, the two of you will find the happiness you deserve."

I swallowed back the sudden emotion that welled in my chest. "Me, too," I whispered. Then lifting my chin, I said, "When can we get you out of here? Can you come walk in the gardens with Beau and me?"

"I would like that. Maybe this afternoon when I've had more time to rest."

"Good, I will come and see you after luncheon."

"I look forward to it."

When I returned later in the afternoon, Jane's fever had increased and she slept restlessly. A tisane to help her sleep had been administered, and I was ushered quickly from the room in case I were to catch whatever affliction ailed my beautiful friend.

They could push me away for the moment, but nothing would stop me from trying to see Jane smile again.

Chapter Eight

Which long this Knight and Lady felt,
at home in country soil.
And somewhat of the cares abroad,
that he perforce did taste:
I mean to write so that as truth,
my verses be embraced.
—Thomas Churchyard, Elizabethan Soldier and Poet

JULY 1, 1558

The air surrounding Hanworth was crisp as I stepped into the dawn the following morning. The sun crested over the hill, and just beyond that would be the orchard—my destination. Unable to sleep any longer, and the house yet abed, I had responded when the sweet scents and peace of the orchard called to me.

My slippers pressed into the dewy grass of the morning, soaking some of the essence through their thin fabric, chilling my toes. I wrapped my shawl closer around my shoulders and hurried my steps, eager to reach the orchard without completely ruining my shoes.

Hidden beneath the folds of my shawl was a book I'd seen in Her Grace's library and impatiently wanted to read, *Le Morte d'Arthur*. While at court, some of the ladies had whispered of the great love story, how tragic it was, and how it moved their hearts. I'd yet to come across it myself, and never before had I cared so much for reading.

But today was different. I knew Jane was interested in the book, and since she was kept in her room, I hoped to read it and retell it to her when no one could listen.

My slippers crunched along the gravel path in the garden, until finally, at my journey's end, the orchard opened up before me. I closed my eyes, breathed in deeply, and sighed.

Peace stole over me. Something about being outside, being one with nature, filled my soul.

"My lady, what brings you here so early in the morning?"

I gasped, jumped, and my eyes popped open. "Ned, you startled me." My hands came up to my heart as if they could still the erratic beating by touching it. The book fell to the ground, pages fluttering.

Ned bent to retrieve it. I swallowed hard. Would he think me shameful for reading such tales, or did he, too, take pleasure in Arthurian legends?

"'And there she welcomed him fair, and either halsed other in arms, and so she let put up his horse in the best wise, and then she unarmed him. And so they supped lightly, and went to bed with great joy and pleasaunce; and so in his raging he took no keep of his green wound that King Mark had given him.'" Ned broke out into a smile, his twinkling eyes catching my mortified gaze.

My face flamed red at the words he read of pleasure. Lovers.

"*Le Morte d'Arthur*. 'Tis a good tale," he said.

I silently pleaded with my body to stop trembling and licked my lips nervously before speaking. "I have heard."

"You have not started to read it yet?"

I cleared my throat, which suddenly felt dry and tight. "Not as yet."

"Come, let us find a bench, and I shall enchant you with the tale until it is time for morning Mass."

How ironic we would read such scandalous tales together—followed by Mass to cleanse our souls.

Ned held out his arm to me, and I took it reluctantly. It was not at all proper to sit with him alone, with no lady's maid to watch over us. But it was not as if he would ravage me in the orchard. And if he tried to kiss me . . . I would let him. Oh, dear . . . I would definitely have to say a few extra Acts of Contrition at Mass.

I licked my lips again. "Perhaps we should . . ." Nerves warred within me, causing pebbled flesh to rise along my limbs—or was that the warmth of his touch where I'd become chilled in the early morning air?

"Is something the matter?" His eyes held question, warmth.

I felt safe with him. "No, 'tis nothing."

He led me through the orchard until we reached the first of many wooden benches and sat down.

"Well, if you have yet to begin, then we shall start at the beginning."

I spread my skirts and tucked my feet beneath them, hoping the covering would warm them. The heat of Ned's body was already warming my arms and chest.

"'It befell in the days of Uther Pendragon, when he was king of all England, and so reigned, that there was a mighty duke in Cornwall that held war against him long time.'"

The tale enthralled me. We read for over an hour, but it seemed like only minutes before Mrs. Helen interrupted us.

"My lady, I have been searching for you."

"And here you have found me." I smiled up at her, still imagining the mighty Uther Pendragon, his court and battles.

"My lady, you must come inside. You should not be here . . . alone."

I was not alone. Not at all, but I knew what she meant. It was not proper for Ned and me to have been alone in the gardens for so long without a lady's maid about to watch over us. Although we had done nothing but read from *Le Morte d'Arthur*, if the wrong person had happened by, trouble would have ensued.

"Thank you for reading with me, my lord."

"'Twas a most joyous pleasure, my lady." Ned stood and grasped my hand in his to help me rise.

Mrs. Helen wrung her hands and looked about, pretending not to be watching.

Ned held out the book to me, his fingers grazing over mine, sending a delicious shiver racing along my arm. "Your book, my lady."

"Oh, 'tis not mine. I found it in the library."

His lips curled. "My mother's? Fascinating. I shall hold on to it then, and perhaps we can meet here at dawn again on the morrow?"

Mrs. Helen opened her mouth to speak, but I rushed to answer. "Yes, I would enjoy that immensely."

"Mrs. Helen, will you oblige us?" Ned asked, flashing a winning smile at the older woman, causing a blush to rise along her neck.

"Yes, my lord."

He swept his cap from his head and bent into an elegant bow. "Until this evening."

"Are you not coming to Mass?"

"I'm afraid I have an errand to run, my lady, but I shall return for supper."

Disappointment flashed within. I looked forward to Mass, when I could watch Ned without anyone the wiser.

"Until this evening then, my lord." I dipped into a curtsy and graced him with what I hoped was a winning and enticing smile.

Every morning for the next several days, we woke early and stole from the manor into the orchards, where Ned wrapped me in his warmth and read to me from scandalous tales of King Arthur. With each passing morning, my urge for Ned to kiss me grew. But he'd yet to do so.

I'd been able to sneak into Jane's room a few times to tell her about the book and my meetings with her brother. She was not yet well enough to come out herself but was quickly on the mend, and terribly excited about my tales of the orchard. Thank goodness for Jane and Mrs. Helen, my two staunch supporters.

Mrs. Helen followed us but stayed well behind and made a point to pretend to take a nap, and sometimes disappeared altogether only to return when it was time for us to make our way to the great hall. I was dizzied by love and hope.

But fate does not always play her hand the way a heart desires. On the fifth day that we sneaked from Hanworth, the duchess was there to greet us in the orchard.

"My, you are up early this morning, Beau." She peered around her son as if suddenly surprised to see me there. "As are you, Lady Katherine." She made a point to crane her neck and squint her eyes. "Is that your lady's maid so far behind? 'Tis almost as if she is not here. What are the two of you about, sneaking so stealthily in the predawn hours?"

My mouth went dry, and I could not find the words to utter. I could tell by the intelligent gleam in her eyes that she knew exactly why we were there. She only meant to drive home the point that we should not be.

"Your Grace," Ned said, tossing his mother a charming smile. "I invited Lady Katherine here for some fresh air. I wanted to show her the orchard with the pink and orange of the sun as it rises."

The duchess narrowed her eyes and pursed her lips. "The world has eyes and ears, my son. You can never be too careful. What may be done in innocence is oft portrayed as wicked."

JULY 7, 1558

The duchess's being called to court to attend the queen for several days left Ned and I more time to spend together. She'd done her best to keep us separated since our encounter in the orchard, for propriety's sake—and while I couldn't blame her, it was still disappointing. But today was all for us.

"More mead, my lady?"

Ned held the corked bottle up, his long fingers wrapped around the clay neck. It appeared the one glass of honeyed wine I'd consumed had made me all too aware of him. The way his fingers were long, strong, the knuckles perfectly proportioned with a light dusting of dark hair.

"Yes," I said, enjoying the warm feeling in my belly.

Ned pulled the cork from the bottle with his teeth and poured the golden liquid into my cup. I took another swill, letting the tangy bite of fruit and honey tantalize my tongue.

"Your face is flushed," Ned observed, his eyes glinting wickedly.

I smiled. "'Tis the wine."

But was it only the wine? I had the most intense urge to lean forward and kiss him. To let our lips press together, to taste the wine inside his mouth.

"Is my face flushed as well?"

"Yes," I lied, wanting him to believe I was flushed from drink rather than desire.

We lounged upon the warm summer grass beside the pond at Hanworth, just under a willow tree to keep the sun from baking our skin. A gentle breeze blew. Swans and ducks floated around the pond, dipping their heads beneath the water, letting the rivulets run over their feathered backs to keep them cool.

Ned plucked a dandelion from the grass and rolled the stem between his fingers. "I think I shall make you a crown of flowers today."

"You needn't make me a crown, Ned." More blood rushed to my already hot cheeks.

"A princess deserves a crown."

I shook my head, terror filling me at the acknowledgment. "I am no princess."

Ned plucked another dandelion, placing its stem behind my ear, his knuckles grazing my cheek. "But you are a princess of the blood, sweeting. Whether you like it or not."

I let out a halfhearted laugh and reached up to touch the flower. "I like it not."

"I wonder how many people there are who wish they could be someone else," he mused, gazing out at the pond. "Do you think the swan wishes to be a duck?"

My gaze was drawn back to the pond. "They seem to float so well together."

"Aye, though the swans are prettier than the ducks."

"But do the ducks know that?"

Ned laughed. "I doubt it." He leaned back on an elbow, closer to me, his face near my shoulder. "I think you are beautiful. You are my swan."

I took a heady sip of wine, trying to distract myself from Ned's alluring scent and charm. "And what are you? A duck or my swan mate?" Oh, dear Lord! My boldness shocked even myself. A lady did not make such forward comments, even if her *beau* had insinuated as much.

I swallowed hard, wishing I could pull the words back from the air. But then my gaze met Ned's. His hazel eyes seemed to darken, the lids growing heavy. The intensity of his stare stole my breath, and I waited minutes, maybe hours, to hear his answer.

"It would be my greatest pleasure to be your swan, my lady."

"Oh," I breathed, unable to speak a word more.

His fingers danced along my jawbone, turning my face toward his, urging me closer. My eyes fluttered shut, my lips parted, and then, sweet heaven, his silky lips brushed over mine. His hand slid to my cheek, cradling me, drawing me in. The wine glass dropped from my hand to splash in the grass, and I let myself sink closer, pressing my body against his.

Ned's tongue caressed the seam of my lips, teasing, enticing. I parted my lips for him, wishing for him to explore me deeper, and he did. The sweet taste of mead mingled on my tongue, on his, melding as one.

The kiss was sensual, moving. I wanted to kiss him forever and never part. But alas, Mrs. Helen cleared her throat from a little ways down the shore, and the spell was broken.

When the duchess returned later that evening, she called me to her solar. I took great care with my appearance, trying to look my best for her. She stood, her back rigid, her face stony as she studied me. I could stand it no longer.

"Your Grace, I beg pardon, but what is it I have done to offend you?"

She tilted her head a fraction of an inch. "What makes you believe I find you have offended me?"

"You do not wish for Ned and me to be together."

A short, bitter laugh escaped the duchess's lips. "My dear girl, my reasoning lies not with you." She looked off into the distance, as if seeing a windowpane to the past. "This queen is . . . volatile.

Much like her father—but I daresay he was a bit more controlled, at least. I fear for everyone close to her. There was a time when I wanted nothing more than for my son to be close to the throne. But now I find times have changed, and I want him further away."

"I want to be further away, too."

"Yes, I am sure you do. But you must understand, you can never be. As long as you breathe, you are a threat. The more works you do with the poor, with the sick, the needy, the more stray animals you take to your breast, the more beloved you become to the people. They see you as a sweet angel come to lay your grace upon their sorry heads, and the queen as but a stalwart monarch, ready to strike should they stray from the path she has set forth."

The shirts I sewed, tinctures made, and animals loved had only ever been done out of kindness. I had never imagined they could be thought a threat to the throne.

"Would that I could run away then."

"But you would be found. Everyone knows you, Kat. Everyone has seen your pretty portrait. They may feign friendship, an interest in your cause, but always the minds of people can be shifted to side with the strongest. Mary is often ill . . . She is weakening." The duchess shifted her gaze to the far wall. "Elizabeth will always be stronger. She is her father and her mother in one. 'Tis a formidable foe those two created."

"What shall I do?"

"What you have been doing. But remember that your actions will affect everyone around you."

"I love him, you know."

She smiled sadly. "Perhaps you think you do. We all fancy ourselves in love sometimes."

"Did you not love Ned's father?"

Her eyes flashed with some unseen secret. "Yes, very much." She turned from me quickly, walking away with brisk clips of her shoes on the stones, but not before I saw tears coming into her eyes.

JULY 21, 1558

A sad case of lassitude had set in about Hanworth. Ned was sent on errands by Her Grace, and she kept to herself. I'd spent the past few days by Jane's bed, reading to her from the pages of the little golden book of Plato my sister had passed to me within the Tower. And yet all I could think about were my mornings with Ned reading *Le Morte d'Arthur.*

In the garden, I gathered chamomile to make a tisane for Jane. This garden sadly lacked the herbal resources I'd built up at Bradgate Manor and even at Pembroke's Castle. I dropped the meager pickings into a pot of boiling water and made my way upstairs to change.

Guilt riddled my mind that I should be so concerned with my time away from Ned, for I had come to Hanworth only to keep my dearest friend company through her illness. But I'd . . . fallen in love. While Jane whiled away in bed, recuperating, I got used to being out in the sun and spending languid mornings beside Ned. Sitting day in and day out in the stuffy castle without his company, at least for a little while, was driving me to the brink of madness.

At least I had my sweet puppy, Beau, to cuddle with. Arabel and Rex had taken to him quite well, nudging him along like two overprotective parents as he bounded with large, gangly feet through the gardens. My tiny monkey, Stew, whom I had had to leave behind at Westminster Castle with servants, would have loved to pick fleas and other such mites off the little bundle.

And in Ned's absence, it was sweet to have a part of him left behind.

I stood from the dressing table and glanced down at the somber blue velvet gown I'd bade Mrs. Helen dress me in. I could not abide any of the more cheerful colors, and while the dress was still a pretty shade of sapphire, it was dark enough to complement my mood. My kirtle of silver silk showed through the split of the velvet down the middle and was edged with pearls. The stomacher was embroidered with silver flowers, and I plucked at the pearls that graced the center of each.

"You are a vision as always, my lady," Mrs. Helen said, tucking an errant strand back into my hood. "This gown always makes the blue of your eyes stand out even more starkly against your fair skin."

She stroked a finger lovingly over my cheek and smiled like a proud mother hen.

"Oh, Mrs. Helen, enough. I do not want to be pretty today. I want to be somber." I pouted, even though I realized what I said was ridiculous. "Would that I could stay in bed with a megrim." I put my hand to my forehead and willed the pains to come, but there was nothing. No reprieve for me today.

I supposed I was being selfish, but I just did not think I could go another day reading aloud inside a darkened room with a little candlelight and the scents of lavender, sage, and roses suffocating me. Mrs. Helen had a free day on Sundays to do as she pleased—even though, more often than not, she refused it. But if I were to be honest with myself, it was not the duties I came here to provide to my dear friend that made me so sour, but missing her brother.

"Do companions not get a respite?"

Mrs. Helen narrowed her eyes. "That is not a way to be thinking about your dear friend. For shame. If she heard your words, you'd bring her to tears. Now go and read to her. Maybe she'll be well enough to come down to the great hall for the nooning, and it will give you a chance to breathe fresh air."

I nodded. "Yes, I must ask the Lord's forgiveness for such self-ish thoughts. It is truly un-Christian of me." And I did feel shame at wishing myself to be in bed sick. I had best make it up to Jane.

I left my chamber and walked down the long, dark corridor. The torches bracketed to the walls were lit only every dozen feet or so. Shadows danced and bounced off of the stone walls, and the eyes in various portraits appeared to follow my path. It was so dark that if I had not known it was morning, I might have thought I had woken in the middle of the night to visit Jane.

Commotion sounded from inside Jane's chamber, and I paused outside of the door, not wanting to interrupt.

What had happened? Had she taken a turn for the worse? I crossed myself and sent up a prayer to God that Jane was well. I knocked lightly, and when the call came to enter, I was greeted by the standing figure of Jane, who had risen from bed and walked about her chamber.

I set down the copy of *Phaedo* I brought with me on a nearby table and walked toward the window Jane gazed out of.

There was a knock at the door, and then the duchess entered. She glanced from Jane to me, her face void of emotion. As always, she was dressed in rich, dark velvet, intricate gold thread embroi-dery and black diamonds sewn on the neckline, waistline, hem, sleeves. Her ensemble could have fed a village for a year if it were sold for coin.

"Jane, your lady's maid informed me you were up and about. Don your new gown and slippers. I should think you have had enough time in this room, and it needs to be aired out and cleaned. Come now, Lady Katherine, do you not agree?" The duchess was like a whirlwind, moving about the room, opening windows, and scraping her finger along furniture.

"Completely, Your Grace." But I dared not say more, for I was truly shocked the duchess would suggest her daughter leave the room, given that she had been the one who ordered her to go there in the first place.

Lady Anne called for servants to enter and listed detailed instructions for cleaning while Jane's lady's maid took her behind a screen to dress.

I watched silently, not really sure what to do, and I had not yet been dismissed.

Lady Anne turned toward me. "You are aware I served many of King Henry's wives, are you not?" She continued without waiting for my answer. "The one most dear to me was my sister-by-marriage, Queen Jane, whom I named my own daughter after."

I nodded, my hands folded neatly at my waist.

"The king had a set of rules about cleaning and what should be done to a room in which an ill person was confined. I think they have helped many—although in the end, the regimen could not prevent dear Queen Jane Seymour from succumbing to childbed fever. I was reluctant at first to follow King Henry's regimen for my daughter, because in the end, it did not help Jane Seymour . . . but now that she appears on the mend . . ." The willowy woman turned from me, and I wondered at her explanation.

"I am positive Your Grace did all you could for Queen Jane."

The duchess didn't say anything, only continued to inspect the servants as they brought in buckets of water and lye soap. I was relieved the conversation was apparently over, as I never knew quite what to say to the duchess.

Jane emerged from behind the screen dressed in an icy blue silk gown with a pearl-crusted bodice and slashed sleeves of silver and white. Her skin was sallow against the pale colors, and the purple circles beneath her eyes flashed like sliced beets above her bony cheeks. The gown sagged on her, showing just how much of her body had evaporated from this illness. But I said none of these things to her, of course.

"Jane, you look beautiful. 'Tis good to see you dressed in finery again. 'Tis as though a black cloud has lifted. I feared—"

"Do not fear for me, Kat."

I rushed forward, taking her hands in mine. I was desperate for her to know what she meant to me. "You have been my hope, my one shining light in this world after so much has been ripped away. For certes, I've other friends at court, but Jane Dormer and Margaret Clifford are mere court ladies. We are of like souls, like minds. I can confess anything to you without fear of my words being twisted and repeated. You've guided me through tumultuous situations, emotions, and Lord knows there have been many. I cannot conceive of life without you. And now there appears to be a positive end in sight."

Perhaps this was what Her Grace could not voice to me. That she'd seen so many perish before her eyes. That her first Jane had been ripped from life, and now her namesake might suffer the same fate. I could well imagine the pain that carved its way through Her Grace's heart, for it was the same pain I myself had had to vanquish time and again.

Hoping Jane might recover from her illness with fresh air, we slowly descended the curving stone staircase. The servants in the great hall bobbed curtsies and bowed as we made our way toward the rear doors that led to the garden pathways—Arabel, Rex, and Beau nipping at our heels.

The sun shone above, and walking several feet behind us through the gardens were servants waving fans and carrying cool flagons of honeyed wine should we need it. Bees clustered on tulips and lilies, sucking the sugary sweetness from their centers.

The rich timbre of Ned's voice broke into my thoughts. "What a trio of beautiful ladies I have fallen upon. Would you accept my offering of an escort?"

I mustered all the decorum I'd had pounded into my head from birth, and instead of whirling and running toward him, I turned slowly, as did Lady Anne and Jane.

Ned approached, looking dashing in his black and silver hose and matching surcoat. He bent over our hands and kissed us each on the knuckles, pausing a moment longer over my hand than that of his mother and sister. Out of the corner of my eye, I saw Jane smile, but their mother had a different reaction. Lady Anne looked on with narrowed eyes and tapped her foot impatiently on the gravel, making a crunching noise. What plans did Lady Anne have for her son—and was I interfering with them? Years before, she'd helped me out of my marriage with Henry using a mock betrothal to her son, but it remained unclear whether she truly wanted us thus linked. Was it possible she saw me as dangerous?

"Beau, cease your hold on my guest's hands. I shan't desire the young lady to become offended by your courtly flirtations," Her Grace said with irritation.

I tugged my hand away, heat blazing my face and chest. Ned grabbed up my hand again, as if in challenge to his mother.

"My dear mother, Lady Katherine does not find me in the least offensive, do you, my lady?" He winked at me, and I nearly choked on the air that left me in a whoosh.

I flicked my gaze away, too nervous to meet anyone's scrutiny, preferring to keep my eyes cast toward the ground.

When I did happen to snatch a glance from the corner of my eye, Her Grace pursed her lips but did not comment further—and Ned dropped my hand. Lady Anne changed the subject entirely, for which I was grateful, so that I did not have to answer Ned's question, which would have been a resounding no.

"I suppose if you insist, we would be pleased to have you accompany us. Do fan your sister Jane. We shall sit in the shade by the orchard," Lady Anne said.

I chanced a peek in their direction and saw that, despite her sharp tongue, Lady Anne had a twinkle in her eyes and was most likely pleased to have her son join us. My stomach, however, flipped when I looked at Jane. Her lips were white and her skin paler than it had been when we'd left her bedroom. A glance ahead showed we were still a ways from the orchard—Jane would not make it that far.

"Perhaps we could stop by the pond?" I suggested, seeing the pond was only a dozen feet away, with weeping willow trees draping their branches over benches that basked in cool shadow. "The ducks are so very friendly."

Jane's eyes lit up with hope, but her mother quickly dashed the idea with a subtle shake of her head. "Nonsense. Those fowl will only beg for bread we haven't brought. Besides, Jane enjoys the scents of the orchard."

'Twas true, Jane did enjoy the scents of the orchard, but I had great cause to fear she would drop in a faint before we made it there. I tried to recall if she'd had a morsel to eat or drink this morning, but I truly could not remember.

"A drink then?"

Lady Anne stopped and turned toward me. "Lady Katherine, I daresay you are out of shape. Can you not walk for another minute or two?"

I swallowed hard, for although she'd posed it as a question, her words were more of a demand.

When I did not respond, Lady Anne said, "Let us continue then."

She lifted her skirts and continued to march forward. Jane looked dejected, her gaze resting on the shaded benches. Her frame was so slight I could see her shoulders lift and lower in a sigh of resignation. Why did she not speak up for herself? Why had Lady Anne insisted her daughter come out of doors to indulge in the fresh air if she would not then be concerned for her welfare?

There was only one thing I could do: create a distraction.

I took a deep breath, closed my eyes, and let out a loud shriek.

"Lady Katherine!" the duchess said, whirling toward me.

I fluttered my arms around, kicked my feet up, swatted at my dress, and turned in a circle, all the while shouting, "Bee! Bee!"

I admit to making a spectacle of myself, but for Jane, I would have done anything, and it was obvious her mother hadn't understood the walk to the orchard would be too much.

"Have you been stung?" Ned asked, alarm in his voice.

I nodded emphatically and whirled again, batting at my skirts.

And like that, the duchess placed Jane on a bench, the latter letting out a loud sigh of relief. Servants rushed forth with the honeyed wine while Jane placed a hand on her brow and swayed on the bench.

The duchess pursed her lips. "Beau, do take Lady Katherine into the great hall and see that her bee sting is taken care of."

With that, she turned her attention back to Jane.

Inside, I smiled. Perhaps had I not been born a princess of the blood, I could have been a lowly actress.

Ned's arm on mine as he gently guided me back to the house was comforting and yet, at the same time, completely unnerving. His fingers burned through the softness of my gown, sending a spiraling path of nerves from my arm to my belly.

"Thank you, my lord, for escorting me back to the house. And might I also offer an apology for my behavior?"

Ned chuckled, his arm tugging me in a little closer, so that our hips bumped together as we walked. My eyes widened in reaction, and I tried to put at least an inch of distance between us, but he only tugged me close once more. I glanced around, hoping no one watched such scandalous behavior. When I saw no one, I let myself sink into that warmth that filled my world when Ned was near. My hip burned, and deep within me, I yearned for something . . . It gnawed at me, like a hunger.

"My dear lady, your performance was quite entertaining."

My lip quirked up at the side at having been caught in my falsehood. "You would call a lady deceitful?"

He shook his head and made a tsk, tsk noise with his tongue. "Only what I might perceive to have been good acting."

I shrugged, still painfully sensitive to our touching bodies. I tried to make my voice as normal as possible, even though I felt like squealing. "Jane needed to rest."

"She could have rested at the orchard."

I huffed. "Did you not see her pallor? Her waning countenance? The desperate glances she made toward the benches situated by the pond?"

"No, indeed, my lady, I admit to being too preoccupied watching you and my mother argue over feeding the ducks."

I pursed my lips into a frown and waved his words away. "Forsooth, you are no gentleman."

His hand came to cover his heart. "Your words do me harm, my lady. I have oft proclaimed myself to be of the utmost in gentlemanly manners and courtly ways."

"And yet you have called me false and nitpicky within two breaths. I promise, my lord, I have been nothing but helpful today." I widened my eyes, using a look that had worked on countless others when trying to divert a conversation.

Ned's head fell back, and he let out a laugh that had nearby birds vacating their tree branches in panic, their loud squalls piercing the tranquility of the garden.

"Do you always stretch your eyes wide and questioning when you're trying desperately to get out of the conversation?"

My mouth fell open. How did this man know me so well?

"Never mind. I shall acquiesce this once. Why do you think my mother so cruel, my lady?"

I squinted my eyes up at the birds, looking for distraction from the intense feeling of need building within me.

I placed a hand over his on my arm and stopped walking, my gaze meeting his. "'Tis not that at all, my lord. Your mother is the picture of kindness and charity. 'Tis only I was worried Jane would not speak up for herself and would not tell anyone of her distress."

"Ah, I see. So you are her guardian of a sort."

Again I attempted nonchalance, even though heat now stroked its way over my chest to my cheeks. "I suppose. Jane means the world to me. She is—" But I could not say it. Could not tell him that she was the sister I had lost. For I still had one sister who lived and breathed, but we were so very different. For a brief, scattered moment, I wondered where Mary was, what she was doing.

"She is what?" Ned urged.

I glanced away, but the gentle, soft pressure of Ned's fingers upon my chin had me turning to gaze once more into his greenish-brown eyes fringed with long, curling lashes.

"She is like a sister to me."

"And I would never let any harm come to her. You know the only reason Her Grace insisted on the orchard was she had set up a picnic there for Jane. She would never wish to harm her child. 'Twas only Mother's excitement that spurred her forward."

"I had not fathomed the notion," I said breathlessly—and only because he would not take his gaze from mine. His full lips beckoned me to taste them, and I knew that being in such close proximity to Ned was dangerous, sinful.

He had a pull on me that no other man, no matter his sweet words of courtly love, could even touch.

"Lady Katherine?" he whispered, his breath hot and inviting upon my cheek.

"Yes?" I murmured, my eyes feeling heavy. My fingers shook. My heart pumped loudly. I desperately wanted him to kiss me. Had missed his lips on mine. Savored every memory of our previous encounters.

"May I kiss you?"

My knees grew unsteady.

I nodded, my eyelids fluttering closed.

I waited . . . *One* . . . *Two* . . . And then there he was. His tender lips brushed over mine and were gone. I'd opened my mouth to protest when they landed once more upon me with subtle pressure. His fingers stroked up my arms to my cheeks, where he took hold ever so gently, rooting me in place. He tilted his head to the side, and I nearly jumped as a soft swipe of his hot tongue slid over the crease of my lips.

And then, once more, it was over—before it had really begun.

Ned put my arm back through his and marched with just as much purpose into the manor house and through the great hall as his mother had mustered on the way to the orchard.

Worry swept through me at his sudden rejection and stern bearing. "What is wrong?"

We reached the stairwell leading up to the bedchambers. Ned's eyes were narrowed, his lips pressed firmly closed, and the muscle in his jaw flexed and unflexed. "You have done nothing wrong. In fact, it was *too* right."

"Too right?" I murmured like an echo, trying to wrap my thoughts around what he was telling me.

"We cannot do this anymore, my lady."

I nodded, even though I did not understand why, and despite the fact that I wanted very much to do it again.

"My mother will not be happy to learn of this. Since she warned me off . . ."

My eyes snapped to his, and I shook my head. The duchess had warned Ned away from me just as she'd warned me away from him. Why?

"She will not know. I will not tell her." To tell would have been to risk my own reputation.

Ned chuckled. "Her Grace knows all, my dear. She has more spies than the queen, I suspect. She has probably already been informed of our kiss just now."

"Oh." My uttered understanding was false, for I could not fathom the placid gardens and house so crawling with spies. Spies were spindly of body, narrow of nose, and dressed in dark colors as they clambered over rooftops and sneaked through windows— and all had faces like William Cecil. I had seen none of this at Hanworth.

Ned laughed again and dragged his finger along my jawline. "You are a breath of fresh air, sweet Katherine."

"Then perhaps you had better kiss me again." I clapped a hand over my mouth.

"Perhaps I will . . ." Ned raked a hand through his chestnut locks. "But not here. Not right now." His eyes burned right through to my soul. "Mother sent me away before when I took the liberty to press my lips to your sweet mouth. I daren't risk her wrath again."

"Why?"

"She has a plan, my lady. She always has, and I am not of a mind to intervene."

"Even if her plans interfere with your happiness?"

Ned's smile touched my heart. "You know a person of noble birth is bound by honor and duty to their family. Happiness never plays a part. But I must know, do you wish to make me happy, my lady?"

His words were heavy, and while my stomach did flip after flip, the truth was, I did so very much want to fill him with bliss. I'd been miserable with my marriage to Henry Pembroke. But with Ned, love was attainable and within reach.

I was not so obtuse as to be shocked Lady Anne did not to want me to have marital notions aimed toward her son. But why? At one point, years before, we'd been nudged toward this path at her urging, even if nothing came of it. And now that he and I had formed an attachment, she was trying to pull us apart.

"Yes, I do."

He smiled and leaned close, pressing one last, earth-shattering kiss to my lips before pulling away. My mind turned to mush.

"That pleases me more than you know."

Chapter Nine

For truth and time that tries out gold,
hath tempered so my talk:
That pen nor muse no pleasure takes,
on doubtful ground to walk.
Now when these states with links of love,
wear tied together fast . . .
—Thomas Churchyard, Elizabethan Soldier and Poet

JULY 22, 1558

The following morning, when I descended—on time, I might add—to the great hall for morning Mass, Ned had disappeared and Lady Anne gave me a sidelong glance.

Had she heard of Ned kissing me in the garden—that our romance remained intact despite her discouragement of it? Jane smiled at me—almost conspiratorial. Her skin had increased in color, and she seemed in better health than the day before.

We sat in the front pew of the chapel, the duchess first, Jane second, and me last.

"I am pleased you were able to rise in a timely fashion this morning, Lady Katherine. Did anything in particular change to bring that about?" Lady Anne's lips twitched in that subtle smile of hers.

I blanched, my fingers wringing together.

"I only wished to please you, Your Grace."

"You have indeed, darling girl. And my Jane is feeling much improved. I think, in large part, we have you to thank for keeping her company and providing succor for her through this trial."

"It is my pleasure," I said quietly as the service began.

While the choir sang out and the virginals reverberated off of every stone, Jane leaned close to me and whispered, "He will be home in time for the noonday meal."

I nodded imperceptibly, so as not to draw attention to myself from the duchess. But I did smile, my eyes cast toward the ground.

After Mass, we broke our fast and then retired to Lady Anne's presence chamber to work on sewing shirts for the poor and blankets for babies. It was good work to keep me still, considering that I wanted to run about the manor. It also reminded me of how much I had and what good I do for those less fortunate. I was filled with a vigor that made my entire body tingle with the need to expel the energy. And yet, I was nervous, my stomach doing flip-flops every time I thought I heard a horse's hooves in the courtyard. Could it be him? Had he returned?

And thus the morning passed, with fourteen pricks to my fingers and five shirts mended with tiny dots of red along the seams.

Finally, Her Grace set down her sewing. "Would you ladies care to take a walk about the gardens with me to refresh our spirits and stretch our legs before the noon meal is served?"

I was more than happy to oblige her and, in my haste to jump to her side, forgot that poor little Beau had curled in my lap to sleep and so fell to the floor with a yelp. I scooped him up and cuddled him to my chest, whispering soothing words in his velvety ears. He licked at my face, forgiving me for my lapse.

In the garden, I felt much as I had in Lady Anne's presence chamber. At every crunch of gravel, I expected to see Ned striding up to us with his long, shapely legs cased in silken hose, his doublet finely sewn and encrusted with jewels that glimmered in the sun. I wanted to see his moss-colored eyes twinkle with humor and mischief and feel the stroke of his fingers upon my cheek or secretly graze over my spine. I wanted his hip to brush against mine as we walked, and God save my soul from purgatory, I wanted his lips to press to mine in a fevered kiss that took the very breath from my lungs.

Alas, every time I turned, it was either a servant, a rabbit, a dog, or just the rustle of the leaves as the wind blew.

Both Jane and the duchess were kind enough to pay no heed to the twists and turns of my neck as I craned to see if Ned had arrived. Instead, they kept up a steady chatter about the coming festivities at court. I was sure to have a strained neck in the morning, for I did not think I had performed this much contorting in my life.

As luck would have it—and given my past, luck was not often on my side—Ned did not come to offer us escort in the gardens as I'd hoped.

In fact, what did arrive was a messenger.

"My Lady Katherine?" He bowed low over a turned leg, flourishing his feathered hat and sweeping it nearly to the ground.

The duchess narrowed her eyes, examining the man wearing Tudor green-and-white livery with the Suffolk unicorn stitched on his breast, her eyes riveted on the rolled parchment in his right hand.

"Yes?" I straightened my back, prepared for bad news, and forced all the fear-forming storm clouds inside my body to hold off until I had at least had a chance to read the letter's contents.

"A letter from Master Adrian Stokes."

My mother's young Master of the Horse husband. My blood ran cold as I wondered what possible cause he would have to write to me. I held out my hand and gripped the smooth, crisp parchment.

"Shall I await a reply?" the man asked.

The duchess interceded. "Go and find refreshment in our kitchens, and we shall have you summoned when she is ready with her reply."

He twirled his hat in a bow again and nodded at the three of us. "Your Grace. Lady Katherine. Lady Jane." Then he retreated to find Cook.

When he'd gone, I stared down at the rolled parchment.

"Will you read it or absorb its contents?" The duchess's hands, although resting calmly at her sides, showed fingers digging into her palms, and her gaze shifted from mine to the parchment.

I'd never seen her look so apprehensive. Her concern made me worry more. My mother's health had not been the best of late, and she suffered bouts of illness from time to time, but I'd never had cause to think I should worry seriously over it. Obviously, Lady Anne had.

I slipped my thumbnail beneath the wax seal and unrolled the letter to find the neatly scrawled hand of Master Stokes. He was an excellent Master of the Horse, no doubt, and obviously, from his neat script, had been well schooled.

I'd not seen much of my formidable duchess mother recently, choosing distance after Jane's death. Somehow, in that time, I'd been able to find some peace and a modicum of forgiveness. I was now glad for my mother to have married Master Stokes—even though, when I was younger, I had been appalled by the idea. After years of unhappiness, my mother had deserved contentment and love, just as I now sought those same things for myself.

My mind wandered since I did not want to focus on what I should. At the sound of Lady Anne's teeth clicking in irritation, I willed myself to read the letter, blood pumping, hands shaking, afraid if I didn't read it swiftly, she would snatch it away.

> *Dear Lady Katherine,*
>
> *'Tis most unfortunate that I should be the bearer of bad news, but given my station as your mother's loving husband, such a duty doth fall to me. The Duchess of Suffolk is gravely ill. She suffers from what the physician has deemed an infection of the lungs. Her constitution never fortified after birthing our two babes, who were recalled to His hands. The physician is not certain that your mother will recover, as her fever continues to rage. I think it best, although I would not presume to make judgments on what you deem most suitable, for you to come and see Her Grace. Perhaps knowing a loving daughter sits beside her and wishes her well will bolster her strength and facilitate her body's return to full health.*
>
> *Respectfully and most honorably yours,*
> *Master Stokes*

I pressed the letter to my heart and closed my eyes, willing the tears away. How could what was contained within this letter be true? The fearsome Duchess of Suffolk had come undone from carrying, birthing, and grieving over her lowly husband's issue.

"May I read it?" Lady Anne asked softly, her touch light upon my arm.

I nodded and handed her the parchment as Jane rushed to hand me a cup of watered wine a servant had passed to her discreetly.

I sipped the wine slowly, unsure of how my stomach would react to anything, my nerves were so on edge. I prayed the wine would help to calm me.

"Is everything all right, Kat?" Jane's voice was soft and reassuring. She led me to a bench beneath one of the willows next to the pond, and I took respite in the cool shade, a light breeze making the summer heat not entirely unbearable.

"My mother is ill. Master Stokes says the doctor is not sure if she will live."

Jane nodded. "Let us pray then that she will."

I nodded, and gripping Jane's hands in mine, we closed our eyes and prayed. *Oh, most gracious and merciful Lord. Save my mother. Let not another of my family die so tragically when there is still so much left to live for.*

Some moments later, I felt Lady Anne's presence beside us. "I have arranged for your safe travel to Sheen."

I nodded, wishing the queen had given Mother back Bradgate, my home, of which we had been stripped after my father's execution. "Thank you, my lady. I shall return before long." If I planned on returning to Hanworth and prayed for my mother to regain full health, it would happen, would it not?

Lady Anne shook her head as if she heard my thoughts. "Katherine," she said informally, "do not rush to return to us when you must take care with what is most vital. We shall await your return whether it be here or at court. Your presence is always welcome. Beau shall attend you on your journey."

I nodded emphatically. "Yes, I had planned to take the pup. I could not leave him behind. We've grown so attached."

The duchess narrowed her eyes a moment and then smiled briefly. "I refer not to your pet, but my son, Lord Beauchamp."

What? I could not have heard her correctly. Ned would accompany me to visit my ailing mother? The duchess had been adamant about keeping us apart, and now she would put us together?

She pressed the parchment back into my hand and raised her brows. "You have my blessing. I have been . . . conflicted on the topic of the two of you. 'Tis dangerous, you understand. But Beau, he is stubborn. And I have a hard time denying him, for he—" She cut herself off abruptly and waved her hand in the air. "No matter. Perhaps he can speak privately with the Duchess of Suffolk and ascertain where she stands."

Jane smiled widely beside her mother, and her glee rolled off in waves.

Inside, my heart soared for a future with Ned, even while it broke for my mother's ill health. But at the same time, my stomach plunged. Though the way she'd spoken leant to sentimentality, I knew Lady Anne better than that. She would only have changed her mind thus if she thought to gain something from a union between the two of us. A cunning woman such as she was not swayed by notions of the heart alone.

"I shan't be bold enough to hope," I responded, though I worked hard to keep the smile from my face.

The duchess raised a brow. "But not too bold to beg for a kiss?"

Heat flared in my cheeks at her words. She had heard.

"Do not suffer so. I have not said it to see my words cause you embarrassment, only to jest with you, child. Though I've given my son leave to court you, I must warn you to tread lightly. Queen Mary is in ill health herself, and I daresay when Princess Elizabeth reigns in her stead, she may not take too kindly to the match."

She did not say more about her thoughts on the matter, but I could guess at what she meant. If we were to wed, we'd need to do it soon. And though she'd given her son permission to court me and ask my mother for my hand, there was no promise my mother would agree, or that the queen would bless our union. Even still, it was a step in the right direction. It appeared we'd leapt over one obstacle and only had a couple more to go before we were free.

I was elated at her approval of a match between Ned and me, and it was so hard not to smile and leap for joy. My mother did want me to wed, and as she'd been a sort of ally to Lady Anne in the past, perhaps this bit of happy news would be just the device to push her humors back into alignment.

Lady Anne and Jane ushered me back inside to eat the noon meal, which I floated through in a haze of dreams—my wedding finery, the groom, our own home, the wedding night . . .

After the noon meal was over, Jane ushered me up to my chamber to order the maids about in preparing for my trip, all the while chattering away. But despite her excitement about my possible betrothal, I could see her color fading.

"Jane, you should go and rest. I shall come to you before I depart, but I could never live with myself if my situation"—I wanted to say good fortune in regards to Ned, but I felt such words negated my mother's suffering—"were to make you ill once more. You've truly come around and are on the mend, but you must rest. Go now. I promise to seek you out."

"Oh, posh, Kat. I am perfectly well." But even as she said it, she swayed and clutched the foot post of the bed to steady herself.

I waved a maid over. "Please see Lady Jane back to her room. Have a posset of sage, wormwood, and comfrey made for her."

"Kat, really." Jane placed her hands on her hips, but the movement proved to unsteady her further, and she nearly fell, save for the caring hands of the maid. "Well, I suppose I am in need of a bit of rest, but you must promise to attend me before you depart."

"I would not dream of doing otherwise."

After Jane left, I flopped onto my bed and closed my eyes. A bit of rest would do me some good, too, but there was entirely too much to accomplish. So many conflicting emotions inside me, too. Fear for my mother. Fear for the future. Uncertainty. Always, always the uncertainty. Then there was excitement for the future—a future with Ned. But then the fear returned. We would not be able to live the life I dreamed of. A life where it was just the two of us, our children, and our pets, living in peace. No, I did not see such a thing ever happening in my life. I was a princess of the blood—remaining within arm's reach of my sovereign was my duty.

I must have fallen asleep, for a knock at the door jarred me awake. I sat up quickly, feeling rumpled and groggy.

Mrs. Helen poked her head through. "My lady, Lord Beauchamp awaits you in the great hall."

"'Tis time already? Yes, of course, come and fix my hair. I fear I've ruined my gown, too."

"My apologies, dear, but I had not the heart to wake you."

I nodded. "We shall be departing for Sheen then?"

"Aye, my lady. Everything was packed in the appropriate trunks while you slept and sent on ahead with a few servants. I do believe the dogs have remained behind to travel with you." Mrs. Helen unpinned my hood and ran her fingers through my hair, and I winced as she caught a few snags along the way.

"You will be accompanying me?"

"Yes, my lady."

I was relieved to have my longtime companion with me, but at the same time, a little disappointed that I would not be with Ned entirely on my own. What had I expected, though? It would have been entirely inappropriate for there to be no one to watch over us at all, and Lady Anne was anything but inappropriate. She lived and breathed propriety. Mrs. Helen finished my hair and handed me a cool, wet cloth to wash my face and hands before straightening my gown and smoothing out the fabric.

"You must have lain very still, my lady, and fallen quite perfectly, for your gown has nary a wrinkle."

I smiled at Mrs. Helen and ran my hands down the front of my brocade skirts. It was time to leave.

"Is Lady Jane still abed?"

"I am not aware, my lady. Shall I check for you?"

I shook my head. "No, I will see to her myself. I promised to say good-bye before I left."

I traversed the dimly lit corridors until I reached Jane's chambers. I knocked lightly and was surprised when Jane herself answered.

"Oh, good. I know Beau has arrived, and I thought you might forget to see me." She put her arm through mine and maneuvered me back down the corridor toward the stairs. "I want to see you both off."

When we reached the great hall, my breath caught in my throat. Ned knelt on the floor, scratching behind the ears of my little greyhound pup. He cooed to the sweet animal and then rolled the creature onto his back to scratch his belly. The scene was sweet, but what took my breath away was Ned himself. The muscles of his calves strained against his hose. His doublet was the perfect cut to show off his broad chest and shoulders, his flat belly. His hair was tousled, as always, giving him a feral look that had my blood pumping rapidly through my body. He looked up when we walked toward him, his smile alluring. Wide, full lips parted to show pearly white teeth. Whenever he smiled, I felt as though he held secrets he wanted to share with me and me alone.

He stood quickly, showing how agile he was, and effected a perfect bow toward us.

"My Lady Katherine. My dear sister. You have caught me at play with that little devil. I say, he has quite stolen my heart." He met my gaze with intensity, as if to say, *and so have you.*

According to the duchess, he would ask for my hand soon. I groaned inside, heat rising in my chest and inflaming my cheeks. Was I ever to have a normal countenance while in Ned's company, or was I doomed to be cherry red?

I curtsied to Ned, and he gripped my hand in his, pulling it to his lips. His eyes stayed locked on mine as he did it, but his lips did not touch me, just hovered, his warm breath caressing my skin and sending pebbled flesh to battle along my arms.

"Lady Katherine, it is an honor to escort you on your journey."

"I am grateful you are willing to do so, my lord. I am most worried about my mother."

He nodded soberly. "Indeed. I, too, would be most apprehensive. Shall we depart?"

I nodded and turned to give Jane a hug.

"Godspeed, Kat. My prayers will be with you." She pressed her lips close to my ear. "And I shall pray not only for your mother's health, but for news of your betrothal."

I tried hard not to smile but failed, and so reached for my pomander to lift it toward my face. But Jane stayed my hand. "We know why you go, but we also wish you happiness."

The duchess entered the great hall then in a stately swish of skirts. She walked straight-backed toward us, her gait purposeful.

"Beau, do take care with Lady Katherine. We want her to arrive at Charterhouse in the best of health."

"Upon my life, Your Grace, I will see her safely there."

My insides shook at his words. To feel safe was a wondrous thing.

"Lady Katherine, I have a letter for your mother. Will you deliver it to her for me?"

"Yes, Your Grace."

She handed me a rolled parchment, and then we all walked to the courtyard, where the horses were saddled and ready for our journey. The sun still shone bright in the afternoon sky. I tucked the parchment Lady Anne gave me into the satchel tied to my mare.

"Cook has packed you some food, as you will most likely need it on your journey," Lady Anne said.

I thanked her, and with last hugs, Ned boosted me onto my mount. I was pleased the stable master remembered that I preferred to ride astride. And thank goodness, Princess Elizabeth did the same, as did Queen Mary, so it was not looked ill upon. I settled my skirts around me, gave one last look at Hanworth and its inhabitants, and then breathed a sigh. This journey would surely change my future—and I had a feeling it would be a most glorious change.

We rode out through the gates, Ned beside me and behind us Mrs. Helen, Ned's groomsman, and a half-dozen retainers for protection. The ride would not be long, and we would arrive before dark, but one could never be too careful upon the road, and although I preferred to forget it, I was a princess of the blood. Plots being hatched and my person being kidnapped for a hefty ransom were always of concern when we traveled.

For the first several miles, we rode in a comfortable silence as I basked in the fresh summer air and the wind in my hair and smelled the various wildflowers we passed in shades of yellow, purple, red, and white. I had been able to sneak away from Hanworth only a handful of times to ride, and my body and mind craved the exercise.

The road was empty save for a few monks on donkeys, the occasional family walking with satchels upon their backs, and merchants pulling carts of half-rotted vegetables. The latter two pulled at my heartstrings. Was the family homeless or simply going on a journey to visit relations? Were they looking for work so that the precious children did not starve? Was the merchant unable to sell the vegetables? Or was he so desperate for money he'd picked the rotted vegetables from a discard pile in hopes of making a few coins?

To the family and the merchant, I tossed a few coins, and though I thought Ned might offer a rebuke, as my father so often had, at my soft heart, he only smiled.

"You are most generous, my lady."

"I feel if I've the means to make someone's life a little more pleasant—if only for a short time—then it is my duty to do so."

"A true lady. Most would keep what precious coins they have for jewels and gowns."

I laughed at this. "Have you not seen I have more than enough?"

"I have noticed you dress most beautifully, but I should never think you had enough. You, my princess, deserve the world at your feet."

I ducked my head. "You flatter me, my lord."

"I've told you before, I wish you to call me Ned. Our servants cannot hear us." His smile sent my heart fluttering.

"Ned, you flatter me unduly."

"I never flatter anyone unduly. You have swept into my life again and again and wound me up in your web, little spider. I am paralyzed by your charm. Do with me what you will." He bent at his waist in a bow.

My eyes widened at his words, at the flirtatious glint in his gaze. I laughed gaily. "You must call me Katherine. Spider simply won't do."

"Hmm . . . Katherine is too formal. May I call you Kat?"

"Indeed, yes, most who are intimate with me do."

"Is that another invitation, Kat?" He brought his horse closer so that his thigh bumped and rubbed against mine, and that all-too-familiar tingling that made me want for him to touch me all the more took over.

I gulped. "Another invitation?"

"To be intimate with you. You asked me to kiss you before . . ."

I looked down at my hands tightly grasping the reins of the horse, my knuckles white.

"I'd thought us already on intimate terms, unless you think a kiss such a trivial thing." *Oh, please do not think it so!*

Ned tossed back his head and laughed. He leaned closer once again. "I think a kiss one of the most intimate things, and I wish to kiss you again." He glanced behind him. "If only we were not so encumbered."

I smiled and met his gaze. "Perhaps we should stop to sup, and I could once more get stung by an annoying bee."

Ned chuckled and tweaked my chin. "You are a little imp, Kat. And the idea does hold merit, for I do not think I can go another minute without tasting your soft lips."

With his words, his gaze went from teasing and flirtatious to one filled with desire. My body reacted viscerally, tingling, hot.

"Oh, Kat, do you have any idea how ardently I admire you?"

I glanced up, lips parted in astonishment and my own deep yearning. "No," I whispered, but I had an idea of what he felt, if it was anything like my own body's reaction.

He held up his hand to indicate for their party to stop.

"We shall rest, and you shall be chased by a bee. Then I will show you." He smiled and winked devilishly.

I sucked in my breath in nervous anticipation.

Ned dismounted in one fluid, masculine motion and then came to my side to help me down.

"We shall rest and refresh ourselves a few moments," he told our entourage, and then taking me by the hand, he led me toward a tree, a couple of apples in his hand. "Will you let me feed you an apple, Kat?"

I nodded and sat beside the tree, smoothing my skirts around me.

I was surprised when Mrs. Helen did not venture close, for we were at an inappropriate distance. Instead, from my position, I watched her flirt with Ned's groomsman as they sat and shared food by the horses.

Beside me, Ned cut into a crisp green apple, the juices flowing over his fingers. He held the slice to my mouth, and I took a bite. The fruit was sweet and tangy, and my love of apples was wholly renewed. Ned took a bite from the same slice, licking juice from his lips. I found myself staring at his tongue, recalling how it had once swiped over my lips in the very same way.

He sliced another chunk. This time, when I took a bite, juice dribbled from my lips over my chin. Ned stroked his thumb over the trickle and then brought it to his mouth, his eyes never leaving mine. He pressed his thumb to his tongue and sucked the juice from it. If I had been standing, my knees would have buckled at so sensual a move. How would I ever be able to eat an apple again?

"Where is that annoying bee when we need him?" Ned teased.

I glanced over to where the retainers, Mrs. Helen, and the groomsman sat chatting and eating. Not one of them looked in our direction. Ned's gaze followed mine. He stood, then he held out his hand. I placed my hand in his, marveling at how much larger he was, how warm his grip was, and how once again I felt such comfort and safety.

He didn't lead me far, just behind the tree, so that parts of us were still seen, but our faces were hidden.

"Kat, I must know, would you have me to wed?"

I was overcome with joy, for to hear him say it—even though he'd been given permission—felt wonderful. "Are you proposing to me?"

"Indeed, my lady. I would have you with me always." He bent to one knee, my hands in his, looked up into my eyes, and produced a pointed diamond ring. "Say you'll be my wife. That day so long ago, when we danced, both of us but babes, I knew then. I love you, Kat, with a fierceness that steals the breath from my body."

I opened my mouth to speak, but no words came out. The emotions boiling inside me grew to bursting, stealing my voice.

"Say something," he pleaded.

I blinked rapidly, willing the tears glistening in my eyes to recede, as I squeezed his hands tight. "Yes, I love you, yes!"

Before I could take another breath, he'd risen to stand, his full height well beyond my own. He slipped the ring upon my heart finger, the metal as warm as his fingers. Excitement and love filled me. He slid his hands up my arms and gently held my face, his mouth coming down on mine so quickly I barely had a chance to take a breath.

His lips were gentle, loving. I was completely swept away, the world disappearing around us, and all I could sense in any way was Ned.

At first I was hesitant, letting him kiss me, letting his tongue taste, but as the sensations whipped around inside me, I grew bolder. I pressed my lips to his, tentatively stroked my tongue over his and was rewarded with a carnal growl from within his chest. His hands glided from my face to my neck and shoulders and then down my back in a sensual caress that sent my body plunging into a pit of craving.

I felt wanton. I felt hunger for more of his touch, and I felt needed, desired.

But the kiss ended all too quickly at the sounds of approaching footsteps.

"My lady?" Mrs. Helen slowly approached, her footsteps loud as if she purposefully stepped on every fallen branch she could find and scuffed her riding boots on every rock.

Without saying more, I knew that Mrs. Helen had allowed us those brief moments alone and that she had not actually taken her eyes off of me once. I was grateful for her gift.

Chapter Ten

And many a sad and heavy thought,
between them both had past,
Of Princes grace and favor great,
(to which regard they took:
As chiefest thing and only cause)
whereon they ought to look.
—*Thomas Churchyard, Elizabethan Soldier and Poet*

THAT EVENING
CHARTERHOUSE

The sun had just begun to set below the horizon, giving Charterhouse a pink-and-orange backdrop cut through by the rooftop and ramparts. It was quite a sight to see. The windows glinted black and glittering. When our horses' hooves pounded through the gate and into the courtyard, Master Stokes rushed from the great front doors to descend the stairs and take my reins himself.

"Lady Katherine, I am so grateful for your arrival, and Her Grace, your mother, when I told her of your plan to come hither at once, did find renewed strength to fight the fever that raged inside her. It has only just broken this past hour!" Sweat poured off Master Stokes's forehead, as if he'd spent the better part of the day pacing in the heat.

"Thank God for such a miracle!" When I turned to dismount, Ned was there to lift me, and along with Mrs. Helen, we followed Stokes into the great hall. "Mary!"

I was pleasantly surprised to see my sister standing in the great hall, as if she'd positioned herself just so and then adjusted her stance until finally coming to be where she stood now. She was still terribly short. It had been at least a year since I'd last seen her, and I had expected her to have grown somewhat, but she had not. At age fifteen, she was the size of a girl half her age. Her eyes, set close together, stared at me blankly.

"I am pleased you have come to see Mother, Katherine," she said. Her voice was high-pitched and gravelly, as if she gargled rocks and speaking was painful.

"Are you ill?"

Her back stiffened. "I had a touch of what Mother suffers from but am much improved."

"I am pleased you are recovered."

And I was pleased, but I wanted to know about her state of mind. Why did she seem so angry to see me? Or was it only my imagination? When we were younger, Mary was the least favorite of our parents. I was well aware of how my mother criticized her small frame and pinched face and how nothing Mary did could be right. My own upbringing had been much the same when Jane was present. The Nine-Days Queen, they called my late sister now.

Back still stiff and rigid, Mary said, "Thank you."

I did not think I was truly strong of mind, but perhaps my fortitude was such that those lamentations of how I should have been more like my sister Jane rolled off eventually, and I'd become the person I was, seeking my own happiness.

But little Mary, she looked as if she was ready for a battle to ensue. I had to find a way to make peace. There was no need for her to be so wary in my presence.

I stepped forward and put my arms around her. "I have missed your company, Sister."

Mary stayed rigid for several breaths, and then she, too, put her little arms around my waist, but only for the briefest of moments. I let her have her way, to make her more comfortable.

Her gaze shifted to Ned, who bowed. "Lady Mary, it is a pleasure to make your acquaintance. I am Lord Beauchamp and most humbly at your ladyship's service."

Mary actually blushed, and a small, tight-lipped smile curved her lips, as she didn't like to show off her little, pointy, rotted teeth. She curtsied in return. "A pleasure, my lord."

Master Stokes stepped forward. "If it pleases, let me show you to Her Grace's sickbed."

I agreed, and my sister, Ned, and Mrs. Helen followed behind me up the winding stair to my mother's bedchamber. The corridor was well lit, and I was pleased to see that the walls and floors looked recently washed—despite the stench. The scent of death hung in the air.

"Are you certain Mother is improved?"

"Aye, my lady."

I pinched my nose and held my citrus pomander to my face. The stench was overpowering. Sweat, blood, dirt, vomit, something rotting . . .

"I had the servants scrub down this corridor to try to alleviate the stench, my lady. My apologies, but your mother's physicians would not let me clean her sick chamber. They advised against even opening a window."

I could hardly breathe. The air was thick and overpowering. "Master Stokes, you will order the servants to clean and refresh my mother's sickbed immediately."

He blanched at my orders, but I could not allow her to spend another minute in this place. I feared I might become ill from visiting—indeed, that may have been how young Mary herself, with her weakened constitution, became ill.

"In fact, Master Stokes, take my mother to another chamber at once. The servants must clean this place immediately. Mrs. Helen, have a bath prepared for Her Grace."

A cloud formed over the former Master of the Horse's face at my giving him orders in his own home. If he wanted to argue, I was ready to do battle with him.

"But the physicians—"

"Frauds! If the queen knew her dear cousin was being treated this way . . ." I shook my head, kept my voice steady. "My mother is the daughter of a queen. She is a princess and should not be languishing in filth. Remove her."

Stokes nodded, despite his glower, and opened the door to my mother's room. A waft of fetid air assaulted us.

"How long has the room been this way?" I asked Mary.

She turned hard eyes on me. "The entire time."

"I fear you grew ill from the stench. Lord knows how much of the sickness is surrounding Mother in a cloud, waiting to settle inside someone's body."

Mary only nodded.

Stokes carried the once-grand duchess, now a withered shape, from the room. Her chemise was stained yellow and brown in some parts. I wanted to shout, knowing that chemise had once been white. Mother's head was turned into Stokes's shoulder, and so I could not see her face.

I did not stay to consider her chamber, knowing if my mother looked so terrible, the rest of the room would be far worse.

I let her servants do their duties, as they bathed mother with warm cloths and rose-scented water. I ordered them to change her chemise, wash her hair, towel it dry, and brush out wicked-looking snarls.

"She has lost much weight," I noted.

My mother had been a buxom woman. Sturdy, my father had called her, but now she was a shell, the illness having melted away nearly half her body.

"And blood," Mary said. "They bled her thrice a day."

I swallowed hard. Had not the Duchess of Somerset complained of that very thing being the cause of the late Queen Jane's demise?

"They shall not bleed her again." I met Stokes's gaze, and he nodded.

I turned to a nearby maid. "Fetch Her Grace some broth and an herbal posset of comfrey and mint."

"But—" Stokes began.

I held up my hand to stop him. "I have been at my dear friend Lady Jane Seymour's side, and the posset has greatly increased her health."

To confirm that fact, Ned spoke up. "Indeed, Lady Katherine has worked wonders for my sister."

Mother turned her glazed gaze toward us, and when her eyes alighted on me, they cleared.

"Katherine . . ." she breathed, wincing at the use of her own voice.

Stokes rushed to her side and gripped her hand. She turned to face him and gave him a wan smile, then turned back toward me. Stokes backed away to allow me space, and I went to her side and sat upon the bed where the servants had placed her. I gripped her bony hand in mine. Her skin was yellowish, made to look more so by the white of her pillow, and the deep-purple smudges beneath her eyes.

"Mother, I am pleased to see you are awake and that your fever has broken."

She nodded and tried to sit up. I plumped the pillows behind her and straightened her coverings.

"Lord Beauchamp," she said, pointing to Ned and coughing lightly. "A pleasant surprise to see you."

"Your Grace," he said, bowing before her. "I provided escort to your daughter."

"And I thank you for seeing her safely to me." She coughed in earnest now, as if before she had been trying to stave off the tickle in her throat.

The broth and posset were brought in then, thank the Lord, and I let Mother sip the steaming herbal. It took some time, perhaps an hour or more, but soon she finished most of the broth and all of the posset.

"That feels nice on my throat," she murmured, then lay her head back, looking exhausted.

"Your coloring has improved already," I said, examining the yellowish-pink flesh of her face. While it had once been full and now her cheekbones jutted, she did indeed look as though blood once more flowed easily through her veins, a good sign.

She nodded. "I am tired, but I feel better. I do not feel as though I am knocking at death's door."

And indeed, judging from the scent of things in her previous chamber, she had been knocking—nay, *banging*—on the door.

I fed her the remaining broth, and I was pleased as Stokes remarked he had not seen her consume so much in days.

I left her then to rest and breathed a heavy sigh in the corridor.

"Should you like to take a short walk, my lady?" Ned asked, seeming to know I needed the fresh air to return vigor to my body and soul.

"I would like that very much. Mary, Master Stokes, would you care to join us in the gardens before we sup?"

Master Stokes shook his head. "I have many duties and paperwork I must see to. With Her Grace so ill, I have put off much. I will have Cook send a tray to my library. Please make yourselves at home." Master Stokes bowed and walked away.

Mary shook her head. "I am weary, Katherine. I, too, shall have a tray sent to my chambers." Mary walked away, her gait stilted.

"I suppose it will be just the two of us then," I said with a smile in Ned's direction.

Mrs. Helen cleared her throat.

"And my attendant, of course," I said with a laugh.

"Always a pleasure to have you with us, Mrs. Helen," Ned said with a wink in her direction.

Mrs. Helen blushed red enough for me to see it in the torchlight and sputtered her gratitude.

Ned held out his arm to me, and I curved my fingers around his upper arm.

"What do you do for exercise?" I asked boldly as we descended the stairs and walked through the great hall to the garden door. The scents of our supper invaded my nostrils—roasted meat, stewed vegetables, and baked bread. My stomach grumbled its approval at the meal we would soon consume.

"I like to ride and hunt. Jousting, fencing, the occasional boxing match."

I turned a teasing smile his way. "Boxing or brawling?"

"Oh, Lady Katherine, you wound me," he said with exaggerated mockery. "To think I would lower myself in such a way. In truth, I have had very few fisticuffs. Mostly, it is for fun among fellows."

"Ah, blood sport."

"You could call it that, but let us not lament on my ungentlemanly endeavors. What do you do to keep such a trim figure?" At his words, his gaze roved over my body, and my breath caught in my throat.

I swallowed hard and tried to find my voice. Would he always have such an effect on me?

"I enjoy walking, riding, dancing."

"I should like to dance with you again, my lady. I recall the last time we did so fondly."

I smiled. "I am surprised we have not had cause to dance again in all these years since."

"As am I. It would be ironic, would it not, if we did not dance again until our own wedding day?"

I sighed to hear him say such words. "Yes."

It seemed too good to be true, that I should be so happy, and that the man I'd fallen for all those years ago, when I had been wed to another, should now soon be the one I would be with for all eternity. I twisted the ring he'd given me around my finger, grateful that since I wore several rings, no one had noticed. I was not sure why I was wary of sharing our secret. 'Twas almost as if I feared that if I did, the dream would be over and I would once again be lonely.

"I will speak to Her Grace and gain her permission before we depart. But I should like to wait until she is a little more recovered," Ned said.

I nodded. "With the posset and a cleaner environment I should hope she is feeling much improved on the morrow."

"You are a little miracle worker, you know that, Kat?"

I was humbled by his praise and mumbled, "I only seek to provide succor to those in need." I liked sharing with Ned my goals, my aspirations to help those in need, to heal the sick if I could, even if I was talking about my mother. I was glad to hear from his own lips that he approved.

"Some might call you an angel for such deeds."

"And yet others might think I interfere too much," I said, thinking of the glower on Stokes's face when I'd come in to take charge.

"He will thank you for it, Kat. His irritation only stems from having not thought of it himself. He loves your mother, I can see, and he trusted the physicians to heal her. And her fever did break, she is no longer on the brink of death, so in a way, they did him a service. But now you are here to lead her back to full health. 'Tis simply a matter of the man's pride, nothing more."

"I appreciate your words, Ned, I truly do. I hope you are right." I tugged his arm closer, feeling the solid strength of him, his vitality, his confidence in me, and his willingness to support my cause.

"I am but your humble servant, love."

Our feet crunched across the gravel in the garden as we meandered into the hedge maze. Little candles upon the ground lit our path as we wandered deeper and deeper among the twists and turns.

I remembered that while I was growing up, the maze at Bradgate had always been lit by candles on those nights when weather permitted it, and my sisters and I had raced through the maze to see who could find their way out first. But now, instead of just being a child's game, it seemed to mean so much more. Now it was romantic, and even a little wicked. If Ned were to run ahead with me, we might lose Mrs. Helen's sight, and who was to say what would happen then? My belly fluttered at the thoughts.

Suddenly, there was a massive rushing along the gravel, and it crunched and crackled beneath footsteps behind us. Several people ran toward us.

I jumped and clutched myself close to Ned's chest, my fingers grasping the soft velvet of his doublet, fearing the worst—the queen's guard coming to arrest me.

Then a bark broke the nighttime quiet, and Arabel, Rex, and Beau burst upon us, all slobbering, kissing tongues, and wagging tails. They nudged their little bodies between us as if to reprimand us for trying to find a moment alone.

"Apologies, my lady. A groomsman let them out, and I could not catch them afore they raced ahead," Mrs. Helen said as she approached, out of breath. Said groomsman rushed toward us, too.

"'Tis all right, Mrs. Helen. They only wished to see that I was well and had not forgotten them." I laughed as little Beau tugged on the hem of my skirt as if to prove my statement, and then Arabel nudged him away so she could rub her soft head against my ankles. Not to be outdone, Rex nipped gently at my toes until I scratched him behind his ears.

"Little rascals," Ned chuckled, picking up a stick and tossing it down the path.

All three dogs' ears perked up, and then they were off to chase the stick.

"Shall we return? I'd hate for Cook to grow angry if we arrived late and the hard work she put into making our meal went to waste," Ned said.

All of a sudden, I recalled the scents of freshly baked bread, herbed vegetables, and succulent meat. My stomach rumbled loudly, and I clutched a hand to my belly, feeling the heat rise in my cheeks.

"I will take that as an affirmative, Kat." He chuckled and took my hand in his. We ran back the way we'd come. "We must hurry, else your insides eat you whole."

I giggled the whole way as we ran, my hood catching on a branch and wrenching pins and strands of hair free.

"My lady!" Mrs. Helen shouted with outrage when I kept going, not bothering to retrieve the shredded fabric.

Ned glanced over his shoulder at me, his eyes catching my golden tresses in the moonlight, and gave me a look of such approval I felt it all the way to my toes.

But Mrs. Helen would not have it. As soon as we reached the great hall, she rushed toward me with a glare fit to make any warrior cower.

"My lady," she said through gritted teeth—and I allowed her this only as she had nursed me as an infant. "You cannot possibly think to dine without your hood!"

"Fetch me a new one then, Mrs. Helen, and do not frown so, it makes the creases on your face more prominent." I gave her a petulant pout while, inside, I laughed.

My longtime companion scowled at me but rushed to find a new hood while Ned and I stood by the hearth.

"She is a dragon, that one," he said with humor.

"Indeed, she is. A surrogate mother to me. She's been by my side since the day I was born. I could not imagine my life without her."

"You are lucky to still have her about you."

"Yes. She could very well have stayed with my sister Mary, as she was her nurse, too, but I was glad she chose to come with me. She has been my rock, especially—" But I cut myself short, not wanting to revisit past horrid tales.

Ned lifted my chin so our gazes connected. "Tell me, Kat. If we are to be man and wife, oughtn't I to know all there is?"

"But you do already. She was with me on many a frightened night when Jane was proclaimed queen and then arrested. I still fear that I will be brought to the Tower for having Tudor blood in my veins." My fear hovered just beneath the surface. In the back of my mind, I always assumed one day they would come for me.

Would I grow to see an elder version of myself in a looking glass?

"I will keep you safe, Kat. Together, we will live in peace."

His words sounded so full of promise, but a niggling fear ate away at me still. If Queen Mary would only live and produce an heir, I would be safe. But her health even now rested on a precipice. My future was uncertain—even if Ned could persuade first my mother and then the queen herself that we should be wed. But then there was Princess Elizabeth to contend with if Queen Mary should not live.

"The sooner we are wed, the better. I fear that if we wait too long . . ."

"I shall speak to Her Grace in the morning and, God willing, with her permission, race for Whitehall to speak with Her Majesty at once."

I nodded. "What about the Privy Council members? Do you think they will agree to the match?"

Ned frowned. "I should think at least half of them will. With the queen's blessing, I won't have to worry overmuch."

Mrs. Helen returned with my hood, pinned it in place, and then disappeared to the kitchens to inform Cook we were ready for the meal to begin. With Mother in bed and Mary and Stokes in their own respective chambers, the evening meal was quiet and intimate.

"You fear Princess Elizabeth?" Ned asked between bites of meat.

"I do not," I replied, half-truthfully. "Why do you ask?"

"What you said before, it seemed as though you thought if she were to become queen before we married that our efforts might be fruitless."

I nodded. "I would never speak an unkind word against my cousin, but 'tis the truth she and my sister Jane—God rest her soul—were at odds, and at times, her ire has trickled down to me. She has styled herself a pious and virtuous woman, even more so after what happened with your uncle Thomas Seymour, and from what I've heard, she prefers all those close to her to be just as virginal and unattached as she is. I am rambling and not making much sense, but suffice it to say, I worry she may deny my request to be married simply on the grounds that she herself is not."

"The council is in constant talks for her to marry. She will be wed soon enough, and then your fears will be forever gone."

I nodded, feeling a headache coming on. Pain seared my forehead, as it did whenever panic began to dig its claws into my person. "As you say."

I did not want to argue with Ned. He was but a man, and a man who believed princesses followed the rule of the council. He'd not spent much time with Elizabeth, I suspected. But I had, and I'd seen the feral outrage that splintered her countenance when the topic of marriage was broached. Of course, it showed for only a moment before the docile, obedient sister to the queen returned, and she'd incline her head demurely. But I'd seen in those moments that Elizabeth would succumb to the rule of no man.

Chapter Eleven

They wayd in balance of their breasts,
what sittest served their corns:
And like as wood takes flame of fire,
and so to cinders born.
So throw the heat of this mishap,
they felt such sorrow thoe . . .
—Thomas Churchyard, Elizabethan Soldier and Poet

JULY 27, 1558

"You wish to ask for the hand of my daughter? A princess of the blood?" Mother's features were pinched as she stared Ned straight in the face.

My feet shifted beneath my vast, rose-colored skirts. I endeavored to keep their nervous swish from notice. My nerves were frayed, and I jumped at every inflection in my mother's tone. She may have become a shell of her former self in body, but in mind, she was as sharp as ever.

"Indeed, Your Grace. I would be honored if you agreed to my offer of marriage to your most virtuous daughter. I have offered her my ring, and she has accepted."

I stood near the back of Mother's chamber, my head bowed as I listened to their conversation. The hand with Ned's ring rested atop my other hand so Mother could see the shining gold and diamonds. Stokes stood beside Mother, his hand resting on the wood-framed, cushioned chair she'd been positioned on. Little Mary had disappeared once again—something at which, I'd come to realize, she was quite talented.

"What, pray tell, makes you a worthy groom? She could marry a prince or a duke, and you are but a baron."

"If it pleases, I am the son of a duke, and my mother, the Duchess of Somerset, descends from kings."

I chanced a glance at Mother to see her reaction to his words—information she most certainly had already known, as every noble made it their business to know the pedigree of every other. Her back was rigid, her clothes billowed on her slight frame, and dark circles ringed her eyes. But her skin had taken on a fleshier color instead of the sickly yellow it'd had upon my first arrival.

"Descended of kings, indeed." She did not snort, but I feared she wanted to. "You are undeniably of noble stock—a drop of royalty even flows through your veins." She tapped her fingers on the arm of her polished chair. "If I were to accept your proposal, what is it you wish in return? Every groom seeks a dowry, and you must know Katherine has one."

"I worry not over her dowry, Your Grace. I am wealthy enough to support us in the style of which she is deserving."

The duchess raised a brow that said she did not believe his denial of wanting the dowry. "You seek nothing but a warm body in your bed? Why not find a scullion to lie with?"

I sucked in a breath, seeing where Mother was going with her words. She *wanted* Ned to want something besides me. She wanted to know that he was shrewd as well as in love.

"Land is always desirable, as is plate, Your Grace."

"And you had something in mind?"

"I would defer to my bride."

"Would you?"

"Since I plan to let her retain any such gain from our marriage, then yes, indeed, I would."

Something softened in Mother's eyes, as if she had hoped for something like this in her own life. A man who was willing to give up wealth for her—true love. She glanced back at Stokes, confirming my suspicions. She had married the man for love, but he'd brought nothing of worth to the table.

"I like a man with conviction. How do I know you will continue to be so chivalrous toward my daughter?"

"Your Grace, I love Lady Katherine. I wish her nothing but happiness, and I hope to be the one who can provide it."

Mother's lips curled in a smile. "What say you, Katherine?"

My eyes widened, and I stepped forward. "Your Grace, I will gladly take Lord Beauchamp to wed."

"Then it is settled. All that is left to do is seek Her Majesty's approval and draw up the marriage contract."

My heart soared. I felt as though my entire body was lifted from the ground. At last! After so many years pining for just this thing, marriage to a man I loved, who loved me in return, a future of happiness and peace! Soon, it would be mine.

"I will ride to beg an audience with Her Majesty at once," Ned said.

The duchess shook her head, lips pursed. I opened my mouth to protest, but thinking better of it, shut it again.

"I would like to write her myself, Lord Beauchamp. The queen is my cousin, and perhaps I will be able to influence her decision before you should need to ask. I do believe she will be agreeable to the match. After what happened . . ." Mother's voice trailed off, and for a fleeting moment, she looked vulnerable. She waved her hand as if dismissing her sad thoughts. "Well, in any case, she has taken a liking to Katherine, and so I think she would be amenable to her marrying."

"As you say, Your Grace. I trust in your judgment."

Mother inclined her head, exhaustion showing at the corners of her eyes. "If that is all, you may leave me."

Why was Mother suddenly so charitable? For once, she was being helpful rather than scheming to see how the turn of events could work in her favor. Was she making amends? Trying to protect me? I wanted to be happy, but part of me worried about her motives.

Ned and I bowed to my mother and inclined our heads to Master Stokes. Before leaving the room, I turned back to Mother. She didn't notice me, but I watched her shoulders slump. The woman had fortitude. She was exhausted but still insisted on maintaining her stoic countenance in the face of others.

I witnessed Stokes lift Mother in his arms, cradling her beneath her legs and back as though she were a babe. They gazed at each other lovingly. I found the scene to be disturbing—only because I had grown up thinking Mother incapable of love. I thought her a cold woman, and to see such warmth on her face—warmth that had never once been directed at me—struck me hard.

"How shall we celebrate, my bride?" Ned gripped my hand in his large, warm grasp and pulled me into the corridor.

He picked me up at the waist and twirled me about, and I squealed with delight. Two maids tittered, their heads together, hands over their mouths as they hurried past.

"It looked to be a cloudless sky this morning. Let us ride."

"Should you like to hunt?" Ned asked.

I wrinkled my nose. "I do not like to hunt."

He looked at me quizzically. "You do not hunt?"

"I like the chase, but wish that it would end there. I cannot watch the killing."

"Well, shall we take the dogs out for a run while we ride?"

I clapped my hands in excitement. "Yes! It sounds wonderful."

"I will see about a picnic from Cook, and you gather up the fearsome Mrs. Helen."

I laughed as Ned wrinkled his nose and did his best to impersonate my buxom companion.

"You are terrible, Ned. If Mrs. Helen were to see you strutting so, she would box your ears."

Ned laughed at that, then gripped my hand in his, gently squeezing as he brought it to his lips. "I think today may be the happiest of my life."

A tingle wrought its way from my hand to my heart. "And mine also. I confess I did not think this day would ever come."

"And yet it has." Ned pulled me close, taking a chance that we might be caught in such an embrace in the open corridor.

He nuzzled my nose with his own and then kissed me swiftly. "I wish to kiss you further, but I do not want to court Her Grace's ire after just gaining her favor."

"Perhaps Mrs. Helen will turn her back while we picnic," I whispered with a mischievous smile.

"One can only hope." Ned's eyes twinkled with mirth. "Truthfully, it is the queen's consent, the priest's blessing, and our marriage bed I look forward to, where I can not only kiss your lips, but kiss . . . other parts of you, with no one denying when and where."

Flames shot from my cheeks, for I had imagined such pleasures myself. My limbs tingled with anticipation.

"Yes," I breathed, for dreams did apparently come true, and I felt for certain I lived inside a wonderful fantasy.

Then Mother's words from so long ago came back to haunt me. *Control, Kat. A woman must always maintain control. Do not allow yourself to be carried away by flights of fancy and pretty words. Your mind is your own and the only place in which you alone are master.*

Somehow, Ned had wiggled his way inside my mind, and I was no longer master there—and I wasn't sure I wanted to be, in any case. His stalwartness was a soothing balm. I quite enjoyed having him to lean against. He was on my side—an ally—the two of us against the world. But our relationship was also so much more than that. Ned was my kindred spirit.

JULY 31, 1558

Over a sennight at Charterhouse in Sheen, Mother's health greatly improved, and Ned and I had a chance to court each other in earnest. Walks in the gardens, reading from books. He sang me ballads while playing the lute and even wrote me a few poems detailing my beauty.

As promised, Mother wrote a letter to the queen—but she had yet to send it off, changing her mind and preferring to speak to her cousin in person. She hoped to be well enough to travel to court when I was summoned.

I tried to hide my disappointment at Mother not expediting the process. Didn't she realize how very much I wanted to marry Ned? Did she have some ulterior motive to delay making our betrothal official?

"My lady?" Mrs. Helen knocked and entered my chambers. She stopped short of where I sat in a window contemplating the rainy day and how Ned and I would not be able to go for our planned chase. Instead, I was knitting blankets for local poor children and babies.

Ned had named hunting "the chase" since I did not like the end result. He was very accommodating to my sensibilities, although I had an idea when one or two of our groomsmen did not return with us, that they were, in fact, finishing off the game we'd managed to corner.

I smiled at Mrs. Helen. In her hand, she held a rolled parchment. "Have you a message for me?" I asked.

"Aye, my lady. 'Tis from Lady Jane."

I jumped from the window seat and rushed to receive the paper from Mrs. Helen. I did so love my correspondence with Jane. She was still my dearest friend, and while I had Ned to confide in as well, Jane would always hold a place in my heart—after all, I dearly needed someone to whom I could confess my secrets.

Jane's letter prattled on about the activities at Hanworth, how she missed me so—but also included a warning. The Duchess of Somerset and she were on their way to Sheen, apparently having been invited by my own mother, who had not informed me of said invitation.

Did Ned know of their impending arrival? When would that be?

As if on cue, the sound of galloping horses and the cranking of a wagon wheel turned in the drive.

"Mrs. Helen, you must aid me with preparations for our guests."

"Guests?" My governess frowned and went to look out the window. "I do not see any guests, my lady, only a few merchants."

"Truly?" I, too, craned my neck out the window to see a wagon full of fabrics and several seamstresses and tailors dismounting from their places astride horses or inside the wagon.

"I suppose Her Grace is in need of a new wardrobe, given her illness caused her to waste away to nearly nothing."

Mrs. Helen made a humming sound in agreement.

"When did this letter arrive?" I asked, holding up the parchment from Jane.

"Just prior to me bringing it to you, love."

"And do you happen to know, Mrs. Helen, when my mother sent a note to the Duchess of Somerset?"

Mrs. Helen narrowed her brow at me and shook her finger. "Now, you know, my lady, I never spy, nor do I gossip."

"Come now, tell me. I must know when they will arrive. The duchess is such a formidable woman. I have to prepare myself in advance . . . Especially now that Ned and I will soon be officially betrothed."

"Seems to me, you are already betrothed."

"In our hearts, yes, but legally . . . If only it were so. You are quite aware we must first gain the approval of Queen Mary."

Mrs. Helen grunted her reply.

I sent my companion a pleading look. "Do tell if you know."

"I believe she sent a note out yestermorn." Mrs. Helen huffed as though I'd forced the words from her.

"Did the duchess send a reply?"

"I do not know, my lady. I was only given your letter from Lady—"

A yelp of pain and loud shrieking from outside interrupted my companion. Shouts and calls sounded from people in the court-yard. Pebbled flesh rose on my arms.

"Oh my goodness, what was that?" I pressed a hand to my chest as I rushed toward the window. Several people hunched over something on the ground.

"Oh, my dear . . . ," Mrs. Helen said, tears in her eyes.

I did not want to believe what I was seeing. I did not want to see the confirmation in Mrs. Helen's eyes, just as vividly as I saw the white paw . . .

I rushed from the room, no care that I'd yet to put on my slippers, and ran barefoot down the winding staircase, tripping twice and nearly pitching forward, only to catch myself with a jarring crack of my hand on the moist stony wall.

"My lady!" I could hear Mrs. Helen shouting from somewhere above me, but I did not stop my descent. I had to get outside, had to get to the poor little creature who'd been crushed beneath—I didn't know beneath what. A horse's hoof? A wagon wheel?

I burst through the great wooden doors, rain drizzling on my cheeks, and rushed down the few stone steps leading to the court-yard, shoving bodies aside before dropping on my knees to the muddy ground.

Although he didn't move his head, Rex turned his eyes toward me, such sadness filling their depths, as though he were sorry to disappoint *me*, the poor creature. He panted, and I reached down to cradle his small, broken body in my arms.

"Oh, Rex. Sweet darling." I turned my eyes on all those gath-ered. "What happened?"

"The hound got in the way of Jasper," said a middle-aged man as he wiped rainwater from his brow.

"Jasper? Who in God's name is Jasper?" I asked, exasperated, glancing around the rain-filled afternoon.

"My horse."

I wanted to shout that the horse should be stomped on, that the man in charge of the horse should also be trampled, but instead, I clamped my lips closed and rested my eyes on my sweet Rex. I'd had him with me since the day Jane—

It was hard for me to even finish the thought. As a gift to pro-vide me comfort, Father had given me the pups from the same litter. I'd held Rex and Arabel to my breast for so many nights as balm for the pain I felt inside. They were so much more to me than pets. They were my dearest friends . . . my family . . . and now . . .

"Oh, Rex," I sobbed into his warm body, feeling his fur soaked through.

Was it blood? I looked in horror, but there was no blood on his body, only rain. I felt his pain as he panted and whimpered against my chest and throat. I kissed his soft head, stroked behind his ears and held him.

Those around me stood in silence, and the few who felt the need to step forward I shooed away with angry slashes of my hands.

Where was Ned?

Arabel and Beau, as if sensing Rex's pain and mine, rushed forward. Arabel licked at Rex's face, and Beau nudged his paws, but the poor dog just rolled his eyes back and forth, as if willing the pain away.

"My lady, I could take a look at him and see the extent of the damage?" The soft voice was that of Mr. Roberts, our stable master and sometime physician to the manor animals.

I glanced up at him with tear-blurred vision and nodded, even as rain fell into my eyes and soaked my hood. My gown would be ruined, but I cared not. He took hold of Rex, and even with his gentle touch, the dog still whimpered in pain. I forced my arms to my sides instead of reaching out to protect him, since I knew that Mr. Roberts would do his utmost to see to the well-being of my Rex. Arabel and Beau slipped their bodies beneath my arms, seeking comfort. Their tails did not wag, and they, too, panted, staring at Rex and Mr. Roberts, awaiting the diagnosis as I did.

"Kat!" Ned burst on the scene, propriety foregone as he knelt by my side in the mud, placing a gently consoling hand on my shoulder. "What has happened?"

His gaze followed mine, and upon seeing Rex prone on the ground, he jumped up to oversee Mr. Roberts.

Mr. Roberts's long, slim fingers probed Rex's wet fur and flesh. Rex whimpered and snapped at him once, nearly taking off one of the stable master's fingers.

Ned cooed to the dog, stroking his white-and-brown head with strong fingers.

The stable master said something in low tones to Ned, and they both glanced up at me.

"What?" I said, my voice becoming shrill. "Do not stare at me and whisper as though I were a child with a weak heart!"

"My lady, I meant no offense," Mr. Roberts said softly, water dripping from the tip of his nose. "Rex, is it?"

At the mention of his name, Rex's gaze flicked from mine to Mr. Roberts. I nodded.

"I am terribly sorry to be the one to deliver such news to you, my lady, but it appears that Rex's rib cage has been crushed. It is a wonder he is still conscious at all, as the bones must have pierced his lungs and other organs."

I went numb. Choked on my breath. The poor pup must have been suffering miserably. I fell to the side, from my knees, and caught myself before I collapsed completely.

"He will die," I said, my voice cracking. Another one I cared so much about would pass from this life.

Ned picked up Rex's body and placed him back in my arms. I cradled him and cooed to him as his breathing grew shallower.

"A finer hound could not be found," I muttered, kissing his cold nose.

Rex's pink tongue came slowly from his snout and licked my face one last time. Our gazes connected, then he shuddered, and his eyes rolled into the back of his head.

"Rex?" I whispered, resting my forehead to his, willing him to open his eyes again. It could not be over! But all the same, I knew it was.

My precious dog had been trampled by a horse. Cruelly beaten for no reason.

My head shot up, searching the crowd. "You there," I shouted, pointing to the man who'd claimed ownership of the horse, Jasper. The man's stricken eyes met mine. "Leave this manor at once! Your services are no longer required."

From behind, Master Stokes approached and said, "But alas, my lady, Mr. Jamison is needed. Her Grace requires appropriate attire."

The man stared at me smugly, straightened his back and smoothed his tunic, wiping water from his shoulders.

"There are other tailors, sir," I replied, keeping my angry gaze steadily on Mr. Jamison.

"None so fine as he, I am afraid. Her Grace requested his presence specifically."

"I assure you, sir, she will not keep this man in her employ after what has just happened."

A loud sigh came from Master Stokes. "On the contrary, my lady. I have just come from your mother, and she has said Mr. Jamison is to stay."

"If he is to remain at Sheen in Her Grace's employ, then I shall take my leave."

"As you say, my lady." Master Stokes turned, dismissing me.

I wanted to shout at him for his rudeness, but I knew when an argument was futile. It was easier for him to dismiss me than to face the wrath of my mother. No man would bite the hand that fed him—unless, of course, that man was my own sire, Henry Grey. And it had been evident from the beginning that Master Stokes was nothing like my father.

"Mr. Roberts, let us see to a proper burial of my poor Rex. Mrs. Helen, pack my things. I am returning to Hanworth as soon as possible. I cannot remain in a place that would harbor a man so careless with innocent life."

Those around me nodded solemnly, some shook their heads, but no one advised against my departure.

Ned lifted me, his strong, warm presence a deep comfort to the coldness I felt both inside and out.

Chapter Twelve

As though hard destiny swore they should,
consume themselves with woe.
The Lady lost her freedom straight,
the Gods had so decreed:
Her knight by sudden flight abroad,
made virtue of a need.
—*Thomas Churchyard, Elizabethan Soldier and Poet*

AUGUST 3, 1558

Mother had not contacted me at all since I'd left her home. Nor had she written or made a visit to Her Majesty regarding our wish to marry, and I feared she never would.

I wrote her a letter, apologizing for leaving her home abruptly, explaining my heartbreak over the pup and that, as he'd been a gift from Father, I felt that I had lost the only connection I had left to my sire. I had hoped to appeal to her softer side, but I was wrong in doing so. Mother might be happy with her new husband, but she'd not changed overly much in her feelings for me.

A letter of reply was sent quickly to me—but not from my mother, rather written by Master Stokes.

The missive was short, to the point, and completely crushing.

Lady Katherine,

Your mother, the honorable Duchess of Suffolk, has bid me reply to you. She was greatly offended to be abandoned by you in her hour of need, especially when it was over a mere animal, no matter who gave it to you as a gift. She has not yet found it in her heart to risk her standing with the queen for such an ungrateful child.

Best that you beg your mother's forgiveness as a dutiful daughter should and pray she finds it in her heart to bless you as you wish in time.

Regards,

Master Stokes

I did reply, begging my mother's forgiveness and telling her I'd been nothing but dutiful, but my mother was known for holding steadfast to her grudges. I did not expect kindness from her ever, but hoped she'd write to the queen before long.

AUGUST 5, 1558

My summons to court was abrupt, and just when I was beginning to enjoy Hanworth again. Jane steadily grew stronger by the day, and when Ned hadn't been sent on some nonsensical errand by his mother, he was happy to oblige me in walks in the garden—but he did not offer up any more kisses.

My lips fairly burned for his to brush against them . . . But alas, he was more gentlemanly than ever. Could it be he would not want to pursue our relationship further should the queen deny our request?

"Her Majesty has not been well since last she thought she was with child. I heard it said she is not expected to recover. Her physicians, in fact, say she is near death's door. And yet, she refuses to name a successor, despite the work of the Privy Council to have her name Elizabeth her heir. Some even fear she may look to her Catholic cousin Mary, Queen of Scots," Lady Anne said as we supped in the comfortable yet elegant dining hall on simple meal of stewed mutton, berry tarts, and almond milk.

I frowned. "When was Prince Philip in England last?" Heretofore, Her Majesty had sent him letter after letter, begging him to return, but all her appeals had fallen on deaf ears. I recalled only a visit the previous year for a few short months, when Mary had once again felt she was pregnant. But alas, this past March, when the child should have been born, there was nothing. Phantom pregnancies were brought on by nerves or the constant problems she'd had with her woman's curse, and some suspected a cancer of the womb. Poor Mary. She'd wanted nothing more than to provide her country and her beloved husband with an heir. Perhaps this was God's way of saying that, indeed, the Catholic church should no longer occupy England, that her wars with France had cursed us—cursed her rule. Her sire, Henry VIII, would roll in his grave ceaselessly if he knew she'd lost him his prize—Calais and the right for English monarchs to style themselves king or queen of France.

"'Twas only those few months last year, prior to her suspicions of a second pregnancy. I do believe he's broken her heart. The ambassador to Spain sent a letter to His Majesty from Queen Mary, begging him to come to her side since she is not sure she will survive, and he has denied her. Some say he's already putting plans into place to win the hand of Princess Elizabeth." Lady Anne's countenance gave no indication of her feelings on the topic.

"Can they be so certain she is deathly ill, Your Grace?" Jane asked, nibbling on a tart, her cheeks full of color. "Perhaps she is with child again and just ill from that?"

My eyes widened at Jane's innocence. Lady Anne tilted her head as she studied her daughter with sharp, dark eyes.

"'Tis not possible for her to be with child, Jane—" The duchess cut off her own words, her lips twitching in a smile. "Perhaps it is time we found a worthy nobleman for you, my dear."

"Oh, Your Grace, I could not possibly marry now . . ." Jane trailed off, not seeming at the moment to land on a plausible excuse. Her face flamed redder than the strawberry tarts we dined on.

"We shall discuss it at a later date." The duchess's shrewd gaze slid to me. "What of you, Lady Katherine? Have you word from your mother regarding . . . ?"

There had been no reply to my last letter to my mother. She was still angry with me. The best I could do was bide my time, with an occasional letter to her of the activities at court and closing with my pleas for her forgiveness. I planned to write to her once a week. I could not let her forget me. I was so frustrated. All my dreams were within my grasp, and my mother was determined to punish me for leaving her house after poor Rex's brutal death. But I could not relay that to Lady Anne. "I have not been made privy to any new information."

Lady Anne nodded. "Yes, I suppose Her Grace wishes to discuss your betrothal with Her Majesty in person. Your position within this realm is of great import. You cannot marry just any nobleman. But I do believe Queen Mary will find Beau worthy of your hand. Her Majesty and I were quite close once, and I would still consider her an ally, as I hope she would find me."

I nodded, wishing Lady Anne could whisper in the queen's ear. "Indeed, my lady. Queen Mary has oft spoken highly of you."

Perhaps it might have been best for Ned instead to seek out the queen, as he'd originally planned. But if he did not have the permission of my mother, we could yet again stir her ire.

As if reading my mind, Lady Anne replied, "Best leave big decisions to those with authority to make them, Katherine. You cannot marry without permission of the queen, and I advise against doing anything rash that would jeopardize either of your well-being."

With that, the duchess stood and excused herself.

AUGUST 8, 1558

The queen's presence chamber was filled to the brim with courtiers, but Her Majesty was not in attendance.

I swept through the crowd and was let into Queen Mary's own bedchamber by the liveried yeomen outside her door. Even from where I had stood beyond the door, the stench of sickness seeped from her chamber. Urine, feces, vomit, disease, rotting flesh . . . The combination nearly had me turning to run for the freshness of outdoors. I was reminded of my mother's sickbed. How could the physicians see this as fitting? I felt the wood-paneled walls closing in on me, the carved-wood ceiling with its paintings of saints and angels falling on top of me. I had to force myself to breathe.

"Lady Katherine," she said from her bed, where I could barely make out her form beyond the drawn, sheer curtains as she huddled beneath large coverings. "Cousin, come closer."

I walked forward, feeling myself hit by a blast of heat—along with the stench. A roaring fire filled the hearth. The shutters on the windows were clamped tightly closed, and candles were lit everywhere. Several priests walked about the room, muttering prayers, incense smoke seeping from the round, silver thuribles swaying from linked chains in their hands.

I walked to the bed and curtsied, taking her gnarled fingers in my hand and kissing the large ruby of her coronation ring. Her flesh looked bloated, and a fetid smell came from her mouth filled with rotting teeth. I tried not to breathe too deeply. Standing opposite the bed was Elizabeth. Her face was deathly pale, lips pinched, and her gaze—directed at me—was full of venom. I forced myself not to take a step back. Why should she be so angry with me? Mary was family. Was I not allowed to console her in her hour of need? Did Elizabeth feel that I was a threat, even now?

"Majesty."

Queen Mary's voice was gravelly as she said, "It has been so long since last we saw you." She took a deep breath, as if talking was a laborious chore. "Did you find Hanworth accommodating? Is Lady Jane's health improved?"

Elizabeth huffed. I followed her with my eyes as she crossed her arms over her middle and walked toward a table set up with wine. I tried to ignore her hatred of me, even though her disgust at the attention Mary afforded me was more than evident. I turned my gaze back to the expectant queen.

"Indeed, Lady Jane's health is much improved, and she has accompanied me to court along with the Duchess of Somerset, her mother."

"Ah, Anne." The queen smiled, nearly toothless, and those teeth left quite black. She appeared to stare at some far-off memory. "We should like to see her. Summon her for us when we are through."

"Indeed, madame, I will."

The queen started to cough with great, wheezing draws of breath that shook her body. When the fit subsided, she waved me closer. "Lift us."

I did as she bade, plumping her pillows behind her so that she sat up in her bed. Was it possible I could approach her about Ned? For certes, if she was as ill as those at court alleged, she would want to see me happily wed? Oh, when would I see Ned again? We'd only just parted, but there was no telling when he would be about again. Not everyone came to live at court, and he had business and learning to attend to, his own estates to look after. How I wished I could be wherever he was.

"What's this?" Queen Mary asked, gazing at my face.

Elizabeth whirled from the table, her venomous gaze catching mine. Surely I imagined her lips turning in a snarl. She set her wine glass down with a loud clink and briskly walked back toward the bed.

My vision snapped back to the queen, and I cocked my head questioningly. "Majesty?"

"We have seen that look before." Her eyes crinkled at the corners as she squinted, and she pursed her lips in a frown. She held her hands up as if to examine the ravages of age on once-youthful skin. Her hands were gnarled at the knuckles, the skin wrinkled and riddled with brown spots. Veins ran the length of the tops of her hands, feeding into the thick fingers filled with rings.

Suddenly self-conscious, I glanced about the room for a looking glass. How did she view me? But instead of a looking glass, Elizabeth loomed in front of me again, examining my face, as if trying to probe my mind, her eyes filled with fire.

With a great, weary sigh, the queen rasped, "It is the look of a woman in love. I myself used to have such a look about me," she said, reverting from the formal use of *we*. "As if the whole world lay open at my feet. You have not gone against us, Cousin, have you? For I gave you no permission to marry. Who is the man?"

Fear snaked its way up my spine and gripped my heart. I clutched my hands in front of me and gazed at the floor, unable to look at the sickly penetrating gaze of the queen.

"Indeed, I have taken a fancy to a particular nobleman, Your Majesty, but I would never go against you nor do anything that would jeopardize my position and reputation within this realm or in your heart. I have been the most virtuous of women and most loyal subject."

"Humph . . . Who is he?" Elizabeth asked.

Mary nodded her head. "Yes, who?"

"Have you received no word from my mother?" I asked, pretending Elizabeth was not there, staring daggers. I truly did not want to answer the queen's inquiry on my own and suffer the wrath of my mother, Frances Brandon—and also what seemed to be the wrath of the future Queen Elizabeth. My fingers twisted in my grasp, my knuckles white.

Mary sucked in a ragged breath, nearly choking on her own spittle. "The last we heard, she was nearing death's door but managed to recover. What has she to do with this? We asked you a question. Are you refusing to answer?" Her voice became shrill and cracked, and she coughed once more.

I waited for the coughing to cease, offered her some water, which she sipped, droplets dribbling down her chin to fall against the lacy collar of her white linen nightgown.

"No, indeed, Majesty, I would never deny you."

"Leave," Elizabeth demanded. "You are making the queen ill."

"You will stay, and you will answer, Cousin," Mary snarled, and I had the distinct impression she thought I meant to steal something from her. Did her jealousy, her suspicions, run so deep? The sisters were more alike than they knew.

"Baron Beauchamp, Majesty."

Elizabeth groaned as if my Ned were a lowly gong scooper. But a smile crept over Mary's lips, and all of her anger dissipated. "Anne's boy."

I nodded.

"'Tis a good match. We've always been close to Lady Anne. Is he agreeable to it? We suppose it does not matter. If we arrange the marriage, he shall do as he is bidden. As will your mother."

My heart soared. *Oh, praise God, let her arrange it!* I did not say anything as the queen continued to mutter to herself, then she dismissed me. "Go tell Anne we wish to see her."

I curtsied and backed out of the room, fearing for what lay ahead. The queen was amenable and would most likely speak to Lady Anne on the subject, but she might also wonder why my mother had yet to approach her. Fear snaked up my spine. Mother was ever watchful of her own reputation. I could only pray she did not trample me in the process of maintaining her status.

A fast clip of heels sounded behind me, and I turned slightly to see who it was. Princess Elizabeth approached, her steps strong, her face angry. She reminded me of a charging boar.

"How dare you come into my sister's sick chamber and make her weaker with your pitiful talk of love? You know all she ever wanted was for her husband to love her, and he destroyed her." Elizabeth was so close I could smell the wine she'd sipped on her breath.

"I did nothing but what I was asked. I am a most obedient and dutiful subject."

Elizabeth scoffed. "If I were queen, I would not allow you to marry for love."

AUGUST 15, 1558

My heart felt as though a thousand swords had run me through.

While Her Majesty had agreed verbally I should marry Ned, she had also sent him abroad to Spain to deliver a message to her husband, Prince Philip, before a contract could be written. We had been parted once more, most likely until winter.

And now, Queen Mary had fallen into a delirious fever. The council ruled, and I didn't dare approach them regarding my marriage.

Must I always be the pawn in the games of those who ruled?

Mother continued to ignore me. What was more, if Mary did not live, Elizabeth would make good on her promise that I not be permitted to marry for love. Was it possible I could speak with Lady Anne or have Ned implore his mother? Most likely not. Queen Mary, in her hopes to keep a tight grasp on her reign as her health failed and with it her dreams of a Catholic realm, had begun in earnest punishing those who would go against her.

No one was safe.

OCTOBER 31, 1558

"The Duchess of Somerset, my lady," Mrs. Helen said as my future mother-by-marriage swept into the room.

I stood from the window seat, where I'd been trying desperately to read Plato without success. The book rested on the bench, one of my fingers absently placed to hold the page I'd last glanced at. Rather than reading, my distracted gaze had been riveted on the window glass, seeing only my reflection and the distant glimmer of a light on the grounds below. The sun had long since set. I'd consumed my evening meal in my chambers as, given the queen's ill health, there were no courtly meals to attend and the maidens' chambers had felt too full.

The duchess walked into the room, her back rigid, her stance filled with confidence and power. I endeavored to keep my head high in her presence and bent to curtsy.

"Lady Katherine."

"Could I offer you some wine, Your Grace?"

"No, indeed, this visit shall be brief." She turned and ushered the footman and other servants away, closing the door behind them. She came close to me and, in an uncommon gesture of compassion, grasped my hands in hers. A chill of foreboding swept through me. "My dear, it appears that Queen Mary"—she paused to cross herself—"is at death's door. 'Twill not be long now . . . Which means Princess Elizabeth will soon be queen."

A rush of relief went through me as, for a passing moment, I'd feared she would suggest I try like my sister Jane to usurp the throne. But a dull throb replaced that fear. Elizabeth had promised she would see to it I never married for love.

I nodded, still not quite comprehending her urgency, her alarm.

"I fear, once again, your marriage to my son will need to be delayed."

My heart plunged. She'd warned me of this before, but I'd lived and breathed in hope the day would never come. Though she did not want to put me on the throne in place of my cousin, she was still using me as a pawn. For what else could it mean that she'd take away her approval of our marriage when we said good-bye to one queen and blessed another?

"But can you not appeal to Princess Elizabeth for mercy?" I asked, letting my hands fall from her grasp. My world started crumbling. So many years had passed since first she'd uttered those words to Queen Mary regarding our precontract. 'Twas as if those teasing words sealed my fate—always to be betrothed but never wed.

How I had suffered with Ned abroad. I received a letter here and there confessing he still loved me, but without his tender glances or a sweet-smelling crown of gillyflowers left upon the threshold of my door, how was I to know?

Lady Anne shook her head, as if I had much to learn, and pursed her lips, making her thin face look all the more taut and gaunt. "Katherine, 'tis no way to begin in a new realm by anger-ing the monarch. You must understand your position. You were named heir by Edward VI. Your position within England is precar-ious, and more important than that of any other courtier. Where you make merry and what you do with each and every minute of every day is observed, reported. There are still some who would see you elevated above Elizabeth—those who think her the bastard child of a whore." She said the last part in a cold whisper, reinforc-ing my own suspicions as to where Lady Anne's loyalties lay.

"What are you saying?"

"Beau is descended of kings. You are descended of kings. For those who may wish to rise against Princess Elizabeth, a mar-riage between you two would appear strong—and treasonous to Elizabeth. I was shocked to hear that Queen Mary agreed. Hold off. Warm to Elizabeth. You are still young yet. Your time will come, but I implore you, for your safety and that of my son, do not do anything rash such as try to marry before Elizabeth has approved of the match."

With those words, and several looks over her shoulders, Lady Anne removed herself from my chambers, taking any warmth it had with her.

NOVEMBER 17, 1558

"The queen is dead! Long live the queen!"

The words rang out through London and the realm. Trumpets blared, cannons boomed, and people shouted. Their beloved Princess Elizabeth would save them from the reign that had been aptly dubbed Bloody Mary's Rule.

Several Privy Council members rode out as if the bats of hell were on their heels, smiles splitting wide their faces, carrying the precious prized ruby ring that had had to be worked with great effort from Mary's bloated finger. They rode for Hatfield—Elizabeth's home—where they would kneel before her and claim to be her loyal subjects.

But while those surrounding me rejoiced in her rule, I could not shout out with joy. Elizabeth had yet to warm to me. In fact, in the last weeks of Mary's realm, when she'd visited her dying sister, she'd sent me hateful glares. Did Elizabeth suspect me of wanting to usurp her?

How could I prove to her I never, *ever* wished to take her place? All I wanted was to marry Ned. And Ned! He was to return to court—summoned when Mary's state of delirium several days prior had become an affirmative that she would pass. I would see him again. I had missed Ned so and prayed he had not forgotten our love.

Dear God in heaven, let Queen Elizabeth allow us to marry.

The next morning, a short note arrived from Ned.

My Dearest Lady,

My mind does spend many moments thinking of your face and replaying your laugh. Would that I could see you soon. Mother has advised me to tread carefully for now. In time, though, we will be together, that I promise.

Long live the queen!

Long live love . . .

Yours forever,

Ned

Chapter Thirteen

And living there with lingering hope,
in foreign country strange:
Where absence might throw present toils,
in some men work a change.
He stood as firm as marble stone,
and kept both truth and touch . . .
—*Thomas Churchyard, Elizabethan Soldier and Poet*

FEBRUARY 3, 1559

Queen Elizabeth breezed by me in her presence chamber, with her ladies in tow, but stopped short to return to where I remained, the scent of roses wafting from her glorious red tresses. I quickly dipped into a curtsy, wondering what punishment she would bestow on me for my tardiness.

"Majesty," I murmured.

"You are late, Cousin. I expected you in my room over an hour ago."

Still looking at the floor, as Elizabeth often seemed in a temper with me, I answered, "My apologies, Majesty. My hound Arabel was ill."

Elizabeth barked out a guttural sound. "You and your silly animals."

Her insult was hypocritical, considering she was also quite fond of her own pets, but one did not argue with the queen.

"I most humbly seek your forgiveness," I murmured, my mind still on poor Arabel. Oh, how she'd retched this morning! I'd been half-convinced someone had tried to poison her.

Elizabeth clucked her tongue, her eyes taking on a mean-spirited gleam. "You are no longer welcome in the Privy Chamber, Lady Katherine. See to it you report only to the presence chamber, or I shall have you removed from court."

I opened my mouth to respond, but Elizabeth straightened and began her procession again in her magnificent white robes, through the castle to the morning service in her chapel. Margaret Clifford, the Countess of Derby, with her chestnut hair pulled back severely beneath a black velvet bejeweled hat, met my gaze as she passed in line with Elizabeth's other ladies-in-waiting. She paused briefly beside me and whispered, "My lady, be wary. The queen has been uttering much against you. 'Twould be best for you to heed her warning and duck into the shadows when she is near."

Lady Derby walked away as if she'd never stopped. Where once I had been allowed to exist beside the body of England's monarch, now I was banished to the outskirts of court, gazing over heads and shoulders of others whom she placed before me. Her ladies whispered and tittered behind her, glancing at me with fingers over their sordid mouths. They would not have treated me thus if not for Elizabeth openly shunning me and making clear my place was *not* anywhere close to the throne. Would she banish me to the kitchens next?

"Do not stare after her so, my lady. Those who have their eye on you might make it their goal to show the queen just how much you resent being lowered in status," Ned said, coming to stand beside me.

Elizabeth had made good on her promise to keep us from marrying. As the court waited for the queen and her ladies to make their procession, I tilted my head slightly toward Ned and spoke to his dark leather boots, which contrasted with the polished stone floors. "Her suspicions of me have not waned, despite my kneeling before her and confessing my heart's desire to serve her and be most loyal to her," I whispered. "Why does she hate me so? I have never done anything but show her that I am loyal and true, and yet she treats me as a leper."

"In time, she will see she can trust you," he murmured, his fingers grazing mine.

"I suppose it is some consolation that she hasn't stripped me of my eighty pounds a year." I did try to find the good in my current circumstances.

"Indeed, my lady, that is a good thing."

"Mayhap it is only because she hasn't seen her treasury accounts yet."

Ned chuckled. "Perhaps that is also true."

It was so frustrating to be true and obedient to Elizabeth and yet have her shun me and wait for me to prove folly. As it was our turn to follow the row of courtiers, Ned took my elbow and escorted me to the chapel. Blanche Parry and Kat Astley, servants of Elizabeth's for years, pointed at me, calling the attention of Lady Fiennes de Clinton and Lady St. Loe. I was to be made a spectacle of. Oh, how crushing. If only I could flee to the country, but I could not, as Elizabeth bade me stay.

Elizabeth glowered, but I pretended not to notice. She could lower me within the court, seek to embarrass me, but I would not allow her to take Ned from me. Not when he was the only thing I had to look forward to.

"You must figure out a way to get closer to Her Majesty, love. The postponement of our marriage is destroying me. I want to take you in my arms and comfort you, to hold you at night after the sun's decline, and wake with you upon its return."

His words washed over me with warmth, and he pressed his leg to mine as he sat beside me. I desired more than anything at that moment to reach out and place my hand on his firm thigh. The thought crossed my mind just as his own hand brushed mine, while he feigned straightening his hose. A tingle of anticipation meandered dreamily through my body, and a burst of heat flooded my face. How could I think such sinful thoughts in the house of God? For shame . . . Perhaps marriage would ease our desire, sharpened as it now was by being forbidden.

From the pulpit, Bishop John Best began his sermon in English, as, once queen, Elizabeth had quickly changed her services back to the Protestant faith. She, so far, was proving to be a merciful monarch, and I had heard her say on more than one occasion that she hoped to gain the favor and love of her people by showing tolerance to those who wished to worship differently than herself, that there was but one God, and that we Catholics and Protestants loved him equally.

Forcing myself to no longer think of Ned and his sensual touches, I focused on what the priest said.

"I have called upon Thee, O God, for Thou shalt hear me. Incline Thine ear to me and hearken unto my words. Show Thy marvelous loving-kindness, Thou that art the savior of them which put their trust in Thee, from such as resist Thy right hand. Keep me as the apple of an eye, hide me under the shadow of Thy wings, from the ungodly that trouble me."

I realized then how I would be able to show Her Majesty that I was true to her, that she could trust me, and that I would never seek to take her place. And while it was immoral to do something for others in the hopes of gaining something in return, I would commit this one act of selfishness and do penance for it later.

The following day, Elizabeth sat in her bath, her eyes closed as she leaned her head back. Rose petals floated in the water as she languished, sighing at the feel of the steamy water against her flesh.

I had given away a pearl-and-emerald brooch to the maid who was to dry the queen after her bath in order to speak with her, and I would not be deterred in my task.

Sensing my presence—or, rather, someone's presence— Elizabeth's eyes popped open. When recognition hit, she frowned, and her eyes searched my person as if expecting me to be wielding a knife and not linen bath sheets.

I set the linens down and knelt beside the tub, laying my hands on the warm metal side.

"Majesty, I implore you, please open your mind and heart to my words, and know that I am ever your most loyal subject and true of heart and would never seek to go against Your Majesty or to succumb to other baser deeds that may be rumored, nor would I seek to destroy your trust. I have watched those before me"—and I dared not name my family—"and seen them perish for foolish deeds, and I have not the heart for it, nor the interest, as I bow to you and your royal rule and claim to this throne."

I was babbling, my heart beating so loud in my ears I could no longer hear the sloshing of the water as she moved. My mouth was dry, and I repeatedly licked at my lips. I hoped my words made sense to her.

Elizabeth pursed her lips, sitting up straighter so her small, pale breasts were no longer submerged beneath the water. "And you thought it best, Cousin Kat, to seek me out in my nakedness?"

I blanched but saw the flash of humor in her eyes, and a small spark of hope started to burn within me. "I did not know how best to speak with you. There are always so many around, and I feared you would not see me."

"I am reminded of myself seeking the ear of my own sister, God rest her soul. Hand me a towel."

Elizabeth stood, her body straight and thin, boyish in its slimness. Water sluiced down her pale flesh, and I moved quickly to hand her a linen sheet lest she catch cold.

"Shall I call a maid?"

"Do you think me incapable of drying myself? You forget, Kat, I was not always a queen, and even when I was a mere princess, I was not catered to every single moment."

I nodded, thoroughly chastised, and stunned into silence. Did she mean to say that I myself had been spoiled?

She dried herself quickly and wrapped the linen around her waiflike figure, stalking to the fire, where she held out her hands. "Besides, if you were to fetch one of my other ladies, would that not defeat the purpose of paying one off to leave you alone with me? Who was it? I shall see her punished. You might have come here with nefarious intent."

Despite the teasing tone in her voice, I still suspected that beneath the surface, Elizabeth believed I was capable of trickery.

"Majesty, I would never," I breathed. "And I reassured the maid I would never betray her trust in me."

"I should hope you are not an assassin. Now dress me. Perhaps I should adopt you as my daughter and marry you off right away."

Did she jest? My mother did yet live, though she was quite ill again and unable to attend court. Had Elizabeth heard that my mother was not replying to my near-weekly correspondence? I shoved aside the icy prickle in my stomach at her words of marriage, for I knew she did not want me to marry Ned . . . No, she would seek some far-off groom to get me out of her sight, and out of England's mind. I prayed the people of England did not wish to see another Grey daughter of the blood be innocently persecuted for someone else's gain.

I pulled on her chemise, tightened her stays, tied on her petticoats, and then began pinning her sleeves, stomacher, and ruff to her gown, all in silence, as I was too afraid of what I would say and what she would take away from me.

"You are a good lady-in-waiting, Kat. You've a spirit that reminds me of . . . myself. Too much sometimes. Perhaps we moved too soon by casting you out of the privy and into the presence. We shall move you back immediately so that I can keep a closer eye on you. Do not think this puts you in favor over anyone else." Her eyes narrowed as she studied me, and I could feel her dislike as keenly as before. "You tie stays like a expert."

I should have been excited at the elevation, but I was not. Elizabeth was not giving me a better position at court because she liked me. In fact, it was for the opposite reason. A cold snake of fear slithered up my spine and wrapped its way so tightly around my throat I thought I might choke from it. Elizabeth terrified me.

Indeed, Elizabeth did move me to a higher position within her court . . . but there were no talks yet of marriage. I supposed I shouldn't be surprised, even if I was disappointed. In fact, all her ladies-in-waiting were counseled to remain chaste. As she had stylized herself virginal, so should we.

That evening, my footsteps echoed in the stone-walled corridor, tapestries billowing at the corners from a draft of an open window. I quickened my steps, quite alone on my way back to my chamber after Her Majesty had been put to bed. The silence was deafening. The hairs on the back of my neck prickled. Torchlights flickered, and a shiver raced along my skin.

Someone followed me.

I took a deep breath, wishing my dogs were with me, but Elizabeth's dogs took precedence, and when together, our animals caused quite a disturbance. Since I was still trying to put myself in the queen's favor, I had capitulated and sent them back to my room. Suddenly, I stopped and whirled. Beyond the reach of the torchlight, the corridor was dark and bathed in dancing shadows.

"Who is there?"

The dark shadows seemed to grow thicker, forming an entity. My breath stilled. An apparition? Of whom? Jane? A man stepped forth and pulled the black hood from his head, revealing his long, slim, calculating face.

Cecil.

"Master Cecil," I breathed out, somewhat in relief, but then my heart sped up again. I kept my hands at my sides, did not clench them as I wanted to, but endeavored to appear calm. Why was he trailing me in the dark? Why was I frightened? After all, he was more than just the queen's secretary, he was her henchman, too.

"My lady," he said in his raspy, soft voice. "Will you allow me the pleasure of escorting you back to your room?"

I wanted to shout no, but how could I deny him? News of my resistance would find its way to Elizabeth, and then she would have cause once again to be suspicious of me. "If it pleases."

He walked up to my side, his long, snakelike fingers coming from within the depths of his endless black cloak to curl around my elbow. "How do you find Her Majesty?"

What sort of question was that? How was I to answer? He propelled me forward at a clipped pace, as though he, too, ran from the shadows.

"Pardon, sir?"

"Do you believe she will be good for England?"

Why, when he asked me these questions, did I feel he meant something else? What did he aspire to discover? I may have been powerless to refuse his escort, but I would not play this game of politics. "Completely. The realm has craved her ascension for some time, and I think she will be the healing balm it needs."

No reaction came from Master Cecil to give me a clue as to how he took my comment.

"What of her refusing to marry?"

I waved away his question. "She is young. She will do her duty when she sees fit. I suppose she wishes to make her own way first. 'Tis the way of our fairer sex when placed in a position that men are wont to seize."

"Ah, but you see, she is not just a woman. She is the queen, and a queen cannot play the same games as a mere lady. No offense to you, Lady Katherine, but this entire realm rests on Her Majesty's marriage."

Again, I had no answer for him. I was not good with politics. It had never interested me. Staying in the queen's good graces was hard enough.

We turned a corner in the corridor, and my chamber door was in sight, thank the Lord.

"Speaking of marriage . . ." He trailed off as we reached my door, and I turned to face him. "I would hold off on any plans you may have until Her Majesty is wedded and bedded, and even best until there is an heir to the throne, or two, in the cradle."

Another obstacle, and years away. I straightened my shoulders and looked him directly in his beady eyes. "Why, sir?"

"You are an intelligent young woman, Lady Katherine. I need not explain it to you. Suffice it to say, Her Majesty's claim to the throne is precarious at best right now. She is still deemed illegitimate by many. She is not married. She has no heirs. You are next in line to the throne. You are legitimate. If you should marry and have children, your claim would be far stronger than hers."

"But I would never, *never* take the throne away from her!" I tried not to shout as I glanced around to see who could have heard his treasonous words. I was so tired of everyone believing I would try to usurp Elizabeth. They could try, as they had with my sister, but I would flatly refuse. I would run.

"And yet, my lady, your sister did not intend to do so either. One can never be safe from the plots of conniving men. As you said, men are wont to seize the power for themselves."

I gritted my teeth but said nothing further. I wanted to rail about injustice. I wanted to shout that I was nothing like those traitors, that I had seen Jane suffer and would not let myself be used as they had used her. I wanted to raise my fist in the air and declare my betrothal to Ned and then rush to find a priest who would marry us straightaway. But I did none of these things, and my head pounded and ached something fierce. My eyes grew blurry with the pain of a megrim setting in. I blinked hard, and when I opened my eyes again, Cecil had melted back into the shadows, his warning given and not welcome.

I opened my door, feeling dizzy and faint. Mrs. Helen rushed to my side, undressed me, and tucked me between my cold sheets. I was now resigned to the fact that marriage to the man I fiercely loved might never be. I'd been born a damned princess of the blood. My life was not my own. How foolish of me to have ever thought I might have a say in my own existence.

MARCH 15, 1559

Our fortunes are changed! Or so it seems . . .

My mother finally sent me a short note that simply read, "You are forgiven." Although she did not promise to seek out Elizabeth on my behalf, I had high hopes that she was willing to do so as soon as she was well.

Ned was named Earl of Hertford by Elizabeth after her coronation. I felt elation for Ned that she would choose to give him back one of his father's titles, something for which he'd longed for longer than he'd wanted me for a wife. The queen had grown fond of him and even more so of me. We had yet to appeal to her regarding our marriage. I was too afraid she'd deny us and send me away forever.

There had been no more visits from Cecil, but judging from what Elizabeth said behind closed doors, he and the council were pressuring her to find a husband. She said she would placate them for a time but would never marry.

What did that mean for me?

Must I, too, remain forever unwed to serve the Virgin Queen?

Or was her virginity something she hid behind? I'd seen Robert Dudley—the brother of my sister's late husband, Guildford—sneak into Her Majesty's chambers. I'd seen the way they danced and looked at one another. 'Twas reminiscent of Ned and me. I was jealous. Why could she do such things and I could not?

Well, this summer we would depart on progress. And Ned had promised he would accompany the queen's court—although I got the sense he was pulling away. He did not always sit beside me and appeared less and less at court. At times, he did not respond to my letters. But I had not seen him with any other female courtiers either. Perhaps he was simply concentrating on his new estates? Or maybe he'd decided our love was a lost cause.

Was it possible Master Cecil had paid a visit to my darling Ned as well? Could his own mother, the Duchess of Somerset, have had anything to do with it? She'd warned me all those years ago that, without the blessing of Elizabeth, she would not support our marriage.

I sighed deeply, feeling listless and completely powerless. Arabel and Beau bounced around my feet, and since the queen was shut away in her room with stomach pains, I had the afternoon to myself. The sun shone bright, and although 'twas not yet spring, the dogs and I both needed some exercise.

I longed for Jane Seymour's company as well. Someone to confide my troubles in and make my days brighter. But she had come down with another ague and had gone home to Hanworth with the duchess for a spell.

"Mrs. Helen, my thick cloak please. We shall take a brisk walk."

I ignored Mrs. Helen's protests, my mind focused on what had to be done until this summer when the three-month progress across the realm would commence. I would continue to gain the queen's favor and look past Ned's distant behavior. He was merely strained with his new responsibilities—that had to be it. A man's love could not wane so easily.

My stomach turned, and I put out my hand for Stew to climb atop my shoulder for a kiss, then handed him back to Mrs. Helen.

Was it possible Ned's love *could* fade?

We'd waited so long . . .

I shook my head and blinked away tears. A walk in the park would do much to refresh my mind. When I returned, I would write Ned a letter, subtly asking for confirmation of his continued love.

Upon entering the garden, my slippers crunching over the cold gravel, I spotted a length of vibrant red hair as the owner twirled. I sneaked a bit closer, Arabel and Beau running off to the grasses to conclude their business.

The queen! And Dudley . . .

They were dancing to a tune in their own heads, their eyes locked on one another, lips curved in wistful smiles. Their bodies swayed like those who were used to touching in such a way, as if they had danced together for years and years. 'Twas unnerving. My lips pressed together in a frown of disappointment. Why should we maids be forced into chastity when our own sovereign danced like a dervish with a married man upon the castle lawn?

Visions of Ned and I dancing at court while Mary reigned came to mind . . . The remembrance of him feeding me apples under a tree, stealing a kiss from beneath Mrs. Helen's nose . . .

'Twas not fair. I was filled with jealousy, outrage, and hunger. I yearned to be a woman and yet was forced to be a maiden. And there was no outlet for my anger. I could not stomp my foot, but must always act in the way Elizabeth bade me. Furthermore, even if I did want to toss her edicts to the wind, the man I longed for was not present, and I could not request for him to come to me, as it would not have been decent.

Come the summer . . . 'Twas time we, too, resumed our courtship, and Elizabeth could go to the devil.

Praise Jesus, forgive me for my harsh thoughts on my cousin.

But the time for courtship was not to come, even when summer arrived . . . The queen kept Ned well away from court on errand after errand. And when he was not working for her abroad, he was kept at his estates with some manner of business or another. We wrote letters, but scrawled words of love were nothing compared with gazing into his eyes.

Chapter Fourteen

To her who found few friends at home,
and hearts disease was much.
Yea though this Knight with offers great,
and treasure tempted was:
(As they full well can witness bear,
who saw those matters pass)
—Thomas Churchyard, Elizabethan Soldier and Poet

THE FOLLOWING YEAR . . .
FEBRUARY 14, 1560

"Do you know what today is?" Queen Elizabeth asked me. Her eyes twinkled, and her lips were set in a self-satisfied smile. She sat upon her carved and polished throne, a purple velvet pillow beneath her behind and another beneath her feet—which were shoeless to show off her new ivory silk stockings, embroidered with Tudor red-and-white roses. Her black velvet gown, embroidered with golden roses and crusted with rubies, was spread out elegantly around her, and as usual, she was beautiful in an ethereal way, her hair crowned atop her head in glorious red curls.

"No, Majesty," I said, watching as she plucked a comfit from her little silver box and popped it into her mouth.

Several of her ladies sat by the window, working on sewing for their own pleasure, a few others played cards, and I, Jane Seymour—who'd recovered enough to return to court—Margaret Clifford, and Bess St. Loe sat at Her Majesty's feet upon embroidered velvet pillows. Winter was full upon us, and the days were short, with the sun setting just before supper. With the temperature outside often unbearable, we ladies of the court spent our days inside beside the roaring fires, talking, working at some craft or other, reading, dancing.

Despite those entertainments, the days were not sweet. Elizabeth was always at my throat for one thing or another. Just three days ago, she'd tossed me from her chamber, claiming I'd tried to portray myself as a prettier version of her with the way I'd styled my hair.

I blistered inside, wondering what she would say to me now.

"'Tis Saint Valentine's Day. Do you know the tale of Saint Valentine?" She held out the box of sweets, offering one to me, Jane, Margaret, and Bess.

"No, Majesty." I plucked a sweet and savored its succulent, fruity taste upon my tongue.

"Well, then, I shall tell you. One legend states that in the third century, Roman Emperor Claudius II banned young men from marrying so he could use them as soldiers to fight his wars. A local priest named Valentine rebelled by secretly marrying young couples in love. When his treachery was discovered, Emperor Claudius had him executed."

My hand came to my chest, and I gasped with the other ladies. Jane and I murmured of the horror. Elizabeth smiled smugly, thoroughly proud of herself for having shocked us. I couldn't help but wonder why she would tell us this tale—beside it being Saint Valentine's Day today. Did she see herself as Claudius? For surely she'd banned plenty of us from marrying.

"Yet another legend tells that a man called Valentine, while in prison, sent the first Valentine's card to a woman who was his beloved and signed it 'From Your Valentine.' But I shall tell you the most romantic story I have heard, and that is of Charles, Duke of Orleans, a Frenchman. And while I do detest the French"—she glowered about the room—"my mother did so love their tales. The duke wrote the poem for his wife while imprisoned in the Tower of London after the Battle of Agincourt in 1415. He wrote poetic words, something such as, *Je suis déjà d'amour tanné, ma très douce Valentinée...*'"

"So romantic," Bess said, her eyes misty.

"What does it mean?" Lady Margaret piped up from her perch beside a window.

"It means, 'I am already sick with love, my very gentle Valentine,'" Elizabeth answered.

"'Tis a beautiful tale," I said.

She narrowed her eyes and studied me, as if she hoped to absorb my mind within her own. "Do you know why I should bring that up to you today?"

"Because you have a Valentine?" As if I needed even ask the question. Everyone was well aware whom Lord Robert Dudley was doting on this day. The sweets she'd offered up had been brought to her by him that morning—along with her stockings, a gift that was quite shocking and indecent. His courting her was quite sad, actually, considering his own wife languished at home while he flirted outrageously with our monarch as if he were not already married.

She tilted her head back and laughed, shaking her head like I was an imbecile. "A queen always has a Valentine, Kat." She gestured to her ladies, who tittered nervously, not wanting to offend either of us. "But today I offer *you* a man to love."

I froze. My eyes widened, and I swallowed hard. All those years ago, she'd sworn I'd never have a man to love, and now she offered me one? "Me?"

Her lips curved again in that secret smile, although now I detected something a little more sinister that made me all the more nervous. In spite of my efforts all this time, Elizabeth still harbored no goodwill toward me. Fear paralyzed me. My head started to pound, and I swore I could hear the rushing of blood in my ears. The megrims that affected me always started off this way and could be quite horrendous.

"Indeed. The Earl of Arran has approached me, asking for your hand. I'm considering it."

My breathing ceased, ice skating across the expanse of my chest. My mouth went dry. She could not do this! She meant to ruin me! She wanted me to be unhappy! She offered me to a man I did not love when, for a fleeting moment, I had believed she might have meant Ned. Beside me, I felt Jane stiffen and suck in a breath.

"No," I whispered desperately, shaking my head slightly, hands gripping the folds of my black-and-russet brocade skirts.

Elizabeth's face went dark with anger, eyes narrowing, teeth clenched. She leaned forward as she hissed so that only I could hear. "I must be mistaken, for it sounded as though my most loyal and obedient cousin has denied me."

I said nothing, for I could not deny her again, but neither could I concede. Mortification heated my cheeks, and luckily, Margaret and Jane turned toward each other and pretended to be engrossed with Bess's new ring of sapphire and gold.

"He is a good match for the likes of you, Kat." Elizabeth glared down at me as she so often had when first she'd been proclaimed queen.

I pressed my lips together and swallowed hard, nausea assaulting me. For certes, she would think the vile man was perfect. He was Scots. A belligerent fool who enjoyed drinking wine by the barrel. He was volatile, prone to fights, and indeed so unmannerly as to belch loudly in my face upon our first meeting. Never could I marry a man so revolting.

Bile rose in my throat, and I worked hard to swallow it.

"Should you not thank your sovereign for arranging a match? You are nearing twenty, are you not? You shall be an old maid soon . . . You shall like Scotland, I think. You can spend much time with our other *dear* cousin, Mary, in the land of heathens."

Mary, Queen of Scots . . . Elizabeth's other rival. The new figurehead of Tudor Catholicism. Although she was not a Tudor directly from the line of Henry VIII, she had been born to Henry's sister Margaret's son, King James of Scotland. All those in England who hated the thought of a Protestant queen looked to Scotland and their new savior, Queen Mary Stuart. It was only a matter of time before rebellion stirred anew.

This was what Elizabeth intended to do? Banish me from sight to spend eternity in dreaded Scotland with Catholics? To be assumed a part of their faction should a rebellion begin? And then I, too, would be put on the chopping block. I understood now she had not meant to bring me closer to her, inviting me into a position with her Privy Chamber as a trusted subject, but only to torment me while she put together this well-laid plan.

She would see me dead, and it had taken her only a short time to figure out how without getting her own hands dirty.

I did not even know how to respond, for to say anything in my own defense was likely to send her into a tantrum of paramount proportion. And yet, I could not agree with her when I so abhorred the idea! Would I never have control over my own fate? The question needed no answer, for I'd never had, and I never would.

From across the room, Jane Dormer, Countess of Feria—and wife of the Spanish ambassador—saved me, although I doubted she had any idea what the queen had relayed to me.

"Lady Katherine, are you quite well? Is it a megrim again? You look positively wan." She put down her embroidery hoop and stepped toward me. "Apologies, Majesty, for interrupting, but I know Lady Katherine was unwell yesterday, and it would appear she is becoming so again. We should not want Your Majesty to become afflicted as well."

I knew then that Jane Dormer had indeed heard our conversation and then most likely watched the color drain from my face, as I had, in fact, been quite *well* the day before.

Elizabeth narrowed her eyes as she, too, tried to assess the situation. "Get thee to your chambers then, Cousin. You shall need to improve as your suitor will be at court in a fortnight."

Jane Seymour helped me to stand on shaky legs, whispering almost inaudibly in my ear, "Do not fret, love. 'Tis only another trick."

"You will remain here, Lady Jane," the queen commanded.

My dearest friend gave me an apologetic look and sat back down on her pillow.

I allowed Jane Dormer's steadiness to carry me to my chambers, trying not to trip on my vast skirts. My megrims were coming closer together. As a result, I was not eating as much and my gowns had grown loose. Mrs. Helen clucked around me as the countess took me to my bed. Between the two of them, they managed to remove my hood and pins, slippers, and clothing down to my chemise and lay me on the bed.

"I am going to go and get her a posset. Will you stay a moment?" I heard Mrs. Helen ask Lady Jane.

"I should be glad to," she murmured.

When Mrs. Helen left, Lady Jane stroked my forehead and said, "I know a way that you can escape this place, escape from the queen's machinations."

My eyes blinked open, and through the blur of pain that seared its way across my forehead, I saw her eager expression.

"How?" I whispered.

"Spain."

"Spain?" I mumbled. Queen Mary had found allies with the Spanish, and I had so loved Mary . . .

"We shall not discuss it here." The countess looked about the room as if expecting someone to jump from behind a tapestry. "I will invite you to dine with us at Durham House next week. My covered barge will carry you down the Thames. 'Twill give you some privacy."

I nodded, not entirely sure what I was agreeing to. Was it somehow possible for Ned and I to marry in Spain? The countess was well aware of my intentions to marry Ned, as I had shared them with her on one desperate night when my heart ached so fiercely in his absence. Elizabeth had yet to offer Ned a place at her court, and in fact, Lady Anne Seymour, his mother, was not here either. I had a feeling she kept them away for two reasons. One, because Lady Anne had been party to Elizabeth's own mother's demise . . . and two, because she knew how I loved Ned.

Mrs. Helen bustled in with a steaming cup.

"Rest, dear Kat," Lady Jane said. "I shall send for you soon."

FEBRUARY 15, 1560

At first light, I called for ink and paper and wrote out a scratchy note to Ned. My writing was long and scrawled, not much unlike when Mr. Aylmer, my tutor, had first urged me to begin my writing lessons. I had not the patience for it that my sister Jane did. Now that I was writing a letter to Ned, I was a little embarrassed at the fact. Taking my time—and balling up seven pieces of paper before I was satisfied my writing was legible—I wrote to him. With a shiny groat, I paid a footman to deliver it to Ned's new house in London on Canon Row.

> *My Good Ned,*
> *Court is vacant without your energetic presence. I find I am without a dance partner who will gift my feet with nary a trod—and so I am left quite sore. Nor a good card player who will let me lose. I pray for your swift return. I long to take pleasure in your company once more.*
> *I must also relay to you, because my heart doth trust yours immeasurably, there are plots afoot, and I fear I am not clever enough to ferret them out. I have been approached by a few courtiers and wish for your guidance and council.*
> *With true heart,*
> *Katherine Grey*

The footman delivered, within an hour, Ned's reply.

> *Dearest Katherine,*
> *My advice would be to seek your cousin and sovereign in these matters. She would know best how to deal with anyone who would endeavor to harm you.*
> *Unfortunately, the business with my estates has kept me from court, but I do have good news! I hope to return no later than the summer progress, as Her Majesty has requested I accompany the court. I am in London at present, but soon will retire to Wiltshire where I have been gifted with a manor much in need of repair.*
> *With most esteem,*
> *Lord Hertford*

My heart crumpled upon reading Ned's distant reply. My worst fears were being realized. Ned had forgotten our love. Or else he was trying to purposefully put distance between us. How could I go to this clandestine meeting with the Spanish ambassador without assistance? I should have liked to seek out my mother—though we did not get along, she was shrewd. But she was too ill, and my step-grandmother, Katherine Brandon, was somewhere north with her husband. I could have turned to Lady Anne, Duchess of Somerset, but I should not have liked to disturb her.

And why should Ned have been so cold? To not have seen me for half a year and shed nary a tear? He did not even seem to mind our separation when once he'd begged for us to marry within an hour. Had his love dwindled so? Did he wish to break off our betrothal, however unofficial it may have been?

I put pen to paper again, this time not taking so much care in the forming of my letters. Another groat, and the footman was out to deliver my letter.

My sweet lord,

Why should I find your letters so cold and indifferent? When once we talked of marriage and shared sweet kisses? Now I find you distant.

'Tis impossible for me to speak with my cousin. She has shown no goodwill or faith toward me and cannot abide the sight of me.

I beg of you, as my betrothed, return to me soon, for fear I shall come undone.

With heart's fondness,

Kat

Not even an hour had passed when the man returned with Ned's reply, sweating from riding hard and shifting his gaze with discomfort.

Dearest Kat,

I most humbly beseech your forgiveness should you have found my last letter to offer you coldness when what you need most is warmth. I remember fondly the taste of your lips and the softness of your hands in mine.

I will endeavor to hurry through my business. And I do testify, I have been forced to leave off from our courtship by Master Cecil and my most respected mother. I should not want to, but I beg of you, Kat, for our sake, for love's sake, take much care. We are being watched.

With humble, loyal heart,

Ned

With a glad heart, I put Ned's letter into the crackling fire in the hearth. He had not forsaken me but was instead trying to protect me. While I may have been on my own with this latest embroilment, I had to trust in God that He would see me through.

I glanced around my chamber, making certain I was indeed alone. The room was empty despite the all-seeing eyes that graced the faces of nobles passed. I unlocked the chest at the foot of my bed using a key I kept on a chain within my gown. I shifted aside some fabrics and ribbons until I came upon the small latch that released the secret compartment and pulled out Jane's Greek Testament. I sat back on my heels and read her last letter to me. Every time I read it, I grew stronger and, in reading, seemed to know just what to do. I could almost hear her fervent voice, desperate for me to listen, to understand.

Be like the good servant and even in midnight be waking, lest when death cometh, he steal upon you like a thief in the night and you be like the evil servant, found sleeping, or for lack of oil, ye be found like the first foolish wench and like him that had not the wedding garment, ye be out from the marriage.

"I miss you, Jane. I miss you terribly."

FEBRUARY 20, 1560

A slight knock sounded at the door, startling me. My nightingale, Cora, who'd been resting on my finger, took flight, her pretty song no longer cheerful. Her frightened trill sent Stew to jumping about the room, and Arabel and Beau began barking at the door, when normally they waited patiently to see who entered.

I'd let Mrs. Helen have half the day off, although she'd insisted on taking only a few hours. One of my other attendants went to the door and opened it to reveal the Countess of Feria dressed in a dark wool cloak with ermine trimmings. She entered the room quietly and met my gaze.

"Gather your cloak, my lady. The barge is waiting."

I'd had no warning that this morning I would meet with the ambassador and so frowned in her direction. "I am not prepared to leave. My lady's maid is not even present."

The countess turned toward the girl who'd opened the door. "Your name?"

The girl glanced at the plush tapestried carpet. "Alice Morris, my lady."

"Alice shall accompany you, Lady Katherine. Come now, the barge awaits, and Her Majesty is resting. You will not be missed if we hurry."

"Fetch my cloak, Alice." My voice was a bit crisp, and I felt sorry for that, but I was irritated the countess would presume to tell me what to do. I was well above her station, and while she had sought at first to protect me from the queen—or at least that was how I was supposed to perceive it—I was also well aware that whatever plot was brewing would benefit her and her husband as well. That meant it could also endanger me in the process.

I turned to the two yeomen at my door. "When Mrs. Helen returns, inform her I've gone to visit a friend and shall return shortly."

The men nodded, keeping their gazes straight ahead.

With my cloak of soft burgundy and spotted white wool, brown ermine fur wrapped around my shoulders, and a fur-lined hood over my head, we stepped from the room. The corridors were mostly empty at this time of day. Courtiers were busy with their plots and secrets while Her Majesty was at rest in her bed. Servants worked to complete their duties. And we three walked stealthily through the corridors into the garden, the palace orchard, and then to the quay, where a barge—without a coat of arms—waited.

"'Tis not marked, so anyone looking from a window will not see the House of Feria drifting over the Thames from Westminster," the countess said as one of her oarsmen guided her aboard.

I followed suit, and we sat comfortably beneath a canopy upon heated pillows, fur blankets on our laps and heated rocks at our feet.

The barge slipped through the freezing water until reaching Durham House, where the ambassador of Spain and his wife, the countess, resided when in London. We exited the barge and were ushered swiftly into the house by several liveried servants. A blast of warm air and the scents of baking bread washed over us upon entering.

"You go to the kitchens. I shall attend Lady Katherine from here," Lady Jane said to my maid, who scurried away without even looking to me for direction.

"The ambassador awaits us in the dining hall."

Footmen seeped from the walls to take our cloaks, and then, arm in arm, we walked through several corridors until we reached a well-lit room with a high, arched, painted ceiling and ornate furniture—fit for a king. I do not know why I was surprised that Durham House should have been so opulently furnished, but I was. It had not occurred to me that those without royal blood could have such wealth.

"Lady Katherine," Ambassador de Feria said with a swift, low bow in my direction.

"Your Excellency," I said in return with a slight curtsy, not as deep as one I would give my own cousin Queen Elizabeth.

Feria's mouth quirked with a knowing smile.

"My lady wife," he said to Jane Dormer, with a bow, and she returned his gesture with a murmur.

"I am glad you have decided to meet with me, Lady Katherine. The countess tells me you may be in need of our assistance."

"Perhaps. I am willing to listen." I did not want to give too much away. I did not want them to perceive that I might understand everything they said. Most at court referred to me as a pretty featherbrain, and while it might have seemed odd to protect that reputation, it was important to me that I did. Most people were willing to say too much or overstep their bounds because of it, which always set me in a higher position, giving me ammunition to wield should I ever need it.

Again, he smiled, but the smile did not quite reach his eyes. "Would you care for a refreshment?" he asked, his accent thick. "We have wine imported from Spain, and 'tis not as watered down as you may find at court."

I nodded. "I should be glad to taste your wine."

His wife indicated for me to sit in one of the plush, carved-oak armchairs near the brilliant hearth, which exuded much heat.

"Is this your work? 'Tis impressive," I asked of the burgundy seat cushions embroidered with gold Spanish pomegranates.

"Actually, Queen Mary made those for me for Christmas several years back. They are beautiful, are they not?"

"Quite. She was very talented with her embroidery." A pang of sadness pinched my chest. I missed Mary, even with all of her neurotic ways. Despite my family's treachery, she had held my younger sister and me close, had even remained friends with my mother.

The ambassador handed me a cup of dark-red wine. I sniffed its fruity essence before taking a small sip. I had never tasted anything so fine. "'Tis very good," I murmured. "If it pleases, Ambassador, I would like to get to the heart of the matter. I am expected back at Westminster presently."

For a moment, the countess's eyes narrowed, and I suspected she thought my terseness a judgment on her, but it wasn't. 'Twas simply a matter of already being in a precarious position at court and not wishing to further Her Majesty's hatred of me.

"You are just as lively as described."

To this, I raised a brow. While most would think the ambassador's representation of me complimentary, from the dark look in his eyes, I suspected quite the opposite. My back straightened all the more, and I glanced at Jane Dormer.

The countess looked down at the rings adorning her fingers. No doubt, she was the one to have provided such a depiction.

"My lady, I understand that within your cousin's court, you are not given quarter. While she has moved you from the presence chamber back into her Privy Chamber, you are still not entirely trusted. Your letters are read"—with this he caught my eye, and at that moment, I realized that my letters to Ned had indeed been read, and somehow he had even been one to see them—"and your whereabouts are marked. What you eat and drink is recorded. Your servants are employed by Her Majesty. They are not loyal to you, but to her."

I knew the latter with clarity—save for Mrs. Helen—perhaps they were even more loyal to the countess and the ambassador than to me, for what power did I really have?

"Everywhere you look, my lady, there are those who watch you, to see if you should slip, if you should cause concern to Her Majesty."

I cocked my head and pursed my lips. "I am well aware that I have more a pretty face than a sharp mind, Ambassador, but did you think such would prevent me from being aware of my position at court and the lengths to which Her Majesty will go to protect herself from what she fears of me?"

From the fleeting look of surprise on his face, I could only surmise that this was indeed the case. Even his wife, sitting so primly on her armchair, glanced up from her bejeweled fingers for a moment, her gaze sharply registering my face as if she'd realized for the first time that rational thoughts might actually flit through my mind.

For shame that she, someone I had considered close to me, should think such. But I suppose all my talking to my pets, flirting with Ned, and otherwise keeping to myself could have made one think little of me. I almost laughed aloud now as I looked back. Friends at court had seen me only ever read Plato, which I struggled with, and my prayer book written in French, which, considering my French was mediocre at best, I also had an awkward time reading. If only courtiers, male and female, would look beneath the surface. Sad that I doubted anyone ever would.

"*Nunca*, my lady, never. I did not mean to suggest that you were not aware. I wanted only to cast further light on the situation. To serve you."

"How can you serve me as you say, Ambassador? I am truly curious. For I have been trying to gain my cousin's favor for years, and while she brings me closer, we all know 'tis not because I have succeeded."

Ambassador de Feria and his wife exchanged a fleeting glance that spoke volumes. They would share whatever plot they'd hatched, I was certain. I was also certain that if I were to listen, I would only implicate myself in said plot. My stomach soured. I took another sip of wine to calm my nerves. Why had I agreed to come here?

Dear Lord in heaven, have mercy on me. Save me from plots and those who would work against me. Leave me not to my sister's fate, but deliver me into the arms of the one I love.

I resisted the urge to cross myself.

"My lady, it may be best you should leave England for a time and go to Spain. The emperor has offered you a safe haven within his realm, indeed within his own court, and he is even willing to offer you a substantial yearly allowance."

I kept my face neutral. "'Tis a generous offer, Ambassador." More than generous. Too generous.

De Feria inclined his head, lips pressed together in a smug smile, as if he'd expected me to be much pleased. Better to keep it that way for now.

"What does Emperor Philip seek in return?" I made my voice quite innocent and plucked at an imaginary string upon the lace at my wrists.

"Nothing, my lady. He only wants your happiness," de Feria said with a flourish of his hands, as if that was all anyone would ever seek.

I sheltered the urge to howl a laugh, loud and unladylike. Where was Ned? He would have so enjoyed this farce. And Mrs. Helen would have been having a ball without a doubt.

"That is very generous, indeed." I tapped my chin. "Do you suppose my pets would be allowed to join me?"

The ambassador raised his brows. "How many pets does your ladyship have?" He shook his head and hands. "No need to answer, my lady. It was most uncouth of me to inquire. All of your pets would be welcome in Spain."

From the corner of my eye, I saw the ambassador's wife nod to her husband, which showed me she had informed him previously that my love for my animals would be a deciding factor.

"Well, that is certainly a relief, as I am very close with my dear pets. They are not usually apart from me, unless absolutely necessary." And while I spoke the truth to a point, I was having entirely too much fun at de Feria's expense. "Stew, my little monkey, short for Steward because he is so much in charge of my household, would be loath to remain at the castle and might, in fact, climb upon just anyone's head and pick the lice from beneath their caps—even you, Ambassador!" I widened my eyes with innocence and nodded, biting my tongue so much that it pained me not to laugh aloud at the disgust he was trying hide.

"Well, *sí*, my lady, there is no reason to worry. You may bring them."

"Marvelous. And how exactly shall we gain Her Majesty's permission for me to up and leave her court for that of King Philip, with whom she is not always on the best of terms?"

The ambassador blanched at the change in conversation, and I could see I had him off his feet. I batted my lashes prettily and took a sip of my wine. "I confess, I have always wanted to see Spain. Lady Jane has told me such pleasant things of your country." I turned and offered the countess a wide, sweet smile.

She smiled nervously in return and smoothed her skirts in her lap with one hand—I suspect she was wiping sweat from her palm—and with the other daintily sipped at her Spanish wine.

"I am most biased, my lady, but I do agree that Spain is a place of beauty, and I think you would be most happy there. Perhaps we could even arrange a marriage between yourself and a most noble Spaniard or . . . prince."

Here we were, finally reaching the heart of the matter. De Feria wanted to see me married to a Spanish prince, which meant that King Philip wanted me to marry one of his heirs. An heir to Spain married to an heir of England, and once again the two realms would be united. Interesting, to say the least.

"Perhaps so, Ambassador," I said, my voice serious, my gaze meeting his without faltering. I had no intention of following through with such a plot. But there was no sense in letting the ambassador and his wife know. It was best to keep my enemies close, as I had learned from Her Majesty.

"For this to be considered, you would have to remain true to the Catholic faith, my lady," de Feria replied.

I inclined my head rather than answer. I'd pretended once before, and I had no problem performing again.

"As I mentioned before . . . your correspondence is monitored," he said.

My ears perked up, but I worked hard to keep my expression plain.

"As a result, I am aware of your . . . esteem for Lord Hertford."

Again, I did not respond, but waited for him to continue.

"If the Spanish are to aid in your plight, my lady, I must gain your promise that you will not marry nor change your faith from that of the true religion without first seeking my counsel."

I smiled at de Feria, a smile I had oft given my father, and Her Majesty, which indicated that I had every intention of following his directive, when in fact, the opposite was true.

"Ambassador, I assure you, I will do neither."

These words served my purpose beautifully as I offered him the promise that he sought and at the same time offered nothing. For in truth, I was telling him I would neither change my religion nor promise to inform him of my prospects.

"Now, if it pleases, we have tarried here overlong, and I fear my absence will be noted, and as you yourself have said, I am watched. I should not want Her Majesty to look at you in a negative light."

He stood and flourished a sweeping bow. "It was a pleasure speaking with you, my lady."

"And you, Ambassador."

MARCH 3, 1560

My footsteps outside the palace were muffled by dew-covered blades of grass. Spring had come. While there were not many flowers blooming, a few buds reached for the sun's sustenance.

A boisterous game of boules was in progress, as today was the first day one might not freeze one's limbs off from being out of doors.

I was relieved to have had no word from Ambassador de Feria, and in fact, the countess had been absent as well, although for different reasons. The ambassador had been recalled to Spain for a time, most likely telling his king that I was amenable to their plan, which, for their sake and my own, I hoped they kept quiet.

It was reckless on my part to play with him, but there had been no way out of it. I had gone to their home. If I had denied him, then it was entirely possible a plot against me would have been hatched. I had trusted Jane Dormer and thought perhaps she had found a way to convince Her Majesty that Ned and I should be together, should we agree to remove ourselves from England. Never in my wildest imaginings had I dreamed such a scheme was afoot.

Perhaps, if I brought information regarding this new Spanish plot to Elizabeth, I would be able to use it to my advantage. I remained a potential victim of such plots as long as I was unmarried. But if Elizabeth were to allow me to marry the ever-faithful Lord Hertford, she would have no cause to worry over me again. Then again, it might give her more cause to hate me.

If I were my sister Jane, or Queen Elizabeth for that matter, I would have known what to do. They were both shrewd and distrustful of others. I tended to believe in the goodness of people.

I envied their abilities to read beneath people's exteriors and see when they meant to do harm. Yet another reason I should not involve myself in the games of politics.

The crack of one ball hitting another shattered the air, followed by loud cheers from male and female courtiers.

I hurried my steps, my slippers becoming damp in the grass. When I reached the field, I saw that Elizabeth had been the one to hit the ball of her opponent, Robert Dudley, from its place, making her the winner.

She glanced up at me then, and her wide smile, showing her youth and energy, was quickly washed from her face. I curtsied low. "Majesty."

"Good of you to join us, Cousin. Should you like to play?"

I was surprised by her invitation, and she opened her arm, indicating I should join her.

"Cousin against cousin!" some idiotic courtier shouted.

I cringed, flashed a glare at the courtier who had spoken. Cousin versus cousin. As if we were not already such in Elizabeth's eyes. Why bring such potent poison to her mind?

"Indeed," Elizabeth said, flicking her hand in the air as though wiping away the courtier's remark.

I smiled halfheartedly. Boules was a game I'd grown quite excellent at, and the queen was well aware of it. But no matter, I would not be excellent today. She needed to see that I was loyal to her, that she had nothing to fear from me, even in a silly game of boules.

The queen always won.

Chapter Fifteen

Yet small account of Fortune new,
he made for still in breast:
Was shrined the saint, that stony walls,
and prison had possessed.
No fear nor friend nor fellow mate,
this troubled mind might move . . .
—*Thomas Churchyard, Elizabethan Soldier and Poet*

July 5, 1560

"He is not coming."

I glanced up from the silk gown of silver I held in my hands to see Jane Seymour's crestfallen face. I knew at once of whom she spoke. The dress fell to the open chest beside my bed.

"Why?" My voice betrayed my pain.

Jane let out a long sigh and came toward me, taking my hand in her reassuring grasp. "He says he has business to attend, but shall join us in the midst of the queen's progress."

"What does that mean?" For months, he'd told me that he would attend court, and then came the promise that he'd be here for the progress, yet I feared he avoided us as though the Black Plague had descended.

I suspected his mother had warned him away from the progress. She feared for our continued affection, knowing that Elizabeth was against it. But it still angered me to no end that Elizabeth would torment us so.

Jane bit her lip and nodded. "I know it appears as if he stays away by choice, Kat."

"'Tis more than how it appears! I have not laid eyes on him in so very long. I feel he has abandoned all promises of affection."

"Do not say such things. He loves you more each day."

"How am I to know?"

Jane frowned, her gaze moving to the tapestry rug. "You are not, if he does not tell you. I fear my brother has never been one to write letters or keep in *communiqué* with anyone. When he was fostered out, my mother did lament of that very same thing. 'Tis a flaw, 'tis a weakness, but it does not mean he feels naught for you, or that he does not think of you."

Hope flared. "Does he mention me to you, Jane?"

Jane nodded, her eyes sparkling. "He says the most wondrous things. He truly is a romantic at heart, Kat. Forgive him his fault of working overmuch and not attending to you. 'Tis not meant as a slight."

"I will try to remember." I sighed heavily and picked up the silken gown. Mrs. Helen had not placed it among my things to be packed for our summer progress, but I could not leave it behind. Squatters came to the castles when we departed. Who would not wish to live in a castle? As cold and bleak as it was, it was an improvement over living in squalor beneath London Bridge. I could not bear for this gown—given to me by Queen Mary—to be stolen or destroyed. "Do tell me the wondrous things he says. If I cannot hear them from Ned, where better than from your lips?"

The smile returned to Jane's pretty face, so much like her mother's but without the bitter pinch of years of strain. "He says how he cannot wait to run his fingers through the silken gold upon your head. How the night sky shines and sparkles and reminds him of your eyes. How his heart aches from not being able to walk with you. That he misses besting you at cards. That he should like to dance the night away with you. Then he whispers that hope and dreams will not die."

"Oh, they will not die!" My breath caught in my throat. I recalled his words so long ago when we were both mere children dancing at my first wedding. He did love me! He did care! And somehow I would have to learn that his flaw of not writing did not mean he was absent of heart and mind, but simply distracted.

Finished in my chamber, Jane and I were passing through the corridors on our way to Elizabeth's chambers when loud shouts, crashes, and shrieks echoed off the walls.

"'Tis coming from the queen's room," Jane said, her eyes wide as saucers.

My heart skipped a beat. I took Jane's hand in mine, and we rushed the rest of the way, bursting into the queen's presence chamber. Courtiers milled about, speaking in hushed tones, gesturing wildly with their hands.

"What is happening?" I asked Bess St. Loe and Blanche Parry, who huddled beside the queen's chamber door.

"Her Majesty has just heard the most awful news," Blanche said, her eyes looking dull and disinterested—almost as if the temper flaring beyond the Privy Chamber door were a regular event.

"What has happened?"

Blanche barely looked at me. "Another threatens her position."

My mouth went dry. Could she be speaking of me? Is that why she refused to look in my direction? But surely not. If it were me she referred to, she most likely would not speak to me at all. To associate with a traitor was to brand oneself a traitor.

The doors rattled as something crashed against them, followed by another round of shouts from Elizabeth and a few choice words. Robert Dudley pushed his way through the throng of courtiers to the Privy Chamber door and was admitted by the queen's yeomen without question.

"Oh, Robin! The witch will have me undone!" we heard Elizabeth lament before the door was closed firmly again.

"What news?" Jane Seymour asked, her gaze pointed at Bess, who would most likely give us a straighter answer than the one we'd received from Blanche.

Bess shook her head. "'Tis quite an offense, truly. Mary, Queen of Scots, is considering not signing the treaty to unite England and Scotland. Upon her crest, she has placed Tudor roses along with the Stuart emblem. She does not recognize Elizabeth as the rightful monarch and instead fancies herself the Queen of England. There are many in the Catholic realms who are backing her claim."

My mouth fell open, and I sucked in a breath. Would Elizabeth finally feel some of the fear that my sister Jane had felt? 'Twas a fitting punishment. If things went wrong, it might be Elizabeth with her head on the block. And yet, though I did not like my cousin, I wouldn't even dream of seeing her in the same position my sister had been in. "Surely you jest."

"I jest not," Bess said, shaking her head. "The queen is most displeased. I suspect she will go after Scotland—Mary still resides in France. Scotland is not protected as well with her out of the country. But I do not claim to know much of politics." Bess waved away her words as if she did not know why she'd spoken them.

Despite the dismissal, I knew Bess was right. Elizabeth would retaliate, and it would not be pretty.

The Privy Chamber door was yanked open, and a well-put-together, despite her fierce show of temper, Queen Elizabeth poked her head out. "There you are, Daughter."

Her gaze was directed at me, but I knew she could not be speaking to me. I turned my head but saw no one standing behind me.

"Come, Kitty Kat. You know I meant you. I told you once before I would adopt you, my fair daughter. Now come."

Kitty Kat?

The queen's eyes were a fiery blue. Indeed, she looked half-mad. I knew then that I must do her bidding. Become like her daughter if she required it. It was the only way to survive. If I did not, she might suspect I, too, was against her. I swallowed hard and walked through the presence chamber, ignoring the whispers and gibes from courtiers. Once more, I was a plaything to a sovereign. I could never escape it. The queen would retaliate against our mutual cousin, and apparently, I was the means by which to do so.

Elizabeth widened the door as I approached, and I walked in somberly to the faces of Master Cecil, Lord Robert, her new henchman Walsingham, Nicholas White, our cousin Lettice Knollys, and the queen's own companion Kat Astley.

The door closed behind me with an audible click that echoed in my ears. I could physically sense the air changing around me. Where the presence was filled with jealousy and thick tension, the privy had a much deeper, darker emotion. I nearly choked on it.

"I have decided that I will indeed adopt you, Kat. Let these people be my witnesses. We will soon draw up the papers."

I started to shake my head, glancing around the room. My fingers started to tingle before going numb. I wanted to shout *no!* To run. But my feet were frozen to the floor. The men in the room showed no expression, except for Cecil, who always appeared to be calculating something. Kat Astley looked at me fondly, most likely remembering Elizabeth when she was younger, as many at court often said I looked like a younger version of my cousin. Truth be told, however, Lettice looked the spitting image of Elizabeth, minus a few years. She was truly beautiful, and while her face showed no hint of emotion, her gaze burned into mine. I could sense from her eyes she resented me, perhaps for taking the place at Elizabeth's side that she herself had hoped to occupy.

"Well, Katherine, do you not have anything to say on the matter?" Elizabeth prompted, although I was not sure why, as she would only toss me in the Tower if I were to object to her plans.

"I am . . . much honored, Majesty." I curtsied deeply, keeping my gaze directed at the floor. There was nothing to do but agree or be beaten into it. The hairs on my arms and the back of my neck rose. I felt as though I were within a den of hungry lions. Any sudden moves and I would be pounced on, my throat ripped out, my cries for mercy unheeded.

"As you should be. You shall ride beside me while on progress, and you will need ladies to attend you—more than you have now. I want all within the realm to know the exalted position you hold within this court. You, Lady Katherine Grey, are a Tudor princess of the blood, and as such, you shall be just one step below me in this court."

Was Elizabeth naming me her heir without saying the words?

My royal cousin turned to Cecil and winged a brow. "She dares to name herself Queen of England? We shall show her that her declarations mean nothing. Send troops to Scotland while we are on progress. By fall, I want this mess disposed of."

My eyes widened only slightly. Bess was right. The queen would strike out while Scotland was weak, and by naming me her daughter and setting precedence with my status in her court, she was showing all of Europe that England was strong.

"I feel quite exhausted now. Leave me. I must rest before we depart nigh on an hour." The group filed from the room, but before I could leave, Elizabeth's long, slim fingers curled around my arm. "Do not do anything stupid, Cousin. I may have elevated you in the public's eyes, but 'tis words only. I know as well as the sun will set and rise that should I turn my back for a second, you will be there with a dagger."

I opened my mouth to protest, but she made a hissing noise with her mouth meant to silence me.

"'Tis no use, Kat. I tried the very same lamentations with my sister, Mary, and in the end, do you know what she did? She imprisoned me. More than once. She did not trust me. Even on the day she died, she begrudgingly handed her realm to me. 'Twill always be the way of things."

How sad were her words. That she had once felt as I did and would still treat me as her sister had treated her. In her eyes, we were destined to be enemies until the end.

"Count yourself among those whom luck has blessed, for I have yet to toss you in the Tower. Do not disappoint me."

Elizabeth let go of my arm. The flesh where she'd held me throbbed, and I had no doubt by tomorrow, there would be bruises on my pale skin. She turned toward the sideboard, and for a moment, her shoulders slumped before she held them rigid again. She picked up an apple and bit into it with ferocity—like a lioness would bite into prey. I'd heard her say on more than one occasion, "I may not be a lion, but I am a lion's cub, and I have a lion's heart."

The energy it took to exude such vehemence, to remain so strict in her resolve, was exhausting simply to think about . . .

An emotion came over me, one I found myself quite surprised by: pity. I pitied Elizabeth her anger, her bitterness, her fear. I knew she had nothing to fear from me, just as she'd known her sister had had nothing to fear from her. But it was this suspicion and jealousy, it was the actions of others that perpetuated that fear. Courtiers and councilmen would prod her into thinking she must bear ill will toward those who might have cause to abuse her. I would never dream of harming Her Majesty, and yet my name had been dragged through the muck, and now I suffered for it.

Mary, Queen of Scots, may have had an entire ocean between her and Elizabeth, but she also had the backing of the French king, and most likely would gain the backing of all those on the continent with ties to the pope. I supposed, in a way, I could blame our cousin for Elizabeth's increased suspicion over my position.

Queen Elizabeth, England itself, represented the bad child. The one who would not bend to her father's will. But the pope was not our father. Lord God was, and Elizabeth would uphold our religion and see that we believed in the Lord our God and that His word ruled. The people of England must not take that away by playing games of politics with those who would destroy us and lay claim to our very lands, forcing their beliefs and wars upon us as Philip had when he was married to Mary . . . And there my thoughts stopped.

He was seeking to do that through me. While I had yet to hear from Ambassador de Feria, or Jane Dormer, as if our conversation had never taken place, I was now certain that word of our meeting, and perhaps even word of what had been said during that meeting, had reached Elizabeth's ears. Was that why she was so pressed to make me her daughter? Not only to show Mary Stuart that she would not yield, but also to show Spain that I would not bend to their Catholic will? That I was with Elizabeth one hundred percent?

The crunch of the apple as Elizabeth bit again pulled me from my thoughts. "Go now. We depart soon."

I nodded, curtsied, and murmured to her of my loyalty, all of which were waved off, her gaze on some far-off place in her mind.

When I returned to my room, a small package sat upon my bed, with a short note that read simply:

To my heart be true, and in your heart spring love.—N

He had thought of me! I ripped open the packaging to find a beautiful brooch in the shape of a nightingale. Clear diamonds glittered along the body and yellow diamonds on the wings and beak. The eyes were crafted with sapphires. I held it up to the light and watched as a thousand prisms shone through the nightingale to dance along the walls. Arabel and Beau jumped along beneath the lighted dots, and I shifted and swayed the brooch to make them run back and forth, laughing as they tried to catch the prism lights.

"Oh, Ned," I said to the air, kissed the brooch, and pinned it to my gown. His note I folded up neatly and tucked into my bodice. My oak chest had already been packed, but when we arrived at the first stop along our progress, I would tuck his note inside Jane's Testament for safekeeping.

JULY 27, 1560

A week went by with nary a moment's rest. We stopped at several houses during that time and were received with feasts and entertainments, until finally we reached Eltham Palace, where we were to remain for at least a fortnight. The gardens of Eltham were magnificent, almost a wild-looking place with rare flowers and trees, unlike the tidier gardens of Greenwich and Westminster. The great hall had a vaulted wooden ceiling like the hull of a great ship, with balconies above for entertainers to play and guests to observe the activities below. Alcoves for clandestine meetings. The walls were covered in thick brocade tapestries and curtains. The palace had an ancient feel to it.

Having been at court for so many years, I should have been used to the fast pace, but things were not so with Mary's court, and this was Elizabeth's first progress. I suspected she wanted to take the next several months to put her face in front of all her people. I

was exhausted, and when shown to my room, I collapsed upon the
bed—and upon a parchment that crinkled.

I pulled it from beneath me and read.

Dearest Love,
This is a poem by that famous lamenter of woes, Thomas
Wyatt, and it reminds me of how my heart beats for yours.

The lively sparks that issue from those eyes,
Against the which there vaileth no defense,
Have pierced my heart, and done it none offense,
With quaking pleasure more than once or twice.
Was never man could any thing devise,
Sunbeams to turn with so great vehemence
To daze man's sight, as by their bright presence
Dazed am I; much like unto the guise
Of one stricken with dint of lightning,
Blind with the stroke, and erring here and there:
So call I for help, I know not when nor where,
The pain of my fall patiently bearing:
For straight after the blaze, as is no wonder,
Of deadly noise hear I the fearful thunder.

I clutched the parchment to my chest. If Ned could not be here
with me, at least he was making a noble effort to remain in my
heart. Jane must have told him how my heart ached from having
no word from him.

I glanced down at his postscript:

I wait on bated breath until I can behold you again. I shall attend
you shortly and leave within a day to meet you at Eltham.

But my joy at Ned's impending arrival was overshadowed by the haunting memory of Master Cecil's words. *You are next in line to the throne. You are legitimate. If you should marry and have children, your claim would be far stronger than hers.* Our child would descend from two royal English houses.

I frowned. Elizabeth would never let us marry unless we had plenty of council members on our side. My mind drifted to the pinched, conservative faces of Elizabeth's council. Ned was a good man. A loyal subject to the crown. His father had been falsely accused, which was widely known, so the blight of treason was not as strong on his head as it was on mine, but all the same, we two came from treasonous lines.

I rolled over and stared out the open window. Luckily, today was proving to be overcast. The sky was gray despite it being just after noon. Thunder rumbled in the distance, and with the impending storm, Elizabeth had taken to her room with one of her megrims—a Tudor female affliction.

For now, I could rest. Ned would be here soon. If I had not been so exhausted, my excitement would have kept me from sleep. I closed my eyes and heard Mrs. Helen cluck her tongue as she tossed a thin coverlet over my shoulders despite the summer months. Her footsteps faded, and then she closed the shutters just as thunder clapped overhead and pellets of rain hit the diamond-shaped panes.

Oh, Ned . . .

A swift knock interrupted my nap, and from beyond my chamber door, I could hear fierce whispers but could discern not who the owners were.

A rustling of clothes and clicking of heels upon the polished, wood-planked floors brought my worst fears to life. I imagined the queen's yeomen coming to arrest me. I sat up straight in bed but was greeted only by the Countess of Feria, Jane Dormer, who was now great with child. Her husband had recently been replaced by

Ambassador de Quadra, who'd approached me a week ago about their scheme, but I had quickly rebuffed him.

"Lady Katherine." She curtsied as low as her overlarge belly would allow. "Please accept my apologies for intruding upon your slumber, but it was imperative that I come to you. I cannot tarry. My husband has demanded I join him in Spain, and with the current state of things at court, it is best I return there. Spain has joined its opinion with France that Elizabeth should be dethroned." Her speech was rapid, her fingers twisting in her hands. "The emperor, via my husband, has offered one last time for you to come with me, to escape this place. They will place you upon the throne—"

"No! Get out!" I covered my ears, not wanting to be a part of what she was saying to me. Her words were treason, and if I heard them, Elizabeth would have cause to toss me in the Tower. "Go now!" I shouted.

Mrs. Helen rushed and ushered the shaken Countess de Feria from my room.

I jumped from my bed and knelt upon my knees, looking up at the ceiling as I spoke rapid prayers. I prayed for her safety in returning to Spain. I prayed no one had heard her or seen her come to my chamber. I prayed Elizabeth slumbered well in her bed. I prayed Ambassador de Quadra would not seek me out. I wanted nothing to do with their schemes.

Mrs. Helen came back in and thrust a cup of warm honeyed wine into my hands, which I gulped greedily, welcoming the warmth and calm it brought my nerves.

"Shall we read from Plato, my dear?" she asked, knowing it was the one thing that could calm me.

"Yes," I said, looking forward to journeying into the philosopher's complex mind.

But before I could rise, another swift knock cracked the door. "No," I said faintly. It would be the guards now for sure. They would take me to the Tower. I would be placed upon the rack, my limbs stretched and yanked from their sockets until I was a limp, fleshy mess of my former self.

"My lady."

It was not the guards. It was the sweet voice of love's ghost.

I turned, still on my knees, as Ned walked into my chamber. Water dripped from the ends of his hair, the tip of his nose. His clothes were soaked through with rain, clinging to every curve of his well-built body.

"Ned," I whispered.

"Oh, Kat," he said with emotion cracking his voice. He rushed forward, bent to his knees by my side, and gathered me in his arms. Neither of us cared that the rain soaking his body seeped into my own gown. I pressed kisses to his face and he to my hair, both of us whispering fervently of how much we'd missed the other. Our lips connected in a fiery kiss, and I entirely forgot where we were, still on our knees, until I heard the soft click of my chamber door closing.

Pulling away, I saw we were alone. Mrs. Helen had, shockingly, left us to our privacy.

Ned's hands held the sides of my face as he gazed into my eyes. "They would keep us apart, but I could not bear it any longer. I had to come. I had to see you."

"It has been too long," I said ardently, pressing my lips to his once more. Oh, he tasted so sweet, and my body soared from the sensations of his mouth on mine, but also from knowing he loved me as feverishly as I loved him. "Do not leave me for so long again."

"I shan't. I swear it."

The time for words ceased as our lips met once more. Passion overwhelmed my senses and my conscience. My fingers divested Ned of his wet clothes as he ripped pins from my gown, tossing pieces of fabric wherever they fell. His lips skimmed down my neck, over my shoulders, to my breasts, which were peaked with need of his touch.

He lifted me effortlessly from the floor and placed me atop the satin coverlet of the bed, his hard body coming down on top of me.

"Marry me, Kat," he demanded, our noses touching, lips an inch away, his gaze penetrating mine.

My breath caught as I gazed into his eyes. To say yes was to defy my sovereign. To say no was to deny my heart. A long time ago, I'd thought to put my faith in love. It would seem now was the time. Every inch of my skin tingled with renewed vibrancy. Hope.

"Yes," I whispered, wrapping my legs around his hips.

Ned pressed a hard kiss to my lips, placing all the emotion behind his question, behind our decision within that kiss. It was overpowering, overwhelming, and I was dizzy with it. There would be consequences. But in his arms, then, I felt we could face the world together. That we were potent. We would overcome whatever Elizabeth threw our way.

He pulled away a moment, his face a mask of seriousness. "I can take it no longer, my love. On the morrow, we shall seek Her Majesty's approval."

I nodded, my demeanor just as grave. "Tomorrow."

"I love you," he whispered, sinking himself inside me, breaking the barrier of my maidenhead.

I cried out at the pinch, but his kiss silenced my pain and made my body shake with a fierce need. With this moment, our declarations changed the course of history. As our bodies rocked together in the ancient dance of love, hope rose. We'd taken hold of our future as much as we'd taken hold of one another. The politics of my birth might have denied me of liberty, tried to rob me of my soul, but Ned had set me free. With him I soared.

Let no man tear asunder.

Chapter Sixteen

This Falcon scorned to pray abroad,
at home he left his love.
Full many a sigh and heavy look.
he sent along the Seas:
And wished himself in fetters fast,
to doe his Lady ease.
—*Thomas Churchyard, Elizabethan Soldier and Poet*

JULY 28, 1560

"Shh . . . In here," Jane Seymour said, waving to Ned and me. We eagerly plunged into the darkness of the closet within the maidens' quarters while Jane stood watch outside.

"I could not wait to see you alone, Kat," Ned said, kissing my lips and cheeks. "Court has kept me busy all this long day."

I murmured my agreement and slid my arms up around his neck. His mouth felt so good against mine, and the stirring of excitement in my loins built as it had yesterday when we'd made love for the first time.

"Oh, Kat," he moaned against my ear. "Would that I could make love to you right here."

"Why can we not?"

My question was all the confirmation he needed. Ned fumbled with his hose, and I hiked up my skirts in a billowy cloud around my hips. He lifted me up, and I wrapped my legs around him. He entered me slowly and continued to move with ease, as if he truly wished our coupling to last forever.

Jane tapped twice, as she'd said she would if someone were to come into the room. We did not move. Ned stayed firmly planted inside me. I could hear muffled voices and the shuffling of feet.

And then Jane whispered through the door that all was well. Ned let out a long-held groan and gripped my hips firmly, urgently. He buried his face in the length of my neck and quickened his pace, until at last, he shuddered and warm stickiness seeped inside me.

"Did you find your pleasure?" he asked, his voice worried, and if I'd been able to see, I was sure his eyes would have shown his concern, too.

I rested my head against his shoulder. "'Twas very pleasurable."

"But did you find completion?" he urged.

I felt complete, so I nodded, although I had not, in fact, felt the pleasurable explosion that I had the day before, which was what he'd most likely meant. Somehow, I knew it would not do to tell him so.

"Oh, good." He set me down and went to work fixing his clothes. I felt around the maiden's closet for a piece of scrap linen to wipe between my thighs.

Ned knocked twice upon the door, and Jane responded with a knock that it was safe for us to exit. When we did, my face felt as if it were aflame, and we must have looked a sight, for Jane blushed clear to her toes.

"Go away from here, Beau. I need to fix Kat up, or else the whole of court will know what you're about. I hope you are urgently preparing to seek the queen's permission, too, else you'll both regret it," Jane said, her face as stern as her mother's. "And if you don't, I shall fetch the priest myself."

Ned bowed over his sister's hand. "My number-one priority is to honor Lady Katherine."

He then bowed to me and blew me a kiss before jauntily walking from the room.

Jane turned to me and shook her head. "You know I love you both, Kat, but you are playing with fire. I meant for you only to meet and kiss maybe, but I can see much more has happened." She pointed to my tousled hair and wrinkled skirts. "We'd best get it straightened out, or even the mice will know you've just rutted in a closet." She closed her eyes and mumbled a prayer.

I rushed toward Jane and hugged her close. "You shan't be sent to the Tower for it, Jane. Now that the queen has adopted me, I have every confidence Her Majesty will give us the permission we seek to marry. It can only benefit her to present me as a strong heir—a married heir."

Jane stared at me a moment, her throat bobbing as she swallowed hard. "I shall pray she does."

She fixed me up in silence, and we headed back to the festivities at court, as if I'd never been gone. No odd glances came my way, as I had imagined they would. It appeared that I had not been missed, despite the dim sense of foreboding that had come over me with Jane's warning. But I could not dwell on her words. I had to think positive thoughts. I had to believe Elizabeth would grant us a marriage, especially given what I'd now done.

And perhaps I ought to discreetly ask one of the less-than-prudent maids how she prevented herself from becoming with child. And then a thought struck me. Might it be better, perhaps, to refrain from taking such measures and instead conceive a child so the queen might be forced to demand our immediate marriage? A soiled, pregnant princess could never become queen, and no other lord besides Ned would wed me if I was carrying his child. The thought had merit.

AUGUST 15, 1560

We arrived at Nonsuch Palace in Surrey, built by my great-uncle Henry VIII. It was a place of magic, with tall turrets, mythological paintings, and garden mazes. Ned and I tried our hardest to keep our distance while in the presence of others, as we feared everyone would see the lust and excitement upon our faces when we gazed at one another. I had yet to approach him with the possible scheme of conceiving.

Queen Elizabeth had been in one of her worst rages to date, although I hadn't been made privy to the cause. Even still, her moods had affected me as Ned and I had been reluctant to speak with her regarding vows. We would have to wait until she was in a better frame of mind to grant us what we wished. Every person in the realm, from noble duke to lowly peasant, knew the queen would deny everything when in one of her moods. I was not willing to risk my future on it. Besides, the little moments we stole together were worth it—I could not imagine life without Ned.

This evening, there would be a banquet and a masque. Our faces covered, Ned and I would be able to dance the night away without fear of reprisal. The ladies would all be working on their masks today, so 'twas very possible they would recognize mine. *But* if I made my mask look much like the others, then there was hope several of us would be thought the flirt.

I sat down upon an oak chair at the table in the queen's presence chamber with the other ladies of the bedchamber and several maids of honor. The table was piled high with ribbons, feathers, sparkling clay jewels, and stiffened-velvet, colored masks. There were pots of fish glue for adhesive, needles, and colored thread.

Over sips of honeyed wine, we sewed, glued, and designed our masks, imagining the night to come. And all while I prepared my Venus-looking mask, I thought of Ned and how happy he made me.

And how I might let him drag me to a darkened corner for a kiss—but nothing more.

As it happened, I had not had to ask a ripe maid for ways in which to keep myself childless for the time being, as my monthly started after the two times we'd been intimate together. I prayed all night and fasted for three days as penance and had denied Ned since. I would let him kiss me, and touch me—maybe—but I would not let him spend himself inside me again until we were wed. It was one thing to beg the queen's permission to wed and be denied, but after some thought, I'd decided that if we were to beg her permission once I was with child, 'twould be a disaster. One likely ending with an ax.

But I supposed that teasing Ned was a lot of fun. Mrs. Helen always lamented: *Who would purchase the sheep if you gave the fleece away for free?* I'd never understood her meaning until now. Why would Ned go through all the work of tending the sheep, keeping it fed, warm, safe in order to obtain the prize if said sheep would simply strip and hand him his coat? I would have to be like the sheep who gave nothing without first being taken care of.

"Oh, what joyous masks, ladies!" Queen Elizabeth exclaimed, coming into the presence chamber to sit with us. She looked flushed, and I noted that Robert Dudley stood in the doorway of her chamber from whence she'd come. They looked much as Ned and I had coming out of the closet.

Lord Robert bowed low to us all, and when the queen's gaze shifted to us, his eyes flicked to my cousin Lettice. She raised her eyes, locking on the queen's sweet Robin. There, her eyes changed, softened. And Lord in heaven strike me down if Lord Robert did not return her affectionate gaze, if only for a moment.

The queen, unaware of the exchange, and acting as if nothing out of the ordinary had occurred—for in actuality, it was not abnormal for Dudley to be alone in her room—picked up a velvet mask and held a brightly colored green ostrich feather to it. She smiled and chattered away as she designed her mask. 'Twas the first time I'd seen her so joyous in a long time.

Images of Ned and me inside the darkened closet in the maiden's chamber flashed into my mind. The kisses . . . warm breath on my neck, firm hands holding my hips . . . his rigid member sinking deep inside my flesh . . .

"Are you quite all right, Cousin?" Elizabeth asked, startling me from my thoughts.

I realized I'd been staring at her with a bemused look on my face and quickly smiled. "I adore your choice of feathers for your mask. They will go well with your complexion."

Elizabeth narrowed her eyes but smiled at the same time, as if assessing me to see if what I said was true. "So you think the green feathers will match well with these purple ones?"

She held up the mask to show all of her ladies. All nodded and proclaimed it was the most beautiful mask they'd ever seen. They tittered to the queen and to each other, and I smiled and laughed along with them, but all the while, my mind was turning. I knew the truth. Elizabeth would not seek out any other dance partner than her sweet Robin, as I would seek none other than my sweet Ned. The trick was finding the right masked man.

When the ladies had left, and when I was alone with Elizabeth, she said, "A masque is a wonderful affair. Did you know my father first saw my mother at a masque? He wanted her from that moment on. She was dressed in white, like a goddess, and she danced elegantly. Her feet were covered in silken slippers so delicate her feet could have been bare. He did tell me once while tickling my toes as a child that my feet were the spitting image of my mother's. Perhaps I shall meet my heart's true love tonight."

The beating of drums vibrated the inside of the great hall. Nonsuch was built on fanciful dreams, with its immeasurably tall ceilings, the paneled walls emblazoned with gods and goddesses as tall as a man and carved from stone. Our host, my own uncle, Lord Arundel, had spared no cost in the added décor of sheer silken cloth of gold hung between pillars in swoops and swags. Sweet-smelling candles of rosemary, honeyed lavender, and vanilla were lit by the hundreds.

Flutes whistled, their song melodic and enchanting, and some-how keeping in tune with the beating of the drums. The ladies of the bedchamber were all dressed in matching satin gowns of sage green. Her Majesty's maids of honor also wore the same styled gown, but in a rose hue. Just as her father had done before her, Elizabeth wore cloth of gold, so all would know just who the queen was, even though no one was to mention it.

We entered the great hall, and standing in a line with Elizabeth between us, we all curtsied to the crowd of male and female courtiers.

Almost immediately, a tall, lithe courtier stepped from the crowd, shamelessly wearing his own cloth of gold, and claimed a dance from Her Majesty. I could tell from both their throaty laughs just who Elizabeth's dancing partner was: Dudley. His behavior, donning cloth of gold to match the queen, would forever scan-dalize this court—for it meant he envisioned himself as king. I could sense it in my bones, beyond any closet kissing I might have engaged in.

He was a married man, for God's sake! His wife, whom I'd never even met because she was not allowed at court, must have been beside herself. I could never imagine Ned doing such a thing to me. And just as I thought of him, a man dressed in black velvet with a great turn of leg encased in ivory hose came to stand before me, bowing low over my extended hand.

He glanced up, and behind his black velvet mask, I recognized enchanting hazel eyes. "My lady, if you would do me the honor of dancing the volta with me?"

My heart skipped a beat. Ned had found me in this crowd, and now we would dance, hands touching, lips close enough to kiss. The volta was a sensual dance. He would hold me close, twirl me about. His hands would touch me as he lifted me and spun me in the air. Pebbled flesh rose on my arms, and I tried hard to find my voice.

"With pleasure, my lord."

With my small hand in his, he led me to the floor and twirled me. He smelled of bergamot and cloves, and when he whispered in my ear of my beauty, I smelled mint. How I wished to press my lips to his.

We twirled and danced to the beating drums and enchanting flutes. One dance after another. We feasted from each other's hands on roasted meat and sweet pies. Comfits poured from trays passed by servants and found their way to our lips.

A better time I'd never known. 'Twas as if the whole world was meant only for the two of us—a reprieve from propriety.

As we continued to dance well into the night, I watched with growing unease as Her Majesty rebuffed our host, Lord Arundel, preferring the company of Dudley. She could do so since she was queen, but as he was our host and had put on such a lavish affair, she should have danced with him at least once.

"Lord Arundel wished to ask for her hand," Ned whispered when he saw where my gaze was directed.

"Are you certain?"

He nodded. "He brought it to the attention of the council prior to the progress, hoping that as Keeper of the Palace, the progress would make a stop at Nonsuch and he could show the queen how much he adored her by throwing her a number of celebratory events."

"And yet she has brushed him aside."

Ned nodded. "There are several other events planned. Seeing how he has been received this eve, he will no doubt have *sweet Robin* engaged otherwise tomorrow." He chuckled and popped a sugared treat into his mouth. "'Tis nearing midnight, Princess."

"Is it? I would never have guessed. I feel so alive!"

Ned stroked the underside of my chin. "You are a wonder to me, Kat. 'Tis why I love you," he whispered into my ear. "Come, let us find a quiet place to be alone."

"I would be more than happy to oblige you, my lord, but I will do no more than kiss you."

Ned's eyes were dark with desire, and he nodded. "I know, my lady, and I would not want to compromise you further without permission from the queen to wed. But days have passed since last my lips touched yours, and I am hungry for your kiss."

I glanced around the room and saw that most everyone was occupied, and those who were not paid me little heed.

I stood without another word and walked around to the edges of the room, moving in and out of the silken fabrics that made the room look every bit like a fantastical dream.

When I reached the darkened corridor, I broke out into a run, laughing as Ned trailed behind me, his own cheerful laughs speeding me on. We found a door to the outside and took it, running out into the grass. The sultry night air, the mixture of wine and sweets in my belly, the comfort of being with the man I loved—all of it filled me with such jubilation my heart swelled and I laughed all the more. We ran through the darkened groves that shaded most of the moon's glow, silvery swords of light streaking down through the branches.

Ned twirled me around and lifted me into the air, a fine mist from a marble fountain sprinkling over our skin.

"Alone at last," he breathed and ripped off his mask and then mine, tossing them to the ground. "Now kiss me, my lady."

"I regret to inform you, my lord, that as I am above your station. I simply cannot bend to your demands." I sniffed, the corners of my lips turned up teasingly.

"I shall bend to my knees then and beg." He dropped to his knees, wrapping his arms around my legs and pulling me close. He buried his face against the junction of my thighs, sending thrills of pleasure racing through me. "May I kiss you, my lady?"

He nuzzled closer, his hot breath seeping through my gown, and my knees wobbled, threatening to give way as I choked on my breath. "Yes," I somehow managed to murmur.

Ned lifted the hem of my skirts and burrowed beneath, his lips pressing hotly against the curls between my thighs. I gasped aloud, my hands flying to find anchor against his head covered in my skirts.

"Ned!" I said in surprise as his tongue flicked out and sparks of fire burned through me.

"Oh, Kat . . . Tastes like sweet honey from my little bee."

My eyes rolled back, and I felt faint as his lips and tongue devoured me. My breaths came quicker. My heart beat so fast I thought it would burst. And then the world exploded around me, and my knees did give way as waves of pleasure descended upon me.

Ned caught me about the hips and laid me on the soft grass. I stared up at the stars, my body still quaking from what had just taken place.

He rolled beside me, pulling my hand to his lips and kissing my fingertips. "That, my lady, was finding completion."

"Indeed it was."

He chuckled beside me, obviously knowing I had not, in fact, found completion in the closet. I had not known a man and woman could be together this way to find pleasure. What a clever way to not become with child.

"Is it the same for a man as it is for a woman?" I asked.

"What do you mean?" He propped himself up on an elbow and stroked a finger over my face.

"Can I give you the same pleasure?"

Ned smiled. "A woman can give a man the same pleasure, but I would never ask it of you, my little bee."

I pursed my lips and tilted my head in question. "Whyever not?"

"'Tis messy and insulting, love."

"Insulting?" I frowned. "How could it be insulting?"

"Most men reserve such an act for their mistresses or for a wench at a brothel, not from the woman they want to marry and who will bear their children."

"But how then can you do it to me?"

He shrugged. "'Tis the way of things."

"We shall see, my lord."

"There will be no *seeing*, my lady. But if you would like me to seek my pleasure without spending myself inside you, let me show you?"

I nodded.

He rolled atop me and kissed my lips, the scent of my nether region still fresh on his mouth. But it was not entirely deplorable. In fact, it made me desperate for him. He stroked a lazy path up my legs and pushed my skirts to my hips. Then he entered me swiftly, and the pleasure he'd brought me moments ago returned.

"My lord, you said—"

"Shh . . . love, I will not spend myself inside you."

He pumped slowly in and out, and soon, I cared no longer what he did, but wanted him only to continue to thrust inside me. I was delirious with pleasure, until my body could hold out no longer, and once again, climax consumed me. Above me, Ned's thrusts grew faster and deeper, and then suddenly, he yanked himself from my body, and I watched with wide-eyed wonder as he stroked his member with a swift hand. His eyes connected with mine until he groaned aloud.

"'Tis how it is done, my lady."

I stared in fascination. "I should like to see it done again."

"You are a wanton princess . . ." He wiped his hands on the grass and redressed himself. "I will be glad to do so over and over with you."

"Let us hope the queen's temperament improves soon."

Chapter Seventeen

What grief of mind and torment strong,
she suffered all the while:
Is known to those that bondage feels,
whose friends are in exile.
Could mischief fall on both the sides,
more harder than it did . . .
—*Thomas Churchyard, Elizabethan Soldier and Poet*

AUGUST 16, 1560

Arundel's plans to distract Robert Dudley so he might act upon his suit for the queen went awry, for he had planned a day of riding in the parks. Now, if he had planned something not having to do with horses, or game playing, the day might have turned out quite differently. But alas, he chose for our group to spend several hours coursing over the fields and through the woods on trails laid out for such occasions.

Male and female courtiers mounted, and the queen—who always insisted on mounting herself—sat astride. But as soon as

Elizabeth saw that her dear Robin was missing, she demanded to know of his whereabouts.

As it turned out, a letter telling Dudley he must return to his wife on account of her health had been delivered that morning, and Dudley was now in his room preparing to leave. A touch of conscience perhaps? Or did he hope it was serious enough she might die and he merely needed to see for himself?

In any case, Her Majesty balked at Robert being left behind. She refused to ride without him. He was her Master of the Horse. How could she possibly ride if he wasn't by her side?

Her temper flared, and she demanded that Lord Arundel go to tell Dudley that he was needed upon this ride. When Arundel argued that the man was going to see to his sick wife, Elizabeth snarled, "As far as we are concerned, he hath no wife and is married to this realm as much as your royal sovereign queen!"

Bows were made and apologies murmured, and Dudley came from the house swifter than a man should whose wife perchance laid at death's door. There was no mention of his ailing wife, no condolences from Her Majesty on the matter. She only smiled and laughed as if he'd never been from her side.

I was stunned, to say the least. Did this mean that Elizabeth truly did not recognize Dudley's marriage to Amy Robsart? My heart wrenched for the girl if she were to hear the words the queen had uttered . . . I could not imagine her reaction. If it had been me, I would have sunk to the floor in a pile of tears and wept like a babe.

Ned glanced my way, worry in his expression. We rode with the crowd, and at one moment, he came to my side, his knee brushing mine. His fingers danced over my arm, and he said, "She has the temperament of an injured lion today. We'd best be cautious, else she forbid us from being in the same county."

I nodded for fear of that being the case, but she showed no further temper the rest of the day. In fact, upon our return from riding, the children of St. Paul's presented us with a sweet play, followed by an evening of banqueting. Ned and I danced—and were explicitly encouraged to dance by Elizabeth herself as she laughed and spun round and round in the arms of her Master of the Horse. Was it because she was growing tender to our plight or because she was allowing herself a fleeting fantasy and so encouraged mine? Or did she only toy with us?

After such a show of encouragement, Ned and I resolved to approach Elizabeth as soon as we returned to London. We had to spend the rest of the progress working to get a few council members to back us. I wrote to my mother—asking the rider to deliver my letter posthaste—informing her that upon completion of the progress, I would visit her at Sheen with Ned to discuss what previously had been forestalled.

As I fell asleep that night beside Jane Seymour, who'd come into my chambers and discussed the lively events of the evening until we'd both collapsed, all I could think was that soon, I would finally have permission to marry the man I loved.

Our return to London could not have come soon enough. Whispers at court were already running wild about Ned and I having formed an intimate relationship. Most likely, they'd been started by those within the council who we'd sought out for support. While we both contradicted such rumors, they were ever present, and the only way to quell them was to keep our distance—which neither of us was willing to do. But we did attempt to keep our clandestine meetings in the groves and various hiding spots Jane found for us late at night or early in the morning when court lay in slumber.

LONDON
OCTOBER 1560

We returned to London yestereve amid loud cheers, music, and people throwing flowers upon the procession as Elizabeth's court rode toward Westminster. Our progress was concluded, and Elizabeth was pleased that it appeared she was still beloved by the people.

After breaking our fast and attending the morning prayer service, Ned and I hurried from Westminster to Sheen, Jane and Mrs. Helen in tow.

When we arrived, Master Stokes took us up to my mother's chamber, as she was not well enough to meet us in the great hall. I was shocked by her appearance. Mother was even smaller than when I'd seen her last. She lay shriveled beneath several coverlets, and still her lips were blue and her teeth chattered.

"How long has she been like this?" I asked Master Stokes.

"For several weeks now." He raked a hand through his hair, pain etching his features. "I had thought she would pass for some time, but having received your note, she has hung on tight to this life."

"Katherine," she croaked. "Come here. Let me see you."

I stepped forward in time to hand her a handkerchief to wipe away the blood and sputum on her face as agonizing coughs wrenched her body.

"I have started to write a letter to Her Majesty."

Master Stokes walked to Mother's writing desk and pulled out a piece of parchment. "I've been drawing up the letter a little at a time, as her energy is not so high. She informs Her Majesty"— he glanced down at the paper and read—"the Earl of Hertford doth bear my daughter, Lady Katherine Grey, goodwill. If it pleases Your Majesty, I would beg of you to give consent for them to wed. For such is the only thing I have desired before the hour of my death and should be an occasion to me to die more quietly."

My mother's fingers clasped mine, and she offered a solemn smile. "I should like to see you take your vows, but I fear that knowing you will do so is all I shall realize."

"Mother—"

"Shh . . . Do not say anything. Just be careful. Hertford is a good man. He will do right by you. And he will do right by your daughters."

A single tear fell down her cheek. Her indictment of my late father rang loud and clear in my mind. Should I be blessed with daughters, Ned would not seek to use them for his own gain. But even knowing this, I prayed for sons. Sons would be treated differently. Sons might be stronger.

Ned and I rode back to court with promises from my mother and Master Stokes that she would finish the letter and send it to Her Majesty posthaste. But when we returned, Cecil cornered us outside the stables, leading us both into a darkened corner between the outbuildings.

"You must cease your queries within the council. Your suit will only agitate Her Majesty. She's had a visit from the Swedish ambassador today who has offered Crown Prince Erik's hand in marriage. She is in quite a state. You would do best to wait."

"Pardon, Master Cecil, but we have been waiting for years. When will there ever be a right time to gain Her Majesty's attention on the matter? Lady Katherine is twenty. Is it not time she was married?" Ned argued.

"Lord Hertford, 'tis not for me to decide. I only warn you off because the council members are wary and must concentrate on finding Her Majesty a groom she deems suitable. She appears warm toward Prince Erik, which is a plus, considering her . . . feelings toward another." He did not need to say who that other was, as all the court knew that if she could have, Elizabeth would have married Robert Dudley within seconds, just as they all knew how much Cecil abhorred the idea. "I should have you know that once the queen is settled, you will have my full backing for marriage. Until then—hold off. Keep to yourselves. Rumor at court is that Lady Katherine is already enceinte."

I gasped at his last words, my hands moving to clutch my flat belly. Absolutely not true! And how dare people speak about me in such a way? Then I lied with an ease that scared me, but which seemed necessary in order to save my own life. "Master Cecil! I am a true, pious woman and would never compromise myself with Lord Hertford without the blessing of the Lord our God in the sanctity of holy marriage. You must tamp down this slanderous rumor before the queen gets wind of it! Threaten arrest for anyone who would say such vile things about a virtuous princess of the blood."

"You remind me of your sister Jane when you speak so heatedly about morals and virtues."

Sadness enveloped me at his words.

"I must go, but please heed my warning. I will not be able to save you should you go against Her Majesty. No one will."

With those words spoken, Cecil disappeared into the bustle of the merchants and servants, leaving Ned and me to stare at one another mournfully. Once again, it appeared all of our dreams would be broken.

"I do not care what he says or that the council warns us off," Ned said. "We will speak to her."

OCTOBER 18, 1560

"What?" Queen Elizabeth sputtered, affronted at the request Ned and I had brought before her.

My eyes widened, and I wished to sink beneath the polished wood floor. My heart felt as though it shattered into a million pieces inside my chest and the shards of the broken organ stabbed and sliced at my insides. Beside me, Ned stiffened, and I sensed his pain as his hope for our future too was smashed.

Our mothers had approved of our marriage. Queen Mary had approved of our marriage, but not Queen Elizabeth. She would not allow it. We'd been warned aplenty, and if I was honest with myself, I should have known this would be the outcome, but I'd refused to see it. I'd been blinded by my faith in love and justice. Hadn't life taught me already that those two things would not triumph?

I felt keenly Elizabeth's hatred of me then. Oh, I'd felt it before, but this time, it was immeasurably worse. She held my life in her hands and squeezed her fist so tight I felt I might pop. Her jealousy of one and all who would dare to marry was scorching. As if all we maidens should be virgins just as she supposedly was.

The absurdity of it left me cold. But I thought I knew why she would bring this crushing blow upon us. For now that her Robert was free to remarry—his wife, Amy Robsart Dudley, having been thrown, or thrown herself, down a flight of stairs to her death—marry the queen he could not. The rumor of his involvement in the death of his wife was too strong, and there were too many who opposed her marrying the lowly nobleman. We should have known not to ask her now, but the time for waiting had come to an end for us both.

"How dare you come to me with such a request?" Her eyes narrowed on us as if we had conjured up a plot to ruin her. "And to think I brushed aside the Spanish plot to kidnap you, thinking you were not willing, and now I might contemplate the contrary and yet charge you with treason! I should never have thought to call you daughter. You are no daughter of mine."

I drew in a deep breath, prepared to grovel if need be, for I was desperate for her to give her blessing. "Majesty, we mean no harm. We have been betrothed for several years, and even your dear sister, God rest her soul, did approve of the match. We humbly beseech your blessing and permission to marry."

If possible, her eyes darkened more, reminding me of a soulless retainer I'd once watched beat a man to a pulp at the order of my father. Would she have us beaten? 'Twould have been ridiculous and uncalled for, but she was the queen. She could do as she wished.

"Then why have you not been married before now? Why at this time do you seek to do such a thing? Ironic that you say my sister did approve of the match but yet did not make you wed." She drummed her long, slim fingers against the arm of her presence throne chair. Her gaze darted from one of us to the other, suspicion in her eyes.

"My queen, please accept my apologies for having distressed you. That was not our intent. Prior to now, we had not thought we were ready for marriage, as I was still studying abroad and Lady Katherine, your dear and most loyal cousin"—Ned indicated for me to step forward, which I did—"did not wish to leave you or your sister. Having loved you both so very much, she wanted only to serve you."

"Why have I no word from your mother? She is my cousin, and yet she has not sent word at all. She might abhor the idea as much as I do."

We had no valid answer for her for why we had yet to marry, as in truth, we had hoped to marry much earlier than now, but at every turn, our desires had been thwarted. And we could not tell her that Cecil and her council had advised against it until she married. But I could explain about my mother.

"Her Grace is quite ill, on her deathbed. Her husband, Master Stokes, did read to me from a letter they had been writing to Your Majesty that states her desire for us to wed."

"I have no such letter, and I am well aware of your mother's health." Why had my mother not sent the letter? She had written to say she'd forgiven me. Why should my punishment be prolonged? *Why?* I wanted to ride all the way to Sheen to find out from her own lips.

"I can only hope she sends it to you soon, or perchance you could inform her she must send it?"

The queen laughed at this, a cold and bitter sound. "I do not think so, Lady Katherine. I care not a fig for your mother's desires. She encouraged your sister to usurp my own sister. Why would I listen to a word she utters?"

I bowed my head, blinking to keep my tears at bay. 'Twas no use. Every word I uttered seemed only to make her more angry.

Ned once more attempted to assuage Her Majesty's nerves. "Majesty, we are your most loyal subjects and regret not having brought this matter to your attention before now, and for that we must seek your forgiveness. Neither of us wished to leave your side, wanting to serve you as best we could, and now we hope that with our loyal service, you might have cause to bless us with your approval of our marriage."

The queen's eyes narrowed, her features stern as she further examined the pair of us for several heartbeats. Then she leaned forward and, in a languid tone, said, "You, my Lord Hertford, are good with your words. Let us think on it as if we played a game of shuttlecock."

Ned looked confused and turned, our gazes connecting for a fraction of a second. My bewildered gaze was mirrored in Ned's eyes. What game was this?

The queen sucked in a deep breath as if we had put great strain upon her with our entreaty. She leaned back on her throne, her nails clicking on the wood arms. "I have thought on it a moment. I have decided against giving you permission to marry." Elizabeth's lips curled in satisfaction.

My knees grew weak, my legs like bread dough—spongy, unable to support my weight. How could she deny us with tactless

pleasure—as if she wanted to hurt me? And how would I muster
the fortitude needed to hold my peace?

"My Lord Hertford, you shall go back abroad where you
might study some more the intricacies of court life and relations
between our allies. I shan't want a man in my court who is not fully
educated."

"Majesty—" Ned started, but the queen held up her hand to
stop him from speaking.

"Do not make excuses. Simply kneel." Her voice was icy and
arrogant.

Ned bent down on his knees and remained there, stock-still,
just as he had before when Elizabeth had taken a sword from one
of her yeomen and placed the blade on each of his shoulders, pro-
nouncing him the new Earl of Hertford. But this time, he was not
being elevated. My heart was crushed at her denying our marriage.

He mumbled his thanks for her consideration, and then the
queen waved him away. I stood to follow, desperately wanting to
hold him in my arms. To run away to France with him or elope to
Scotland. Even reinvent the Spanish plot if need be. Anything so
that we might be together.

"Lady Katherine, you are not dismissed," came Elizabeth's
harsh tone.

I stopped dead in my tracks, my skirts swishing against my
ankles. I was unsure of how to react to her tone. My insides warred
between the need to follow Ned and the duty to obey my queen.
Ned turned once, our gazes locking for several crushingly painful
moments.

He dipped his head and smiled sadly, a smile that promised he
would find me later, before he was swarmed by courtiers seeking
news and he was no longer within my sights. Before plans were
finalized for him to go overseas and leave me behind to an uncertain fate.

I turned slowly and approached the queen once more, trying with great difficulty to hide my anger at her decision. My shoulders were straight, chin sturdy, jaw clamped tightly shut, and I refused to cry. I would not let her see the pain she caused me. I could not. For then she would win, and while I'd always played her way, she'd beaten me today with her hatred. She'd shattered my dreams, but I would not concede my tears to her. Those she could not have.

"You shall be married, Cousin." Her words were clipped, and her eyes bored into mine, her essence daring me to deny her.

My voice dripped venom. "I assume since you waited for my betrothed to leave the room before you mentioned it that you have a different groom in mind?"

"Three old shrews deciding the two of you should marry does not a betrothal make."

I blanched and, with stalwart grace, managed not to snarl my reply. "My apologies, Majesty."

Ned and I would never win. She would have her way. She did not want us to marry, due to the justifications Cecil had again repeated about Ned and my marriage being a threat to her own reign—and also due to her jealousy of our love.

"There's a Scots nobleman who is still in need of a wife, and we are in need of peace with the barbarians once again. I will soon make arrangements for you to marry the Earl of Arran. You do recall our previous conversation, do you not? He has been imprisoned in France, hence your not marrying him earlier, but I have it on good authority he is at this moment being reunited with his family. I intend a formal betrothal betwixt you both when all is sorted out."

She'd threatened me with marriage before to the belligerent fool, but nothing had come of it. Now it appeared she would make good on her threat. My only solace was I might still have some time to change her mind.

I bowed my head, but said nothing.

"I have need to quell our dear cousin Mary's rebellion in Scotland. Best to fortify the deal with a marriage. 'Tis how it has always been done."

"As you say, Majesty."

"Look at me, Katherine."

I glanced up into the hard eyes of the queen.

"You are still a virgin?" Her tone was accusatory, as if she did not believe it to be the case.

How could I answer her? If I admitted to no longer being pure, she would toss me in the Tower. If I lied and said I was, and then she found out the truth, I'd be tossed in the Tower. I was damned either way.

I looked back at the floor and said meekly, "Yes, Majesty."

Elizabeth scoffed. "That is not what some courtiers are reporting."

My stomach did a little flip. Several moments passed before I could answer. "You yourself know of rumors that get twisted on the tongues of those who wish to gain favor and power, Majesty."

"Are you saying they lie in order to gain my trust?" Her nails, clicking in a rhythmic pattern on the arm of her chair, quickened their pace.

"Is that not how it has always been?"

"You are more cunning than I gave you credit for, Kitty Kat."

"Thank you, Majesty."

"Do not think flattery will change my mind. You will marry Arran. Remove all thoughts of your lover from your mind, and do not let me see you with him again. Be gone with you."

I barely made it back to my room. Upon my exit from the queen's throne room, where we'd been lucky enough, at least, to meet with her alone, Jane Seymour clasped me about the waist, along with Bess St. Loe. They lent me their strength in walking back to my chamber. I was numb. Completely and utterly numb. My hands shook, my eyes glistened, but other than that, there was no outward appearance that I was disturbed.

"Where is Mrs. Helen?" I asked weakly. "I have a megrim. I need her posset."

Bess went in search of Mrs. Helen, who'd been seen taking some of my gowns out to the laundress to be cleaned.

"What happened?" Jane asked, sitting beside me and taking my hand in hers.

"She has denied us, Jane. She has forbidden us. But what's worse—and my dear sweet Ned does not even know it yet—she is truly forcing me to marry that Scot. She meant it when she threatened me before."

Jane sucked in her breath. "No," she breathed out, "'Tis not possible."

I let the tears come then, sobbing uncontrollably as Jane stroked my hair.

"I love Ned so much, Jane, and she would see me forever steeped in misery. I have done her no wrongs. I have only ever borne her goodwill and charity, and she would seek to stomp on my heart and feed it to her dogs."

At the word dogs, Beau and Arabel trotted toward the bed, jumping up to form a comforting barrier against my back.

"You cannot marry the Scot."

"I have no choice. The only way out would be to take my own life."

"No!" Jane shouted. "'Tis a great sin to take one's own life. You shall never gain God's great reward if you do. And I shall never forgive you, and Ned shall never forgive you."

I shook my head. "I know of no other way."

"Perhaps she was only saying she would marry you to the Earl of Arran to hurt you. She has said much in the past, and it did not come about. And if it should—" She gulped loud enough for me to hear, stroking my hair and wiping my tears with a handkerchief.

"If it should come to pass, at least you have had time with Ned before then, so you might close your eyes and imagine your husband is he."

Footsteps sounded outside my chamber door, and in rushed Mrs. Helen with Bess behind her. Mrs. Helen shooed away Jane and Bess and settled into giving me slow sips of her herbal posset until I fell asleep, pain gone for the moment. But even slipping into oblivion, I knew 'twould not last. My life thus far had been moving from one agony to the next, a few sweet interludes gifted between.

Chapter Eighteen

The one from joy and worldly pomp,
in prison closely hid.
The other forced by fatal chance,
to seek his fortune out:
And shunning danger found despair,
in wandering world about.
—*Thomas Churchyard, Elizabethan Soldier and Poet*

November 4, 1560

"My mother has petitioned the crown to sell off some of her jointure property," I told Jane. "She seeks to leave an inheritance for Mary and me, to pay off some debts and leave her stable boy husband well cared for."

"I thought you were starting to like Master Stokes."

I sighed heavily. "I am. 'Twas un-Christian of me to call him a stable boy."

"He has not been ill toward you, has he?"

"No, unless bid so by my mother," I said, recalling the death of Rex and the way I'd been mortified in front of the nasty merchant.

"Then why are you so overcome with bitterness?"

Leave it to Jane to be so forthright. I set my embroidery hoop on my lap so I would not stab myself. "Her actions mean she does not expect to live."

"Oh," Jane said softly and patted my hand.

"I have yearned, since I was a young child, to be close to my mother. But she's always remained at a distance."

Jane nodded, most likely relating to such feelings with her own mother.

"To know the one thing that she wanted to see before the hour of her death was that I should gain Her Majesty's permission to wed your brother, and that I did not, breaks my heart. If we could not be happy together in this life, I wish that we could have been upon parting."

"Perhaps you can."

"'Tis not possible. I shan't seek out the queen about it again, else she hastens to see me matched to that pugnacious Arran."

Jane frowned and picked up the ruff she was sewing silk edges to, as two other ladies-in-waiting entered the queen's presence chamber. I had once again, for the time being, been ousted from Her Majesty's bedchamber, punishment for daring to find love before she could.

Lady Lettice Knollys and her younger sister, Lady Elizabeth, set themselves up across the room arranging flowers. Jane leaned in close to me. "What if you were to marry my brother? In secret."

"What?" I asked a little too loudly, catching the attention of Lettice and her sister, their burnished red curls bouncing beneath their hoods as they turned.

"Shh . . ." Jane giggled. "I'm certain you do not want *them* to hear."

"What do you mean, in secret?" I whispered from the side of my mouth, pretending to be completely engrossed in the velvet piece I was embroidering as a pillow—a present for Ned come Christmas, so he might always have a piece of me by his side while he slept.

"What if you were to meet Beau at his house on Canon Row and marry? I will bring the priest. You cannot marry another. You've already been unvirtuous with my brother."

Jane's latter words made my stomach plunge. "Unvirtuous? Isn't that a bit harsh, Jane?"

"Well, it may be harsh, Kat, but can you deny it?"

I turned away from her stern gaze. "No, 'tis true."

Jane gave a curt nod and succinctly said, "Then I shall seek out my brother. I would see you wed in truth before the year is out."

My breathing quickened, and I felt I would be sick. To marry without the queen's permission was treason, and I could lose my life for it. But to live without Ned as truly mine would mean the death of my soul.

In a fit of tempter, Elizabeth would most likely toss us both in the Tower, but she might eventually let us go, and then we'd be together. Or she could execute us for treason.

NOVEMBER 20, 1560

I rushed to Sheen, where my sister, Mary, was already in attendance. We held Mother's hands, we kissed her brow, and even though she did not open her eyes, her lips curled into what we discerned as a smile. Her fingers twitched in our grasps, and we knew she was aware of our presence.

A priest stood vigil and whispered prayers.

The dowager duchess, our step-grandmother, arrived late in the evening, and she, too, knelt, reciting prayers.

Master Stokes cried until his eyes were swollen and red.

The following morning, my mother, the great Duchess of Suffolk, princess of the blood, breathed her last. A little knot formed in my throat. But I'd learned a long time ago not to cry when I lost someone. Showing sorrow could lead to someone taking advantage of my pain and weakness.

A letter was sent to the queen, who promptly agreed to pay for the funeral expenses—a parting gift to her cousin who had never sought to personally take the crown from her own hands. I doubted she would do the same for me. She saw me as the enemy, where my mother's marriage to a groom had forever sealed her fate as a noncandidate for the throne. I couldn't help thinking what my life might have been like if I'd done the same. If Ned had been a common man . . . But there was no use thinking on what if.

I recalled little of the funeral ceremony. It was pious, officiated by the new bishop of Salisbury, John Jewel. I was chief mourner, followed by my tiny sister, Mary. We rode in a grand procession that befitted my mother's station through Richmond to Westminster Abbey. After the service, read in English, Mother was buried in St. Edmund's Chapel at the abbey. Mary and I held hands, and I whispered the words that would soon be engraved as her epitaph:

Nor grace, nor splendor, nor royal name,
Nor widespread fame can aught avail;
All, all have vanished here. True worth alone
Survives the funeral pyre and silent tomb.

Mary and I were all that was left now, a sad duo if ever there was one. Two princesses of the blood, one shrunken and ill formed, the other ill fated to love and lose. Truly what had Her Majesty gained in keeping me at arm's length and alone?

Nothing.

When I returned to court, a short note was waiting for me from Ned.

My Dearest Lady,

She stood in black said Troylus he,
That with her look hath wounded me.
She stood in black say I also
That with her eye, hath bred my woe.

Seeing you grieve for your mother has left my heart in pain. I would see you smile again.
Your loyal heart,
Ned

His note settled my misgivings about whether he still thought of me. I wanted to smile. To love. I would take my fate into my own hands. Just as my mother had—perhaps if I could learn one thing from her life, that would be it.

NOVEMBER 29, 1560

A thousand butterflies twisted and turned in my belly. Sweat collected on my brow, and I could not stop fidgeting. I did not recall being this nervous when I'd married Henry, and I had *not* wanted to wed that day.

Today was a day I'd dreamed about. A secret day . . . For there were only four of us who knew so far, and the priest would make five when Jane found him. There was something about it being clandestine that stole my breath away. From the beginning,

Elizabeth had not acknowledged my betrothal to Ned, despite her sister having approved and both of our mothers being pleased for the union. Then again, Queen Elizabeth had also taken away many privileges that Mary had given me. The only thing remaining the same was my being housed at court, my eighty pounds per annum, and that I was sometimes given the privilege, depending on her mood, to be a lady of the bedchamber.

A frown creased my brow, and I pressed it away with my fingertips. Today was not the day to worry over such things, for there was little I could do to control the moods of my sovereign.

I would take for myself what I wanted. I would let happiness into my life and cherish it, even if I had to do so in secret.

A soft knock landed on my door, and I called for the knocker to enter. Jane opened the door a crack, and I beckoned her to come inside.

She stepped in, and I waved away Mrs. Helen, who had fitted my headdress securely with pins and had been putting the finishing touches on my hair. My longtime companion curtsied and left Jane and me in privacy.

"It is done. The queen is headed off to Eltham for the night, and she has excused you for having a toothache and me to take care of you. Truth be told, she did look relieved you would not be accompanying her."

I was too happy to care that Her Majesty did not want me to go. I would be married today!

"You look beautiful, Kat." Jane's eyes shimmered with unshed tears, and she pressed her fingers to her lips. "I cannot believe that, in under an hour, you will be my sister."

I put my arms out, and Jane came forward. We enfolded each other in a sisterly embrace, both of us breathing deeply and blinking rapidly so that tears would not fall. I recalled another Jane whom I'd wished to embrace in similar fashion on my last wedding day, and my eyes stung anew. My late sister would not have approved of Ned's and my marrying in secret. Whose side would she have taken—mine or Elizabeth's?

But I could not think only of my sister and what she would have done. For I'd made that pact five years earlier with myself. And seen it through. My faith was my love, and I had not strayed.

"You have no regrets." Jane's tone revealed this was more of a statement than a question.

"None." I pulled away and let her see the genuine happiness in my smile. "Your brother is the best man I've ever known, and I have prayed night and day that he would become my husband. Today is that day."

"Do you not fear Elizabeth's reaction?" Jane wrinkled her nose.

Not wanting to frighten Jane, I said, "I admit to a bit of fear when she finds out. But we shall keep it quiet for as long as we can. Perhaps, in the meantime, Ned will gain more support from the council, and I can continue my attempts at gaining Elizabeth's approval if not her respect. Perhaps then we may have hopes of her agreeing to a match between him and me."

"She will not like being deceived. I know this was my idea—and really, you have no other choice since the two of you have already . . ."

"I know, and no, she will not be pleased. But there is no other choice. As we speak, Elizabeth is attempting to arrange my marriage to that belligerent Scot. In less than a year, she would have me shipped north. There are worse fates than her wrath."

Jane nodded, her eyes sparkling with pleasure. "You are indeed the perfect match for my brother. Your spirit and tenacity equal his."

"Will your mother be displeased?"

Jane shook her head emphatically. "Who do you suppose gave me the idea of a secret wedding? Now, I must admit she did not mention the two of you, and she did say the queen would never agree and that she would never condone it. Nevertheless, she said something to the effect that two people who love each other, if they cannot get the masses to agree, might marry behind closed doors."

The duchess. She had had to play a part in everything. She was not one to wait around for fate to find her and, instead, had made her own destiny and seen to that of her children. Of course, she would have had to save herself by saying she would never condone such a plan. I wondered if she, too, had grown tired of waiting for us to marry. Nearly seven years had passed since first the topic was broached.

"Come now, soon-to-be Lady Hertford. My brother awaits, and a priest must still be found. All of the servants have been ushered off for the next couple of hours so you might have some privacy."

I felt the heat rise in my cheeks, for I knew the reason for that privacy. We should wed and consummate the union this very afternoon. Then Jane and I would be smuggled back to Her Majesty's court before my absence was questioned.

We pulled on our cloaks, making sure our hoods covered all our hair and faces. Jane threaded my hand through her arm and walked me to the door, opening it to reveal a dark and empty corridor.

I took a deep breath and left my chamber. Several steps down the corridor to the circular stone stair, and then we walked through the palace gardens. The sun was out, but hidden behind clouds. A chill wind swept its way up my skirts to freeze my bare flesh. We had made it this far. I was really going through with the secret wedding. Passing through the orchard, no birds singing us praises, we descended the steps to the river. We walked with hurried steps along the sand as the tide was out, and taking a barge would have only called attention to us. No one must know what we were about, and eyes were everywhere.

My nerves were so frayed I barely felt my slippers sinking into the sand or the slight dampness collecting around my toes. I glanced at the vast gardens of those houses that backed the Thames.

The trees were bare of leaves accept for a few brown hangers-on. The flowerbeds were mostly brownish, too, except for the hedge bushes that kept their vibrant green colors all year round. Did the rotten scents of the Thames reach into those gardens? I crinkled my nose, knowing that if I had been sitting among pretty spring blooms, I wouldn't have wished to smell decaying things.

We made a left onto Canon Row, leaving behind the scent of the butchers' slops and other foul wastes tossed into the Thames. The reality of what was to come struck me suddenly, and I stopped for a moment.

Jane turned and beckoned me farther. "Come. We cannot stop."

I nodded and hurried to catch up.

Our hoods covered our faces, and our cloaks covered our gowns. To those who passed us, we nodded, and our simple coverings let us blend in quite well with the common folk. A few merchants yelled out their wares, and a stray dog jogged alongside us, sniffing at Jane's ankles, but she shooed it away.

Jane stopped in front of an impressive stone house that was three stories high, with beautiful glass windows that reflected the morning light.

"This is Hertford House. Soon to be your house. Are you ready?"

I stared up at the stones, my breath catching with excitement. "Yes." I kept my voice as steady as I could and squared my shoulders. I was more than ready.

Rather than knocking, Jane opened the door herself, and we entered unannounced. Ned waited eagerly in his drawing room. He wore his finest doublet of black velvet, broidered with cloth of gold and crusted with rubies and pearls. Upon seeing me, his eyes lit up, and he stepped forward, taking my hands in his. He smiled widely and pressed his lips to my fingers. "Good morning, wife."

"Not yet," Jane replied. "I shall return momentarily with the priest."

Jane stepped from the room, and we heard the click of the front door close behind her.

Ned chuckled. "She will drag inside the first priest she sees."

"No doubt." I laughed. We were like two giddy children eating comfits without permission.

Ned leaned in and kissed me soundly. "'Twill not be long before I can say I have the right to kiss you thusly."

"And hopefully not much longer before Her Majesty gives us her blessing."

Jane returned with a disheveled priest who looked as if she'd roused him from bed. He held his prayer book in hand and a leg of roasted meat in the other. He looked distracted, nervous.

"I am to wed you, my lord, to this young lady?" The priest examined us both, his vexation apparent. "And 'tis with permission from the crown, I assume. You are not marrying because you have already compromised this gentlewoman, are you?"

We nodded and shook our heads at all of his questions until he was satisfied. Then he tossed his leg of meat to one of Ned's hunting dogs and flipped through the pages of his prayer book. The ceremony was short and sweet, and when over, Jane handed the priest a very large purse filled with coins—obviously his price for performing such a clandestine exchange of vows.

When the priest exited, Jane offered her congratulations and had a couple of the servants who'd returned bring in trays of comfits, meats, and wine. But Ned and I could barely eat a morsel or drink a drop. Our eyes were locked on each other, smiles frozen upon our faces. We'd done it! I was his and he was mine.

"I shall leave you two for a time . . ." Jane continued to speak, but I could not hear what she said.

The moment had come—the time to consummate our marriage. Ned led me to the stairs, and those few servants who had returned early lowered their gazes as we ascended.

When we reached the top of the stairs, Ned gripped my hand in his, and we ran toward his room. He slammed the door behind us, and laughing, kissing, and touching, we hastily disrobed. A small fire crackled in the hearth, emitting the only light, as his shutters were closed and no candles lit. He carried me to the bed and laid me down, a pin from my hood catching on one of the silken pillows—we had not even bothered to remove it!

"I shall make love to my wife in nothing but her stockings and hood. And every time hence, when I look at you with your hood atop your head, I will remember this moment."

"Ned! You are wicked . . . I wear my hood everywhere."

"I know," he said with a wink.

The next several hours were filled with making love on first one side of the bed and then the other, Ned atop me. Then he showed me how to make love astride his hips. Sated and spent, we lay, limbs entwined, my head resting on his shoulder. My fingers danced circles over his chest, and he stroked my back.

"I do believe I shall enjoy being married," I said with a smile.

"Your words wound me, my lady."

"Why?" I asked, propping up on an elbow.

"I should think you find me worthy only in bed."

I let out a lusty laugh. "Well . . ."

"You little tease," he said, pulling me down on top of him for a kiss. "I shall prove to you over the years I am capable of much more than excellent lovemaking."

"And I truly look forward to it," I said seriously. "I will count the moments until we can live truly as man and wife."

Ned kissed me tenderly on the forehead, drawing his thumb over my new wedding ring. "Did you notice your ring, my lady wife?"

I held my hand up for us both to see and studied the gold ring of intertwining circlets. "'Tis beautiful."

"I had it made especially for you. For us. Let me show you." He slipped the ring from my finger and then mesmerized me when he opened the circlets to reveal the lines of verse wound round each ring.

As circles five by art compact show but one ring in sight,
So trust uniteth faithful minds with knot of secret might,
Whose force to break but greedy Death no wight possesseth
*   power,*
As time and sequels well shall prove, my ring can say no more.

Tears came to my eyes. "So beautiful."

"I mean every word, Kat. I love you deeply, and now that you are truly mine, I shall not let anyone tear us apart."

"I love you, too, my sweet Ned."

We lay in the silent glow of our emotions for some time, drifting in and out of light slumber. Ned's voice broke our reverie. "I hate for us to part, but the hour grows late, and if you do not return to the palace soon, your absence will be noted."

"Mrs. Helen said she'd hold them off, but you are right. She cannot do so forever."

DECEMBER 15, 1560

"Lady Katherine, I should like to read your fortune. Let me see your hand," Blanche Parry said. The ladies of the bedchamber and several council members lounged in the queen's presence chamber, whiling away the afternoon. Blanche was fond of telling fortunes, and she'd already told those of Lady Fiennes de Clinton, Bess St. Loe, and Her Majesty.

I laughed a little and took her hand. Over her shoulder, I spied Cecil, who stared at me intently. He'd come to me that morning, as I'd expected, as he'd approached Ned the day before, asking again about our relationship. Ned had denied his concerns. But still Cecil had approached me and said in serious tones that he adamantly advised me to beware of keeping company with Ned. We were wed just over two weeks and yet a secret.

I turned my gaze from Cecil as if I had not seen him standing there watching me and smiled at Blanche. How like the man to spoil our fun.

"Tell me my fortune. I do so want to know." I held out my hands palms up, and Blanche ran her fingers over their surface.

"There are many things I see here," she whispered. Then suddenly, Blanche pulled her hands away and looked up in horror, her eyes wide.

I narrowed my gaze and glanced up at Cecil. I looked toward Queen Elizabeth, who occupied herself with chatting with Robert Dudley, thank goodness.

"Your palms say, Lady Katherine, that if you should marry without Her Majesty's permission in writing, you and your husband will be undone and your fate worse than that of your sister Jane."

I stood abruptly, upsetting a dog that lounged behind my chair. I had thought Blanche a friend, but it appeared I was wrong. "How dare you say such a thing to me?" I responded in an acid whisper. "How dare you speak my sister's name? You are no fortune-teller. Only a licentious, slandering viper. There are far more unseemly relations at this court. I expect an apology for such abominable words!"

Several eyes moved to the queen and Robert, firmly grasping my meaning. No one spoke. Did they all suspect Ned and I were married? It was clear they suspected at least we planned to be.

Queen Elizabeth swiveled toward our group, her eyes spearing me with daggers. "What is amiss?"

"Nothing, Majesty," I said, more sternly than needed.

"Did you not like the fortune Blanche read for you?" The queen left Robert's side and came to stand before us. "What was it?"

My eyes flashed to Blanche's, imploring her with my gaze not to say anything. I could barely breathe. Was everything to fall apart right now?

"I believe she suggested to Lady Katherine that her marriage to Lord Arran would be fruitful," Cecil interjected before Blanche could answer.

Several courtiers tittered and nodded. Blanche's face paled considerably, and she swallowed hard. "I meant no offense," she muttered.

Queen Elizabeth laughed. "I can see why Lady Katherine would be so offended, since she is hardly grateful for my choice of her mate."

I felt faint, as if I might collapse on the floor within moments if I could not escape the venomous pit. "Majesty, I beg of you to excuse me to my chambers."

She waved me away as if I were a fly she would squash. By the time I made it to my chambers, Ned was there, waiting. "Word travels fast," I grumbled.

"Never faster than at court." He laughed. "Let me pour you a glass of wine."

I nodded, leaning against his arm, and we entered my chamber, sending away the servants.

"I'll be right outside the door should you have need of anything," Mrs. Helen said quietly. I was grateful for her diligence since, at that moment, I couldn't have cared less if someone were to burst through the door. I reached up and fingered the gold chain with my wedding ring on it, buried safely beneath my bodice.

Ned handed me a cup of wine, then walked behind me to rub my shoulders and kiss my neck. I reached up and held his hand in mine. Ned was my rock. If it weren't for him, I wasn't sure I could have gone on at this vicious court with my head held high, feeling I had no friends other than his sister, Jane.

Then he made me feel loved all the more when he carried me to bed in the broad daylight—though we did not completely throw caution to the wind, for we'd both decided that a pregnancy would do nothing to further our cause and would only further infuriate our volatile monarch.

Chapter Nineteen

But weighing well a subject's state,
and what was duties bounds:
He yielded straight to open harms,
for fear of secret wounds.
And venturing life, yea lands and goods,
to keep his name from blot . . .
—*Thomas Churchyard, Elizabethan Soldier and Poet*

FEBRUARY 13, 1561

A second month had passed that I'd deceived the keepers of my linens . . .

I poured a few drops from a vial of deer's blood onto my sheets and smeared it on my chemise, then stripped the wretched fabric from my body, bundling it up and tossing it on the bed.

The vial, which Jane had managed to smuggle to me from only God knew where, had prevented suspicion about what I was nearly certain was my current state.

I was with child.

I wanted to be happy. I wanted to bear Ned an heir.

But if the queen found out, I would be tossed in the Tower, Ned as well, and our child most likely murdered after he took his first breath—or before.

I dropped to my knees and prayed, naked and shaking upon the cold stone floor.

MARCH 30, 1561

Whispers sounded around me. They gave off an eerie hiss, and I felt as though I must be dead.

But I couldn't have been dead. Dead people did not feel pain. My pain was deep, and it wrenched my insides. My head felt as though an executioner had taken off the top but hadn't finished the job. Indeed, my entire being felt as though I'd spent the last sennight in a torture chamber in the bowels of the Tower of London.

But 'twas not that.

My heart ached with a pain more fierce than when I'd lost my mother, my father, or my sister.

My dear, sweet Jane Seymour had died.

Just a week past, she had been well and merry, guarding my chamber door when Ned and I were alone. Sharing secrets with me in the gardens and prolifically writing letters to her two sisters.

Now she was dead, finally succumbing to the illness that she'd slowly wasted away from over the years.

The only witness to Ned's and my marriage, for none of us knew who that priest was, and should I ever have seen him again, I did not know that I would recognize him. The queen would have no reason to believe us now.

I placed a protective hand over the small knot in my abdomen.

I did not want to ever leave this darkened chamber, the comfort of my counterpane pulled up around my shoulders.

But I should have to rise in a couple of days for Jane's funeral procession. The queen had promised a funeral befitting Jane's royal deference, and she would be buried beside my own mother in St. Edmund's at Westminster Abbey. Ned had already commissioned a lovely monument for her body.

But for now, I mourned, curled into a ball beneath my coverlets and refusing to come out. Not until I must.

MID-APRIL 1561

"I will not leave you, Kat." Ned paced the orchard, the trees and flowers just starting to bloom and filling the air with succulent scents.

"You must, Ned. The queen has arranged for your trip abroad. Many courts are awaiting your arrival. She demands you go. You must do her bidding. You shall see the world and return to me a man with much education." I smiled, trying to ease the tension.

"But you may be with child, Kat. God knows we were not overly careful, and we've carried on like a couple of sensual halfwits."

His words stung, however true they were. We'd succumbed to passion and foregone caution only one time. It did appear that once was all it took.

I gritted my teeth a moment and then lied. "I have no way to be certain if there is a babe within my womb, Ned. I desire for you to go abroad. I shall be fine, and if it comes to pass that I am with child, I will send word straightaway."

With Elizabeth's current state of mind, we'd both see the scaffold before the end of the day if I told him the truth, for Ned would not leave me to bear the lion cub's wrath alone.

He swiped a hand down over his face. "But what of the queen?"

"There is no remedy for her ill will toward me, Ned. We shall have to pray for Her Majesty's mercy if it comes to that."

Which it would, and I was in no way ready to face her.

"I only wish you could say precisely whether you are with child, then I would not depart this realm for anything. I would stay with you, Kat. You should not have to go through with it alone."

Did he realize the accuracy of his words? I was truly alone now. My dearest friend and confidante gone, my mother gone. My sister Jane gone. My sister Mary . . . remained deeply cold toward me. I could not count on her council, as she kept to herself—self-preservation having kept her well away from court since she was a child.

"I cannot, Ned."

He sighed loudly, raked his hands through his hair, and then placed his hands on his hips.

"Then I should go, wife. The queen bids me visit other courts to gain knowledge and better serve her on my return. I cannot refuse to go unless you are certain of your state."

'Twas insanity that I should be in this predicament, but I could not bid him to stay and invite the queen's wrath. Perhaps once he was abroad, I could meet him and give birth in secret. I'd heard rumors of ladies doing this before.

"I agree, you must go."

He came to stand near me, taking one of my hands in his. He kissed me gently on the fingertips. "I will not tarry long from you."

But I already knew he would be gone for some time, perhaps a year or more. Cecil once more had come to see me to insist that Ned should leave. He believed that once Ned was out of sight and obediently doing her bidding, the queen would grow more fond of him. And once more, Cecil warned against our relationship.

I did not know what I should do. I'd even been too afraid to tell Mrs. Helen, and I'd continued to use the vial of deer's blood, but it would soon be gone.

"I have written this for you, for your protection." He handed me a rolled and sealed parchment, his crest stamped in the wax.

"What is it?" I gripped the smooth parchment in my hands.

"It is a jointure for you, Kat. It states that, as my lawfully wedded wife, you are entitled to all of my lands should something happen to me while I am abroad. And take this, too."

He reached inside of his doublet and handed me a heavy velvet purse. "'Tis enough to last you for a time. If you should need more, simply write to my steward and ask him to send it. I have informed him he must deliver to you whatever you need."

I nodded, feeling a small pinch in my heart. He'd made a good effort to pretend he did not want to go abroad, but it was now obvious he had planned to do so all along. But how could I hold it against him? Cecil was a very convincing man. He was also a threat, and Ned most likely felt he had no other choice but to do the queen's bidding. I almost laughed aloud. Whom was I fooling? The queen always got her way. There *was* no other choice. He would go, and I would wish him well. And I would not bother asking him to write to me often. We'd traveled down this path before, and asking for an empty promise would only set me up for heartache.

I lifted my chin and swallowed hard. "Thank you."

"You do not have to thank me for doing my duty."

I nodded, biting my lip. "Return to me, Ned."

"Oh, Kat," he said, true regret shining in his eyes. "Would that I could stay by your side forever." He came forward then, without a care for who might have been spying in a nearby hedge, pulled me into his embrace, and kissed me.

MAY 13, 1561

"My lady." Mrs. Helen stepped into my chamber and startled me enough that I shrieked.

The clock had long since struck the midnight hour, for which I had waited before arising and lighting a single candle to work by. Ned had been gone for a little over a week and should by now have arrived in Paris.

My fingers were covered in pinpricks.

"Mrs. Helen, what is it?" I looked behind her, worried that something horrible had happened and someone other than she had brought news.

"There is no one here but me." She stepped inside and closed the door.

"What is it, then?" I said, irritated that she'd interrupted me.

I could work on letting out my dresses only when no one would see. And 'twas hard work. I would be doing it for several more months, and soon, I would have to somehow figure a way to add another panel in the underskirt. Luckily, split overskirts was a popular style at court and left more room for my growing belly.

Her gaze went to the gown in my lap, then flicked up to meet mine, lines of worry etched on her brow. "What are you about, Kat?"

"Nothing." I did not answer to her. I was her mistress, not the other way around.

"Might I speak freely then, as I always have in the past?"

I sucked in a deep, cleansing breath and let it out slowly. "Hurry through it, Mrs. Helen."

"You are letting out your gowns at night?"

"'Tis none of your business."

"You are with child."

I narrowed my eyes. My stomach clenched. Had the gowns given it away, or was it obvious in other ways?

Mrs. Helen had been the only person I'd ever been able to trust completely. I could trust her in this, too.

"My lady, please. I have known you since you slipped into the world. I was outside the door when you entertained your husband. Let me help you."

I put my sewing down in my lap and covered my face, rubbing my eyes.

"Yes, Mrs. Helen, I do believe I am with child."

"How far along do you suspect?"

"Three or four months."

"But, my lady, your courses. I've seen the sheets."

"Deer blood, Mrs. Helen."

"Oh," she breathed, her eyes wide with terror, no doubt picturing me upon the scaffold as I, too, pictured myself.

"Are you here to assist, or will you weep in the corner?"

"Oh, no, I will help you, my lady." Mrs. Helen pulled up a chair and took the gown, needle, and thread from my lap. "You'll lose your fingers if you keep up with that. Now go back to bed."

I stood up and kissed Mrs. Helen on the cheek. "I am grateful for such a one as you."

"You've long been like my very own. Now to bed with you."

I crept back beneath the covers as Mrs. Helen bent to the task of letting out my gown. When I awoke the next morning, Mrs. Helen had deep-purple bags beneath her eyes, but every one of my gowns was let out, and I could choose between them all for comfort.

Summer Progress
August 11, 1561

Every muscle, joint, bone, even my very flesh ached. A woman in her eighth month of pregnancy, as I determined I must be, should not be riding a horse as vigorously as I had been for the past two months on progress with the queen. Though there had been rumors regarding my situation, none had confirmed it—nor approached me. With the help of tight stays and loose overgowns hiding my waist, I managed to keep from showing my swollen belly. I'd had good luck, thank God, to carry deep and, as such, didn't show as much as some women did throughout their pregnancy.

But it was becoming harder to breathe with tightened corsetry, and riding was becoming downright dangerous. I requested to speak with Her Majesty in private, but she denied me repeatedly, and so finally, I sent her a note.

> *Your Majesty, Queen Elizabeth,*
>
> *I beg of you to let me stay behind and not travel on with court when we should leave in two days' time. I am not well and suffer from fevers, aches, and other more unfortunate bouts of unpleasantness. My physician feels I should take my rest here. I will be glad to join you once I am recovered.*
>
> *Your most loyal subject,*
> *Lady Katherine*

Her reply came only a couple of hours later, written in her secretary's hand, although signed by Her Majesty.

> *Lady Katherine,*
>
> *As Queen of England, we bid you remain on progress with the rest of the court. We will not waver in our decision, as we believe your illness is of your own doing. See that you take these two days to recover your strength.*
>
> *Signed,*
> *Queen Elizabeth of England*

She knew. She must have known for her to deny me comfort, and to state my illness was of my own cause. I was beside myself. I could not go on much longer. I felt as though the horse dragged me behind his rump on the rocky ground rather than me riding upon his back. And my belly . . . oh, how my skin strained to fit over this child.

I lay down in the bed provided for me at Christchurch Mansion in Ipswich and shuddered a sigh. Mrs. Helen came in with food, but I waved her away, certain it would hurt too much to chew.

"Come now, you must eat, my lady."

I shook my head, turning into the pillow and smelling the scent of the soap used to wash the linens. "I cannot."

"'Tis not good for the babe if you starve yourself."

I closed my eyes, hoping Mrs. Helen would just go and leave me in my misery.

"You cannot go on like this, sweet child." I felt the bed dip as she sat beside me. "Someone is going to notice soon. Have you any plans?"

"I have written to Ned, begging him to return, telling him that I am in great need of his assistance, and my letters go unanswered. He has sent reports to Cecil, so I know he writes. He has sent jewels to the queen. A few baubles have come my way, but no words of comfort or guidance. He is not coming home. Why must he forsake me?"

"Oh, my lady," Mrs. Helen said, stroking my brow and coaxing me to sit upright. "He has not forsaken you. 'Haps he is on his way already. We cannot know his plans. He may have thought it too dangerous to send you a note, thinking it might give away your condition."

I pursed my lips. "I do not think so. My own letters gave away my condition. My belly swells from guilty actions, and without witness to a valid marriage, my babe will be born a bastard in the eyes of the court." Angry tears slipped down my cheeks. "My husband, whom I cannot prove to truly exist, is gone away. The babe will surely come before his return."

"Have you thought about going abroad or into the country for a time?" She spooned a bit of stew into my mouth and broke off a piece of bread for me to nibble on.

"I have, but the queen will never allow it. She will not even allow me a few extra days of rest. She has guessed at my condition. She keeps me close to humiliate me. People whisper when I walk by. They call me a whore. Every nobleman talks of my indiscretions with Ned—I am certain that all know of mine and Hertford's affair. Anyone who claims me as an enemy, who was threatened by my family, will tell the queen. I am doomed, Mrs. Helen. Now leave me."

Mrs. Helen took away the tray of food, which was empty—to my surprise, since I'd barely realized I'd consumed it. I was glad for the solitude. I had much to plan. I should rest a few days and then seek guidance from friends at court. Bess St. Loe was once close to my mother. Perhaps she could advise me. Then there was Robert Dudley as well. As much as I abhorred the man, he was once my brother-by-marriage through my sister Jane's marriage to his brother Guildford. Would he not take pity on me, remember our lost siblings? Since he was close to the queen, perhaps he would make a plea for mercy? I would have to trust in God and the assistance of these people. There was no other way. The babe would be here soon. As if to express that point, the child kicked hard at my ribs.

I pressed a soothing hand over my belly, feeling the little feet and hands as the child moved with vigor. He would be an active one. What little joy I found for the moment was fleeting.

I could not allow the queen to name him a bastard.

AUGUST 13, 1561

"Bess!" I hissed in a whisper.

Bess lifted her head from her pillow and turned to stare at me with squinted eyes. I held the candle up to my face so she could see me better. She frowned, her eyes drawn to my rounded belly, made obvious without my stays.

"Kat?"

The fact that she'd used my nickname made me smile. I thought I had chosen the right person to confess to.

"Yes. I must speak with you."

"Come in then." Bess sat up and fluffed her pillow and patted the bed beside her.

I padded into the room in my slippers, nightgown, and robe and set the candle on the bedside table before climbing in next to her.

"What is it, Kat?" Bess's brows drew together, and she looked concerned. Her throat bobbed as she swallowed as if expecting grave news—and what I had to tell her was grave indeed.

In hushed tones, I told Bess everything. "What should I do?"

Bess's hands came to her chest, and her mouth fell open and closed like a fish out of water. The look of horror on her face was profound. Then she burst into tears.

"I had hoped it wasn't true! You understand you have committed treason! Why did you not accept the queen's denial? Nor made her privy when the deed was done and child planted? Oh, for the love of God, you will be the undoing of us all!" She shook her head, and I saw in that instant that Bess did not care so much for my well-being as I'd thought. She was only concerned that her name would become aligned with mine and soon be dragged through the mud of slander. "You were warned. And by so many. All of us beseeched you to remain chaste. We told you of our concerns about your relationship with Hertford. How could you be so reckless?"

"We love each other."

"'Tis madness. Go! You must away from my room." She jumped from bed, tears streaming down her face, and shooed me out.

I, too, burst into tears, now completely helpless. "Do you not know I am filled with horror? With fear that I should be in this alone, with my husband so far and the queen's dislike of me known in every corner of the realm? What is to become of me, Bess? I should die like my sister!"

Bess's gaze caught mine, stricken. "I will speak with my husband. Mayhap he knows better than I."

But the next morning at chapel, it appeared the only thing her husband knew best to do was tell the whole of court. Everyone whispered behind hands, eschewing me as though I had the plague.

Even Bess. She walked right past, her nose in the air. Betrayal had never felt so keen.

I begged leave of the court and stayed in my chamber the rest of the day, praying for mercy and writing an urgent letter to Ned that all had become known. When night fell, once more, I left my chamber in search of an ally. This time, Robert Dudley. I did not knock, knowing instinctively he would not agree to see me. Instead, I bribed his guards to let me in, and the two men gave me leering smiles.

I ignored them and entered, finding Robert reading in his window seat, still full dressed, and his legs propped up casually. He startled when he saw me.

"Lady Katherine! What are you doing in my chambers?" He glanced behind me as if expecting someone else to be there.

I rushed forward and dropped to my knees in front of him, tears of despair streaming down my face. "Please, my lord, I beg of you, as my brother-by-marriage, on the souls of our two siblings, that you present my confession to the queen and beg her for mercy and forgiveness."

He slammed closed his book and tossed it aside. "Madam, rise! What is this you speak of?" Robert stood and helped me to a chair.

I let spill the same story I'd told Bess and, to my dismay, was given the same response.

He jumped from his chair and pointed toward the door. "I'd heard rumors of this . . . The whole of court is wondering of it. Leave! Lest they think I am the father!"

"But, my lord, please, you must help me, being that you are in great favor with Her Majesty!"

Robert swiped his hand over his face, jumping when a log snapped in his hearth. "I shall speak to her on the morrow. Now get you gone. Go!"

I hastened from his room, feeling ashamed and frightened. I almost did not go back to my own rooms. I wanted to run away. But to where could I run? I slunk back to my bedchamber and crawled between the sheets, but sleep did not come. Tomorrow, my fate would be decided.

So many years ago, I had lain in bed with fear of arrest when Queen Mary had come to take her crown and, in so doing, had arrested my sister. I felt the same now, so young and naïve, and once more, here I lay in fear of arrest. And this time, it was my own doing. Reckless emotion governed my life.

A loud banging came at the door, and I closed my eyes, willing it away.

"My lady!" Mrs. Helen said, fear filling her eyes, for she, too, had been expecting this moment.

"Let them in, Mrs. Helen."

I stood from my bed, slipped my feet into slippers and pulled on my robe. At least I would be taken away partially dressed. The queen's guard filed into the room. Sir William St. Loe—Bess's husband—came to stand before me, unraveling a parchment.

"Lady Katherine, you are hereby arrested in the name of Her Majesty, Queen Elizabeth I of England, and charged with treason."

I stood tall, my chin lifted, one hand on my belly. "I have committed no treason."

"You have unlawfully wed, conceived a child, and plotted against Her Majesty to overtake her throne."

I gasped. "I have done no such thing!"

Sir William glanced at my large, obviously pregnant belly and raised a brow.

My chin rose higher. "I have never plotted against Her Majesty. I confess I have loved and wed without Her Majesty's permission. But the child growing inside me was conceived lawfully in the eyes of God."

"We shall see. You are to be given no manner of favor. Let us go quietly to the Tower."

Two guards stepped forward, one on either side, and gripped my arms. I was surrounded by an armed guard as if they expected I, a slight, heavily pregnant woman, would fight them.

"I am perfectly capable of walking on my own."

"Queen's orders," Sir William responded.

"Oh, have mercy on a princess of the blood! Let her go fully dressed, sirs!" Mrs. Helen shouted.

They allowed me only a few minutes to dress, and they did not leave the room, but stood guard in case I decided to place any weapons on my person.

"What of my maid?"

"She will follow with your things and other tirewomen."

I swallowed hard. So Elizabeth would have me go completely alone. But at least my solitude would not last long.

They said no more but marched me through the palace and gardens to a waiting wagon and horses that would take us to London. The long, windy, bumpy road jostled me relentlessly. I clenched every muscle to keep from falling over. Several times, I feared flying out of the wagon. There was no covering, and dust, rocks, and bugs collected en masse upon my face, hair, and gown. No matter how much I attempted to wipe the debris away, more collected.

As we passed a creek, my bladder screamed for relief, and my flesh yearned to be washed.

I mustered up the strength and tried to speak. The first words came out a croak, my throat was so dry from lack of drink. No favor had been granted me indeed. I cleared my throat and licked my lips. "I must stop."

One of the guards riding in the back of the wagon grunted, not even bothering to look. "No stopping."

I squared my shoulders and glared, willing him to meet my eye. "It is not a request."

His eyes rolled, then he shouted to the wagon driver. "Lady needs to take a piss!"

The other guards laughed, and heat flamed my face. How dare they treat me this way? My own cousin was the Queen of England, and I a princess of the blood! But to them, I was only a prisoner. I'd be lucky to make it to London in one piece.

They pulled the wagon to the side of the road, and only after I awkwardly tried to dismount from the back of the wagon did the lead guard offer me assistance.

"Thank you."

He did not respond, only held on to my elbow and led me toward a cluster of trees.

"Some privacy, if you will."

"No, my lady. Best to get it done quickly." He boldly watched me as I wobbled on unstable legs, trying to squat, skirts bunched up around my knees.

Angry tears threatened to spill. I wanted to pick up a sharp rock and hit him on the head with it. When I finished, and somehow managed to stand, I held my head high and swept past him, intent on reaching the embankment.

"Where are you going? Back in the wagon," the guard ordered.

"I need some water."

He huffed and grumbled but did allow me half a minute to splash water on my face and take a sip before yanking me up and lifting me back into the wagon. "We won't be stopping again."

True to his word, we did not stop again, and it actually felt as though the men drove faster, rougher than before. My limbs screamed for a soft mattress, and my throat burned, it was so parched. When we reached London, they forcefully pulled me to the ground, amid crowds of jeering people. The mobs did not know me from any other prisoner, and my once-well-tailored gown was covered in dirt and torn in places where it had caught on the wagon.

I closed my eyes, wondering if this was how my sister Jane had felt. Was I following in her footsteps after all? We boarded a moored barge for our final leg of the trip: a short ride down the Thames to the Tower. The guards made me stand so that all along the banks could see me. I stared straight ahead, refusing to be cowed. But then the Tower came into view.

The imposing white walls loomed up into the sky, the four corners of the towers each topped with a metal spire stabbing the clouds. For the space of a moment, my heart stopped beating.

I swallowed hard, a solid rock of nausea forming in my belly. I had not been back to the Tower since Jane was imprisoned there. The barge slowed to a pace so lagging we could have been moored. Ages seemed to pass before we pulled into the gate. *Traitors' Gate.* A name so aptly picked for those who normally traversed its opening. Traitors. But I was no traitor! I'd fallen in love, married, become with child, and my queen sought to punish me for it. In her mind, I had betrayed her. Betrayed her morals, her wants, her desires. Loved when she could not, and for that reason, I was a traitor.

The barge pulled up to the quay, and several guards marched up. They took me by the arms, and every muscle screamed as I hobbled up the stairs. By the time we entered the courtyard, the Lieutenant of the Tower, Sir Edward Warner, greeted me kindly, taking my hands in his. He did not seem to notice that my clothes and skin were covered in a film of dirt. As if to complete my humiliation, my belly growled for sustenance.

"'Tis a pleasure to make your acquaintance, Lady Katherine. I only wish it were under different circumstances."

I nodded, unable to speak from my parched throat. The Lieutenant waved over a guard and grabbed a tankard from him, bringing it to my lips. I swallowed heavily of the brew, even though its strength on a normal day would have made me wince.

"Thank you," I murmured.

"I shall see to it you are properly cared for, my lady. We have contrived to make your room as pleasant as possible with a few relics you might appreciate. We have placed a few tapestries on the stone walls, one sewn by your cousin, our late Queen Mary, God rest her soul. There is also a bedstead covered with a red and gold quilt, which should please your ladyship. A crimson velvet chair to rest your bones and two green footstools that your great-uncle Henry VIII used to rest his feet upon."

It sounded heavenly, but I was so exhausted and filled with fear that I could barely nod my head in thanks that he'd bravely overlooked the decree I be shown no favors.

"What of the queen?" I asked.

"She will continue on her progress while we question you and Lady St. Loe. Lord Hertford has been recalled immediately to court."

"Lady St. Loe?"

"She, too, has been arrested."

Oh, what horror was this? Had Sir William taken pleasure in arresting me since his own wife had been taken to the Tower as well? "May I send a letter?"

"I will have to read the letter, my lady."

I did not want him to read the letter. I wanted to write to Ned and tell him to stay away from court as long as possible since his arrest would be imminent. That I had been thrown into the Tower. What I could not write was that I feared our child, whom we had created with so much love, would be born behind these prison walls and perhaps named a bastard if the queen sought to dissolve our marriage. I wanted my letter to arrive before his recall from the queen, so he had warning. Despite the lack of response from Ned when I'd written of my troubles, I still loved him. He was still my husband, and we were still going to have a child. If it went out now, my note should arrive right on the heels of the queen's summons.

"Sir Edward. I beseech you . . ." I trailed off, swallowing my pride.

"Lady Katherine, I harbor you no ill will. I will send one letter for you without reading it. But one only," he whispered.

My shoulders sagged with relief. He would not make me beg. I wanted to hug the Lieutenant and fall down sobbing all at once.

"Your women should be arriving soon, my lady, and I have given them permission to collect your pets."

I gave him a wan smile. At least I would have the comfort of my ever-loving animals.

Chapter Twenty

And to requite with hazards hard,
the love that he had got.
From Spain with speed he did return,
and setting foot on land:
He put his cause in justice doom,
and noble Prince's hand.
—*Thomas Churchyard, Elizabethan Soldier and Poet*

AUGUST 22, 1561

They questioned me repeatedly, but I had only the same answers to give. What did they want from me? I did not know, but I refused to give in. I would say as little as possible. I would maintain my innocence of any plots.

I had already been tried and judged and found guilty in the mind of the queen, who was as harsh as her father. The questioning was simply a formality. Or perhaps they were waiting so they would not be committing murder of the child within my womb when my own death was ordered.

I could only pray Ned stayed away from this place.

SEPTEMBER 5, 1561

Posies. And a note.

> *My darling wife,*
> *I have tried for long to stay away as you wished, but I found I could no longer let you suffer alone. I am here within these Tower walls and wish I could be within your arms. My jailers will not let me come to you now, but I have a feeling I shall see you quite soon. I must beg your forgiveness for having left you within the horror of this realm and the awfulness that is your situation. You must think me an abysmal husband, and I fear I will seek your forgiveness until my dying day. Might I dare ask you to show me mercy when none was shown for you by those of this court?*
> *A loving, remorseful husband*

I held his letter to my heart and cried all the more. It would seem as I neared the end of my pregnancy I was forever in tears. Since the queen would have me stay here forever, as she had told all and sundry, I did not often have cause to rejoice.

But rejoice in his letter, I did.

> *My loving husband,*
> *I forgive you, my sweet darling. I confess to feeling anger toward you while you were away, for not writing to me, for not returning to me, but in truth, I could have asked you to stay, told you the truth of my situation, and we could have risked her wrath all those months ago instead of dragging it out. But to*

dwell in should-haves and would-haves will get us nowhere. All
we can do is pray for mercy. I hope to see you soon. I pray you
are allowed to visit me. It has been too long.
   Loyal heart

But no visits were allowed, only the passing of our honeyed
words back and forth. And Ned's shocking and heart-wrenching
report that he'd received none of my letters while abroad. In my
naïveté, I'd not once thought that my letters had never been delivered. Read, perhaps, and so I'd not quite come out to say anything
that could have been used against me. But stolen—destroyed—this
was different. Love and my belief that Elizabeth would one day see
me as I was, and not as her enemy, had left me vulnerable. I knew
who held those letters in her possession, knew all of my secrets,
and toyed with me.
   The queen.

SEPTEMBER 21, 1561

Unbearable, searing fire burned its way from the middle of my
back to my abdomen and then radiated down my legs. "Oh, God,"
I whispered, sitting straight up in bed, sweat drenching my body
and causing my linen night rail to cling to my limbs. "Have mercy."
   I looked about frantically, clutching my belly and panting at
the pain. The room was dark. Not even shadows were visible, as
my maids had closed the window drapes tight, and not a candle nor any embers in the fire burned. I listened intently for any
movement within my room. Had I been stabbed in the belly? Had
someone come to kill me and my child, knowing we were a threat
to the queen's realm? I could hear nothing. Not even Mrs. Helen's
habitual snoring.

I felt as though my insides were shredding. I slid a hand over my very rounded belly to the place between my legs. Sticky, warm wetness met my fingertips. Blood?

Panic surged through me, and I scooted forward, trying to ignore the pain, and somehow managed to move my legs over the side of the bed. Another wave rocked me, and I rolled back on the bed, my legs coming up until I curled in a fetal position, rocking back and forth.

"My baby!" I was surely dying, and the babe would die, too!

I groaned, my head falling back to hit the headboard painfully.

"Help me!" Tears burned a trail down my cheeks, and then, just as suddenly as the pain had arrived, it eased. Still, no sounds came from me. Would no one come to my aid?

"Mrs. Helen!" I shouted. My throat clenched tight, felt dry, and my voice, although I shouted in my head, came out in a hoarse whisper.

I sat up, and my fingers fumbling on the table beside my bed, I came in contact with a candlestick. With all the force I could muster, I hurled the candlestick. A second later, a loud crash sounded and then the yelping of my dogs as they called out in alarm.

"My lady!" Mrs. Helen's voice was loud and filled with concern, cutting through the terrifying silence.

I heard her and my maid Alice rustling in their bedclothes. I fell back again, my arm flung over my forehead, clutching my belly as once more pain ripped me apart. Someone struck a flint, and light shone red behind my eyelids, but I could not open them. Could not bear to see the world and the blood I was sure soaked my entire night rail. Death was upon me. The heir I'd so wanted to grace my husband with would be gone forever.

The child wouldn't even have a chance to breathe the putrid, suffocating air of the Tower. He would be called to heaven, and yet my body would birth him anyway, making me bear the pain of such an ordeal and not even gain the fruits of it.

"My lady—" Alice gasped with shock.

"You are soaking wet, my child." Mrs. Helen's voice was calm and soothing, like she'd taken her soft, wrinkled, old hand and stroked it over my nerves. "Get her a cool cloth," she barked to Alice.

I tried to sit up, as once again the pain had abated, and Mrs. Helen shifted me back toward my pillows, fluffing them behind my head. She brought a cool metal cup to my lips, and I drank greedily, letting the watered ale dribble down my chin. Alice came toward the other side, sitting on the bed, and wiped a cool cloth over my forehead.

"Mrs. Helen. The babe. I am dying. It is dying." My voice shook, but I needed her to know. "Get the priest."

Mrs. Helen only smiled and insisted on me taking another sip of ale.

"Did you hear me, woman? We need a pries—" My words were cut short by another bout of searing pain.

I shouted out, my head falling back, and I gripped my belly tight, my legs coming up. "Jesu, have mercy on me!"

"Oh, love, shh . . . Breathe easy now. Breathe . . . ," Mrs. Helen urged. "Baby is fine. Mama is fine."

The woman must have been insane. I was not fine! I was bleeding—gushing blood! The baby, the pain! 'Twas not normal!

When the pain passed, I opened my eyes and pinned them on Mrs. Helen, letting all my anger and frustration spill out onto her in that one glare. She chuckled.

I wanted to hit her.

"My lady, the baby is coming."

Air left my lips, and I looked down, seeing there was no blood, but I was quite wet. "What?"

"Your bag of waters has broken. The heir is coming."

I looked back up at Mrs. Helen, confusion filling my face, and my mind whirled. I would give birth. The babe was still alive. I was not dying.

"You must stop fighting it. You must gather your courage and save it, for the hardest part is yet to come."

Her words, although meant to soothe, only had panic rearing again. This was terrible! It hurt like the devil. I felt as though I were on the field of battle being murdered by a thousand swords, and she was saying it would get worse? Just then, Arabel jumped onto the bed, Stew not far behind. Arabel licked and licked my face and arms and the bed while Stew picked at my hair.

"They know the baby is coming. They offer their support," Mrs. Helen said with a laugh.

I lifted my eyes then toward Beau, the beautiful greyhound Ned had gifted me. The dog stood by the door. His calm eyes rested on me, but his muscles stood rigid. He protected me. He protected the babe. And yet, at the same time, his gaze was soothing, as if he were telling me to stay calm, that he had everything in hand.

I smiled then, somehow reassured. "Send word to His Lordship. His heir is coming."

Alice nodded, knocked on the door, and spoke with the guard. Mrs. Helen squinted her eyes in Alice's direction. Between pains, I deduced why. Alice must be sweet on the guard outside my door. A short, uncontrolled laugh escaped my lips. As she was enjoying the romancing of a guard, she was also doing my bidding, for a man in love would be more apt to get a message to my husband than one surly with stiff muscles and no one to rub away the strain.

The queen had meant to punish Ned by having him taken from his studies in France. But she had been wrong in her thinking, for he did not want to be so far from me. He'd confessed it himself, and now that he knew I was bearing his child, he was grateful to the queen for summoning him back to England, even if it meant he must reside in the Tower.

I sat up with the next pain, reveling in it. For I was doing my duty. A duty Queen Elizabeth, and even Queen Mary, had not done.

"Push, my lady, that's it." Mrs. Helen, having helped many a birth, stood between my thighs and, over the next couple of hours, coached a head full of blond curls from my womb.

I pushed with all my might, feeling as the head emerged, and then the shoulders. I pushed again. And again, until the rest of the body slithered from my own. I fell backward, blessed relief filling my mind and body. I had borne my child!

And I lived!

The child wailed a moment before Mrs. Helen placed it in my arms, wrapped in blankets.

"'Tis a boy, my lady." She beamed a smile, proud of me for having borne a son and most likely proud of herself for having provided assistance.

"A boy. Hello, my son." I choked on a sob and pressed a kiss to the soft, warm forehead of my infant. He stared up at me with eyes a murky blue, red lips open in a contented sigh. "We shall call you Eddie, short for Edward."

SEPTEMBER 24, 1562

I kept Eddie's cradle in my room and woke with him every time he cried. The nursemaid stayed with me and scooped the bundle of my baby against her chest, making my own breasts ache with longing and need to feed my child. But it wasn't proper, and I'd been forbidden. As it was, the nursemaid would turn glowering eyes on me when she saw me cuddling him.

"Don't want him to get used to your scent, my lady, and then reject what I've got for him."

Did that mean I was not to hold my own child? I ignored her. Eddie was a lusty eater and did not at all turn away from the milk his nurse offered him. When I held him, he rooted slightly with his bow-shaped mouth, but mostly, we stared into each other's eyes. Our connection was powerful. I could not believe that Ned and I had created this child with our love. That he'd grown in my womb into this perfect, supple, soft, sweet-smelling being.

He was the perfect miniature of Ned, and I could not wait for my husband to see his child and prayed that it would be soon. Instantly, I frowned at the wall. We were imprisoned. The Tower held us captive, as did our queen. She would not allow us to share in this moment together. I swallowed hard and pressed my hand to my clenched heart. I tossed back the blanket and placed my trembling feet on the cold floor. I had to write to her, begging for her forgiveness and mercy.

"My lady, no, do not get out of bed. It is too soon," the nurse-maid said, holding out her hand.

"I must write a letter." I tried to stand, but my legs couldn't hold me, and pain radiated through my feminine parts.

"Your labor was intense, my lady. There was some tearing. You must rest."

"I have to write . . ." I trailed off, sitting back down and then lying, hoping the sting between my legs would recede.

"Must you write now? 'Tis well past midnight and not yet close to dawn."

My days and nights seemed to have blended together, and it wasn't until that moment that I gazed around my room and noticed that the only light came from a few candles, and the windows, which were usually covered with blinds, had no slits of light peering through.

I yawned loudly and curled up on my side. "It can wait until morning, I suppose."

I closed my eyes and drifted into a restless sleep in which my husband and baby were taken and I sat in a darkened room, coughing, sick and alone.

I awoke the next morning, covered in sweat, and tears streaked down my face. My maids fussed around me, thinking I might be sick with childbirth fever. I pushed them away, asked for parchment and ink and wrote a letter to the queen, begging her, my tears smearing the ink. Then I wrote a letter to Ned, lamenting our situation and questioning how we might escape this place.

"The chief warder will read your letters before they're sent," Mrs. Helen warned, eyeing the rolled parchments in her hand.

"Burn the one to Ned," I ordered her, my voice gravelly.

Mrs. Helen nodded, and I watched her toss the parchment into the fire. It crackled and hissed as my plea to my husband turned to ash.

"I have been given permission to visit with some friends later in the week. I shall make sure a message to Lord Hertford is delivered."

I looked up sharply. "How?"

"Do not fret, my darling. I shall seek out the duchess."

I nodded, and when all the maids finally stopped wiping my brow and shoving herbals down my throat, I took out the circlet ring Ned gave me on our wedding day, opened up the links, and read his words of love and comfort:

As circles five by art compact show but one ring in sight,
So trust uniteth faithful minds with knot of secret might,
Whose force to break but greedy Death no wight possesseth
    power,
As time and sequels well shall prove, my ring can say no more.

OCTOBER 1, 1561

Elizabeth arrived alone, cloaked in black and a simple gown beneath, as though she hoped no one would guess who she was. I had not expected to ever see her within these walls. The queen never visited the Tower, not since she'd been imprisoned here, the memories too painful. Did she not realize I felt that same pain? My sister had been imprisoned here. Murdered here. The way her lips quivered on the verge of a smile, I got the sense she enjoyed seeing me suffer.

"Kitty Kat," she drawled.

"Why have you come?"

Elizabeth looked taken aback by my blunt question. I watched a flicker of question cross her countenance and realized I'd never quite shown her the real me.

"Why would I not?"

"Does this place not hold memories you'd rather forget?" I couldn't help myself. "Do you not see the irony? You inflict on me the same pain that you yourself experienced. We are much more alike than you realize. Both of us unjustly imprisoned."

"Unjustly?" Elizabeth sputtered. "Quite the opposite in your case. It has been a long time coming for you, Kat."

I could only shake my head, words unable to form on my tongue. Was she so stubborn?

"Give me the marriage license. I would see with mine own eyes that the deed was done, now that you have brought a bastard into the world."

"There is none, Majesty." I glanced about my Tower prison room, hoping the spot I'd hidden the jointure document would not be discovered. 'Twas not a license, but could be close enough to be seen as proof of our being wedded. Why I should not want her to see it, I did not yet know, but there was something in her tone, in her eyes, that warned me against presenting it to her. I feared she would burn it.

"You do not have one?" she repeated. "How could you marry without a special license signed and approved by the archbishop?"

"Perhaps we did, and I left it at Hertford House, after the fact. I cannot recall . . ." My fingers trembled, and I hid them in the folds of my skirts.

The queen glowered. "If indeed there ever was one. Who can bear witness?"

I shook my head, sadness filling my heart and making it heavy. "My lord husband's sister, Lady Jane, was our only witness."

"And she is dead." Elizabeth stated the fact as flippantly as one would announce stewed beef was for supper.

I nodded.

"The priest's name?"

"I do not recall, save for he was a common priest walking along Canon Row."

Elizabeth visibly gritted her teeth. "For shame, you married like a common harlot when you have royal blood in your veins. 'Tis heinous. Nevertheless, I shall send men out to locate him."

Fear snaked around my spine, but I nodded my assent, as I really did not have a choice in the matter. I prayed she did not mean to do the man harm.

"You and your Lord Hertford shall languish and rot together forever, until the truth be told to me. To think you could plot against me."

My eyes widened. "Together?"

She barked out a short, bitter laugh. "Certainly not. Together behind the walls of the Tower, rotting in his bed of treason and you in yours. He'll get nowhere near your skirts, Kitty Kat."

I pressed my lips together to keep from crying out at the pain in my heart her coldness forged.

"Did you honestly think I would let you remain together? Your marriage shall be deemed invalid, your child a bastard. And for good reason. I'll be damned if I will have an heir whose lineage was the cause of my own mother's undoing. Your bastard's grandsire testified against my mother."

Elizabeth rarely spoke of her mother, and never of her demise. I thought she'd made it a point never to speak of her for fear of bringing anger and bridled hatred to the surface once more. But I realized, as I never had before, that Ned's presence must remind her that his own aunt had been the one to replace her mother. Her mother, Anne Boleyn, had been beheaded because of the king's lust for Jane Seymour, and now here I was, flaunting Seymour lust once more beneath her nose.

The look in Queen Elizabeth's eyes was feral, angry. I bit the inside of my cheek hard, drawing blood, and dared my knees to quake, lest they give away how deeply her wrath affected me. And just as suddenly as my fear of her enveloped me, something inside snapped.

I met her gaze without wavering and let her see the true Katherine Grey, if only this once. "You think a marriage before God and a child born of it a scandal, but what of you and the rumors regarding Lord Sudeley? What of the whispers of your own pregnant belly?" Elizabeth's mouth fell open, but I did not let her speak. "You feel I fell in love unsuitably and yet you romp alone in your room with a man who may have killed his wife and openly flirts with anything wearing a skirt." I stepped forward, drawing my shoulders square, though I did not come quite close to her height. "You and I are no different, Cousin, save for the fact I had the courage to love while you force everyone you can to share your loneliness and dry out with you."

By the time I was done, my breathing was erratic, my heart pounding, and dizziness threatened to drop me to the floor. Somehow, I managed to summon the courage to continue standing.

"How dare you?" Elizabeth spat, her lips thin. Her fingers clenched at her sides as if she itched to strike me.

I swallowed hard, having seen her so unhinged before, and waited for her to slap at my face.

I bowed my head but did not speak, the fight gone from me. She still had the upper hand and, because I'd lost my temper, would most likely imprison me behind these walls until God lifted me up into heaven.

There was nothing I could say to make my decisions seem right in her eyes. Nothing I could do to take back the venomous words I'd spoken. Elizabeth was not a forgiving woman. She would not understand. She did not choose to love or to marry. The one she wanted was forever forbidden her—especially after the suspicious death of his wife. 'Twas that event that had sealed her fate, and Elizabeth had vowed never to marry. She did not express an interest in being a mother. And she would never understand why I had chosen love over following her demands.

"Have you nothing to say?" Her voice was shrill.

I opened my mouth, but nothing came out, only a shuddering breath.

"Speak!" Elizabeth's voice boomed from the rafters.

"Most Gracious Majesty—" I had to apologize for having spoken so offensively to her lest she have me killed this same day. Had to salvage whatever small speck of respect she had for me. If only so my child could see the light of the sun on his face and not the shadows of the Tower walls.

"Do not use flattering words on me, dear Cousin, for I shall not be gracious to you in this respect. You have poisoned my court with your wantonness and given your sacred body of royal blood to a man I have not approved of. Now you flaunt your Satan child in front of me. I had thought you a silly, witless, parentless girl. Now I see you for what you truly are. You are filled with the devil, Katherine Grey."

I raised my eyes to Elizabeth's, imploring her for understanding and mercy. "I am no devil, and my child is not an evil thing, my queen, but an innocent child born of love."

The queen's lips curled menacingly. "Love, you say? Is that the reason for you to spread your legs and threaten *my* realm? After all I have done for you? You were fully aware of my plans to adopt you as my own child, my plans for your marriage alliance to the Scots earl, and you have tossed *my* love to the wind, with nary a care for my feelings." Tears welled in Elizabeth's eyes.

While I was hurt by her words, her actions, and angry at her for being so selfish and lashing out at me for falling in love, I also felt sorry for her. Did she truly believe that she loved me? Elizabeth had no idea what love was.

"I must beseech your forgiveness, Your Majesty." My words were not filled with the conviction they should have. I knelt before her, gaze on her feet, praying she would press her hand to my head. The stone floor cut through my gown, angering my knees, and my womb contracted painfully at the position so soon after giving birth.

"I cannot forgive you for your outburst, nor for committing treason against my crown. Mayhap you are no better than your sister Jane, the usurper." She spat the latter words in a way that showed she still harbored much anger at Jane for having been her rival when they were children.

Jane had told me on many an occasion how Elizabeth was jealous of her relationship with the dowager queen, Catherine Parr, the only mother figure Elizabeth ever had, and until that moment, I had thought it mostly an exaggeration on Jane's part. But now I could see it was not. Elizabeth felt deeply on the matter, and her anger ran thicker in her veins than I could ever hope to soothe. Not even Jane's death had mollified Elizabeth.

I shook my head slowly, placed my hands over my heart, and gazed into her eyes, seeking to appease her. "Majesty, I am always your servant and seek no more power than what you would give me to serve you."

"But you have betrayed me!" England's anointed monarch looked so much the lion then. I dared to hope she would see reason someday, but I knew today she would not.

"I spoke out of turn. A childish rant, but I did not mean a word of it," I lied. "'Tis true I fell in love and followed my heart. 'Tis a fact I married without permission and have been blessed with a child out of that union, but I never did seek to hurt you or betray you."

Elizabeth rolled her eyes heavenward. "I expected more from you, sweet Katherine. I had thought you different than the rest. You were my heir!" She bellowed the last.

I sucked in a breath. She'd never thought me different and had made a point of telling me that I was below all for years. Did she think me so unintelligent?

"Now you shall linger here in the Tower as my prisoner. You shall think about what horrors you have brought upon my realm with your wicked ways, your fornicating. Your bastard shall languish with you, and you should pray that he succumbs to an early death, for I will see to it that he remains in this Tower for all eternity. Just like the two young princes haunt these halls, so shall the fruit of your womb."

Chapter Twenty-One

Though in the yoke with free consent,
the humble heart did fall:
The heavens stood so out of tune,
he gave no grace at all.
And clapped up full fast in hold,
a prisoner's part he plays . . .
—Thomas Churchyard, Elizabethan Soldier and Poet

OCTOBER 25, 1561

My eyes widened as the door slowly opened to reveal the tall, lithe form of Cecil. He bowed briefly before standing tall once more. His willowy form was so erect I doubted the brief bow could have been from anything other than his muscles straining at being moved from his normal, statuesque pose.

"Master Cecil . . ." I trailed off and inclined my head out of manners, although I wasn't sure what to say. He was the last person I'd ever expected to see. Even Queen Elizabeth herself was higher on the list of those who might darken my doorway.

The light from the candles flickered, creating dark, dancing shadows along the walls and floor and over Cecil's face. I squinted, but between the trick of the lighting and the set of his cap, it was difficult to gauge his attitude.

"My lady." He stepped into the room and closed the door with long, pointed fingers. "You seem shocked to see me." So very blunt he was, and yet his voice held a hidden note. "Mayhap I have come at the queen's behest."

I pursed my lips and gave the secretary a smirk. "My dear sir, we both know that is not the case. My cousin wishes for me to rot eternally in this prison."

Just saying the words aloud brought on a pang of sadness. My baby was with me now, but my husband was not—if I could even call him such since Queen Elizabeth was bent on having our union proclaimed invalid. *No!* I would not let her take that from me. We were lawfully wedded, and I should forever lay claim to our union. And when would she take my child from me? For that threat had been evident in her sharp black eyes when last I'd seen her.

Cecil waved away my words and walked deeper into the room.

"I forget myself, Master Secretary, would you care for wine?"

He looked around, appearing to search out the goblets and decanter as though I might have poisoned the wine already—or as if surprised I might be afforded such luxuries.

"My thanks, my lady. However, my visit to you must be brief, and kept . . . quiet."

My eyes narrowed at his words. "Quiet?" After all I'd been through, I was not about to get myself embroiled in more court scandal.

"Indeed. If Her Majesty knew of my presence here, we would both regret the outcome." He took a deep sigh and went toward the window, closing the shutters and curtains, then peeping about to make sure we were completely alone.

"Why have you come?" My voice came out harsher than I intended, but the greatest spy known to Elizabeth's realm made me quite nervous.

Cecil came to stand in front of me, and I had to crane my neck to see his sharp, angular face, his nose so long that the tip threatened to poke my eyes out. "I have come to strike a bargain with you."

"A bargain? With me?" I could not hide the bewilderment in my voice or my expression. I even stepped back and shook my head. "No, Master Cecil, 'tis not possible. I am a *prisoner* of the queen. Bargains are best left struck with those who maintain free will."

Cecil chuckled, but his face did not show any merriment, only determination.

"Lady Katherine, you still have free will. You must be careful only in how you use it."

I continued to shake my head. "Your words puzzle me, sir. I am a prisoner. Please tell me how I might have free will when I am forbidden from leaving the Tower grounds and cannot even leave this chamber without permission. The queen herself has told me I will never gain her favor again, that I am a traitor in her eyes."

"May I speak plainly with you?" His tone broached no argument, and so instead of answering, I simply raised my brows and spread my arms wide in invitation.

He nodded briskly and stroked the length of his pointy beard. "The queen is headstrong. Stubborn. She has trouble seeing past her own ego and toward what is right."

He paused, once again taking in our surroundings.

"I assure you, there is no one here. The nurse has my babe in the antechamber, and I have no other visitors."

His lips twisted in what looked more like a grimace than a smile. "You can never be too careful. I am a spy, my lady, and I know how spies operate."

His words sent a shiver up my spine. Could I trust this man? He was so intense . . . His words frightened me and left me on edge, unsure of how to react. I found my own eyes wandering about the room, fearful some man dressed in black would jump out from the shadows and charge me with some other imagined insult.

"As I was saying, the queen is headstrong and follows her heart. She is a good sovereign, but one who is volatile and often makes decisions based on her own feelings."

"I fail to see where you are going with this, sir, other than to say our queen is a female with normal and rational female emotions?"

"You turn out to have a sharp tongue much like your cousin. I see why she fears you. You are also beautiful, and our good queen fears beauty in others. But that is beside the point. I have come to strike a bargain with you, and I would know that you are open to such before I proceed."

"And if I am not?"

"Then I will leave here now without either of us mentioning our chance meeting."

Chance meeting? It was almost laughable, as there was no chance about him happening to travel to the place where I was being held prisoner. And yet I was intrigued by his words. My future was bleak. My heart ached. What did I have to lose in making a bargain with this man, other than my life?

"Do you offer me your support? Will I be kept safe?"

"I cannot make promises, my lady, but I will do my utmost to see to your safety should you agree."

"Then, yes, I am willing to hear your bargain."

He chuckled, the sound grating along my nerves like a sword scraping over cobblestones. His lips twitched and a true smile emerged, but there was no twinkle in his eye, as though he was made happy not by merriment, but by something dark, something deep inside his soul.

"Excellent. I will have that glass of wine now, if it pleases."

I nodded and walked to the small sideboard, pouring two glasses of red wine—although quite watered, as my new warden seemed to hold a tight purse. I handed a glass to Cecil, who drank a tiny sip, swishing the liquid in his mouth.

"Why do you do this, sir? Do you taste for poison?"

His eyes locked with mine, as if he was trying to decide how to answer. He gave a quick nod and then took a larger sip, this time swallowing normally.

"Come sit." I walked to the two armchairs that sat close by the hearth and indicated for Cecil to take a chair. Even when he'd folded himself into a sitting position, his spine was erect and he appeared stiff limbed.

"My lady, you have borne a son. At this point in time, your boy could be our next king."

My eyes widened in shock, for while I had thought such a thing when his large blue eyes gazed into mine, I had never heard the words from another's lips.

"The queen refuses to marry. She says she is married to the crown, and all of England's people are her children. Such poetic words are sweet to the people's ears, but when it comes to a strong and secure throne, they are like bait, luring any would-be usurper and bringer of riots to the surface. It is my plan to have the queen write a new will in which she names your sons in the line of succession unless she marries and produces children."

I shook my head vehemently. "She will never agree to it."

"Such is the case right now, but if you were to continue bearing sons, she would see the error in her thinking."

"Continue? 'Tis not possible. My husband is kept from me."

"I can make arrangements for you to meet on occasion."

"How is that possible?"

"Leave the details to me. All you have to do is follow my orders. You will be with your husband, and you will be doing England a great service."

I nodded, but not necessarily because I was in agreement—more due to shock and fear.

Elizabeth would surely kill my son now. And if I were to have more children, she herself might swing the ax at my neck.

With one hand, I touched my neck, feeling the long delicacy of it. With the other, I brought the wine to my lips. I gulped greedily, choking on it when I breathed in a ragged breath.

"Fear shows courage, my lady. Let the people see you have the latter in abundance." Cecil stood. "I shall return when I have more news."

JANUARY 3, 1562

"My lady, I bring you news," Cecil said as he entered my Tower chamber. I'd heard nothing from him since his previous visit some months before. As days had turned into weeks and months, I'd concluded he'd been trying only to draw information from me.

My eyes widened, and I set little Eddie in his nursemaid's arms and turned to give Elizabeth's man my attention. "Tell me." A flicker of hope crept through my voice.

"'Tis not good tidings I bear."

My smile faltered, and I swallowed hard. "Tell me."

"The commissioners in charge of your interrogation have drawn their conclusions, my lady. They have stated that no one appears privy to the marriage, nor to your love of Hertford and his love of you, other than a few servants who saw you together after the fact or those who are dead. As such, and there being no evidence of declaration of marriage prior to now, they have declared your marriage invalid. The archbishop of Canterbury has stated that Hertford had undue and unlawful copulation with a princess of the blood and that because of your excess, you shall both be punished."

I was shocked. I had thought the commissioners would see the logical sense in our case. I nodded, accepting his words, even though inside I was crushed. How could they deem our marriage invalid? My eyes swept to little Eddie, nestled in the arms of his nurse.

"If husband and wife swear under God that they are married in truth and act upon that truth, how is it that anyone should then conclude they are not?" I whispered. Why should I have been shocked, though?

The queen always won.

"My lady, you have much support from the people, who do believe your marriage is valid. There are streams of people who believe Her Majesty's treatment of you is cruel and unnecessary. That she is acting out on a bruised ego. Indeed, why should man and wife be prevented from coming together?" Cecil walked to the window and looked out onto the grounds below. "They are comparing your plight to that of Hertford's innocent father and of your sister Jane. Others who have been harshly imprisoned for nothing other than someone else's gain. And you have a legitimate male heir—despite what Her Majesty says—my lady, an heir to the throne, while Her Majesty's bed remains cold. And it would seem it shall stay that way."

"She is the queen." She was the ruler, and she showed no mercy. She would not rule with a man by her side. She'd seen all too cruelly how marriage could be for a woman.

"Mary, Queen of Scots, claims you proudly as her rival. And I will tell you, you have many powerful allies at court. We encourage Her Majesty daily to name an heir, in favor of you and your son. You declared during your interrogation to the archbishop of Canterbury that you are married. Many would see that as valid. Indeed, I would wager most do, which is why the queen lets you languish rather than ending things. We need only bide our time, my lady. And you shall soon see your husband once more—in truth."

"What are you saying?" I hissed and glanced again at my maids. He talked of my being named heir to the throne, of accepting Hertford into my bed when forbidden by the queen. We could all have been arrested for his words. "'Tis treasonous talk."

Cecil's eyes flickered to the maids. "They are in my service, my lady. All I am saying is your time will come."

LATE FEBRUARY 1562

"Kat," Ned breathed, his beautiful lips parted, and I had to hold myself from running to him, to kiss his mouth for all the time we'd lost, for all that we had suffered thus far, and for all the pain that was still to come.

"My lord." I dipped into a curtsy, not sure how to react with him, since we had not seen each other in nearly a year.

He sauntered forward, all power in his long, lithe legs, and I noted that he still kept a trim figure.

"There is no one here, my lady wife. You needn't be so formal." He gripped my hand in his and pressed a kiss to the knuckles, which had me fairly swooning. How I had missed him.

I smiled up into his joyful face, my excitement to see him breaking free and bubbling to the surface. I threw my arms around his neck and pressed my lips to his. His hands came swiftly around my back to pull me closer.

My head swirled, my knees weak. The world seemed to spin in a way at once both heavenly and dangerous. Ned kissed me with a passion we had not shared in our previous joinings, as if he would melt everything he felt, all the kisses we'd missed, into this one press of lips on lips.

"Oh, Kat, my love," he whispered, his lips pressing my forehead as his fingers stroked the length of my neck. "How I missed you."

His voice crackled with emotion, and I pressed my hands to his cheeks, forcing our gazes to connect.

"Ned, I missed you so much. I am . . ." My emotions swirled through me like the tide crashing up the sides of a mountain. It was hard to express exactly what it was I felt. "I felt as though I'd died inside, and when Cecil approached about it being possible for us to be together . . . I did not think it true, and yet here we are."

"How is our son?" He looked around, eyes settling on our baby's cradle.

"He is good, healthy, strong." I smiled with pride, watching Ned approach the child we'd created.

He stared down into the cradle for several minutes before turning eyes prickled with tears on me. "He is beautiful."

I pressed my lips together to keep from letting my emotions flow out.

Ned reached inside, lifting out a squirming bundle and holding it close to his breast. Awkward for but a moment, he quickly curled his arms around our baby and cooed softly. A natural.

"Have you been a good babe for your mother?"

"The very best," I said, coming up behind him and placing my hand on his back. I peered over his shoulder.

Little Eddie was gazing blissfully up at his father. After they'd had some time together, I asked the nurse to take the baby for a stroll in the courtyard so Ned and I could be alone.

A wicked glint entered Ned's eyes when the door was closed, leaving us alone, and I felt heat rush to my cheeks.

I smiled shyly. "It has been such a long time since we were alone."

"'Tis my greatest wish, the one thing that has kept me from despair over these last months."

I pressed my hands to his shoulders and then patted down his arms and over his ribs, examining him. "Have they kept you well?"

"Aye, wife, I am kept well, and I have paid dearly for it, too."

My brows shot up and then wrinkled together with concern as I imagined the jailers prodding him and tormenting him. "How have they made you pay?"

Ned reached out and stroked the back of his hand over my cheeks. "'Tis not as bad as what you imagine. Ever the one to let your fancies get away with you. I meant only that I am paying for our keeping. 'Tis expensive to keep a family of nobles comfortably, and all this"—his hand swept out, indicating my rooms, the food, the wine, the fabrics—"I give coin from our coffers to keep us well placed."

"I had no idea. I simply thought the queen did not want us to win sympathy from the people for being kept in poor conditions."

Ned laughed quite loudly at that. "Elizabeth is intelligent and cunning. She knows what the people would think, so she forces her noble prisoners to pay fines and to pay for their housing. 'Tis not a choice. She'd take my land to pay for it if I didn't give it freely. Ruthless is what she is. She will stop at nothing to see that she reigns until her hair is bleached white with age and more lines appear on her craggy cheeks than the maps in Cecil's study."

I giggled at the image he painted. "Surely there are more than just the poor who consider her kind."

"What of you, my lady?" He walked toward the table laden with wine, cheese, fruits, pasties, and crusted bread. He popped a grape into his mouth and then poured two goblets of wine, bringing one to me. "Do you consider her kind for forcing you to live in the Tower, for not recognizing your marriage? For allowing you to give birth while imprisoned and then calling your son a bastard?"

I took a sip of the wine, letting its tangy essence rest on my tongue before swallowing. The wine carved a warm path down my throat into my belly. "I try not to dwell too much on the path that has been given me. I am happy to be your wife and know in truth that I am married, that God knows we are, and on Judgment Day, the queen will know, too."

I walked toward a window, staring out the diamond-shaped paned glass. "I spent many days, weeks, months wishing for change when my sister was imprisoned. Wishing for our monarch—Queen Mary, God rest her soul—to see the truth. To know that Jane meant her no harm, but 'twas all for naught. Now I refuse to wish and dwell on things I know very well I cannot change."

Ned came to stand beside me, his hand pressed to the small of my back. "You know you do not have to keep all the burdens to yourself. We may not be allowed to live together daily as husband and wife, but with Cecil behind us, we shall see each other more and make something of a life out of what the queen has given us."

I gazed up at Ned, knowing my deepest fears showed on my face. "What of our Eddie?"

"She will not harm him, Kat. I swear, he is protected."

"How can you swear when you are imprisoned yourself?"

"My coin pays not only for our comforts, my love, but for our safety, too."

"Oh, Ned." I buried my face against his chest, unable to bear the thought that we had to pay for protection inside these Tower walls. That even now, if Ned hadn't seen to paying off the guards, we would be in danger, our child's life in danger.

Ned pressed his lips to my forehead, pulled my hood off and tossed it somewhere, before I felt his chin rest on top of my head. It felt good to be in his arms, safe. Pain sliced through my heart, knowing our time was limited this afternoon and that soon he would be taken back to his own prison chambers. But I refused to let it upset me now. I could not dwell on being apart when my arms at that very moment were wrapped tightly around him. I had to soak in every moment, for I had not a clue when he would be returned to me. Cecil had promised that we would see each other more often but had not specified a schedule. Would it be once a month, less? Or, dear Lord, could it be that we'd see each other even more often than that? I squeezed my eyes shut, my stomach doing a flip of excitement at the thought of seeing Ned on a weekly basis.

"Do you think she will ever let us out?" I asked.

Atop my head, I felt Ned's chin move back and forth. "No." His tone was resolute and quick.

"You answered too fast."

"I am sure of it, my love."

"Why? You do not think she will have a change of heart?"

"Not unless she marries and bears herself two or three princes, and even then, perhaps not. But alas, such fancies are merely that, since she appears to have no interest in a husband."

"But why? Why must she leave us to languish?" Tears of frustration and grief prickled the backs of my eyes.

Ned sighed deeply, his arms pulling me tighter against him. "Because, Kat, you are the next in line to the throne, put there by her father and her brother, and our own Eddie at this moment in time could be crowned king. We are a threat to her. A deadly threat. She will keep us contained for as long as she can."

I imagined then the two little princes in the Tower so long ago, they who'd been a similar threat to then-monarch Richard III. Did Elizabeth intend for the world to forget about us if she left us in here long enough? She'd certainly said as much. But I hadn't believed her.

I envisioned her cool, dark eyes. Calculating eyes. The way she'd spoken to me, the way she grasped her throne and held on tight. She was scared. She was alone, and everywhere she looked, traitors lurked.

The fact that she would never let us out solidified in my mind with a sense of foreboding.

I must live for every moment then. I reached up and traced the outline of Ned's face. Loving the noble, angular lines, the straight nose, his full lips. He was a beautifully made man. I pressed my lips to his, my shyness forgotten and a bold woman coming forth in the heat of the moment.

At first, our kiss was tender, as if we wanted only to remember this moment, to soak each other in, to express our love and sorrow at the hand fate and the Queen of England had dealt us. But with one subtle swipe of Ned's tongue, all thoughts of tenderness escaped.

Ned's hard physique pressed to mine had my own body reacting violently, and I wanted nothing more than for him to make love to me right then and there. As if in answer to my silent call, Ned scooped me up in his arms and carried me to the down bed that my maids had fluffed and sprinkled with rose water just that morning, in preparation for his visit.

When we'd divested ourselves of clothes, he lay beside me, a lazy, gentle finger tracing circles around my navel. He whispered, "I love you. From the moment I first saw you, and until the day I breathe my last, you are mine, a part of my very being."

My heart squeezed tight in my chest. A tear wove its way down my cheek, and Ned smiled at me tenderly as he brushed it away with the pad of his thumb.

My throat constricted, and I felt as if the words would not come out, but I had to speak them, had to tell him how much he meant to me. "We are one soul, one body, one heart. No matter how far apart they may place us, you will always remain here." I placed his hand to my heart, let him feel the deep flutter within.

Never had the words meant more to me. I pulled him closer so that we might once again lay claim to that which was ours.

Sir Edward Warner, our warden, let Ned and I meet nearly once a week for several months, each time under the cover of darkness, so that no one would be the wiser. Ned joined me in my room, and after we'd made love, we held each other. He visited with our son, Eddie, loving his beautiful boy. Sometimes, we'd hold the babe between us in the bed, stroking his wiggling body, his flexed toes and fisted hands. It was a wonder we were able to find a sense of peace between us, being that we were imprisoned. I was grateful to the warden, for without him, we would have been lost, but together, I felt whole again.

I'd even had a portrait commissioned of Eddie and me. I was quite proud of how it turned out. We both looked well and happy. You would not have known we were imprisoned from looking upon its grace. For the sitting, I wore around my neck a portrait of Ned on a length of corded silk. It was plainly visible in the painting, so all who looked upon it would know that this child was ours. My little boy with his jaunty cap of black velvet and pearls. I had much hope for his future and prayed that one day, he would not remember these stone walls.

For as long as we lived here, though, we'd make a life. The warden might yet let me plant an herb garden, and with the romps in the yard, my life was not all that different than when I was essentially imprisoned at court. Yes, indeed, we would make a life here. As good a life as we could. At least we were all beneath the same roof.

Chapter Twenty-Two

Where griping griefs and grievous groans,
consumed his gladsome days.
Whilst he aloof full long remained,
and out of danger crept:
The doleful Dame in deep despair,
his absence sore he wept.
—Thomas Churchyard, Elizabethan Soldier and Poet

MAY 16, 1562

The deed had been done. We'd achieved that which Cecil had bade us do. My belly was swollen with child once more.

And it could not have come at a worse time.

The queen was once more at odds with our cousin Mary, Queen of Scots. I was told that a massacre of Protestants in France had begun—and someone kin to Mary was involved. Elizabeth and Mary were at each other's throats, which meant Elizabeth would be at mine soon. When one body seemed to be her enemy, so did all.

What was worse was that had this political and religious war not happened now, Ned and I could have been hopeful that our marriage might at last be claimed valid and our children legitimate. As Cecil had said some months back—when we were first questioned—we'd declared ourselves married in front of England and God, with many witnessing our proclamation of it. Cecil had claimed Her Majesty was close to letting us go free.

But no longer.

There was a pamphlet just printed by John Hales, claiming our marriage as valid and that my child should inherit. Her Majesty had seen him promptly imprisoned. For how dare someone publicly and so righteously have claimed what she had denied?

I prayed for Mr. Hales in his foolishness that having been so rash in his opinions, he was not hanged or burned at the stake. I could never have forgiven myself had a life been taken because of me.

The people should remember as I did. The queen always won.

OCTOBER 12, 1562

I must have been halfway through my pregnancy now, and this babe did act up as much as little Eddie, who turned one last month. I prayed for another boy. Two princes to be born in the Tower, and to live, unlike those two who were unlawfully imprisoned before my time. My princes would live, and should be set free. They must.

"My lady." The warden opened the door and stepped inside. "I've news for you."

I smiled sweetly, for the man had tried his best to keep me informed of courtly news.

"The queen is very ill. Delirious with fever. Smallpox. She is not expected to live."

My heart skipped a beat, at once fearful for her life and excited that our torment might soon come to an end. "Thank you, Sir Edward."

"Is there anything you need?"

"Not right now."

He bowed low and then left the room. I walked toward the makeshift altar Sir Edward had provided me. But I found it hard to pray for the queen's good health, because that health ensured I would remain a prisoner, and yet, I could not wish for her to die.

My hands settled on the swell of my belly. Thus far, I'd kept my second pregnancy hidden for fear the queen would have me poisoned. 'Twas a valid fear. She wanted me gone. But now it would appear God had struck her down.

Perhaps, in this game, the pawn should gain ground.

DECEMBER 1, 1562

The queen had recovered, and another pawn—not me—had made the first move.

Sir Edward delivered news with a large basket of Spanish oranges. My cousin Margaret, the Countess of Lennox—and Catholic—had a handsome young son, Henry, Lord Darnley. She wanted him to wed Mary, Queen of Scots, as she'd not yet remarried after losing her French royal husband. And Elizabeth, having declared she would never allow me or my children near the throne, implemented a plan of her own. She was in agreement with Lady Lennox and would name Mary her heir, despite all of their warring.

Did she not see that England did not want a Catholic heir? Her actions were at odds with each other, as she also raised money to fight in the religious wars in France—against Catholics.

Would the queen not make up her mind? Her hatred of me almost made me laugh. She abhorred me so much that she would have her people doubt her rather than name me or mine heir.

I missed the guidance of Ned's mother. The Duchess of Somerset's sage words would do me good as well. But for fear of her own imprisonment, she kept well away from me. Still, though, Sir Edward told me she had pleaded for mercy on behalf of her son and grandson.

Ned's allowed visits dwindled to perhaps once a fortnight, then to even as far apart as a month and a half. The guards were becoming increasingly wary of the imminent threat of Elizabeth learning of our deeds. I missed him dearly. I missed those summer days at Hanworth when we'd had nothing to fear but discovery by a servant.

There was little hope now. I had been locked in the Tower for so long . . .

I thought it would be the last thing these tired eyes of mine saw.

JANUARY 25, 1563

Lady Katherine Grey,

I write this letter to you because I cannot bear to dishonor myself with your presence. My attention has recently been brought to the fact that you are once more with child, which should be impossible, given you are imprisoned and separated from Lord Hertford, whom you claim to be your husband, though this marriage has been deemed invalid.

You are not the Virgin, immaculately impregnated, but a whore who has sullied and brainwashed the men of my Tower.

You shall now lay others' suffering upon your conscience, as they will be severely punished. Sir Edward Warner, your jailer, has been arrested and charged with treason. Your fornicator, Hertford, shall also appear before the Star Chamber and shall be fined 15,000 pounds for his part in conspiring to have access to your person and impregnating a kinswoman of the queen, not once, but twice.

If you had ever thought to see the light of day upon your face again, you can erase such from your imaginings, for as long as I live, you will remain hidden and repent for your whoredom.

Elizabeth, The Queen

February 10, 1563

A boy. *Thomas.*

I gazed into his precious eyes, seeing myself in his innocent face. For the moment, my joy was unending. Eddie bounded on the bed to meet his new brother, wrapping a soft, downy curl around his chubby finger.

"Baby?" he asked.

"Brother," I replied and kissed them both on their foreheads.

God grant him His great paternal blessings.

August 22, 1563

"Dear God in Heaven, have mercy on us. I pray to thee, keep us safe," I whispered fervently, hearing the shouts and pleas throughout London.

The scent of death was in the air, nearly a thousand dead a week.

I knew Elizabeth wanted me and my children dead. At this moment, I did not even know if Ned was alive. His visits had ceased when Elizabeth found out about our babe Thomas. And our new guards would give me no news, fearing for their own lives after the punishment of their predecessors.

The plague was upon us. Elizabeth had fled London for Windsor with her court and threatened to hang anyone who would dare to bring the disease near her.

A knock at the door had me rushing to my children to cover their faces with the bits of fabric I'd cut to keep them from breathing the plague-filled air.

"My lady," a guard said, looking haggard and ill.

"Do not come any closer!"

"You are to leave this place."

"To be thrown in the streets? Dead within a day?"

"No, Countess." The Duchess of Somerset, Lady Anne, walked into my chamber, looking every bit as imposing as she always had. Her use of my title was shocking—she told me in that one word that she believed in my marriage to her son. "The older boy, Lord Beauchamp, is to come with me."

"My Eddie?" I looked down at the boy, almost two years old, in my arms. "Why should we be separated?"

My mother-by-marriage's expression did not change. "The queen wished me to take both, but I insisted you have Thomas for a while longer."

"Why?"

"Because I could not bear for her to tear them both from you." She sighed. "I know I have kept well away from your situation, Katherine, and for that I am sorry. Sometimes one must protect oneself from . . . injustice."

Pain circled in my chest, gripping, tightening. "My lady, I understand, and I do not blame you, but why should the queen want to take my children?"

"For the same reason she has kept you imprisoned so long."

Revenge. Hatred.

I nodded, begrudgingly accepting another calamity that I could not change—even if it tore my heart out. My boy would be well cared for with his grandmother.

"What of Ned?" I feared her answer.

Lady Anne looked down at her hands, an odd move for her, since she was normally so bold. Oh, God! My love was dead!

Finally, she answered, "He is to come with me also."

I smiled, filled with joy that he was alive. Lady Anne looked startled for a moment at my smile before covering her emotions.

"I am pleased little Eddie shall have time to spend with his father." This was a good sign, wasn't it? The queen was punishing me, but even still, she was giving us a gift. Perhaps she meant to punish me for only a short time more. There was a chance that, with Ned going free, he would be able to persuade the queen to set me free as well.

"Yes, 'tis a good thing he should have his father to see him reared," the duchess said.

"Where am I to go?"

"She has arranged for you to reside with your uncle Lord John Grey at Pirgo in Essex. But you are there to remain a prisoner with no contact with anyone outside his household. Not even from me. Nor your sister Mary. Nor Ned or Eddie."

I bowed my head. That was worse than the Tower, where Ned and I had managed to send some letters to one another. To see one another in the flesh even, prior to the queen's show of temper.

"All the same, I shall write the queen and thank her for removing us from this wretched place and from the plague. And let her know that with upstretched hands and down-bent knees, from the bottom of my heart, I still most humbly crave her pardon."

September 3, 1563

I'd not been at my uncle's home for long, and yet already, a melancholy had taken control of me. I'd no hunger for food, for drink, for any of the things I once enjoyed. I thought maybe it might even be better if I were to waste away to nothing and then float off into the heavens. Would not my children and Ned be better off without me? The queen must have held a special place in her heart for him if she would let him stay with his mother and one of our sons.

"Good madam, you must eat something." Uncle John's face was pinched with concern as he stared at me over the great table in his dimly lit dining hall. We'd eaten many a meal like this, my uncle and I alone in his grand dining hall, with only the servants hovering near. Mrs. Helen had already tucked Thomas into bed for the eve.

I sighed and stared over the table at my uncle, shoving my plate away. I relayed the same message as I'd done the night before. "Alas, Uncle, what life is this to me? I am grateful for your hospitality, even though you truly had no choice, as I am a prisoner. But I live with the queen's displeasure always. If it were not for Lord Hertford and my children, I would pray for death."

It was true I was not housed with other prisoners, that I lived in physical comfort. I had the use of the gardens, could walk freely about the house as long as one of Uncle John's servants followed. No horseback riding. But I was lonely. My family torn apart. And part of me was giving up. I stood from the table, no more than six bites of my food gone. Perhaps oblivion was the better option.

"If you please, I have a megrim."

My uncle nodded, but I knew he did not understand. I felt his eyes on me as I left the room, my limbs weak from lack of food and my mind heavy for what I thought I must do.

In a few days, my Eddie would be two, and I would not be there to share his birthday. What kind of a life was that to lead? At least at the Tower, there had been hope of seeing Ned, and both my babies had been within my reach. Here, I was glad to have Thomas, but Ned and Eddie were so very far away.

Indeed, I had no hunger. Not for anything.

NOVEMBER 14, 1563

I waited with bated breath, wearing the carpet in my bedchamber bare from pacing. This past week, I had been diligently working with the assistance of Cecil on a drafted letter to Her Majesty, begging forgiveness and mercy and acknowledging my rash and disobedient behavior and praising her long reign. Robert Dudley even promised to deliver it to Her Majesty on my behalf. It appeared that those closest to Elizabeth agreed my punishment had lasted long enough.

With the backing of Cecil and Lord Robert, it seemed I might be reunited with my family at last, and I had even agreed to live in exile if that would assuage the queen's fears.

"My lady." Mrs. Helen interrupted my pacing to produce a package. "Lord Grey has given this to me to give to you. He says you are lucky to have received it."

I gripped the package, thankful for small miracles. The queen had ordered Ned and I to have no communication—and yet, a gift! Tearing open the paper revealed a brown leather book of poetry, coins, velvet fabric, and diamond earrings, as well as a small wooden horse for Thomas.

My lady wife, Katherine Hertford,
I seek to know how you fare, given word from Cecil via your uncle that you have not been well, and I pray to the Lord that you are healed soon and delivered into health.

I miss you dearly, my love. I miss lying beside you, holding your hand, and sharing a laugh. While it was a life behind walls, and while they were much too infrequent for satisfaction, those few visits we were allowed in the Tower were some of the happiest moments of my life.

Soon, my faithful love, we shall be together again, making merry, and I swear, one day, we shall live as we always hoped— as man and wife, beneath our own roof with our own children prancing like pagans around us.

With much love and concern for your well-being,
Ned, Lord Hertford

Oh, what sweet joy in his words! Just seeing Ned's concern for me had my strength renewing, and a new vitality filled my veins. Knowing my letter might well not be delivered, I sat down with ink, quill, and parchment to pen a reply to Ned.

My dear husband,

No small joy, my dearest Ned, is to me the comfortable understanding of your maintained health. I crave for God to give you strength, as I doubt not that he will. Neither you nor I have anything in this lamentable time so much to comfort us, in our pitiable absence from each other, as the hearing, the seeking, and the countenance of good health in us both. Though of late, I have been unwell, now, thank God, I am restored to health. I long to be with you, as you do with me, as when our little, sweet boy in the Tower was begotten.

I wish you to be as merry now as I was heavy when you came to my door for the last time, and it was locked. Do you think I forget what matters passed between us? No, surely I cannot but bear in memory far more than you think, for I have good leave to do so when I call to mind what a husband I have in you. Very well, though I write you are good, you be my naughty lord. Could you not find it in your heart to have pity on me, to have given me more pains for more children, so fast, one after another? No, but I would not have regard to rest my bones . . . I should have remembered the blessing of God in giving us such increase. I do not doubt I should rather have been glad to have borne a great deal more pain than thought any too much . . . to bring them, so much is my boundless love to my sweet bedfellow that I was wont with joyful heart to lie by and shall again . . .

Thus most humbly thanking you, my sweet lord, for your husbandly sending both to see how I do and for providing coin. I most lovingly bid you farewell, not forgetting my especial thanks to you for your book, which is no small gift for the heart as well as the eyes. I can very well read it, for as soon as I had it, I read it over even with my heart as well as with eyes, by which token I once again bid you vale et semper salus, my good Ned.

Your most loving and faithful wife during life,
Katherine Hertford

DECEMBER 13, 1563

The queen would not forgive us. I was ill and wretched of body and mind for what she put us through. So long now! And to continue so. I wished to be dead and buried. To just be done with it all. I had no energy left for it. I prayed to God to take me that moment instead of leaving me to languish in continual agony. What few small joys I had were not enough to keep me from this bleak and dark mood I seemed to have spiraled into.

I was fully aware that there were those in the world who suffered more greatly than I. Prisoners even who starved and languished in cold, dark cells. I was weak. I hated myself for being such—and that disgust at my own weakness only made death more appealing.

I threw myself on my bed, weeping. For I had truly hoped, with Cecil's assistance and the backing of Lord Robert, at long last we would have been pardoned. But Elizabeth continued her zealous cruelty toward me. She had cursed me the day I was born, I was certain.

"My darling, you must stay strong for your children," Mrs. Helen whispered, stroking my hair.

But I continued to weep. If these tirewomen would leave me, for they were always watching, I might have thrown myself from the window.

"I pray God shortly will see me buried." Hopelessness consumed me. And once more, I was clutched by the notion that if I were to perish, my family would be let free. I was the threat to Her Majesty. If I were gone, so would be the threat—for Elizabeth had deemed my marriage fraudulent and my children illegitimate. A bastard would never be allowed to inherit her throne. Not even the most overzealous of rebels would dare to put a bastard in Elizabeth's place.

"I am the reason my family is suffering. Without me, they will thrive."

At my words, Mrs. Helen gasped, her hands slapped to her mouth, and she, too, started to weep. She waved a maid to take Thomas from the room, and then Mrs. Helen gathered me in her arms, cradling me as she'd just been cradling my babe. My stout and busty companion, and me wasted away to nearly nothing. She rocked me and prayed for life, while I silently prayed for death.

SEPTEMBER 21, 1564

Eddie was three today.

I had not seen him since before his second birthday.

What would he look like? Would that I could have seen his smile. Did he think of me?

Thomas was little consolation to me. Nothing was. Hope was no longer even a thought. Even still, I held Thomas close, squeezing his little body against mine, feeling his sweet breath on my cheek, watching his wide, happy eyes take me in. I never wanted him to know how weak I was. That I had given up.

Whatever moments we had together, where I could gaze into his crystalline eyes and imagine a different time and place, went by too quickly. Even though I smiled at him and kissed his tiny nose, he still sensed something was amiss. He stroked my cheek and gazed intently in my eyes.

I could not hold his gaze for long. He reminded me so much of Ned, of Eddie. Of the innocence of the world and the joy that life could bring that I could no longer accept. I turned from him and told one of the maids to alert the footmen which trunks were ready to be moved.

"Mama?"

"Yes, Thomas?"

"Where go?"

"A new place, Thomas. We shall watch the leaves turn colors from a new window." How did one explain to a babe that we were prisoners, that this was not our home, that we had no home?

"Leaves? Colors?"

"Yes, they'll turn from green to red, orange, and yellow."

"'Lellow.'"

I smiled as he rolled the word on his tongue and frowned. "You shall see, I promise. Now run along."

One of the maids gripped Thomas's hand and led him away with promises of milk and sweet bread.

I sighed deeply and glanced about the room all in disarray. My body felt so heavy. I'd have to use great effort to put one foot in front of the other. I was to be moved to Ingatestone, away from Uncle John. My new jailer would be Sir William Petre. Someone had taken it upon himself to further my misery by publishing a pamphlet proclaiming my claim to the throne as being stronger than that of Elizabeth and our cousin Mary, Queen of Scots. No one thought of the little lives they were ruining, my children's lives. Poor Thomas did not even know his father or his brother.

I feared it would not be much longer before Elizabeth would have me beheaded.

And soon, little Eddie would not know the love of a parent. In retaliation for the pamphlet, my good Ned was being removed from Eddie. Ned would be housed with a man who despised him and had been the one vicious tongue to the queen approving of our imprisonment, Sir John Mason. Cecil told me this man once proclaimed that prison was too good for us. I could not imagine what horrors he would see my husband put to.

'Twas my fault he suffered.

At least Eddie would be able to remain with Her Grace, Lady Anne. I'd sent countless letters begging for Eddie to be returned to me, but Her Majesty sent only a curt reply: no. To make matters worse, Uncle John had been arrested. Supposedly, they thought him linked to the disdainful manuscript because of the harsh words he'd written in a letter to Cecil about the queen—of which she happened to get hold. Now I questioned my trust in Cecil. In his letter, my uncle had complained bitterly to Cecil of my lot, wishing he could be the queen's confessor and lament to her of her cruelty and that God would not forgive her unless she freely forgave all the world.

Foolish man.

So many suffered because of me.

I felt numb.

I did not feel at all.

AUGUST 15, 1565

Word had come to me that my sister Mary had been married in secret to Thomas Keyes, the queen's sergeant porter.

Forsooth, the queen would surely blame me for setting a bad example.

Keyes resided in Fleet Prison, and Mary had been placed under house arrest. God keep them safe and save them for their foolish ways.

"Lord Thomas awaits you in the gardens, my lady."

I nodded and stood to join my son in the gardens for our daily walk, which I did on the days I was not confined to bed. I did it for him, for I gained no pleasure in worldly things.

I'd not heard from Ned in at least a year. No word from the duchess, either, concerning my Eddie. Half my days were spent wondering. Were they sick? Did they live? Where were they? Did the queen treat them well?

I no longer dabbled with herbs or sewed shirts for the poor. My head pained me much, and I was weak, prone to illness and megrims. I was reminded of my dear friend Jane and how she'd been ill so often. One of these days, I would let it consume me.

My gaze was drawn to my Thomas. Poor child. It would have been best for him to go to the duchess, too.

Little Thomas took my hand in his, holding tightly to my fingers. His hand was small and warm, and I rubbed my thumb over his knuckles.

I looked down at him, his head covered in a miniature cap that looked very much like the ones Ned used to wear. Velvet, trimmed with an austere silk ribbon and a brightly colored feather stuck on the side. He looked up at me with his clear, blue, innocent eyes.

"Want to play dice with me, Mama?"

My eyes widened as I took in his prideful expression. He even puffed out his little chest. "Dice? Where did you learn to play dice?"

"The footmen play it, and they showed me how." He stuffed his hand in his pocket and pulled out a pair of dice. "See? They even gave me some to play with."

I smiled at his excitement, trying to let it show in my voice. "You will have to show me how then."

He jumped from foot to foot and yanked his hand from mine to clap. "Yes! I will show you!"

He gripped my hand again and started to run. I lifted my skirts with my free hand and ran beside him. His exuberance for life, for fun, was intoxicating. I hoped he could always be this way. Alas, innocence was taken from us all at some point. But for now, I would enjoy this moment of angelic peace.

JUNE 16, 1566

There might have been an end in sight to my despair.

Little Thomas and I had been moved once more, because Sir William Petre had become quite ill. But we had not moved far. We were at Gosfield Hall, which reminded me so much of Bradgate Manor, and I was pleased for my little three-year-old Thomas to see such a place as this.

My new wardens were elderly: seventy-seven-year-old Sir John Wentworth and his wife. They were not be able to keep a good eye on me, and I had had word that Mason, Ned's jailer, was dead, and his widow now kept my husband as prisoner. We once more were able to write, after nearly two years since last I'd had word from him.

Ned had sent me presents of jewels and fabric and furs, as well as fabrics for sweet Thomas. He'd even said we might soon be together, though I scarcely dared hope. Despite the good news, my megrims grew worse, and I'd developed a persistent cough. Perhaps I should pick up my herbs again to aid my tightening breaths.

For the moment, Elizabeth's attention had been turned from us. There was much turmoil at court as Mary, Queen of Scots, had also given birth to a son.

But I was not worried about the Queen of Scots. No matter how much people might try to force it upon me, I did not want the crown. All I wanted, all I *craved*, was to be merry once more with my Ned and to play together with both my sweet boys.

MARCH 3, 1567

My darling wife,

At long last, our time to celebrate may be at hand! One lord, who dared to come so close to Her, has sent his older brother to speak with me in regard to forming an alliance. They have decided to back you in the matter of freeing you and in the matter of the succession, in light of the news of the death of the Scots queen's husband. They have even gone to speak to the duchess, my mother, as well. Cecil is pleased at this turn of events since you know he has oft lent a hand to our side. We may soon be free! Pray, my love. I shall see you soon. I pray for it nightly.

Your Loving Husband in Truth

Could it have been true? Lord Robert had attempted to aid me before, and now he would seek to do so again? What would he gain from it?

My heart soared at the thought of a reunion with my husband and eldest son, but I tamped down the excitement burning within me. I had oft been disappointed, and the crushing blow of denial had become harder each time.

And yet, hope still sizzled within me, and I vowed to hold on to this life for a little while longer—even as my coughs turned wretched. I hid the small droplets of blood on my handkerchief, but I knew Mrs. Helen would see them eventually.

JULY 27, 1567

"Master Cecil," I said with surprise as he entered my chambers while I sewed Thomas a new coat of russet damask for the coming winter. Thomas played with a carved wooden horse and knight at my feet, making neighing and clashing sounds.

"My lady." He bowed low.

Master Cecil had aged much since the last time I'd seen him. Wrinkles were deeply cut at the corners of his eyes and around his mouth.

"My lady, are you well?" he asked, his eyes roving over my thin form.

"I am," I replied, contradicting what he saw. I knew I was much too thin. I knew deep-purple bruises and bags marred the flesh beneath my eyes and that my cheeks were hollow, gaunt. As if my body wanted to shout out my lie, I started to cough, and it was a great feat not to double over with the effort of it.

What did one expect of a woman imprisoned for love, marriage, and bearing children? What did one expect of a woman deprived of those very things?

Arabel and Beau, as if sensing my distress, hobbled to stand beside me. They still doted on me in their old age.

"I have come on behalf of your husband."

I looked down at my sewing, and now that the coughs had subsided, I made sure to keep my breathing even.

"My lady, he has been moved once more and is no longer able to write to you. Seems the queen has caught wind of more plots and schemes."

I pressed my lips together, refusing to cry, and sank the needle into the fabric, pulling the thread through tightly.

"She will never set me free, Master Cecil. You had best find a new cause."

"Nay, my lady. I shan't. I do not give up hope that Her Majesty will do the right thing." He glanced at Thomas meaningfully.

There was silence except for the soft pull of the thread through fabric as I sewed. Even little Thomas quieted his playing, as if sensing the intensity of Cecil's words. Finally, I said, "Then you will be the only one, for all else, God and sovereign, have. Leave me."

Cecil opened his mouth to speak, but I waved him away and looked out the window, pretending he had already gone. I could not have heard another word from him. So long had he promised me freedom. So long had he tried to provide relief. All for naught. There was no use.

All was lost. I hated myself for being stupid enough to believe there might be a light at the end of this very dark tunnel. I was without hope.

And I feared I shouldn't ever gain it back again.

SEPTEMBER 1567

Whatsoever may seem to be too good to be true shall soon turn to bad.

That was the story of my life.

With thoughts of a reunion with Ned shattered and now my kind jailer, Sir John, dead, I was sick with megrims all the more.

Political and religious strife ran amok, but I cared not to hear about it. And it appeared my supporters were once more banging on the palace gates.

Why not ask me what I wanted?

Let Elizabeth rule! Give me back my family! I was no queen. I was no monarch. I was a simple woman with simple desires.

My sister Mary remained imprisoned, but even she had been moved to stay with our step-grandmother, Lady Katherine.

But it was hopeless for me to even wish for such things or lament my desires to anyone. For the queen should keep me locked in these invisible chains, alone, forsaken, for my whole life, which shouldn't be long. I could feel it. My coughing had grown worse, the blood droplets more frequent, and I was no longer hungry for food or even breath.

I just wanted to sleep now.

To lie beneath the coverlet and let the darkness sweep in. 'Twould be better that way for everyone.

"My lady, Kat, child, you must eat something."

Mrs. Helen placed a tray of food upon my table, but I shook my head. Food held no interest for me. What little I managed soon came up besides. It'd been weeks since my last true meal.

"You must gain vigor! You must!"

I smiled weakly at the woman who'd been by my side so long. "There is no need." I'd already decided.

"No need? My lady, there is plenty of need. You shall live a long life, and soon you shall be free."

"No," I said softly. "No, Mrs. Helen. I shan't. Go and play with Thomas. Feed him. There is no life in this world left to me. Nothing here but misery. Her Majesty has seen to that. But I will pray for my soul, for in the life to come, I hope to live forever in peace. I *long* for life everlasting."

The words of my sister Jane echoed in my ears . . .

Trust not that the tenderness of your age shall lengthen your life, for as soon as God wills it, goeth the young as the old. My good sister, let me entreat you once again to learn to die. Deny the world, defy the devil, and despise the flesh. Delight only in the Lord. Be penitent for your sins, but despair not.

Mayhap, with death imminent, Jane had been able to see the future.

Chapter Twenty-Three

Yet great regard to promise paste,
she had as world well wist:
And therefore often wrong her hands,
when that her knight she missed.
But now began the boisterous blasts,
to blow in bloody breast . . .
—*Thomas Churchyard, Elizabethan Soldier and Poet*

COCKFIELD HALL, SUFFOLK
JANUARY 12, 1568

Inside these prison walls, darkness fell within my mind just as out-side it crept over the realm.

What had started out as a desperate thought in a time when I felt I could go on no further had taken root, and now I knew I must die in earnest. To be rid of this despair. To release my family from this imprisonment. If I had to die so that the three of them could be together, then so be it. The queen would never let us all be free.

And now I was letting go. I had not the strength for anything.

If I had to die—then it would be of my own choosing. I would take back the power over myself that had been wrenched away by my cousin, Elizabeth, and in the end, *she* would know I had finally wrestled my freedom from her.

It had been weeks since I'd eaten, my body slowly slipping away. My wishes to see my family before I let go had been sent and ignored. And now I feared the time was near, and yet I'd not seen Ned's nor Eddie's face in years.

The queen's anger came down swiftly and mightily. And still she did not come to see me herself. Only sent her guards to Gosfield Hall today to have me dragged, half-dead, to this new, cold place, with my new jailer, Sir Owen.

My mind lazily rolled around a phrase my father had frequently uttered. *Fear is often the greatest tool in the armory.* At the time, I had thought he meant for fear to be used as an offensive measure, but it would appear that my sovereign ruler, Her Majesty, Elizabeth I, did use fear as her defensive weaponry.

Her fear ruled her. And had she but asked me, I would have told her she had no need to worry of me. Though, I supposed, I had expressed as much to her quite often.

The throne had never been what I coveted. I would have tried to bear my duty well had she passed it along to me willfully, but never would I have taken it from her. And now, I never would.

Angry gray clouds closed in around Cockfield Hall as if they meant to converge overtop of us, meshing together like fingers enfolded. Then their mighty storm crashed down on our heads with colossal force. I lay upon the bed, lips numb, body shivering. A blizzard whipped the wind outside my window, shaking even the rafters above. Large chunks of ice fell from the sky and pinged against the glass windows. I flinched. A mighty gust sent my sweet pets, Arabel and Beau, rushing toward my bed, tails tucked between their old legs. My monkey screeched and hopped around.

Somewhere in the background, I heard Thomas mock sword fighting with a guard. They'd all taken to my little charming prince. I was sad for him. 'Twas wretched that he should see me this way, but it would all be for the best.

I dropped a limp arm over the side of the bed, and the dogs nuzzled my fingers with their cold, wet noses. I tried to murmur sweet words to my loyal babes, but only my lips moved, no sound issuing.

My eyes began to adjust to the sudden darkness brought on by the storm. There were no candles lit in this dank, musty-smelling room. Mrs. Helen wanted to light them, knowing the storm was coming, but I did not let her and bade her leave my room. Better she save the precious tapers for herself. Hide them away deep in her own trunk, for they were the costly sort, lavender and beeswax—something she might pamper herself with when I was gone.

I squeezed my eyes shut. They burned. Partly from too many tears left unshed, partly from the smoke in the room from a hastily put together fire and a chimney partway clogged.

I rolled onto my back and stared up at the cracked plaster ceiling. In some places, large, missing chunks showed the rotting wood beneath. How much coin was Sir Owen Hopton being given for keeping me prisoner here? He would most likely need it to repair his roof. Rain would soon fall on me in torturous drips, no doubt.

Why had he agreed?

I almost laughed at that thought. No one *agreed* to do what Her Majesty demanded. A body only obeyed in this realm.

Except for me.

How I wished I could take back every sniveling, pleading letter I'd sent her. I wanted to relive that moment in the Tower when I'd stared her down, spoken my mind, but this time, I would have kept going. Just to tell her the truth, that I would do it all again. That her unhappiness in love did not mean I must suffer. Love was rare, a thing of beauty, and she would only see it marred.

I knew why. Everyone did. She had loved—she did love. And she had not been able to grasp it, only to hold it in her hand but for fleeting moments that disappeared like water through her fingers.

Robert Dudley. My own sister's brother-by-marriage. Oh, how Elizabeth must have been tormented to know that Jane slept each night with her own Dudley, while she, the princess of the realm, had had to do without.

I could never fathom her attraction to the man. For certes, he was beautiful of face and body, but he was a rogue, a lecher. He flirted without qualm with any woman—especially Her Majesty— all while his wife had languished far away, and not even in her own home. And he'd most likely made a bedfellow of our cousin Lettice Knowles, for I'd seen love in their eyes.

Why would our virginal queen have chosen this man to love? What good could he have done her? What joy had he brought her other than showing her that love could never be hers?

Throughout the years of her reign thus far, she'd insisted her ladies remain unattached, and more than one—I was not the only lady to be chastised—had succumbed to their hearts and married in secret. Of course, none had been so harshly punished as I had been.

I had had hopes once. Hope that she would set us free. Hope that she would see we had not married and produced our beautiful children to offend her. Hope that she would forgive me.

But my hopes had long since burned to ash. If there was anything I'd learned, it was that Elizabeth would not give up this fight. She was not willing to risk what doing so would have said about her, what doing so could have implied to those within and without her realm.

She thought to punish me by not naming me heir, by removing me from the succession, by excluding my children from their rightful places in the realm. But what she did not understand was what I *truly* wanted. I simply wanted peace. I was happy for her to rule this realm. I would have been happy to take my children to my husband's home and live there the rest of my days, never setting my foot in court again.

Arabel and Beau jumped up onto the bed at a flick of my fingers and cuddled beside me, their warmth seeping into my bones, which never seemed to feel anything other than the cold these days.

"My babes," I whispered—because my voice was not strong enough to speak—partly to my pets as endearments and partly to the sweet cherub who'd been ripped from my arms and the one who was still with me, who had grown these years without seeing his family together.

Snow and ice splattered and pinged against the shutters, and gusts of wind blew in from some narrow, unseen crack. Perhaps by the time the tenacious drops slipped their way through the eaves to drip upon my face, I would no longer be in this place, my soul having escaped my body. As if the Lord heard me, my chest tightened painfully, and I felt for a moment as though my whole throat was closing up, cutting off my air. I coughed, deep, heaving coughs that shook my whole body, made me ache in spots I had not known existed. The sound emitted from my hacking coughs was wholly unnatural and splintered fear throughout my spine.

I closed my eyes, let the coughing take hold until my belly and ribs ached and red and yellow sputum dribbled from my lips.

From somewhere, I heard a door open, the wood cracking against the wall. Feet rushed forward, heels clicking on the wooden planked floors, but my world floated around me, and I could not make out much more than a hovering face and probing hands.

Someone wiped at my face, around my lips, upon my brow with a cool cloth. A cup was brought to my cracked lips for me to drink. I tried desperately, because an overwhelming need for drink took hold. I gulped at the cool liquid, but none of it made it past my mouth, instead gushing from behind the wall of my teeth and lips to form warm, spittle-filled paths down my chin.

"How could she insist my lady be brought here today?" an anguished Mrs. Helen said.

There was silence to her query.

A rustling of skirts. "I demand you send a messenger to Her Majesty! You must request a physician. My lady will not—" Mrs. Helen's voice caught, and she did not finish what she was going to say.

But she need not have finished, for I knew what words she clamped behind frozen lips. I would die.

Not a one was willing to say thus to me, but I knew. I could feel it in my bones, in each aching muscle, in my chest that hurt, my lungs that refused to breathe. And I felt relief.

"Oh, the babies . . . Poor little Thomas and Eddie!" Mrs. Helen wailed. "His Lordship! And they only wished to be happy . . . The poor girl has lost so much. She sought only her own happiness. And that woman—"

"Do not blaspheme, madam. We can all only do as Her Majesty commands, and if 'tis God's will to take this child from our presence, then so be it."

Mrs. Helen gasped, and I imagined her running at the man full force, pummeling his chest, but my consciousness was beginning to wane.

"I will send for a physician. And a priest."

I murmured my thanks for the latter. "My time has come. Even now, I am going with God as fast as I can." I was not sure if either of them heard me, for I did not hear myself, and I barely felt my lips move. Nevertheless, I had thought it, wished for them to know that while all else had abandoned me, I was grateful for their presence.

And for sleep . . .

"I cannot bear it!" The distressed cry from Mrs. Helen woke me with a startle.

The crease of my elbow stung, and I tried to move, to pull it away from the source of the pain, but I could not. Was I completely paralyzed? I had felt the numbing tingles in my lips before. My toes were too weak to wiggle, and I was powerless to move any part of myself.

A whimper escaped my lips, loud enough that I heard it. I wanted to tell them to stop. To no longer attempt to save my life, for I was through with it. Ready to die. I had *learned to die.*

Mrs. Helen heard it, too. "She is awake!"

I heard the swish of her skirts as she approached my side, felt the air move against my cheek, and then her old, callused hand upon my brow.

"Careful of the blood bowl, madam," a stiff male voice commanded.

Blood bowl?

"I shan't be in your way," Mrs. Helen replied tartly.

The man grunted.

"They had cause to bleed you, my love," she whispered.

That must have been the reason for my stinging arm. I tried to nod, but instead felt my head roll to the side.

I blinked open my eyes, the light harsh. Everything was a bleary mass of white. I blinked some more, but my eyes refused to cooperate. I looked around, panicked, but could get no certain image of anything in particular. Shadows with the light . . . Flashes of movement . . .

I let out a moan when I had truly wanted to ask what was happening. Pain. Blindness. This was my new world? No, he could not yet have taken me. *Why, Lord in Heaven? My sweet Jesu, I beseech you. Take me away to paradise.*

"Hush, darling girl, 'twill be all right," Mrs. Helen soothed.

But it would not. Where were my babies? My Ned?

Precisely when I started to think the only thing I would ever experience again was the sting of my arm as the physician sliced my flesh and bled the life from me, I felt something else. Something warm, wet, then cool against my cheek.

Tears.

Warm, weathered fingers wiped at my cheeks.

"Can you not be done with this foolishness? You are traumatizing my lady, Dr. Symondes," Mrs. Helen pleaded.

"'Tis how we heal a body, madam. She must be bled. Her humors realigned." There was no emotion in his voice, almost as if he'd tired of the argument and now had only a practiced response.

I had not realized my eyes had closed again until the snap in Mrs. Helen's voice woke me. "I recall another great lady, a royal of this realm, who was bled in her bed when ill. The physicians bled the very essence of her soul from her body. Would you do such a thing to my mistress? A princess of the blood?"

My vision cleared slightly, and while things were still a blur, I was able to make out faces, able to make out the blanch of the physician's face at Mrs. Helen's words.

"Surely, madam, you are not referring to whom I think you might be referring?"

I blinked to try to understand what it was he meant. What great lady?

"That I am, sir. That I am. The king did not take kindly to his physician bleeding her, and I suspect our current monarch will be just as angry with you."

"I never—" he blustered.

"That is just the issue then, is it not, sir? You never—you never thought to do anything other than bleed her. Do you even know what is wrong with her? You never thought to even ask me what was the matter, just took out your knife and sliced away at her precious arm. She is weak enough as it is, having eaten barely a thing in months, and now ill, and you would let the only thing keeping her with us flow from her body."

"Madam! This is an outrage! I am a trained doctor, schooled by the very best in all matters of modern medicine. You are little more than a housemaid, and you dare to tell me how to treat a patient?"

"When that patient is a princess of the blood and you are killing her, then yes!" Mrs. Helen's hands came up to rest on her bountiful hips.

What little breath I had came quick at this exchange. He was killing me. She was trying to save me.

But I saw what she could not, what she refused to see. I perceived in that one moment that Mrs. Helen was scared, that she was searching for someone to blame for what had happened to me. There was no one to blame. There could be no one to blame. Had the doctor not come to bleed me, I would still have been lying here, ill beyond measure, not long for this world.

I smiled, or at least I hoped I did. Through sheer force of will, I beckoned Mrs. Helen to me with tingling fingers.

"Oh, my lady," she gushed, rushing over and dropping to her knees beside me. "It has been days since you last awakened."

She gripped my hand in hers as the doctor rushed to press a wad of padding to the incision on the same arm's elbow. She kissed my fingertips and whispered, "I am afraid."

I licked my lips and tried to speak, but all that came out was a raspy whimper. I closed my eyes. Swallowed. Took a deep breath. Reopened my eyes and tried again. "Do not be afraid, dear friend." My voice came raspy and gravelly.

The physician reached for a cup and held it to my lips. I drank a few drops but choked and sputtered. I had things to say, and if my cough should return, I would not be able to get my words across. He put the cup back on the table and mumbled indiscernible words before quitting the room.

"You have been good to me."

Tears spilled down Mrs. Helen's face, and she shook her head. "I should have stopped you. I should have never let this happen."

I smiled sadly, knowing the struggle this poor, loyal woman had gone through. She'd been with me my whole life. Nursed me as a babe, and now here she knelt beside my deathbed. My whole life, I'd been searching for someone who loved me truly. And while I had found that in a man, in my dear sweet Ned, who would always be more of a Beau to me, I had overlooked the one person who'd stood by me through the entirety of my life. Here she was. The last person I would see.

I squeezed her hand. "You have been like a mother to me, but know there is—" A cough interrupted my thoughts for several minutes, and once again, the cup was put to my lips. "You could not have done anything. He is my love, my life. My soul. I could not have lived without him." I recalled then the words he'd inscribed on the ring he'd given me nearly a decade before, "Whose force to break, but greedy Death, no wight possesseth power." By the end of my words, my voice no longer held strength, and so *power* came out on a breath.

"You always were a stubborn child," Mrs. Helen chided. "I remember watching you frolic in the gardens, picking posies and weaving little crowns. Your sister Jane scoffed—even at the tender age of six—at your antics, and when Mary came along, she was so shy and timid she would only stare after you. Everyone claimed you were the beauty, Jane the brains. But I knew there was more to you than lustrous hair, fair skin, and delicate bones. You have heart. You have strength beyond measure, and you are true to yourself. You would not let anyone tell you the rules of your life. Though you had to follow the demands of your parents and sovereign, you always did so in your own way."

I chuckled softly, but it came out sounding like only a raspy grunt.

"And now here you are, you stubborn chit, and still my sweetest little lady, lying upon your deathbed and telling me you would lie here still if you had it to do all over again."

Tears gathered in my eyes, and once again, I felt their hot journey carving a path of sorrow on my cheeks. But not sorrow for the life I had lived. As Mrs. Helen had said, I would have done it all over again. No, my sorrow was that I would not get to finish this life. That I would not see my boys ride their first mounts, parry in their first sword match, nor have them in my arms again. And Ned! My sweet husband . . . That I should never set eyes on his beautiful face again. Never feel his soft lips on mine. Never feel his arms slide around me and bring me to the heights of passion as he whispered of his love in my ear. And most of all, that I should not see any of their faces and have the chance to tell them myself that I loved them—tell them that this was good-bye in this life, that I would see them once more in heaven.

"Go within my chest . . . There is a small box."

Mrs. Helen went to the chest and rummaged through. I saw from the corner of my eye that Sir Owen, master of this house, had entered my room.

"Take out my ring, Mrs. Helen, and give it to Sir Owen." I felt faint and weak, as though any moment, I would be called to sleep once more, but not to wake.

"Is that your wedding ring?" Sir Owen asked, shock resounding in his voice.

I nodded. "Give this to my lord husband, the loving, natural father to my children." I sucked in a breath, feeling as though I could not get enough air into my lungs. But I wanted my words to be heard. They must be heard. "And then take my plea to the queen, which shall be the last suit and request I ever make to Her Highness, be it from the mouth of a dead woman. Plead with her that she forgives her displeasure toward me, that I hope she has already. I must needs confess I have greatly offended her in that I made my choice without her knowledge. Otherwise, I take God to witness that I had never the heart to think any evil against Her Majesty. Beseech her to be good to my children and husband

and not impute my faults and transgression upon them. Tell her I give their care wholly to Her Majesty, for in my life, they had few friends, and fewer shall they have once I am dead except Her Majesty. I desire Her Highness to be good to my Lord Hertford, for I know my death will be heavy news to him. I pray that Her Grace will be good enough to send liberty to gladden his heart. Beg her to show mercy . . ."

"I shall impart your message to the Queen's Majesty, my lady," he said through a choked voice.

My eyes blurred, and I sought Mrs. Helen through waning vision. I held out my hand for her comfort.

"I am here, child." She gripped my hand in hers.

"You will tell him . . . tell him I love—" My voice broke, and I sucked in a breath. Unable to get enough air into my lungs, I sucked again. But I was so overcome with emotion, so filled with it, eating away at my insides, sorrow took control, and I could no longer speak.

"I know, my love, I know." Mrs. Helen gathered me in her warm and comforting arms, and we cried together, our tears mixing, both of our chests shaking and rumbling with grief. "You needn't worry over a thing, love. I will tell him. I will tell all to everyone."

She pulled me close, wiping away the endless stream of tears, stroking my once-lustrous hair.

Extra weight made the mattress sink lower as Arabel and Beau slipped onto the bed to curl up along my back and legs.

There I lay, with my precious dogs and Mrs. Helen, those lovely creatures who had been my comfort and security through the years of misery and doubt.

And there we stayed, a deep sigh on my lips as, for a final time, I fell asleep.

THE END

Epilogue

And now the golf of sighs and sobs,
burst out with great unrest.
For loe, one house held both these bearers of ill-fortune,
yet both asunder were:
And both in like displeasure stood,
yea each of both in fear.
Of Princes wrath and worlds disgrace,
a heavy tale to tell,
A plague past hope of heaven's bliss,
a torment and a hell.
—*Thomas Churchyard, Elizabethan Soldier and Poet*

COCKFIELD CHAPEL, SUFFOLK
MARCH 1, 1568
ELIZABETH I, QUEEN OF ENGLAND

I am come hither to bear witness in truth to that which hath been relayed to me. That mine own cousin has died.

Katherine. Kitty Kat.

My eyes must be deceiving me, for here at her tomb are many flowers, many candles lit. The people did favor her much as their heir to the throne. I was right to have feared for my life with her alive. And yet, my heart doth die a little more, if it were possible, to ache for the love she did receive from the people and from her lover.

The small chapel has been cleared, save for a priest who hovers in a corner, his eyes wide and unbelieving at what he sees. I have traveled here in secret, but it shall no doubt be told at many a hearth that I came to offer a prayer for Lady Katherine's soul.

A draft wafts up the aisle of the church, and despite the coming of spring and my thick ermine cloak, my bones are chilled. A small dog, looking very much like Katherine's old mutt, rushes from beneath a pew to bounce around the hem of my skirt.

"Shoo!" I hiss, not wanting to play. But he does not leave the chapel, although he does stop yanking on my skirts. He runs up to Katherine's tomb—and so he must be hers—and there he lays his head on his paws and whimpers.

Even the dog misses this woman. For shame! Will every living, breathing being attempt to make me feel regret for what has transpired? I have protected myself and my crown just as any other great monarch would have done!

I caress the cold stone of her tomb and shiver a little at a flash of something that I fear may come to pass. Lord Hertford shall never forgive me for keeping them apart, and while I do not fear what he can do to me, for I am Queen of England and ruler of this realm, I do fear what his great sadness will do for the people of this land.

How like them, to bring attention to themselves and their cause. But does no one think of me? I have given up so much for the greater good!

Yet their love affair will be revered and spoken of for years to come, and I shall most likely be slandered. And I shall lie beside no one, never experience the love they had for one another, for I am married to this crown, to this country.

I reach for the hard gold of my simple coronet. There is comfort in something always constant.

I must make certain 'tis not possible for Hertford and Kitty Kat's story to be immortalized. I shall make him remarry if I have to—to forget her. For this is a terrible thing I have done, and yet there have been so many terrible things, and I'm sure there shall be even more to come. But I must protect myself. I must protect my lands, my rights, my inheritance, my people. And if in achieving those goals, some must hurt, then so be it.

My knees quake and threaten to spill me to the ground. My breathing is shallow and rapid, and my eyes sting with unshed tears. Guilt riddles my bones, but I must be strong and steadfast. For what good is a monarch if not for their word, their rule?

But my heart aches for one so young. For a love lost. For two children, now motherless as I was at their age. I have deprived them of that. I have resigned them to a fate I would not wish on anyone. But at least those two young boys will have the love of their grandmother, Anne Seymour, Duchess of Somerset, if you could call her a loving guardian. I have yet to see true joy in the woman's face.

Still, it is more than I ever had, left only to those servants who would care for me and a few brief, happy moments with my stepmother, Queen Catherine Parr, who eventually pushed me away.

A deep, ragged sigh draws itself from my chest.

I am forever alone, and yet surrounded.

If they had come to me today with news of their secret marriage, would I have denied them what I did in years past?

Again, I reach out to run a hand along the marble stone. All that is left of dear Kat, that little girl I had once thought to adopt as my own. My own blood.

I know this: If I were once again to endure the pain of seeing two so in love, who had gone against me and stolen my trust, then indeed, I would keep them apart.

My spine straightens and I frown as I realize this. I cannot regret my decisions, only learn from them. Harsher punishments may come to those who deign to act in secret. I *am* the Queen of England. I *am* their sovereign ruler and head of the church. It is *I* who decides the fate of this realm and those who are fortunate enough to live within it.

And never shall I let the young Edward and Thomas Seymour rule. They are the product of everything I could never have. Love, passion, a family.

Love, that one selfish indulgence that as Gloriana, the Virgin Queen, I shall never fully be allowed to feel.

"A pox on love!" I say acidly.

With head held high, I whirl from the tomb of one of my greatest personal enemies. I will leave this place, and with it, I abandon the pain, too.

Even in death, these two will defy me. It is a premonition, a knowledge that makes me shudder. I've created a legend. A tragic tale of star-crossed lovers.

And those throughout history will always remember me as a monster in this, and not a woman born of jealousy, pain, and regret.

God Bless you, Kat. And see you safely to heaven.

Author's Note

As I do with all my historical fiction titles, I took creative license to write my story *Prisoner of the Queen*. But to be honest, the story of Katherine Grey and Edward Seymour, Earl of Hertford, was so dramatic, so filled with passion, treachery, pain, and love that I needed to change and add very little.

At the beginning of each chapter is an excerpt from a poem written by Thomas Churchyard, an Elizabethan soldier and poet. The poem tells the tale of Katherine and Ned's tragic love story. The poem was published in 1575 in *Churchyardes Chippes* and is titled "Doleful Discourse of a Lady and a Knight." Churchyard got into a bit of trouble with Her Majesty when it was published. It is a very long poem, so only about the first quarter or so is pasted within the manuscript (with the exception of the lines gracing the beginning of the epilogue, which are the last lines of the poem). Additionally, I have translated the poem into modern English, as it was quite difficult to read the way it was originally published. Finding period accounts is a must for me when doing any project, and what a stroke of luck it was to have found Churchyard's gem.

There are many who in history and in fiction have portrayed Katherine as frivolous, "featherbrained," promiscuous, selfish, and covetous of the throne. I feel this is false. She watched her sister be thrust into power and die from it. Why would she want that for herself? She willingly chose to marry the man she loved behind Elizabeth's back, knowing there would be consequences. While some of her behavior may have been brash and reckless, she was an intelligent woman. She was, in fact, well educated. She did spend more than she had and was often in need of funds. But this was said of many during that time period—including Lord Robert Dudley and even Henry VIII.

I think there was a lot more going on in Katherine's head than she is given credit for and that she never guessed Elizabeth would punish her as harshly as she did. I think she hoped that while Elizabeth would be angry, she could convince her cousin that she did not covet the throne.

All through her trials, she remained loyal and faithful and loving to her husband. They corresponded (and saw each other in the Tower) whenever they could. As far as their visits in the Tower, by her own admission and his, it was only two times, and on the third attempt, the door was locked. I increased this for purposes of my story, because they were able to conceive another child under such circumstances, and perhaps I wanted to grant them a little more joy.

I have changed a few dates to make the story flow better but, for the most part, have remained true to the timeline. There are several letters quoted in this story that were actual letters written by the characters, and then there are also many letters I've written myself. The letter from Jane to her sister is, in fact, real, although I cut a large part out of the middle to avoid repetition. In addition, Kat's long letter to Ned after they are removed from the Tower was written by her hand. The circlet ring with the inscriptions was real.

Her lady's maid, Mrs. Helen, is a fictional character based on the woman who most likely foster-mothered and nursed Katherine and her sisters.

According to some historians, Katherine did plead that her marriage to Henry Herbert had been consummated, even though it had not been. She begged for the marriage to remain intact, under the pretense that they loved each other deeply and that she could be with child. I considered putting this into the story but chose not to for purposes of making her love to Ned unique. Also, if the plea was made, it was likely made in desperation for her life and safety.

Some say that Katherine starved herself to death, and others believe she died of consumption. In either case, I believe her heart was so badly broken that when death presented itself, she embraced it with open arms.

I do not know if Elizabeth I ever visited her cousin's grave, so the epilogue in Elizabeth's point of view is entirely a figment of my imagination.

In eternity, these two lovers do reside together. Kat and Ned's grandson, William Seymour, had his grandmother's body moved to be with his grandfather's. There is an effigy that can still be visited today. This was Ned's wish, and he shared that with his grandson, bidding him to have this effigy engraved:

Incomparable Consorts
Who, experienced in the vicissitudes of changing fortune
At length, in the concord which marked their lives,
Here rest together.

Ned began drawing plans for this tomb many years before his death—planning for his final resting place to be beside the woman he had never forgotten. The love of his life. He worked just as diligently on this tomb as he did on restoring the legitimacy of his two sons and the validity of his marriage to Kat. Though the queen did have him remarry, that union resulted in no children, which makes his last wishes all the more poignant.

While Elizabeth was a strong ruler, I like to think that she did regret and struggle with having been brutal. She loved her cousin and, at one time, wanted to adopt her, so when Katherine married secretly, she took it as a personal affront and felt betrayed. To add salt to the wound, the fact that Katherine bore two healthy sons made Elizabeth only more angry and fearful for her crown. When it came down to it, she was bound to the throne and loyal to nothing else. I'm sure she struggled with that every day. But in the end, she didn't choose Katherine's sons to be her heirs and instead united Scotland with England in a move that shocked many but ultimately brought the country to where it is today, a united island. Perhaps she had a greater vision for England's future than any previous monarch.

What a different world this would have been had Jane Grey overpowered Mary's run on London—or if Mary had named Katherine queen.

Thank you for reading!
Eliza

Acknowledgments

Some people say an author's career is a lonely job; it is anything but. I'm surrounded by people who've helped me along the way and offered support in so many capacities. I could not do it without them.

There are many people I wish to thank for helping in bringing this creation to life. First, foremost, and always are my husband and daughters, who have been such a huge support to me over the years and endured the hours I spend researching, writing, and talking endlessly about my characters. You all are my mountains!

Prisoner of the Queen was a true labor of love—which I considered turning into an alternate history because the ending was so difficult to write. My critique partners talked me off that ledge! As this is the second book in the series, the same people who assisted me in writing the first were instrumental in this work as well. I could not have written and published this book without the help of the following people: Stephanie Dray—a huge supporter and friend! She read endless chapters and helped me to revise, listened to me vent, and once again talked me down off ledges. Kate Quinn for taking the time to read my book and pointing out places for improvement—you're a gem! My critique partners, Kathleen Bittner-Roth and Tara Kingston, who read the chapters of this book in its beginning stages years ago. Without your encouragement, I'm not sure I would have kept on going! My first copyeditor, Joyce Lamb, who bled with me once more over tense issues. A special thank-you to my editors with Lake Union—many thanks to Jodi Warshaw for taking a chance on my series and on me! It has been such a pleasure working with you. Thank you to my editor Anna Rosenwong for working with me on making this new version of the book wonderful! I'm thrilled for the new and improved version! Thank you to my Lake Union copyeditor Laura Petrella, a word genius.

And last but never least, my wonderful readers. Without your dedication to my books, your support, and your pure awesomeness, I would not be able to do what I do. Endless gratitude!

About the Author

Photo © 2011 Katherine Brandon

E. Knight is the award-winning, *USA Today* bestselling author of the Tales from the Tudor Court series. She is a member of the Historical Novel Society and Romance Writers of America and the creator of the popular historical blog *History Undressed*. Knight lives in Maryland with her own knight and three princesses.

For more information, visit www.elizaknight.com.